To Paul,
I knew you'l
and this isn't a
in a way its?
painting! As well as othe.
things.

A message
from Carlos

Hope you enjoy.

Denys Lingard

Denys
13/12/23.

Other books by Denys Lingard

The Fraser Trilogy

A Beautiful Obsession – Book 1
A Perverse Enmity – Book 2
An Enigmatic Endeavour – Book 3

Shackled
People, Times and Places – A Memoir
That's my Biography – Jimmy Gilbert
(Compiler and joint author)

Dedicated to all my children and their spouses - Jenny and Naj, Mat and Sarah and Sally. To my grandchildren and their partners Sophie and Luke, Josh and Agata, Sam, Maddy and Jess and my great grandson Jonah.

But above all Sally for her unstinting help in so many ways, particularly in the preparation and publishing of this book.

List of characters

Marie d'Albeigne Shawcross – well-connected, successful, fine art expert employed by insurance companies to work alongside police in recovery of stolen paintings etc.

Andreotti an attempted assassin

Sid Atkins, London mobster leader of the Telford Association

Cyril Atkins, Sid's younger brother

Giacomo Balscalso, Lodgehouse keeper

Dimitri Beltrovich, a wealthy Russian oligarch living mainly in London.

David Barber, archivist at Dakins Auctioneers

Belvoir Syndicate, A group mainly operating in Europe that specialise in acquiring works of art on behalf of collectors.

Peter Bird, recently deceased, a friend of Simon Brookes..

Tim Bird, brother of Peter and Yvonne Simmonds

Nicolas Bredask, Beltrovich's business manager

Guy Brodie, friend of Michael Marchant

Simon Brookes, retired, living in the Cotswolds

Benjamin Burns, picture gallery owner and frame maker in Gloucestershire

Antonio Castelini, lives in Rome where he is "known to the police."

Dakins, auctioneers & estate agents in Norwich

Peter Davenport, manager at a City construction site

Trevor Davidson, London manager of JSI based in Camden Town office

Guido Foresta, a guest in the Firenze Porta Baltica Hotel

Hearn & Miller, house clearance agents and dealers

Felix Holder, English owner of apartment in Florence

Edward Holt, Beltrovich's chauffeur/bodyguard

Jeremy Idle, expert in the Italian masters

Harold Jenkins, recluse and art collector

Guido Lambertini, successor to Marcus Welland as Manzini's UK agent

Quinton Leasdon, deceased wealthy businessman

Isambard (Izzy) Leasdon son of Quinton

Letitia Leasdon widow of Quinton

Lord Lionel Leddingham of Dellshot Hall, deceased

Lord Richard Leddingham, Lionel's son

Teodoro Manzini, original and now part owner of Ca' Manzini, a Grand Canale palazzo in Venice.

Carlotta Manzini, deceased mother of Teodoro and sister of Angelo de Vincentti

Michael Marchant, friend of Roberto Vincentti

Reggie Marsden, owner of Ragmar Galleries, based in Norfolk

Alessandro Pagnetti, major domo for both Teodoro Manzini and his father

Yvonne Simmonds, sister of Peter and Tim Bird

Angelo de Vincentti, younger brother of Carlotta Manzini. Dealer in Fine Art

Roberto de Vincentti, son of Alessandro (above). Dealer in Fine Art

Marcus Welland, deceased, former UK agent for Manzini family

Police

In Venice – Commisarrio Albertini, Inspecttore Noblisio

In Florence - Inspettore Superiore Ricci, Sourintendente Calassio

  In London – Met Police - Detective Superintendant Wilkins DCI Major (Serious Crime),

DI Sheila Nelson & DS Denis Price (Met Police Arts & Antiques Unit)

DI Peter Percival, DS Riley (City of London Police)

In Gloucestershire – DI Morgan

Contents

Chapter 1

It was the worst kind of January day, cold and overcast with dark clouds bustling in from the northeast bringing with them spasmodic heavy rain. A dutiful few had ventured out from the church after the funeral service, following the coffin to its final resting place fifty yards away. Wind driven rain found its way past the angled umbrellas, the inadequate hats, adding weight to sodden trousers and stockinged legs and continuing to drip inexorably into squelchy shoes.

Wiping an errant trickle of water from his neck, Simon Brookes pulled his upturned coat collar even tighter and thought that this was the most miserable situation that he had ever found himself in and he hoped his recently deceased old friend Peter Bird, whose funeral this was, would appreciate the effort he was making.

Very conscious of the appalling weather that those gathered around the grave were having to withstand, the vicar speeded up the proceedings as quickly as decency allowed and quite soon the group were running for their cars to drive a few hundred yards to The Pheasant Hotel. They joined earlier arrivals at the reception who were drying off in front of a roaring log fire in the lounge bar, sipping hot coffee and a tot, or a glass of wine, whilst savouring the contents of a varied buffet.

Simon had first met Peter at University when they were in the same College and became good friends and it was in this period that he had also met other members of the Bird family. Later their careers took them both abroad, Peter to academic appointments in the U.S , with Simon spending long periods in Australia and then Singapore, but they always arranged to meet up at least once a year, usually in London. They had both married in their twenties, but both had been widowers now for some years. Simon had three children, all now grown-up, whereas Peter had no offspring, so it was not surprising to Simon that he didn't recognise any of the other people in the hotel lounge.

He chatted to a couple of men who, like him, were on their own. One an ex-colleague from Peter's working days and the other a close neighbour in the Norfolk village, before an attractive lady, he guessed in her mid-fifties, approached and asked "Is it Simon Brookes?" It turned out that she was Peter's younger sister Yvonne, whom he had last met forty years earlier when visiting Peter's home whilst they were at university, and she had still been at school.

They laughed about that and about Peter's idiosyncrasies and then she said "I'm glad I caught up with you because he's left you a painting that you apparently said you liked on a number of occasions. It's quite an attractive piece, not I think by anyone well-known nor valuable, though Peter liked it a lot, in spite of its size and the ghastly frame."

Simon responded at once "Yes, I remember it well' it was of a girl sitting in a garden, she had a particularly intriguing face with a half-smile and laughing eyes, but I know what you mean about the frame, an unusually thick, dull blue/grey thing that did nothing for the picture. Though how generous of Peter to remember me in his will, quite unexpected."

She went on "My husband and I are staying at Peter's cottage for a day or two sorting out some things. It's going to be some time, we think, before we get probate on his will because his estate is rather complicated with properties abroad and so on and where his bequests are small items and have little or no effect on the value of the estate. As an executor I'm hoping to distribute these quickly and wonder, as I gather you've come by car, if you wouldn't mind taking the picture with you?"

Simon agreed and followed the couple back to Peter's cottage where he was duly handed the picture which was somehow much larger than he had remembered being about a metre high and 70 centimetres wide in its bulky frame. He was given an old raincoat to wrap round it and protect it from the relentless rain as he returned back to his car.

A few hours later back at home, he had the first opportunity for many months to examine his newly acquired painting and delight in the generosity of his old friend. It was everything he remembered, a portrait of an attractive oval faced girl looking slightly to one side of the artist, with an intriguing half-smile and eyes that seemed to be full of life and laughter that had been caught so well in the painting. It was difficult to date it, the girl didn't wear a hat or gloves - often a give-away – and her shoulder length hair with a slight wave in it didn't point to any particular time. The lines of her pale blue dress with three-quarter sleeves and a wide neckline had been suggested rather than painted in detail on the slim figure, so no clues there, although the dress length was a little longer than was generally fashionable nowadays.

He really liked the picture and couldn't believe his luck that he was now its owner, though why Peter had left it for so many years surrounded by such an unattractive thick and clunky frame, he couldn't understand. He determined there and then to take the picture the next day to a framer, consult with him on a suitable replacement frame and leave it with him to carry out the work. In the meantime, he could decide where it was going to hang in his Cotswold cottage – pride of place over the mantelpiece in the sitting room, on a side wall, or in the entrance hall to attract the eye of any visitor perhaps?

The next morning he re-wrapped the picture in the old raincoat and drove with it to the nearest town where there was a gallery and picture framer he'd used many years before called intriguingly Glass & Burns. Mr Burns suggested several suitably sized and coloured frames and mounts to compliment the picture and, with difficulty he made his selection and returned home impatient for the week or so to pass before he could put it on display. He was surprised therefore to have a phone call from Mr Burns three days later asking him to call and look at something he had found whilst taking off the old frame. Burns sounded quite excited but refused to be drawn, so Simon agreed he would be there first thing in the morning.

Glass & Burns didn't open up until 9.30am much to Simon's irritation as he had arrived outside the shop at ten past and had to wander aimlessly round the town to fill in twenty minutes. It was in fact nine thirty-four before Burns pulled up the blind and unlocked the door to admit him and it only added to Simon's impatience and surprise when the proprietor after greeting him with a wide smiley "Good morning" added "I'll have to go and get your painting from the safe, I shan't be long," and ambled off towards the back of the premises.

"Why on earth would he need to keep my painting in a safe" thought Simon looking round at the many paintings – originals and prints that lined the walls of the gallery which dominated the front of the shop, or were stacked framed and unframed, in racks against the walls.

A few minutes later Burns beckoned Simon down to the back of the premises and showed him into a workshop where the frames were made, explaining on the way "I thought it would be a bit more private to show you in here as I'm sure you will be as surprised and excited as am I at what I discovered." The painting was laid lengthways on a cleared workbench, covered by a white cloth which he whipped away like a conjurer showing off his prowess. The painting was face down with the wooden backing loosely laid in its original position but with the retaining paper tapes neatly cut through and four retaining screws extracted.

Burns gently removed the wooden backing and a pad of tissue paper that he had placed behind it, to reveal another painting in a slim wooden frame, face up and without any protective glass – no wonder, thought Simon that the original painting had been fitted into such a deep frame. He then reverently lifted the newly discovered picture out and onto the work bench so that they could see it better.

"How very strange" remarked Simon as he moved in closer. Burns was almost beside himself as he pointed excitedly with both hands at the painting and said "But look at the composition, the style and the setting, it looks like the work of one of the Italian Rococo artists of the eighteenth century like Tiepolo. If it's genuine, it could be worth a small fortune!"

Simon peered at the painting which portrayed a group of men sitting around a long table "But there's no signature that I can see, how can you possibly identify who it's by?"

"They often didn't sign their work in those days" Burns went on excitedly "and Giovanni Battista Tiepolo was no different. Before you came this morning, I looked him up. He was prolific in his heyday, around the 1750's, and examples of his art are held in all the world's great galleries, and highly prized. I couldn't see this particular painting listed – it represents, as you have probably realised – the Last Supper – with Christ in the middle surrounded by his disciples. He painted a similar piece between 1745 and 1747 which differs from this one in both its colouring and the positioning of some disciples, although the figure of Christ in the centre with a halo seems to be much the same." Simon continued to gaze at the picture in amazement "So do you think it's genuine?"

"Ah I can't say for sure, that would be up to the experts, and I should warn you that there are a lot of clever forgeries about, indeed you can order on eBay a reproduction, hand painted brush mark by brush mark, of your favourite Tiepolo for less than £500 and only an expert could tell the difference."

Burns continued "However, from my own observations it looks like an old canvas and the style and painting seem to be of the right time, but the most encouraging sign to me is that Tiepolo might well have painted a very similar scene to his well-known "Last Supper "- part of a series- and for some reason put it to one side and kept it. The reason will remain a mystery, but it certainly doesn't lessen the interest that this work will arouse in the art world and beyond."

Whilst he was talking Simon continued to gaze at the picture, wrestling in his mind with the implications of the find and what he should do, and then said, "I understand that in matters of verifying whether or not paintings are genuine, provenance is often the key, are there any labels or markings on the back of this frame that might help?"

"I must confess that I haven't looked" said Burns," because once I saw this painting I was stopped in my tracks, but yes, we must look at the back, but before we do that I think as a matter of record we ought to take a photo of each stage of our discovery, it might perhaps help in tracing the provenance." Simon agreed and the backing was put back on loosely and both of them took pictures of the whole backing, the cut securing tape and the screws, before the back was again removed. Then Burns, donning a pair of cotton gloves, delicately lifted the picture out of the timber frame and laid it on a pad of tissue for protection so that they could look at the back.

It was a slim dark frame, and the back of the picture was held in place with some form of black cotton or linen tape typical of 18th century paintings which was good news. Elsewhere on the back was a partially torn paper label on which one could just discern :

Galleria Aspid......and part of a date, ***22 guigno 17***

Could this be an art dealer's ticket? On one side of the frame barely readable against the dark wood was written in black:

" Ritornare a Residenza Barantella via dela Fava."

(Return to Barantella Residence on dela Fava Street)

Could that be where Tiepolo was living?   It was something –
but not much to go on - and then, another discovery.

Chapter 2

Simon spotted it first. Near the top right corner of the frame's back was a patch that was paler and smoother than its surroundings, shaped rather like a small lollipop. Looking more closely it seemed that this area had been chiselled out and then filled in with some sort of sawdust and filler mix that had hardened and rubbed smooth so that it was barely discernible from the rest of the wooden frame.

"What is this do you think?" he asked.

"Well, I can only guess that something small has been hidden in the frame and covered over."

"Will it affect the value in some way if we explore?"

Burns considered for a moment before responding "I don't think so, after all we're only excavating a small corner of the frame to find what, if anything, lies beneath and it can be restored much more cleverly than it was originally. However, we must take pictures as we go to show what we have done."

Having taken additional photographs in which they tried to highlight the pale area, Burns selected two small chisels from an adjacent bench.

He began carefully, first to outline the pale area with a straight half-inch blade inserted, then using a curved blade to do the same on the rounded lollipop outline. After taking another photograph he then began tapping gently with a quarter-inch chisel to loosen and excavate the cavity and soon disclosed an old key about five centimetres long, made out of two metals.

The bit or blade which fitted into the keyway of a lock was formed in steel or perhaps polished iron which astonishingly, was still gleaming and untouched by rust. This was attached to the shoulder of the key which took the form of an elaborate circle of brass with filigree work. In its centre was a small, enamelled plaque that featured a rearing horse and the letters "de V".

"What do you make of that?" asked Simon twirling the key between his fingers.

"It's too small for a safe key so I would have thought it fitted a lock on a cabinet, a drawer or maybe a box of some sort for jewels or valuables. It's rather elaborate and the little enamelled button with the horse symbol and the lettering would suggest it belonged to someone of distinction."

"It's certainly intriguing and makes me even more curious to discover the provenance of the painting, who owned it, where and when," said Simon.

"I agree" responded Burns "but I think the first step, before we get too excited, would be to have it confirmed by an expert on the artist, as a genuine piece of work by Tiepolo. As I said he is often faked or copied and only an expert eye and scientific tests will prove one way or another. Lack of provenance is going to be a problem and the way that it has been hidden away in this manner doesn't help.

However, if you like I'll make some more enquiries and see if I can locate an expert in this country who is prepared to give an opinion?"

"Would you do that please and of course I will happily pay for your time and expenses on the research. May I leave the two paintings in your safe keeping for the time being?" continued Simon. That was agreed and Burns promised to be in touch as soon as he had any news.

Simon returned home turning over in his mind the events of the morning. He was excited by the possibilities that had opened up but was conscious that there were other questions to be resolved. Had Peter realised that hidden beneath the painting that he had bequeathed to Simon was another potentially much more valuable piece? Should he not, in all honesty, tell Peter's executors and inheritors of his estate of what he had found at this stage, even though the picture had not been authenticated; or should he wait until it was identified as the real thing or not, and valued accordingly?

He wrestled with his dilemma for another day before deciding to contact Peter's sister, Yvonne and update her on his current findings. She had seemed a reasonable, pleasant woman who would, he thought, take the rational view that Peter had bequeathed in his will a framed painting to his friend Simon, and whether or not he knew that the frame also enclosed another more valuable painting, was irrelevant.

And so it proved. Simon phoned her and told her the whole story, she was intrigued by the discovery and seemed quite delighted by Simon's good fortune should it turn out to be genuine.

At no time did she express any doubts or second thoughts about the bequest in the changed circumstances, merely wished good luck with the authentication and valuation process and a request to let her know in due course what happened.

Meanwhile, Benjamin Burns had been using his contacts in the art world to find an expert on Tiepolo in the UK who would be prepared to give an initial opinion on the painting. At this stage he knew it was unlikely, without a detailed forensic examination, to get someone to give a more definite answer as to whether it was a genuine Tiepolot, but a "favourable possibility" or even a "negative impression" would be helpful in deciding how to go forward.

His enquiries led to him to Jeremy Idle, an expert on the paintings of Italian Masters, who until quite recently had been with Sotheby's the art auctioneers and happened to be involved when a large Tiepolo painting was sold at auction in 2019 for $17.3 million. He did not claim to be a top expert on Tiepolo but was very familiar with his work.

When Burns told Idle about the painting and the circumstances in which it had been discovered, his curiosity and interest were aroused and he was agreeable to having a quick look, particularly as he was in Gloucestershire the following week. He arranged to call on at Burns' premises the following Friday afternoon, Burns told Simon, who would also make sure he was there.

When Idle, a colourful figure in his brick red trousers and yellow jacket first saw the old painting, he tugged hard with his thumb and forefinger at his flamboyant handlebar moustache whilst looking closely through a torch lit magnifying glass held in his other hand.

He slowly tracked to and fro and up and down as the others looked on, for fully ten minutes, before turning the painting over to look at the back.

After turning the painting over again and laying down the magnifying glass on the bench he looked at the others, tugged at both sides of his moustache and backed towards a handy chair. He sat and uttered one word "Remarkable."

"You mean" began Simon hesitantly "that you think it might be a genuine Tiepolo?"

Idle replied, "Well, the brushwork and the masterful and almost unique way that a central figure has been highlighted with others painted in unusual positions are very persuasive. I don't know whether you know that Tiepolo painted a series of six paintings on *The Life of Christ* between the years 1745 and 1747. I think most of them are in the Louvre, but certainly the painting he made of *The Last Supper* is there, and this is another version of the same scene with, if my memory serves me correctly, another figure shown and the disciples arranged around the table slightly differently, but with Christ in the centre as before."

"Why would he paint another version of the same scene?" asked Simon.

"Any number of reasons, and it is not all that unusual, although if the artist was unhappy or dissatisfied with a painting nearing completion, he would generally paint it over or change it as necessary. I suspect in this case, having finished the painting, somebody else – possibly the patron who had commissioned the work – didn't like something about it and asked him to slightly change it and the artist who liked it, rather than make changes, painted another to the patron's requirements."

"Would you at this stage be prepared to state that in your opinion it is a Tiepolo?" asked Burns.

"I can only reiterate what I said just now. Nothing I have seen rules it out as a Tiepolo, but it would need some scientific tests to be made of the paint used, the canvas and so forth to verify that it is broadly contemporary with his other works in the same series. Possibly X-Ray and Infra-red photography as well, and most importantly it would have to be accepted by one of the recognised experts on Tiepolo as one of his."

"Can you point us in the right direction to get those things done?" asked Simon.

"Yes, I think I can help you there, but you must realise that a real stumbling block to gaining its verification as a genuine Tiepolo is the complete lack of any provenance for the picture. There is no reference, as far as I know, of the picture being painted, and no entry in any Tiepolo catalogue or gallery sale reports on of another version of *The Last Supper*. It leaves a big question mark and would entail a great deal of original research to come up with something on the provenance that would satisfy the experts."

Simon asked him "To what extent can you help us Mr Idle? I would of course recompense you for your time, expertise and all the necessary tests and examinations by experts that are required to confirm or deny that it is a Tiepolo."

"That's fine" responded Idle "I can certainly do that for you, but establishing a provenance for the painting is, I think, going to be a long, difficult and – I have to be frank – quite likely a fruitless task, and I haven't the time that needs to be devoted to it.

It is almost certain to require research abroad in the archives of galleries, art dealers and auction houses and so forth and will need the dedicated work of someone who is prepared to go the extra mile in persistence, questioning and following up clues. I don't honestly know if there is anyone I can recommend in this instance .

I can give you names of several people, so called experts in their field, who will write you beautiful reports on what they are doing and how hard they are working, who will charge you very high fees for their travels, their stays in the best hotels and their researches and probably, very little to show you in return. You don't want that, I'm sure."

"Well no," replied Simon "but what do you recommend I do?"

"It is quite simple and clear to me – do it yourself." said Idle. "I gather you are retired with no ties to keep you from travelling, Mr Brookes and you are keen to uncover the hidden history of the painting, I think there is nobody better for the task."

Simon was slightly taken aback "But I'm no expert, remember, until a day or two ago I knew nothing of Giovanni Battiste Tiepolo or any other painter for that matter, and I've no experience and probably not the patience for researching through old documents in archives overseas."

Idle smiled reassuringly "It's not as bad as it sounds, all the leading galleries and auction houses keep their archives well indexed and cross-referenced and employ very helpful and well-informed archivists. Look on it as a treasure hunt where every discovery is a step towards establishing a provenance and where each step will quite often point towards other avenues worth researching.

Knowing every last detail about Tiepolo's work is not of first importance. Although you can read-up on that, it is research that is the only key to provenance if none has so far been established."

" But I wouldn't know where to start" protested Simon.

"You've got an address in Venice and a key which is something, but if I were you, I'd start with the girl painting. Where and when did your friend acquire the picture, surely somebody in his family or a friend must have a clue and this big clumsy frame must have been especially made for it with space to accommodate the hidden Tiepolo."

With some trepidation, Simon agreed he would make a start and agreed that Idle could take the Tiepolo painting away to have the various exploratory tests carried out and seek expert acceptance. A special padded carrying case was to be made to hold it by Benjamin Burns, who would also carefully de-construct the big frame to see if there was any clue as to where and by whom it had been made. They arranged to meet up again in a few days when Burns would have the carrying case ready.

When Simon returned home there was a message on his answer phone from Yvonne Simmonds, Peter Bird's sister asking him to ring her urgently.

Chapter 3

When Simon rang Yvonne, she immediately began the conversation with an apology.

"I'm really sorry to involve you in this, but in handing over that painting to you, according to the lawyer who is an executor of Peter's will together with my other brother Tim in Australia, and myself, I was acting prematurely, before probate is granted, and he gave me a sharp rap over the knuckles. Legally speaking – would you believe – you should hand it back only to be given it again after probate!

A load of codswallop I agree, and told the solicitor so, but anyway he now requires a letter from you confirming that you have taken possession of the painting in accordance with Peter's will. He's sending you a draft to follow and when he gets that back he will send on to you a letter that Peter had written you to accompany the bequest.

"Again, I'm sorry about all this but the solicitor wishes to make it all legal and proper."

Simon agreed he would respond immediately he heard from the solicitor, thinking as he ended the call that Peter's letter might answer some of the questions about the older picture's provenance or at least provide a clue to follow up.

The next day, a phone call from Benjamin Burns. He had completely dismantled the thick, dingy blue frame and whilst doing so had discovered on an inner edge a small, thin brass label that read – *'Burlingham Gallery'.*

"Wow" responded Simon "a clue at last. Does that indicate, do you think, where the picture of the girl was bought or where the frame was made?"

"It could be both" replied Burns "and thinking along the same lines I looked up some references to see whether I could find a gallery operating under that name but I'm afraid found none. On the other hand, if that picture was painted as I suspect between 1920 and 1935 it would be unusual for a small art gallery and framer still to be operating to-day over a hundred years later, and under the same name. I sound a bit negative I know, but I thought I'd let you know as soon as I'd found it."

After the call, despite Burns discouraging conclusions, Simon felt that the brass plate was a good place to start.

He googled "Association of Art Galleries and Framers" and turned up The Fine Art Trade Guild, an organisation which represented Fine Art Galleries and Framers. If Burlingham Gallery was a former member then it would be listed somewhere. The Guild address was in Wandsworth, south London, and he phoned to find out whether they had records of former members. They had, and he was welcome to look through their old membership lists if he called in. He decided immediately to travel up to London the next day and do so.

Justifying a full day in London with a couple of other appointments that he was able to make, he caught an early train into Paddington and then took a taxi to the Wandsworth address.

They were very helpful and sourced membership lists for the years 1900 through to 1920, which covered the early years in which Burns had suggested the girl painting was created. He initially drew a blank, but in the lists for 1920 to 1930 he was delighted to discover, in 1926, a first entry for Burlingham Gallery & Frame Maker, listed with an address in Norwich. He quickly checked in successive years and the name was consistently recorded as a member.

With the help of the Guild staff, he was able to establish that the Burlingham Gallery was still in business until 2002, when their membership ceased. There was no other information available at the Guild so with many thanks for their help he left, had lunch with an old friend, kept his other appointments and caught the train back to Gloucestershire.

On the journey home, he thought about his next step. Although Burlingham Gallery had been out of business for twenty years, it was possible that a member of the business owner's family or a former employee might remember something about the strange thick blue-grey frame that had been fabricated in their workshop to unusual inner dimensions. He was not optimistic about finding any accounts or records after all this time, they would have been destroyed long ago but there was a tiny chance, and it was certainly worth exploring.

He looked in his diary and saw that he was clear the following week from Tuesday until Friday and decided he would drive to

Norwich on Tuesday and booked a room at an hotel near the city centre for two nights.

He calculated that with a stop for coffee en-route, it would take him the best part of four and a half hours to drive from Gloucestershire to Norwich, so left home at 7.30 am. However, he drove into the hotel car park just after half past eleven, time to book in and take a walk before lunch in the centre. He soon found the address where Burlingham's had been situated some twenty years before in Exchange Street, it was now a charity shop.

He talked to the shop manager who, although she had lived in Norwich much of her life, did not remember the premises being a picture gallery and framers before it had become a charity shop. She remembered it as a lady's dress shop and she thought before that a book shop. She addressed one of the older volunteers working in the shop "Val do you remember a picture gallery and framer called Burlingham, being in these premises some years back?"

Val, a grey-haired lady with a pronounced stoop, turned out to be a fountain of knowledge with a good memory and replied "Yes, I remember it very well, but it closed about twenty years ago. It was a very smart shop, always worth looking in their windows as they had interesting pictures and prints on display. As a matter of fact, a neighbour of mine, Bill Marsden worked for them for many years until they closed down."

Simon's heart gave a bound "Is this Bill Marsden still your neighbour?"

"No, he was well into his eighties when he died two years back."

Simon immediately felt deflated and having started to thank her before leaving was conscious that she was paying no attention and was lost in thought before she suddenly came out with "Now it comes back to me, Bill had a son in the business.

"Reggie joined them as an apprentice frame maker. Then he had a row with both old Crossthwaite who owned the business, and his father, and left. They never made it up properly, father and son I mean, particularly as Reggie set up his own business as a frame maker here in Norwich and, from all accounts has done well."

"Is he still in business?" asked Simon.

"As far as I know, you quite often see the ads in the local paper, for Regmar Galleries, and I suppose he's still involved although I haven't seen him for years. His business is on the other side of town, and I haven't ever been there." She was able to give him the approximate address and he thanked her profusely for her help before setting off for Regmar Galleries, which was situated on a spacious, well-designed combination of business and retail park.

The Galleries occupied a central position amongst exclusive shops and a top supermarket branch and was larger than Simon had surmised. It had separate sections – rather like an arcade – offering not only a large area devoted to paintings, prints and framing, but also some fine furniture, a design studio, some antiques and a pretty tearoom overlooking a garden at the back. Having made a cursory walk-through,

Simon approached an older assistant in the Art Department and asked if it was possible to see Mr Reginald Marsden.

The assistant looked Simon up and down before he asked, "Have you an appointment sir?" Simon said no but was very keen to have a brief conversation with Mr Marsden about a period some forty years ago when he worked at Burlingham's.

His explanation however cut no ice with the assistant who responded imperiously "Mr Marsden is a very busy man and I doubt very much that he has the time to deal with casual callers. I suggest you write to him with your query and if necessary, he will make an appointment to see you."

Whilst he was delivering his rudely dismissive message, he was unaware that a man had emerged from a door behind him and was listening. The man then said sharply "Thank you Jarvis, I will now look after this gentleman." As the man moved forward and out of the half shadow Simon suddenly realised that he knew or at least recognised him, but from where?

Chapter 4

At six foot three Reginald Marsden topped Simon by a couple of inches, and his chiselled features with silver grey hair would make him stand out in any company, but Simon couldn't momentarily place where he had met him and admitted as much.

"You are right" Marsden said "we have met, and not that long ago. Are you local?"

"No, I live in Gloucestershire" replied Simon. "So unless you have been down my way, we both must have travelled to be in the same place at the same time."

Marsden pondered a little and then exclaimed "I've got it, and you are right we both travelled to be guests at my niece's wedding in Bedford last month, I guess you were on the groom's side?"

"That's right he is my nephew. Well, I'm glad we sorted that out."

"Yes, it's irritating when you can't place someone you've met, and embarrassing sometimes." They both laughed and Marsden went on, "but I gather from what I heard of your conversation with Mr Jarvis that you wanted to ask me something about when I worked at Burlingham's.

"That's a long time ago now, and I was only with them for a few years, but I'm happy to help if I can remember. Perhaps, now that we've established that we are almost related, you'll join me for some tea whilst I tax my memory. We can go into our teashop just along at the back here" and led the way.

When they were seated at a table overlooking an attractive garden and with an order given to the waitress, Simon explained the situation and described the unusually large and thick frame that bore the "Burlingham" label and held a painting of a laughing girl in a garden. He omitted to mention the other painting hidden in its interior. Marsden's reply was a surprise.

"Yes, I remember that unusual frame, it was a special commission that had been made to very precise measurements, I remember it particularly well because it was made by my father, some years before I joined Burlinghams. It stood, covered in a cloth, paid for but unclaimed, in a corner of the workshop for a long time."

"Did they not give a name or an address when they placed the order?"

"No, it was all rather strange. According to my father a man called Wendell (somehow that name stuck in my memory) walked into Burlingham's one day, asked if they could make a picture frame for him to precise measurements which would, he knew, make it unusually thick and heavy but that is what he wanted. He produced drawings with the exact measurements which my father looked at and agreed that it could be done although it would not be a particularly attractive frame to compliment a painting.

"Wendell was clearly not interested in the look of the thing, and when asked about the picture it would hold, admitted, surprisingly, that he had not chosen that yet and perhaps my father would help him.

"My father told me that Wendell was less interested in the subject matter and more in the size of the painting. He eventually settled on that attractive picture you described, of a smiling girl in a garden. It had been painted in the twenties or thirties by a local artist, and later acquired by the gallery from a private sale. Wendell took my father's advice on the mounting but was initially adamant that the frame itself should be left plain wood, only agreeing reluctantly to the suggestion that it should be painted a plain light blue."

"As it was such a special commission that couldn't be sold elsewhere, my father told Wendell that it would have to be paid for in advance and that it would take him a while to work out the cost. Wendell however, responded that he was in a hurry and would be happy to pay there and then, in cash, Dad's highest estimate for picture and frame.

With little chance to think, my father mentioned what, in retrospect, he termed 'an absurdly high figure'. Wendell didn't show any reaction except to withdraw a fat wallet from an inner pocket and count out the notes on the counter. He accepted a receipt and the assurance that it would be ready for collection in ten days and left."

"So, what happened to the framed painting, after, as you said, it had sat for a long time in the corner of the workshop?"

said Simon.   Marsden thought for a moment before he continued. "It was in 1992, my last year at Burlinghams, so it must have been about seven or eight years after the frame had been made.

"I took a phone call from someone with a heavy accent – I think Italian – who asked if we still held a painting called "Laura" by Lawrence Dence set in a deep frame, made for a Mr Wendell, that should have been collected some years before. I asked him if he had the receipt and he confirmed that he had, adding that he was very pleased that we still had it, and apologised for the very long delay in collection which he said was due to an accident involving Mr Wendell and a consequent loss of the receipt for some years.

"He then asked if it was possible for Burlingham's to construct a timber crate to hold the picture and frame, suitable to ship it abroad. I confirmed that we could do that by the following week and he said his agent would pick both of them up and pay what was due for the crate. As agreed, his agent, someone from Stephenson's the specialist fine art shippers, came, produced the receipt, and departed with the framed painting and crate. That would be in 1992, and that's the last I saw or heard of it until now." He poured both of them another cup of tea.

"That, if I may say so, was a most detailed yet succinct account - Bravo!" said Simon and silently mimed a round of applause.

Marsden smiled and went on "I'm glad to be of service, but I'm just surprised that it is so important to you to learn when and where the frame was made, and the picture bought?"

Ignoring the question Simon asked Marsden another "Why did you think that such a clumsy design of a frame had been asked for?"

"Well, it was pretty clear both to my father and me that it could only be to carry another picture concealed behind the picture of the girl."

Simon thought quickly. Although Marsden had told him everything about the frame and the picture, it didn't take him much further along the road of discovery, and he decided to tell Marsden the whole story – it might help.

"You're right, Mr Marsden" he said and went on to tell his companion the full background to his enquiries including the hidden painting – hopefully a Tiepolo.

When Simon had finished, Marsden commented "That's a fascinating story and I can see how important it is to for you to trace the provenance of the old painting to help prove it is by Tiepolo. I'm only sorry that I haven't been able to help much other than to tell you where and when the frame was made and when it was eventually collected."

He stopped abruptly as a thought struck him and after a pause went on "I'll tell you what though, I know the local manager of Stephenson's the fine art and antique shippers, we have dealings with him from time to time. Maybe he can trace from his records the name and address of the person or company who arranged for the framed painting to be picked up. If we are lucky, we can find out where it was shipped to. Do you want me to try him?"

Simon enthusiastically agreed and they left the tearoom and went into Marsden's office where he telephoned his contact at Stephensons only to find he had left for the day. Marsden promised to ring him again first thing in the morning and then to phone Simon.

Walking back to his hotel, Simon was not disappointed at what he had discovered so far and there was a slim chance that, if the records still existed, he may find out who instructed Stephensons and to where and to whom the painting had been shipped.

The next morning, as promised, Simon received a call from Marsden who had spoken to his contact at Stephensons and was told that all the archived records and documents from all the branches pre-2010 were held at a storage unit in Essex. He doubted that that they would still hold anything from as long ago as 1992, but he was checking. An hour later he called Simon again to say that they did indeed still hold the records for that year in the archives.

But there was a snag, they would only allow a search of the archives to be carried out by someone who was personally known and could be vouched for by a manager at Stephensons. Whilst his contact was willing and able to vouch for Marsden, he could not do the same for Mr Brookes. With some reluctance however, it had been agreed that Mr Brookes could accompany Mr Marsden providing that he in turn would vouch for Brookes, which he happily did.

Simon's immediate response was "Oh no, that is too much to ask you to do. It is extremely good of you to offer, but really, I cannot agree to putting you to all that trouble."

"It is no trouble at all I can assure you. I've become quite intrigued in the whole business and after all," he added with a laugh "we're almost related so I'm helping family, aren't I?"

After a few more expressions of doubt and reassurance, Simon accepted the offer, and it was agreed that they would go to the archive unit the next day. It was quite near the junction of the M11 and the M25. Simon would drive them both there from Norwich in a couple of hours or so and having completed their search would take Marsden to Chelmsford to catch a train back to Norwich.

They had an early breakfast together at Simon's hotel over which they agreed to use Simon and Reg in future and were away before 8.30am. It was an agreeable journey together and it seemed that the time had passed very quickly when they drew up beside the Stephenson Archive Storage unit. Necessary verification completed, they were quickly seated at a table drinking coffee and awaiting the arrival of the records for the office covering Norwich for the year 1992. The documents had all been digitised after about 2010 but these were all original documents, copy invoices, statements, customer records and notes and there were an awful lot of them.

Reg recalled that it was summer, probably June or early July of that year when Stephenson's picked up the picture and crate, so they made a start by looking through the order book and the invoices for June, looking for any reference to an instruction to pick up from Burlingham's, or an invoice covering the transaction. They looked without result and turned to the July records. There, to their delight, they found an order entry for the 5th that read:

Order No. 92FA 7432.   Giancarlo Balgazzi A.d'A.I.

1. Collect from Burlingham Gallery, Norwich, after 15/7/92 framed oil painting - Maria by Lawrence Dence plus special shipping crate.   Pay charges.

2. Ship crated picture to Pagnatti, Palazzo Ca' Manzini, Canal Grande, Venice. Italia."

Simon looked at Reg, both were smiling broadly, "Bingo!" he said. "It's a bonanza – you've got so much information there," responded Reg.

"If we look in the copy invoices for the end of the same month or August we should find an invoice made out to Mr Balgazzi, which might tell us more. "

Sure enough, a swift search revealed a copy invoice dated 7/8/92 made out to Mr Giancarlo Balgazzi, at Agenzia d'affari Italiana, with an address in London W1. It reiterated much that had been on the order, with the additional information that crate and contents had been despatched airfreight from Gatwick to Marco Polo airport Venice on the 4th August.

Simon quickly googled Agenzia d'affari Italiana to find that the company had ceased operating ten years before, so there was no chance of speaking to Signor Balgazzi, not that it was strictly necessary as they now knew where the painting had been sent.

Simon said that he had now more than one reason for visiting Venice quickly and told Reg that he intended to fly out the next week. Rather diffidently Reg responded, "I wonder whether you could put up with a companion on your Italian research, only I'm due some holiday and frankly am fascinated by this whole thing and would like to tag along if you are agreeable."

"Delighted" replied Simon, and they made a plan to meet up on the following Tuesday in a Venice Hotel.

After taking Reg to Chelmsford station Simon drove home to Gloucestershire and to a mixed bag of news.

Chapter 5

On the front door mat, amongst the newspapers, bills, unwanted catalogues and take-away menus, was a card from the postman, who had been unable to deliver a letter, as a signature was required and a consequent trip to the sorting office needed – which was a nuisance. But the most unnerving thing was a rather garbled message on the answerphone from Benjamin Burns.

It started "Mr Brookes - Simon. I'm terribly sorry but I may have been indiscreet and said more than I should have done. About your painting I mean - .to the wrong person. Oh dear, I'm not making much sense. Can you ring me back and I'll explain. Thanks - and oh this is Benjamin Burns if you haven't gathered. I'm sorry again."

It was too late to phone him then, but the following morning he rang to find Benjamin full again of apologies and not making a deal of sense, so, Simon interrupted him and said "Ben, calm down and just tell me what has happened."

"Yes, sorry, well it was just as Jeremy Idle was picking up the Tiepolo painting and its carrying case that I had made. Whilst he was signing for it, he remarked how fascinating this whole business was – finding the hidden painting behind another one and the fact that it was possibly a lost masterpiece by Tiepolo.

"He had become quite excited and was speaking in a loud voice that could easily be heard in the rest of the gallery although I wasn't aware there was anybody in there. Anyway, he left, and I found – to my horror - that there had been another customer in the Gallery who had heard every word of our conversation. In most circumstances that wouldn't really matter, an overheard conversation would usually be quickly forgotten, but most unfortunately the eavesdropper was a local newspaper reporter who quite often drops in for a chat and to garner any local gossip that is newsworthy.

"After Idle went out of the door, the reporter immediately approached me and said, "That sounds an interesting story, can you tell me more?" I told him "No, at this stage it is subject to client confidentiality and mainly conjecture and I would appreciate it if you forgot what you overheard.

"However, Tomkinson – that's his name – was persistent and said he would write about what he had heard after a bit of research on Tiepolo and so on, on the basis of it being a strong rumour and put it to me that it surely would be better to ensure that the known facts on authenticity and provenance issues were correct from the start?"

He went on "I tried to persuade him to delay publication by agreeing that, after the research work on the painting and its provenance had been accepted or rejected, he would be given exclusive access to those involved to write a full story, and in the meantime I would give him an outline of what had happened so far. The best he would promise however would be to delay anything appearing in print or on-line for a couple of weeks."

"Well, that's something" said Simon "and I don't really think that a couple of paragraphs in a Gloucestershire newspaper is going to be much of an encumbrance to our research, so don't worry Ben, and thanks for letting me know. As you know, I'm off to Italy in a couple of days and if you want to contact me, here's my mobile number."

Simon didn't think much more about Ben's gaffe and soon set off for the sorting office, to pick up his recorded letter. He could see from the envelope that it was from the solicitors who were executors to Peter Bird's will and doubtless it contained the letter that was to have accompanied the bequest. Back in his car he was tempted to open it there and then but restrained himself. He drove home and sat down with a cup of coffee before he slit open the outer envelope which sure enough contained a covering letter from the solicitor and another envelope addressed to Simon in Peter's hand.

As he opened it, he fervently hoped that it would explain everything and provide at least a guide to the provenance of the old painting, but it did nothing of the sort except in a cryptical sort of way. It read:

My dear Simon,

I'm sorry we never had a chance of saying "good-bye" before I shuffled off, because I have highly valued our friendship that has continued over the lord knows how many years, but there it is.

I wanted to leave you a token of my respect and affection and knowing that you rather admired the painting Laura by Lawrence Dence, or 'The Girl in the Garden' as you called it, I have bequeathed it to you.

Whilst I hope you enjoy it gracing the walls of your cottage I should tell you that it is surrounded by a mystery I have found impossible to solve. If you seek to learn more, I sincerely wish you every success in your endeavours, possibly under Adriatic skies, but take care, there are always those who would thwart your efforts.

Sincerely,

Peter

This seemed to indicate to Simon that Peter knew about the hidden painting within the frame – the mystery. However, he'd failed to solve it, presumably he had been unable to prove authenticity or trace its provenance. But why be so secretive – why not state where and why he had failed? The only pointer was his reference to Adriatic skies – i.e. Venice, and he thought, I'm going there anyway in a couple of days despite the strange warning.

Simon had agreed with Reggie that they should make a holiday of their few days in Venice in addition to the research. They had booked rooms at a luxury hotel overlooking the Grand Canal, the Ca' Sagredo, a 15th century palazzo which, appropriately, had many walls and ceilings painted by old Venetian masters including Gio Battista Tiepolo. Flying in from different UK airports, they arrived at the hotel just two hours apart and met up in the bar before dinner.

Greeting each other with enthusiasm they ordered drinks and sat at a table so that Simon could bring Reggie up to date on the letter from Peter Bird, Ben and Idle's indiscrete conversation and the consequences that had followed from the eavesdropping Tomkinson.

As they talked Simon's mobile rang, and looking at the screen he remarked "Talk of the devil – it's Ben – I'd better take this, if you don't mind" and turned away as he pressed the button and began "Hello Ben, you find me sipping a drink in a Venetian bar, are there problems?"

"Hello Simon. Yes, I hope you had a good trip and I'm sorry to disturb you but thought I better tell you that there has been an unfortunate development. You remember I told you Tomkinson, the reporter had agreed to delay publishing anything about the painting for a couple of weeks. Well, his editor, on hearing the story, overruled him and has gone much further by contacting a national newspaper with the story – I think it's *The Times* – which likes to feature stories on rediscovered masterpieces, buried Saxon caches of gold or Roman mosaic pavements.

"Anyway, it looks likely that some sort of story is going to appear in the paper any day now. I doubt it will mention names, but it will without doubt mention the Tiepolo painting and the circumstances of its discovery. I really am sorry that this has happened and if there is anything I can do to help..." his voice tailed off.

"Thanks for letting me know Ben, there really is nothing we can do except wait and see what appears in the paper, I'll keep in touch," said Simon and ended the call. He told Reggie precisely what Ben had said and they discussed the implications.   A story about a newly discovered Tiepolo painting in *The Times* would certainly be picked up by Italian newspapers, particularly those circulating in Venice, but they felt it was unlikely to hamper their enquiries much, even if people put two and two together and realised they were connected.

After dinner in the hotel, the duo admired the Tiepolo ceiling and frescoes and learned that the artist was equally if not more famous for this type of elaborate decorative splendour than his smaller work. Having discovered that the Palazzo Ca' Manzini was less than half a kilometre from their hotel along the Grand Canal and it being a warm evening, they decided to walk that way and have a look at the one of the places that they planned to visit and make enquiries the following day.

Venice is a fascinating city, particularly at night alongside and at the back of the Canal Grande. There are a variety of contrasting building. Some are built in the Moorish style, illuminated brightly in pink or yellow, others are of more sober architectural fashions ranging from Baroque to Renaissance and Gothic and they take on a special air of mystery that fires one's imagination. As it was not possible to walk the whole way beside the Canale they experienced some extraordinary sights as they traversed bridges and travelled up little side canals, finding their way.

The palazzo Ca' Manzini turned out to be a rather rundown, formerly grand palazzo, the lower floor of which housed some sort of business with apartments on other floors. It was ill-lit externally and there were no obvious clues that they could see as to who lived or worked there. All doors were firmly locked and anonymous. A few lights could be seen on the upper floors, which confirmed that at least someone lived there, but they were a little disappointed as they turned to make their way back to the hotel.

When they were in the bar again having a nightcap, Simon's phone pinged and showed a message from Ben "Look at article in *The Times* tomorrow.   Fear the worst.   Ben."

Chapter 6

Simon enquired from the concierge at what time of the day English newspapers became available and was surprised to learn that using the latest technology, a European edition of The Times that was printed in Rome, generally arrived in Venice by about 9am. There was a well-known shop at the back of St Mark's Square that always had the earliest copies.

Soon after breakfast he and Reggie were walking the short distance from their hotel to the newsagents to find that copies of *The Times* had just arrived. They bought one each so that they could quickly scan the pages to find any article relating to the Tiepolo find. Reggie spotted it first – a quarter page spread including a reproduction of the known Tiepolo painting of *The Last Supper* that was part of the series of the Life of Christ held in the Louvre. There was also an account of how "what is strongly believed by experts" to be another version of the same scene, had been discovered in Gloucestershire, hidden behind another painting in the same frame.

No names were mentioned or any clues as to ownership, but the article made much of the sale of Tiepolo's larger *"Madonna of the Rosary with Angels"* at Sothebys in 2019 for $17.4 million.

The headline and article speculated that the value of the newly discovered smaller painting, if verified, could be "well in excess of £5 million."

They discussed the implications over coffee, and neither were inclined to change their view from the previous evening. They made their way back to their hotel, where Simon picked up his carrying case for his i-pad and notebook before they retraced their steps and made their way again to Palazzo Ca' Manzini.

The old palazzo was no more impressive by day than it had been at night, in sharp contrast to its neighbouring building that featured a frontage of Moorish shaped pale stone framed windows encased by bright red stucco walls that had been beautifully restored. The dull grey stone Manzini building was accessed not only by the Grand Canale but also at the rear by a small canal linked by a narrow calle and it was from there that the business that seemed to occupy much of the ground floor operated. High folding wooden doors were partially open and a lobby behind displayed the sign" Palazzo Computer e Innovazione".

Further down the calle at the corner of the palazzo, where it met the front overlooking the Canale, they noticed a line of black iron railings and an elegant wrought iron gate which carried at its centre an enamelled coat of arms that looked familiar to Simon – a rearing horse and the letters de V against a blue background. He felt in his jacket pocket and brought out something he now always carried with him, the key that had been buried in the picture frame, the enamelled image on the key matched the other precisely.

They passed through the gate which gave onto a narrow path and steps leading down to the water and also to the pillared front of the palazzo. They walked up to a tall arched recess and the grand front door. Beyond this lay a tall spacious lobby with a spectacular sweeping staircase and to one side of this a rickety old-style lift with metal folding doors.

Displayed on the lobby wall were the names of occupants of the appartamenti, of which there were two on the Primo piano, four on Secondo piano and six on Terza Piano. There was a rich assortment of names from many countries, but only one caught Simon's eye. It was a Manzini, presumably of the family that had built the palazzo in the 17th century, still in residence in one of the second floor apartments, but no Pagnatti.

There was no sign of a building manager or concierge so they decided to make a few enquiries first with the computer company occupying the ground floor hoping that there would be someone there who could speak English. They were in luck as there were several. It turned out that the company did not only repair computers but employed a team working on creating and producing graphics for computer games, where it was important to speak good English.

The General Manager, a Signor Mantovani, was particularly forthcoming. He had been one of the original team that started up the company six years before and had negotiated with the palazzo owners to lease the ground floor for the company. The terms of the lease had allowed them to make extensive alterations within the shell of the old building to accommodate a modern IT company. This included strengthening the whole structure which had been welcomed by the owners and had resulted in very favourable terms on the lease.

Simon remarked that whilst the ground floor was internally now very modern and stylish in the furnishings and decoration, it stood in stark contrast to the rest of the palazzo which, externally at least, showed signs of dereliction over many years.

Mantovani agreed and went on "It is all due to an on-going disagreement between the joint owners, a property developer, SSIV, and the remaining members of the Manzini family. SSIV acquired from the family a sixty percent share in ownership of the palazzo some seven years ago, which allowed for considerable improvements to be carried out inside and out, but they had never started. As part of the deal SSIV wanted to develop the first floor with its imposing entrance on the Canale, and its high lobby with sweeping staircase as a fine restaurant, leaving the second and top floor to be made over into eight modernised apartments. The palazzo sales agreement allowed for "significant development" only to take place with the approval of two-thirds of the shareholders and the Manzinis wouldn't agree.

"So the palazzo falls further into decay whilst the wheels of the bureaucratic, creaky Italian judicial system grind slowly onwards. Hampered at every stage by amendments, claims and counter claims until the judges in their wisdom decide on what constitutes a 'significant development.' In the meantime, because promised improvements have not been carried out, half of the present apartments have become empty – it's all rather sad really."

"I agree" began Simon "I see from the residents listing that one of the apartments is still lived in by a Manzini – is he or she a member of the original family that lived in the palazzo?"

"Yes indeed" responded Mantovani "that is Teodoro Manzini, now in his eighties, who lives in some style in his second-floor apartment. I think he is the last of the old family here in Venice." "He would be able to tell you something about the Signor Pagnatti you seek, as I believe he has lived in the palazzo all his life. Mind you he doesn't welcome visitors and his housekeeper is a dragon gatekeeper who rarely lets anyone through the door to see him."

Thanking Mantovani profusely for all his help and information, Simon and Reggie took their leave and walked again along the side of the palazzo to the little wrought iron gate with its coat of arms. They had quickly agreed that a visit to the elderly Manzini was the next obvious step to take, and that there was no time like the present, so they pushed open the little gate and entered through the palazzo front door and on into the lobby, past the beautiful staircase to the small lift beside it.

The rickety lift conveyed them slowly to the second floor where an old sign pointed them along a corridor to the junction with a wider one and the top of the staircase. To the left, facing each other were high, elaborately carved double doors to Apartamenti 1 and 2, each with large highly polished brass knockers in the shape of sea serpents. As there was an old fashioned bell-pull on the wall beside the door to number one Simon gave it a tug and could hear a faint tinkling from inside which showed it was working. Nothing happened for a couple of minutes, so he gave it another tug which resulted in the door being opened a few inches to reveal a rather annoyed looking woman's face. After eyeing them both up and down she merely asked "Si?"

Lifting his Panama hat politely Simon responded with "Bon giorno Signora, do you speak English?
"Si....yes a little" she replied.

Simon explained that they would like to speak to Signor Manzini for a few minutes if convenient, only to be told that he was not receiving visitors that day and she would not agree to make an appointment as his health was poor.   Simon persisted however and spoke much louder in case Signor Manzini was nearby and heard him, "I assure you Signora I would not detain him long as I merely wish to ask him about a Signor Pagnatti and a painting that was sent to him at this address from England about thirty years ago. I'm sure he would be interested in what we have to tell him."

His gamble worked as a small dapper man with grey hair and a well- trimmed Van Dyke type beard and moustache pulled the door wider, stepped beside the woman and in impeccable English said "I am intrigued by what you say sir, so gentlemen step inside."

He ushered them from the small vestibule into a sitting room where he began "I am Manzini, and you are?" he put out his hand as Simon introduced himself and Reggie. Manzini gestured to chairs for them to sit down and asked the housekeeper to bring coffee whilst they talked.

"Now Mr Brookes, you mentioned Pagnatti and a painting that was sent here thirty years ago. I would like to know why you are asking these questions and from where you have obtained your information before I respond, you have the floor."

Simon embarked upon a summary of what had happened and how it had led them to this palazzo, bringing in Reggie at several points in his narrative. Manzini put several questions for clarification and at the end asked if he could see their i-pad image of the painting which Simon was happy to produce, together with pictures of the big frame and the girl in the garden painting.

After viewing these Manzini sat back silently in his chair for a few moments before he began. "You have been very frank and open with me gentlemen in your story, and I must congratulate you, Mr Brookes on your diligence and persistence so far, and I must match your openness and candour."

"You may perhaps be aware that this palazzo has been in the hands of my family for most of the four hundred years since it was built. The Manzinis are one of the oldest original families in Venice and count two Doges in times gone by as members of the family. I mention this not just because I am proud of my lineage and the history of this place but to explain that over time family fortunes and circumstances have changed.

"My ancestors built up a considerable fortune trading from this ancient port and owned much land in the Veneto and beyond. The family continued to prosper until well into the 19th century, even though the world was changing fast.

"It was in the early years of the 20th century that my grandfather began to dispose of some of our farms in the

Veneto, and other properties in order to make necessary repairs and renovations to this palazzo and reinvest family capital in new ventures. Few of these, I'm sorry to say, prospered and he was badly affected by the Wall St crash. This in turn led to further disposals of both land and properties and the sale of many of the pieces of art - old master paintings, sculptures and other objets d'art from our family collection.

"The photo image of *The Last Supper* that you showed to me is, as you say, a companion piece to others in a series on the Life of Christ held in the Louvre, and an alternative to the one with the same title in that series, which has always led to some controversy and differing opinions as to whether it was a genuine Tiepolo. We have always maintained that it was and there was a story passed down that it was originally acquired directly from the painter."

Manzini had been talking non-stop for fully five minutes and was obviously tiring from the effort as his voice had faltered and his words came more slowly. He rang a little handbell that stood on the table to summon his housekeeper and as they waited, explained he was going to have a glass of Grappa, inviting them to join him unless they would prefer a glass of wine.

After the housekeeper had left with the order and their empty coffee cafetiere and cups, Manzini asked for a few moments whilst he collected his thoughts, so nothing was said until she had returned with a large tray holding a beautiful vintage Murano glass decanter in green and gold with a matching glass, two antique fluted stemmed glasses and a bottle of Pinot Grigio nestling in a glass bucket full of ice. They helped themselves, Simon and Reggie to the wine and Manzini poured himself a substantial Grappa which he sipped. It obviously helped to revive him as he then continued in a stronger voice.

"I should explain here that all the negotiations to sell our paintings or sculptures, mostly by private sale, were conducted over many years on behalf of both my father and me, by Angelo de Vincentti a respected art dealer who also happened to be my mother's younger brother. He was, as a member of the wider family a well-loved and trusted friend and agent. Which turned out to be our big mistake.

"In retrospect we were naïve and too trusting in his honesty, but he was after all my uncle and until too late we had no reason to question the valuations and advice from him and other experts that he introduced. But when by chance his duplicity and fraudulent behaviour was exposed nearly fifty years ago, we discovered that he been systematically robbing us over many years of a substantial portion (in some cases up to a third) of the sales figure he had obtained for works of art that we had owned and entrusted him to sell. They included a Canaletto, a Raphael, drawings by Titian – I could go on.

"It appears from the investigation that followed his exposure, that he had kept two sets of books, one genuine showing the actual sales price that he had negotiated with prominent galleries and wealthy collectors in America, Europe and other parts of the world. The other books recorded much reduced sales figures to the same people for the same works supported by forged invoices and sales receipts to satisfy tax authorities as well as sceptical clients.

His criminal activities were not confined to the Manzini collection and there were many other people he had swindled in the same way. In consequence he had amassed a fortune running into many millions of dollars by the end of his activities. He had plenty of warning that he was under suspicion and suddenly disappeared and despite the best efforts of Interpol and other investigators there has never been a trace or a sighting of him to this day. By his own declared calculations, he left still owing us revenue from sales amounting to nearly two and a half million dollars although his crooked machinations might easily double that figure – we don't know.

"I expect he is dead now or well into his nineties and I don't suppose we'll ever learn any more about his activities or be able to fill in the blanks of which there are a few when comparisons are made between the two sets of books. There are sales of paintings that appear in the genuine books that have been checked and are accurate, but don't appear at all in the fraudulent record. On the other hand, there are two paintings that are listed as sold to the same buyer in the fraudulent list in 1972 but neither appears in the genuine sales book. These were *"The Last Supper"* ascribed "after Tiepolo" meaning there was doubt it was by the master, and the other painting was a disputed Tinteretto.

"I remember being particularly disappointed by the figure he negotiated for the disputed Tiepolo of $22,000 which, had it been confirmed as genuine with a full provenance would have been expected to fetch nearer half a million dollars in those days. I was genuinely fond of the picture and regretted that Angelo had let it go at such a low figure, to such an extent that I actually asked him to contact the buyer and negotiate its return, but he reported back that the American collector wouldn't sell. Some years after Angelo's disappearance I tried again only to find that the name and address of the American buyer in the fraudulent books and papers was fictitious."

Manzini took another couple of sips of Grappa and shrank back into his chair looking exhausted again after his efforts and closed his eyes. Simon and Reggie talked quietly together awaiting his resumption, but after a few minutes the elderly man gave a snort and slumped to one side. Alarmed, they both got to their feet, Simon to check that Manzini was still breathing and Reggie to furiously ring the little handbell.

When the housekeeper came into the room she rushed to attend to her employer as Simon explained what had happened.

"I think he is just sleeping" she said "but I think he is exhausted with much talking. You gentlemen must go now," and gestured towards the door.

"Of course," Simon said "but I believe he wished to tell us more and when he is feeling better, we would appreciate it if you let us know. We are staying at Ca Sagredo," and left his card on the table.

"I doubt he will feel well enough for some time to come" said the housekeeper and quickly showed them out.

Chapter 7

Jeremy Idle felt a real shiver of excitement when he drove away from the Glass & Burns premises near Stroud, with the case holding *The Last Supper* painting stowed in the boot. If his instincts and experience were proved correct, he had taken charge of something that was worth several million pounds and had aroused considerable interest in the minds of the three carefully chosen people that he had, in strictest confidence, discussed it with. Two were Tiepolo experts, one based in London and the other in Florence, and the third was a Professor specialising in the investigation of materials and techniques at The Courtauld Institute of Fine Art.

Her department used everything, from the spectroscopy of pigments used in oil paintings which can be dated by the types of colour used at the time, and the palette normally used by a particular artist. These results combined with the examination of art works under x-ray and infra-red for clues on painting techniques and brushwork, could often identify very accurately an artist's work.

Idle knew that the Professor had already carried out examinations of Tiepolo's work in order to expose a forgery a few years before.

She had made comparisons of techniques and materials used by Tiepolo by taking tiny fragments from genuine paintings by the artist around the dates alleged for the fraudulent piece. These dates happily coincided with the time that it was believed *The Last Supper* had been completed. Fortunately, the professor was intrigued by Idle's story and agreed to prioritise examination of the piece.

Nevertheless, it was about a week later that, prompted by a phone call, he presented himself at the Courtauld to hear the verdict which he was delighted to learn was a yes to both pigments and techniques - they both tended to confirm that it was a Tiepolo and moreover, the canvas used was dated as being contemporary with the six *Life of Christ* Tiepolos in the Louvre. Triumph!

But she reminded him, all she could do was confirm that nothing she had seen went against the proposition that *The Last Supper* was a genuine Tiepolo, and that it was up to the authorities on Tiepolo to pronounce that it was a genuine work by the artist. She wished him luck with that and in finding a provenance to back it all up.

He lost no time in emailing Simon in Venice about the successful scientific tests and details of his plans to see the Tiepolo experts in London and Florence. He also asked how the search for a provenance was going.

Simon's mobile pinged with the message whilst he and Reggie were in the impressive Correr Library and Museum on St Mark's Square which held a vast collection of books, legal documents, maps, letters and other items relating to the history of Venice and its residents from its very earliest days, besides paintings and other works of art.

There were two prime reasons for their visit, both gleaned from the back of the frame on Simon's old painting. The first, now faded but still discernible were the written words **Ritornore a Residenza Barantella via dela Fara** and the second a torn fragment of a label that read **Galleria Aspid…..20 guigno 17……**

A modern street map of Venice showed neither de la Fara as a street or calle nor Residenza Barantella, hence a search of old maps was needed and a follow-up through contemporary records of the eighteenth century, to find a gallery beginning with the letters *Aspid…*

The answer to the first question was quite quickly found on a map dated 1796, where Via de la Fara was shown as a short, narrow street running parallel to the Canale Grand with Residenza Barantella marked at one end. The whole area had been cleared in the early 19th century to make way for new cottages to be built, so it was very unlikely that anything relating to the house that stood there or its residents remained after demolition. So, disappointingly, no result there.

Records relating to the 18th century didn't reveal any reference to a gallery or a dealer in paintings in Venice beginning *Aspid…*, but one of the curators promised to dig around in the archives amongst the papers they held relating to several artists, including Tiepolo, who were producing works around the middle of the century. He would look to see if any mentioned *Aspid….* as a dealer or middleman handling their paintings. He didn't hold out much hope but would be in touch if he found anything relevant.

Rather disconsolate, they returned to their hotel to find a message from Signor Manzini's housekeeper telling them that he was feeling better, and against her advice, insisted that they continue their conversation at his apartment two days hence at 11am, which improved their mood considerably.

Simon spoke on the phone to Jeremy Idle to let him know what progress they had made on establishing a provenance for the picture, and Idle was encouraging, particularly as they were seeing Manzini again.

That night for dinner Simon had one of his favourite dishes – Moules Mariniere or as the Italians would have it – Cozze alle Marinara and one or more of the mussels was bad, because overnight and in the morning, he suffered a severe stomach upset and on doctor's advice remained in bed for the morning. It was Reggie who took the call from the curator at the Correr Library who told him that he had found a couple of references which might help, and Reggie arranged that both he and Simon would go there at 3pm.

Simon was still feeling far from well when the afternoon arrived so it was agreed that Reggie would go on his own, borrowing Simon's Panama hat, at his urging as some protection against the particularly hot sun that day.

He never came back.

Chapter 8

It was as Reggie turned with his back to the Grand Canale to walk up into St Mark's Square that the first bullet hit him in the right thigh and the second below his kneecap as he fell on the spot. Most people in the vicinity ran in panic to the edges of the square taking refuge under the colonnade beneath the Doges palazzo or into one of the restaurants on the opposite side, but two people, a man and a woman, came directly to Reggie who was writhing in pain and shock.

The woman turned out to be an American doctor on holiday who quickly assessed the situation and producing a pair of scissors from her bag, cut and then tore away his right trouser leg exposing gaping wounds caused by the bullets that were bleeding heavily. Then, using the trouser fabric, she cut off a length that she then applied as a tourniquet. Meanwhile the man rang for ambulance and police to attend, and both arrived together five minutes later with sirens sounding across the water as they came into to dock at the nearby landing stage on the Canale.

He was taken to the Ospedale of St Giovanni & St Paolo in a spectacular speedy journey accompanied by the police launch with siren wailing along the canal. Two other policemen stayed behind to question witnesses and try to discover from where the shots had been fired.

It was late afternoon before a call came through to Simon from the carabiniere police who had found an hotel keycard in Reggie's pocket and had rung reception. They said that Reggie had been shot at whilst walking into St Mark's Square and had bullet wounds in his shoulder and leg. He had undergone surgery to remove the bullets and received attention to both wounds and was recovering in hospital. Simon would be able to visit him that evening. In the meantime, they would like to talk to Simon and, as they were aware from the hotel reception that he was unwell, were prepared to come to him at the hotel.

As he put down the room phone Simon was both shocked and bemused as he tried to understand how such a thing could have happened to Reggie. His assassin could not be a madman spraying bullets all around otherwise there would be other casualties surely, but then who would want to single out Reggie and try to kill him and why? Stomach pains forgotten, he wrestled with the puzzling facts as he awaited the arrival of the police.

If he had not been so concerned, Simon would have been highly amused because Commissario Albertini and Inspector Noblisio were a perfect double act. The senior officer was tall and suave with wavy thick hair speaking passable English whilst his bald companion was short and fat with seemingly little English but a habit of nodding enthusiastically and saying "si, si" as his boss ended a sentence.

Albertini summarised again what had happened, adding that, as yet, they had not found the gunman although they had found an open window above the café at the entrance to the square, below which they had found two spent cartridge cases. The window gave a perfect view of the place where Reggie had been shot.

Enquiries were of course, ongoing, but the police wanted to know whether Simon knew of any possible reason why his companion would have been a target for a gunman. Had he any enemies or people who owed him a grudge perhaps? Simon described his friendship to Reggie as very recent and he knew very little about his background or family. He went onto to explain that it was a shared interest in finding out the provenance of an old painting that had brought them together in Venice. He was able to tell them Reggie's address in Norwich, and that he was a widower, but little more.

Relieved that at least Reggie's injuries were not life threatening and that he would be able to see him in hospital, Simon rang the curator at the Correr Museum to apologise for the non-arrival of his colleague with a brief explanation and to arrange another appointment for the following day.

As Simon was tidying up his room prior to going downstairs for an early evening meal, he picked up his Panama hat that the two police officers had recovered from where it had lain on St Mark's Square after the shooting. Then it suddenly struck him. He and Reggie were about the same height, invariably wore similar light-coloured trousers and shirts. Indeed, the only thing that would identify them apart would be that Reggie was generally bareheaded whereas Simon would be wearing his panama with its distinctive MCC red and yellow hatband. It was he, Simon that the bullets had been intended for, not Reggie.

The cold realisation that he was, for whatever reason, somebody's target, slowly percolated through his body, it was so frightening, he could hardly think straight.

After a while though, the initial panic subsided, and he was able to think more rationally. Of course, it made more sense that he was the target and not Reggie.

He was the prime mover in this search for provenance for the old picture and despite their original decision to keep their exploration quiet, the news of the picture's discovery had been emblazoned across newspapers. Even though names had not been disclosed, for somebody keen to discover who was involved, it was not too difficult a task. Clearly such cover as he had was now "blown" and somebody was anxious to stop him finding out more. But who and why?

Simon took a water taxi to the hospital, moving quickly from the shelter of the hotel and down to the waterfront and for once not wearing his distinctive Panama hat. He found Reggie still drowsy from the effects of the anaesthetic and distinctly hazy about what had happened to him in St Mark's Square except that he had been shot, the memory of that was clearly still very painful. "What I can't figure out is why?" he said quietly.

"I think I can answer part of that Reggie," Simon began. "They were looking for me and when you appeared wearing my Panama, they made their mistake and I'm afraid you took the bullets intended for me. I suspect that someone has traced the story about the painting to me and wants to write me off or at least stop me doing my research, although I can't fathom why, any more than who would gain anything from doing that."

They talked for another quarter of an hour until Reggie drifted off to sleep and Simon took the hint and left, returning to his hotel again by water taxi.

The next morning before setting off for his two appointments at the Correr Musuem and then with Manzini, Simon phoned Commissario Albertini to tell him about his latest thinking on the shooting. Albertini agreed with his reasoning and told Simon that he was in considerable danger and that he would organise protective measures. In the meantime, he told Simon not to leave the hotel. Simon immediately objected to this confinement as he had appointments to keep, and after some wrangling it was agreed that for that morning, Simon would be accompanied by a bodyguard who would take all precautions in leading him via diversionary routes to keep his appointments. The situation would then be reviewed.

In the event, two men came from the Venetian police to escort him. One scouted ahead surveying likely sniper or ambush points and the other bodyguard and Simon followed as they wended a circuitous way down calles, over bridges and down back alleys until they reached St Mark's Square from a totally different direction. Only a short distance of the square itself needed to be traversed before they entered a side entrance to the Correr.

After expressing his horror and concern at what had happened to Reggie, the curator, who had trawled through many files of documents and notes made by or concerning painters contemporary with Tiepolo, for any reference to an agency or Gallery with a name beginning *Aspid*, had managed to find three references which were relevant and had translated all of them into English.

The first was in a letter written by the great Canaletto to a friend in 1742 "I left two pictures with Farracini at his new Aspidistra Gallery on the advice of Gianbattista T., who says he's good – we shall see."

Another was in an undated scribbled note from "Francesco" (believed to be Guardi) to Guiseppi Crespi "Have you heard anything good about this gallery that Ferracini has opened? Some say he's a crook….." and in the same file a thin card was discovered handwritten with an elaborate script across the centre reading: *Galleria Aspidistra* followed by a name - *Alberto Farracini* and a description *Artist, Negotiator, Agent*, and an address on Via dei Limoni.

Simon was delighted "That's great, it confirms that there was a place called Galleria Aspidistra in Venice in the mid-18th century and for a time my painting was exhibited there and, indeed, may have been sold from there by this Alberto Farracini." The curator agreed adding that Guardi may have been right in quoting some suspicions about the business as it didn't seem to have lasted long. He went on "the street is still there and quite a few of the old buildings are much the same as they were two hundred and seventy years ago."

With the curator's agreement, Simon carefully photographed the original documents, making a note of the file references and taking possession of the translations. Then, after thanking him for his valuable help, Simon re-joined his police bodyguards and began another circuitous walk via calles, bridges and back alleys to keep his appointment with Teodoro Manzini at his palazzo.

As they reached the lobby at Palazzo Ca' Manzini Simon told his two escorts that he had no means of knowing how long he would be with Signor Manzini, maybe more than an hour, and suggested they go and have a coffee or a drink somewhere and he would phone them when he was about to leave.

At first, they refused the 20Euro note he passed to them, but then agreed after insisting that they would see him into the door of the apartment he was visiting and assuring themselves that no assassin was hiding inside. Having exchanged mobile numbers, the three of them made their way up to the Manzini apartment.

When the bell pull brought to the door the same angry-faced housekeeper it was no surprise to Simon that, when asked if the two police officers could quickly look round the apartment, she refused point blank. Simon used the ploy that had worked well on his earlier visit by speaking slowly and loudly in the hope that Signor Manzini would overhear. This worked again, as against the background of the two indignant policemen flashing their warrant cards and exchanging insults with the housekeeper in rapid high-pitched Italian, Manzini joined the group around the door lifted his arms and brought them down with a loud "Silenzio!"

Then turning to Simon he asked what it was all about. Simon explained briefly at which Manzini gestured for them to look round, accompanied by the housekeeper and led Simon into the sitting room where coffee, Grappa and chilled white wine awaited.

Manzini expressed his surprise and condolences for the attack on Reggie and fully understood the police concern, particularly when Simon explained that the attack had probably been intended for him.

Pouring coffee for them both, Manzini asked whether Simon suspected that the attack had anything to do with his discovery of the Tiepolo painting.

"I'm forced to believe that it must be, but I'm at a complete loss to understand who would do such a thing and for what purpose."

As he passed a coffee to Simon, Manzini began "I am an old man now and experience has taught me that if one views other people with a degree of reserve and caution, one will often be pleasantly surprised. Whereas an open acceptance of people on their face value leads inevitably to bitter disappointment or worse. I purposely said other people because unfortunately I have to include under that collective term friends, colleagues even relatives. Where there is suddenly the possibility of a large sum of money becoming theirs, attitudes may change, moral issues can fly out of the window. But I side-track, you must have already thought on these things."

"No, no you are quite right I haven't thought deeply enough, and your thoughts are a timely reminder."

"Good. Now there are other things that I intended to tell you at our last meeting but was overcome by tiredness for which I'm sorry. Help yourself, by the way, Mr Brookes, to a glass of wine."

He paused as he poured himself a good measure of Grappa. "You mentioned a Signor Pagnatti to whom the crated frame with the two pictures inside it was consigned from England to this palazzo in, I think you said 1992."

"Yes"

"Well Pagnatti was in those days a valued employee and had been for twenty years. He was a sort of major domo. We owned the whole palazzo in those days and there were several family members living here. Pagnatti used to look after most things, the building, staff and a good deal of family business – as I say he was a trusted employee. But I'll come back to him after I have filled in the background history a little more.

"I've already told you that my mother's brother Angelo de Vincentti, who was an art dealer, was entrusted successively by my father and then myself to dispose of many items from our family art and sculpture collection as the need arose over a period of fifty years. His fraudulent actions over much of that time, not just from our items, meant that he had amassed a considerable fortune and had cost us at a conservative estimate $2 million. When all this came to light, he was, of course, long gone, and enquiries carried out all over the world told us nothing of his whereabouts. He'd covered his tracks very cleverly.

"Examination of his books, and questions directed to the new owners of our paintings confirmed that his sales (all of which were to private clients) were bona fide but at prices that were up to a third higher than the sales prices shown in the duplicate books he kept to show to us and the tax authorities. He, of course, pocketed the difference." Manzini stopped abruptly and then carried on with an apology "I think I may have told you all this before, if so I am sorry, blame it on an old man's memory."

"No, no please carry on" said Simon. Manzini took another sip of Grappa and continued "I think I have already told you that *The Last Supper* painting and a disputed Tinteretto were entered into his accounts as sold to an American collector, but they were not, and for many years we heard nothing of them despite continuing enquiries by our agents around the world.

"And then, out of the blue, our correspondent and agent Mr Wendell in England, spotted in 1983 or 1984 that, listed amongst a number of paintings in an auction in Norfolk was what was described as *'an Italian painting in oils, probably a copy of a Tiepolo – depicting Christ and disciples.'* He had obtained a copy of the auction list which reproduced an indistinct black and white photograph of the painting which he thought might be our missing *Last Supper*, the guide sale price was £1600- £2000.

"From the description and the size of the painting we thought there was a good chance that it was indeed our lost picture and Mr Wendell, was instructed to bid for the painting up to a figure of £2500, and to arrange for it to be suitably packed, crated and sent here. At the same time I asked him to find out as much as he could about the seller, then to go and see him or her and ask them when and how the painting came into their possession.

"Wendell reported back that he had successfully acquired the painting for the bargain price of £1720, and because of its potential value, was having a special frame constructed around another cheaper painting, behind which the older painting would be hidden safely for its protection and that he would ship it over when completed.

"He had learnt that the sellers of the old painting were a house clearance and second-hand furniture dealers in Norwich. He was making more enquiries and would report back but he was not optimistic about learning very much in the circumstances. He enclosed a bill for his costs in acquiring both the paintings, for the framing, crating and shipping and his services which was paid by me plus a bonus and an encouraging letter to speed on his research about the previous ownership.

"Conscious of the fact that he had not told us the name of the firm that was making the frame who were, presumably, holding the Tiepolo painting, we wrote to him again a few days later, asking for this information together with details of the shipping company.

We found out that he had banked the cheque but heard nothing more from Mr Welland, until we found out that within two weeks of completing that transaction, he was dead.

.

Chapter 9

At this point Manzini paused to take another swig from his glass of Grappa, sat back and closed his eyes. Simon was not surprised but hoped that the elderly man had not overtaxed himself and that this was to be just a short rest.

After a few moments Simon quietly stood up and walked around the room looking at some of the beautiful and varied items that were on display in cabinets and shelves around the room. From intricately carved Japanese ivory and jade to tiny, jewelled boxes and miniature painted portraits, the number and variety would not be out of place in any of the great museums. Almost hidden between two cabinets was hung a larger montage from which he immediately recognised the beautifully jewelled and enamelled figure of the rearing horse and the letters **de V** against a striking blue background.

As he gazed at this, Manzini opened his eyes and commented "That is the symbol of my mother's family the de Vincenttis whose fortunes were lost as a result of two devastating blows, the Wall Street crash in 1929 and a great fire that engulfed and utterly destroyed their family seat in the Veneto in 1938. Fortunately, my mother and her brother were away staying with relatives, but her father and mother perished in the blaze, together with virtually all their possessions.

That family crest was one of a handful of things recovered, and here and there around this palazzo you'll see a few reproductions in wall plaques and wrought ironwork that I arranged to be brought here and installed as momentos of my grandparents and their old home."

"I wondered about the symbol and the connection, particularly as I found this embedded in the back of the frame around *The Last Supper* painting when we discovered it behind the other painting" said Simon and brought out the key from his jacket pocket passing it over to the old man, who examined it.

"How extraordinary" he began "you say 'embedded,' was it difficult to find?" Simon described how it was spotted and recovered before Manzini went on. "Who could have put it there and why I wonder? I can only surmise that when Angelo de Vincentti was entrusted by my father with the picture to find a buyer, he put it there, but for what purpose I can't imagine."

He was now wide awake again and handed the key back to Simon remarking "Sorry about just now, I just closed my eyes for a moment to concentrate my mind so that I didn't overlook anything that I intended to tell you."

"Of course, Signor Manzini, please take your time but don't exhaust yourself – I really do appreciate you telling me all this," Simon responded.

Manzini continued his narrative "Welland's death was reported to be as a result of a massive heart attack he suffered whilst out walking his dogs in an isolated spot, so that his body was not discovered for some hours. Both his dogs were found sitting quietly beside him, so the story goes.

We were naturally shocked and saddened by his sudden death but also acutely conscious that we had now no clue at all as to the whereabouts of the paintings.

Welland lived near Brighton in Sussex. We surmised he would have had dealings with local frame makers and immediately instituted enquiries amongst those in the area as well as around London and also amongst shippers of fine arts, but completely without result. Sadly, I had once again to face the fact that we had lost Tiepolo's *Last Supper*.

"Now Mr Brookes," he went on "we come to Signor Alessandro Pagnetti who you mentioned at our first meeting. I explained he had, for many years, been a major domo at this palazzo working for the family under both my father and me. I would like you to reiterate please exactly what you know about him."

"Well, very little I'm afraid. It was only that from our research we discovered where the new bulky frame had been made, in 1983 to Welland's order, to surround a newly purchased oil painting of a girl in a garden but providing space for another painting behind. This had been held by the maker unclaimed, for years until somebody rang on the telephone to claim it, and had it picked up by the shippers who then according to their records despatched it to Signor Pagnetti at this palazzo. That's all I know."

Manzini looked keenly at Simon "So this would have been in 1992" he asked. "Yes, that's right, in fact it was my companion Reggie Marsden who took the original telephone call at the frame-makers where he then worked, and later handed over the picture in its frame and a new crate to the shipping company's representative in Norwich.

It is as a consequence of that connection that, fascinated by the story as it was unfolding, he asked if he could accompany me here to Venice.

"I see" said the elderly man who paused before going on "Would it surprise you to know that I knew nothing of this until you told me. Pagnetti, as I have said, worked for my father and then me, here at the palazzo for nearly thirty years before telling me without prior notice, late in 1992 that he was leaving my employment with immediate effect, due to a serious medical condition that had just been diagnosed. He didn't disclose any details, merely that he was going to live with a nephew and would be vacating the small apartment he occupied on the top floor of the palazzo the following day.

"He had been well paid for his duties and would be in receipt of a good pension on retirement, so I had no qualms on that score but nevertheless presented him with a cheque and our thanks as a family for his services over the years, when he left. I don't mind saying that his sudden resignation was a shock both on a personal level and also because of the difficulty we would have finding someone suitable to fill his role.

"In the weeks and months following his departure various things came to light which made us question the former complete confidence we had in him as someone who was absolutely honest and had the best interests of the family at heart. Nothing major, you understand but small discrepancies in his book-keeping records, payments made without receipts. Small things, but sufficiently niggling to undermine his former impeccable reputation.

"But when you told me that it was about that time that the special frame that Wendell had ordered had been found, and that the frame makers had received a phone call asking that it should be forwarded to Pagnetti at this address, it made me think and wonder. Pagnetti was, of course, familiar with the story of Wendell's find, his order for the special frame to hold two paintings and his intention to ship it over to Venice.

"He also knew that Wendell had not disclosed where the frame was being made before his death, and indirectly, Pagnetti was also involved in the immediate attempts that were made to find the frame, or any reference to it or the painting, amongst Wendell's effects at both his Sussex home and London office. That search was both extensive and thorough and included a trawl lasting several months of all known picture frame makers in and around London and in the Sussex area, but it turned up nothing.

"Wendell's successor as our English agent, was an old Venetian friend of Pagnetti, Guido Lambertini, who came to us highly recommended. He already spent most of his time in the UK and could conveniently fit in our work, which of course included supervising the search which went on for several months until I decided it was leading nowhere.

"I suspect he was privately told by Pagnetti to keep on with the search in another direction where Wendell might have kept things. It was known that Wendell had a 'pied-a-terre' somewhere near Manchester which he used quite often when his work took him in that area, and two other small apartments, one believed to be in East Anglia and another vaguely thought to be in the Scottish Borders, but he was a very secretive man, and nobody knew exactly where they were."

He paused, laughing "not even his wife who is said to have admitted to close friends that she often suspected that he had a woman in each one."

He continued "I now surmise that Lambertini, by dint of persistent searching and the use of private investigators, eventually discovered where at least one of Wendell's other boltholes was, probably the one in East Anglia. He then gained access to Wendell's papers that included the address of the frame-maker in nearby Norwich and informed Pagnetti."

Manzini paused and asked, "Do you know if the caller to the frame maker had a distinctive accent?"

"Now you mention it, yes. Reggie said he spoke with an Italian accent." Manzini took another sip of Grappa and went on "At this point Pagnetti made a big mistake I suspect. He assumed, quite reasonably, that the frame held both pictures, but as we now realise, Wendell intended to pick up the frame, insert the Tiepolo behind the other picture, reseal it all and then take it to the shippers and of course, never did.

"Originally Pagnetti must have told the agent to have the frame and contents shipped to him here at the palazzo, but because of the risk of discovery he then told the shippers that he would pick it up from the airport himself rather than having it delivered. After your first visit to me, I had one of my staff check with Stephensons, who confirmed from their archived papers that Pagnetti had indeed arranged to pick up the crate himself from the airport – the delivery documentation was endorsed with that information.

"One can only guess at the shock and disappointment he felt when he took the back off the frame only to find there was only one painting of no particular value and the dream of having one that potentially, was worth a small fortune, was shattered.

"I'm confident now that is more or less how it happened, and that he would have lost no time in making contact with Lambertini in England to ask him where the devil the old painting was. Lambertini would have replied that he didn't know what Pagnetti was talking about, and would claim that after tracing the whereabouts of the frame, he had it picked up and despatched to Pagnetti as instructed, and he knew no more than that.

"Now I strongly suspect that in going through Wendell's papers, Lambertini had not only found the address of the frame-maker on the invoice but, to his great surprise, the Tiepolo picture as well, and decided to keep it for himself. After all, nobody other than he knew where the painting was and I'm sure that he kept it in a very secure place in England until he could arrange a private sale. It was, I believe, a case of the double-crosser, double-crossed, but of course I can't prove anything."

Simon had followed Manzini's assumptions and argument closely and couldn't fault the logic behind most of it even though there was no proof. "I think you have built up a strong and fascinating case around what probably happened but much of it needs to be confirmed of course, and I have a number of questions, and will be taking notes if you are agreeable."

The old man nodded his agreement and for a further ten minutes Simon posed his questions and carefully noted the answers plus names and addresses for further research.

Simon's final question was "Assuming that the events happened broadly as you have described, why do you think that eventually the frame with its two pictures enclosed turned up in England?"

Manzini, who by this time was looking distinctly tired threw up his two open hands as if in resignation and said "Who knows. It could have been Pagnetti in a fit of pique who sent it back to Lambertini telling him to redouble his efforts, find the Tiepolo, put it into the custom-made frame and send it back, I have no idea whether Pagnetti is still alive or dead, in Venice or elsewhere and am frankly not bothered. I fear Mr Brookes, it is down to you in your search for a full provenance to find out anything more."

Manzini then stood, a little shakily, and extending his hand said "I wish you good luck and god speed in safely carrying through your quest. Take good care of yourself because you are clearly in some danger and let me know please how it proceeds." Then he handed Simon an envelope with the words "you may find this useful."

Simon shook his hand and thanked him for the invaluable help he had given and promised to stay in touch. Then Manzini resumed his chair, rang the handbell and closed his eyes, and a moment later the housekeeper arrived to show Simon out.

Down in the lobby he rang his two guards who arrived very quickly from a nearby cafe and escorted him back to his hotel.

He noted that there had been two missed calls from Reggie whilst his phone had been turned off but decided not to ring him back immediately. He wanted to write up his notes whilst Manzini's talk was fresh in his memory and to make a couple of other calls so that he would be able to describe the progress he had made in detail when he, plus his escorts, went to see Reggie in hospital in the early evening.

Simon opened the envelope that Manzini had passed to him which contained a statement signed and witnessed the same day, it stated that he, Manzini had reimbursed his agent in England, a Mr Welland, in 1983, the sum that Welland had paid at auction in Norwich for an oil painting which it was speculated could be the missing *Last Supper* by Tiepolo. It may be construed that in this way that he, Teodoro Manzini was the owner of the aforesaid painting and he wanted to make it clear that that if he had any rights over the ownership of the painting, he gave them up entirely in favour of its present legitimate owner Mr Simon Brookes. Simon was both pleased and gratified by this clarification which could prove very helpful at some stage and wrote a letter to Signor Manzini to express his thanks.

Promptly at 5pm the two policemen arrived in a water taxi at the hotel and rushed him out and on board and they sped off down the same narrow canal as before on the shortest route to Ospidale St Giovanni & St Paolo.

On the third floor where Reggie occupied a private room, the three of them were met by a group of carabinieri in the corridor, who of course, recognised Simon's companions but were very reluctant to let him pass, demanding to know who he was, which sparked a rapid exchange of angry Italian between the two sets of policemen at the end of which Simon asked for an explanation.

Apparently around midday when the police guard was momentarily away, a man with a handgun had forced his way into Reggie's room, with the purpose of shooting him. Only Reggie's presence of mind saved him by him saying "I'm not Simon Brookes you've got the wrong man I'm Reggie Marsden. Look at my passport." This was fortunately, on the bedside table and he tossed it across to the man holding the gun.

Clearly thrown off-purpose by Reggie's response the gunman lowered the gun to look at the passport, at which moment an armed policeman peering round the door shouted to him to drop the gun, and as he made to level it again, shot him in the arm. He fell and was jumped on by another policeman, who disarmed him, cuffed and arrested him.

.

Chapter 10

Reluctantly the police allowed Simon in to see Reggie who, despite recent events was sitting up and delighted to see his colleague. He immediately launched into a description of what had happened, ending with "I'm sorry that I redirected him towards you but when someone is pointing a gun at your head you grasp at any possibility."

"You were quite right to do so Reggie, you were never the target. Have the police questioned him yet and found out anything like, why was he after me and who he is working for?" asked Simon.

"I've heard nothing since they took him away and left me guarded by this platoon of policemen, which now seems rather unnecessary" he replied, and went on "Oh yes, and I must tell you that I'm being flown back to the UK by air-ambulance tomorrow. It seems my anxious son, after my phone call yesterday, contacted the insurance company who after some urging from the police here – no doubt keen to see the back of me – arranged it all. Although I'm sorry to leave you, I'm really not able to give you any help in my present state, and I'd be a liability if I stayed on. My son is keen to get me into an English hospital as quickly as possible, even though they have been first class here."

Simon thought it was an excellent idea, adding that he had no doubt that the local carabinieri would be very pleased if he, Simon, would quickly follow suit but he was anxious to tie up some loose ends here in Venice before he picked up the trail again back in England. He went on then to describe his latest discoveries regarding the painting's provenance and had barely finished before a nurse came in to tell him his time with the patient was up, as he needed rest before his journey the next day.

They bade each other an emotional farewell, Simon wishing Reggie a good journey back home and a quick recovery from his injuries and a promise to keep him up to date with progress. In turn Reggie pressed Simon to take all the precautions he could, to keep up the good work and return to England as quickly as possible.

Simon re-joined his two police bodyguards and made a speedy return to his hotel. On the way they told him that Commissario Albertini wished to talk to him the following morning and they would be at the hotel to pick him up at 8.30am. Meanwhile an armed officer would sit outside his hotel room until then.

When they arrived at police headquarters the next day, Commisario Albertini rose from behind his desk with the nodding Inspector Noblisio standing by his side as Simon was ushered into his office and, gesturing for Simon sit in the chair opposite, began "Good morning, Mr Brookes, I hope my people looked after you and that you slept well last night despite everything that has happened."

Simon assured him that he had indeed slept well and thanked him for the excellent security that had been provided for him.

"I'll come onto that it a moment" said Albertini "but I expect you would like to know what we learned from Mr Marsden's would be assassin, a man called Andreotti. We agreed to lower the charge against him from attempted murder to issuing threats plus carrying and discharging an unauthorised weapon and causing bodily harm. This would change the likely sentence when convicted from twenty years to seven and he quickly, as you English say "spilled the beans."

Noblisio said "si" three times, smiled and nodded enthusiastically as Albertini went on "he had been hired and paid to kill you here in Venice by a gangster contact in London who in turn had been instructed by somebody in Sydney, Australia. He also admits to shooting and injuring your colleague in mistake for you. Does this make any sense to you Mr Brookes?"

"No, I can't say it does" said Simon "I'm hard put to think of anyone I'm even vaguely acquainted with in Australia and can't think of anyone there or indeed anywhere else that would want me bumped off."

"Well, I think Andreotti is telling the truth about this business. I don't think he has the imagination to come up with such an unlikely story, and we managed to extract from him the name of the man in London who hired him" he looked as his notes "a Mr Gordon Portman - which I have already passed onto a colleague with the Met in London who told me that he is a well-known gangster.

With Andreotti being held in custody awaiting his court appearance I think you are unlikely to be in danger here in in

Venice for a day or two, until the man in London somehow learns of his arrest and makes alternative arrangements.

However, without appearing inhospitable I hope you can quickly complete your business over here and return to England."

"I can well appreciate that and plan to leave within the next three days" replied Simon, and then thinking quickly added "one of the things that will delay my leaving is my need to trace somebody that was, up until 1992, employed by Signor Manzini at the Palazzo Ca'Manzini as a major domo and lived at the palazzo until then. He said, at the time that he was moving to live with a nephew somewhere in Venice but I have neither the nephew's name or address. Is there any way you can help me with that?"

"Will that speed your departure?" asked Albertini, with the ghost of a smile.

"Undoubtedly" said Simon.

"Perhaps we can help you.   His name please, and it is from 1992 up to the present?"

"Alessandro Pagnetti, and yes from 1992.   I don't know his age now, but my guess is that he must be well into his eighties, if he's still alive."

Albertini wrote down the details and handed the paper to Noblisio with rapid instructions in Italian then, getting up from his chair he spoke again to Simon. "If you will go with the Inspector and wait a while, we will search through all available records for this man. I will arrange for a bodyguard to be with you for the next few days, but I hope you will stay alert and not take any risks. Please inform me when you have booked your flight back to England where you need to get into touch with Chief Detective Inspector Clough at New Scotland Yard, here is his number.

"He may arrange to have you met off your flight, I'll keep him informed."

He handed over a card and they shook hands before Simon followed Noblisio out of the room and down two floors to a waiting room, where after supplying him with coffee, and a two-day-old copy of *The Daily Mail* the Inspector indicated in very broken English that he must wait there and after a flurry of nods and 'si's', he was left alone.

Two hours later, after Simon had long devoured the old Daily Mail from front to back, and done all the crosswords and puzzles, the door flew open to admit a beaming Noblisio waving a piece of paper. "Successo, successo," he began and handing the paper to Simon continued "Ze addresss of Signor Pagnetti, he is at nephews in Murano!"

Thanking the delighted Noblisio for his help, Simon left accompanied by many 'pregos' and quick bows to find his waiting bodyguard. He knew that Murano, famous for its glassware manufacture, was a small island in the Venetian Lagoon and asked his bodyguard if he could use their boat to go there straight away. They raised no objection and were soon on their way to the island, just a kilometre and half north of Venice. After they had moored their boat adjacent to the Museo de Vetro and the bodyguard had quickly found that the address in Via St Stephano was less than five minutes' walk away, they quickly found it.

It had helped the police researchers that the nephew was also called Pagnetti, Matteo Pagnetti, who was the son of Alessandro's brother. However, the door was answered by a young boy who explained in answer to their request to see Signor Pagnetti that his father was at work.

When Simon suggested Signor Alessandro Pagnetti, he asked them to wait, and he would fetch his mother. She asked what it was about as Signor Alessandro was an old man who rarely saw visitors. Between them they told her that his old employer of many years back, Signor Manzini had suggested that they call.

At this she gave an incomprehensible shrug and said something sotto voce before uttering the single word "Come" and ushered them round a corner to the side of a small canal where an elderly man huddled into a heavy coat was sat on a bench in the sunshine, reading a newspaper. She spoke to him rapidly in the distinctive Venetian dialect before he put down his paper and looked closely at them for fully half a minute before Simon broke the silence with "Buon giorno, Signor Pagnetti, do you speak English?"

The old man responded in English "It is nearly thirty years since I last heard from that mean old bastard and then he sends an Englishman to talk to me. Remarkable!"

Simon jumped in quickly "No, no, I'm not here representing Signor Manzini. When I spoke to him yesterday, he thought you might help me, but had no idea where you were or even whether you were still alive. I managed to trace you to your nephew's house here in Murano."

"Mmm. So how is he? Still trying to dictate terms on his sale of the palazzo I gather, meanwhile the old place deteriorates around him.

I'm still interested in the building as I served both he and his father for many years in managing the palazzo and hate the thought of it going to rack and ruin. However, he thinks I can help you in some way, what is that?

Simon summarised what he had learned from Manzini concerning his health and the palazzo, and chose his words carefully when he came to the Tiepolo painting, his ownership and the part that Pagnetti was alleged to have played in 1992, when the painting had come to light again. Simon added that he had been told that around the same time, Pagnetti had left his employment with Manzini and had personally collected the crate containing both paintings from the airport. Was that correct, he asked tentatively.

Pagnetti seemed momentarily taken aback by Simon's bald statement of the facts as he knew them, and his rheumy eyes seemed to well-up briefly, before he smiled weakly and replied "You seem to have done your research well Mr Brookes, but I think the facts have been rather juggled and coloured by Signor Manzini's imagination.

"By way of an explanation if not a justification of my actions, I should tell you that I worked thirty years for the Manzinis as major domo looking after the palazzo, its residents and contents in every conceivable way including financial matters in return for a very meagre salary. True, I had the use of a small flat on the top floor of the palazzo and the promise of a pension on retirement, but too late realised how small this was going to be. Whenever I raised these issues with Manzini I was fobbed off or given a tiny increase and have to confess that in later years in order to augment my income I adjusted the books here and there, gained a small commission from regular suppliers and so on, to make up a little on my income.

"I'm not proud of that, but felt I had no alternative in the circumstances. He was such a mean man Manzini, that on the day that I left, he made a great play of presenting me with a parting cheque in a sealed envelope.

"He inferred to me, and others that this was for a truly magnificent sum reflecting my past loyal service. When I opened it later, I found it was for 50 Lira – less than £25 in your money at the time. Not much for a lifetime's work, was it?"

He ruminated for a few moments before resuming "You can perhaps understand that when an opportunity came along that offered me the possibility of making an appreciable amount of money even though it was at the expense of the Manzini family, the temptation was great.

"In your enquiries I expect you will have heard of Angelo de Vincentti. He was the younger brother of Signor Teodoro Manzini's mother, and was also an art dealer who was entrusted with the sale of almost all the art treasures that Manzini family found necessary to sell during the 20th century. You may have also been told that he turned out to be a rogue and fraudster who managed to skim a large amount of money from all the transactions he conducted on behalf of the family, and other people, over a period of many years. Then when suspicions had been aroused, he disappeared and was never found despite the most intensive search."

"Yes" said Simon "I had heard as much."

"Well" Pagnetti went on "I know now that Angelo went off to live somewhere in Brazil, where he married a local woman and they had two children. Angelo had continued to stay in touch with a couple of his old friends in the art world here in Venice after he had left and although he died of cancer about thirty years ago his eldest son Riccardo maintained the contacts, displaying a keen interest in the art market like his father before him. I'll explain his connection in due course.

"When, what was thought likely to be *The Last Supper* painting by Tiepolo turned up in a country house auction sale in England and was spotted by Welland, Teo Manzini told him to buy it. As you now know, Welland, as an extra security precaution, bought another painting and had a special frame made to house both paintings with the Tieopolo hidden behind. Unfortunately, nobody knew of this arrangement and Welland had a fatal heart attack and died having told nobody and apparently without any record. So, the new frame and its contents sat gathering dust for several years at the frame-makers unclaimed.

"Manzini and I spent a good deal of time and his money on trying to trace the Tiepolo's whereabouts but without success, until Manzini eventually decided to give up the search. However, I privately thought it was worthwhile continuing the search and as our new English agent was an old friend of mine, got him to agree to look in new directions.

"I knew from previous conversations with Welland that he owned at least a couple of other places in England apart from his offices and showroom in London and his home in Sussex. He quite regularly stayed in these in connection with his art and antiques business, but I had no idea where or what they were, cottages, flats or just rooms, and his wife claimed to have no knowledge of them.

"I told my friend Lambertini, our new English agent, that if he would finance and oversee a new search using specialist agents in England to locate Wendell's other addresses he would be handsomely rewarded. My promise was that if he was successful and it led to finding the Tiepolo painting (I was very confident it was genuine) he would be rewarded by receiving ten percent of the selling price. – at least $200,000 I reckoned - when it was brought to the market.

"I didn't discuss this with Mazzini as I was confident he would be more than happy if it worked out and I believed he would reward me with a similar amount when the painting was sold.

"As you know, Lambertini's new search was very successful and he found Welland's flat in Manchester, and a cottage in Norfolk. He personally searched both, the latter successfully disclosing the address of the firm in Norwich who fortunately still had the specially framed picture awaiting collection.

"I told him to have it crated up and despatched to me at the palazzo and a few days later had an altercation with Manzini. I had found out after much pressing, just what my pension from the Manzini family business would be on my retirement and was shocked by how small it was to be, certainly too tiny to live on. I found myself angrily pressing Manzini on the matter at a meeting when I had intended to tell him about the recovery of the painting. There and then I decided to say nothing, to resign my position and leave immediately on the excuse of a worsening medical condition and go and live with my nephew.

"I would pick the crated painting up from the airport myself and then think over how I would handle the situation from there on".

Pagnetti shifted his position on the bench to try and be more square-on and face Simon. "At this same time, and certainly not by coincidence, I had a visit from Roberto de Vincentti, the son of the late Angelo de Vincentti , who had friends still in Venice with ears close to the ground in the world of art. These friends had passed on to him rumours that were circulating about the emergence of a missing Tiepolo. He had put two and two together and guessed Manzini and I were involved and sought me out.   Surprisingly he also knew that Manzini and I had parted company.

"He asked me outright whether I knew where the painting was at that time, and I avoided answering him by saying that I would be in a better position to answer him in a few days time, without disclosing anything else. He went on to suggest that if I obtained possession of the alleged Tiepolo painting and was prepared to cut Manzini out of the picture, he would assist me to sell it privately and quietly for a figure likely to be well in excess of $2 million, for which discreet service he, Pagnetti, would take a fee of 20% of the selling price.

You can imagine Mr Brookes, my inner excitement at the offer, particularly as I told myself that Manzini had already written off any chance of regaining the painting, and anyway I still felt bitterly that he owed me something for my years of devoted service.

"I told Roberto that I would email him in a few days time after I had time to consider his suggestion and the next day went to the airport to claim the crate which had arrived two days earlier. The shipping company had sent me an email earlier asking me to confirm either that I was still picking up the crate personally or to authorise them to pass the crate over to a Signor Bertasconi who claimed to be acting as my agent.

"I told them I would still be picking it up personally and that in no circumstances should they hand it over to a third party. I thought at the time it was just an admin error but when I arrived I found it had been a very determined attempt to get the crate. It gave me more food for thought but that was quickly forgotten when I got the crate back home, took out the framed painting and removed the back to reveal that it contained no hidden painting.

"My reaction was a mixture of frustration, disappointment and anger and my immediate, if stupid action, was to send off an email to Lambertini who I thought had double-crossed me saying that I was returning the crate with the girl picture so that he could send it back again to me together with the Tiepolo hidden in situ. I took the crate back to the airport to be shipped to him the same day.

"Of course, I had to tell Roberto de Vincetti that I couldn't help him and added much of the background story. I never heard from him again, or from Lambertini for that matter. Slowly over the following days and weeks I realized that untold riches were not going to fall into my lap, and for years now haven't really thought much about it until you came along."

He lifted his head to look Simon in the eye and asked two direct questions which hitherto Simon had dodged. "All that was twenty years ago and I don't know what happened to the painting after that. Are you now sure that it is a genuine Tiepolo, despite the doubts that have been expressed down the years? Secondly, I think that you have been very assiduous in your research to establish a provenance for the picture, are you in fact the current owner?"

Chapter 11

Simon hesitated briefly before answering and decided to be frank and open with the old man whose story so far, though interesting, had been more of a plea for recognition that his questionable actions had been self-justified, and had not, so far, filled in any gaps in the provenance trail. He hoped for more information and told Pagnetti that yes, all the extensive investigations carried out on the painting had indicated that it was a genuine Tiepolo, and all that was required now was the verdict of a panel of Tiepolo experts on the painting backed up by a provenance without any embarrassing gaps.

It was also a "Yes" to his second question. Simon was the present owner and he explained how this came about, adding that he had a signed statement from Manzini disclaiming any rights he may have to the painting, which cleared up any possibility of a claim from that direction.

"That was unusually generous of the old bugger" remarked Pagnetti "either he's changed a lot over the years, which I frankly doubt, or it is a meaningless gesture, designed to mislead you. My advice to you is to be very cautious in your dealings with him and do not take things at face value."

Pagnetti went on to say that he was not able to add any more details on the provenance of the painting than those Simon had already gleaned from Manzini, that it had been in family possession for around two hundred years before being reluctantly passed over to be sold by Angelo de Vincentti in 1972. Vincentti, he added, claimed to have sold it for a disappointingly low figure to a private client, but it was a fraud no trace of a sale had been found and as now he was dead there was little chance of tracing where it had actually been.

Pagnetti said "I asked his son Roberto at our meeting, what had actually happened to the painting after his father had taken possession of it to sell. He claimed his father would not speak about it, other than to say it had been sold, and there was nothing found amongst his papers that referred to the painting."

Simon realised that, disappointingly, Pagnetti seemed to know nothing more and little was to be gained by staying any longer. A thought occurred to him, and he asked "You say you emailed Riccardo when you opened the crate and found only one painting in the frame. Did you happen to keep his email address?"

Pagnetti fumbled in his pocket and brought out a museum piece of a mobile phone and handed it over to Simon "Have a look in there. I rarely use the thing, but I don't think I've purposely eliminated anything. My son insists that it's charged up and that I have it with me all the time."

Simon struggled to find his way through the phone's old system, but eventually found the email address was still listed there and transferred It to his own phone. Then, thanking the old man who had returned to reading his newspaper, he slipped away to re-join his bodyguard who was leaning against a wall nearby.

As Simon joined him, he gave a small nod in the direction of three men who were looking towards them from the corner of the calle and remarked "Those three guys have been taking a lot of interest in you and the old man for the last few minutes. I think we should move quickly back to the boat but in the other direction. Follow me." He then moved very smartly away along the canal side to another calle into which he turned in the direction of the busier area beside the museum where their boat was tied-up. The three men were taken by surprise by their sudden departure, but from half-way down the calle and looking back, it was obvious that they had decided to follow.

Led by the bodyguard, Simon scooted up a small turning and then into another at right angles between overhanging buildings. From there they ran onto the main quay where there were quite a few people moving about. They slackened pace and walked in a more leisurely fashion to their boat and cast off just as the pursuers reached the water's edge and looked on as the boat accelerated away into the lagoon back towards Venice.

"I thought we were in for a spot of trouble there" said the bodyguard "they clearly didn't like you talking to the old man and I'm glad you finished when you did. You are not very popular with some people in this district at the moment, and I hope for your sake you will be leaving shortly before something nasty happens."

"I think you're right" responded Simon "and I'll try and arrange a flight out as quickly as possible when I get back to the hotel."

He managed to book a mid-morning flight back to England for the following day and, as promised, phoned Commissario Albertini's office to let him know.

Albertini returned the call twenty minutes later to assure Simon that his bodyguards would be with him in good time to escort him not only to Marco Polo airport but would by-pass security and customs and see him directly on to the aircraft. Furthermore, having spoken to CDI Clough at New Scotland Yard, he was able to tell Simon that he would be met off the flight by police officers and to sit tight until they arrived on board. Finally, Albertini wished Simon godspeed and a return to Venice only when his safety could be assured.

Everything went according to plan and Simon was indeed met off the plane by two plain-clothes police officers who escorted him speedily through security and passport control and then to his car in one of the car parks. As he left Heathrow a police escort car swung in behind him and accompanied him to Membury Services on the M4. There the Met Police handed the escort duty over to an unmarked Gloucestershire Police car that saw him home.

The two police officers came into his cottage with him to examine that his alarm system and security on windows and doors were adequate and all working, but explained that as there had been no explicit threat to him on British soil they would not be posting a police officer on his premises, but police patrols would regularly keep an eye on the property during night and day and he was given a special number to ring should anything unusual or suspicious occur and get an immediate response.

Simon was frankly relieved that he was being left alone for a change but settled down with a cup of coffee to make some telephone calls. First, he phoned Addenbrookes Hospital in Cambridge to check on Reggies's progress and had some initial resistance to overcome because he was not a relative.

However, after some fast talking, including an embroidered version of his involvement in Venice at the time of the shooting, he was put through to Reggie's room. Despite his travels, the patient declared he was feeling much better and that the medical prognosis showed that he was making good progress with no complications.

Simon rang off and decided to phone Benjamin Burns with a view to going round to his gallery and bringing him up to date on what had happened in Venice and their discoveries. Burns' wife answered the phone and shocked Simon with what she told him.

The previous evening after locking up the gallery, her husband had taken their dog for his usual walk around a nearby park, something that usually took about half an hour, but after nearly an hour had passed she heard their dog barking and scraping at the back door. She found when she let him in that he had a gash at the top of a rear leg and was limping badly and she immediately surmised that the dog had been in a collision with a car or had been severely kicked.

As she cleaned the wound and attended to the dog, she became increasingly worried about Ben who should have been home some time ago. Was he perhaps looking for the dog who might have slipped his lead or was something else delaying him? She rang a friend nearby explaining her concerns and wondered if he would accompany her to the park and retrace Ben's steps.

She described that It was now dark and the large torch that she took with them to sweep either side of the path and into the woodland proved invaluable, as after ten minutes slow progress they made out a figure dragging itself with difficulty from amongst trees onto a grass verge that lay above the path.

They rushed towards the figure and found Ben bruised and much bloodied about the face and head. They afterwards discovered he was also suffering from two broken ribs, a broken arm and a twisted ankle.

They immediately phoned for an ambulance, making Ben as comfortable as possible lying on their two coats laid on the grass and quickly added a request for the police to attend. Between painful gasps for air, Ben told them that he had been attacked by three men who had followed him into the park, grabbed him and force-marched him into the woodland where they tied him to a tree, gagged him and then subjected him to a beating with a baseball type bat and some sort of chain. All the time questioning him about the Tiepolo painting, its whereabouts and where Simon Brookes was staying in Venice. Mrs Burns said that her husband was still in hospital in Gloucester and that a police investigation was underway.

Simon was temporarily lost for words as he contemplated the fact that he was now indirectly responsible for two innocent friends being injured and hospitalised. All because of the discovery of the Tiepolo and his subsequent investigation into its provenance.

He apologised profoundly to Mrs Burns for the injuries that her husband had sustained if, as it seemed, they arose from his association with Simon, but she said that nobody could have anticipated such an attack and that Benjamin she was sure, would agree with her. Before ringing off Simon assured her that he would go the next day and see Ben in hospital.

After he had replaced the receiver Simon realised that he was faced with some new questions.

The man who had hired Andreotti to shoot Simon in Venice and who had shot Reggie by mistake, already knew where to find Simon so was this someone new wanting to find him? The Gloucestershire Police were already investigating the attack on Ben and would have quickly established his connection to Simon – why had they not said, because it clearly made Simon more vulnerable?

His contemplation of these uncomfortable facts was rudely interrupted by a thunderous knocking and bell-ringing at the front door. When he opened it he found the two policemen who had been with him earlier, standing there.

"May we come in Mr Brookes, we've just heard from HQ of a development which may place you in greater danger so one of us will stay here with you throughout the night ."

"Would that have any connection with the attack on Mr Burns that his wife has just told me about on the phone?"

"Why, yes sir" the policeman agreed "someone just made the connection with you and called us right away."

"Well, you are very welcome" said Simon, and the two men began to make another security check in the house and garden, before one of them left to return in four hours to change places with his colleague.

As Simon began to prepare supper for two the phone rang. It was Yvonne Simmonds the sister of Peter Birch who'd left him the paintings, once again sounding agitated.

She began "Thank goodness you're there I been trying for days and didn't want to leave a message."
Simon began to explain that he'd been away but she interrupted him. "I haven't much time but wanted you to know that my brother Tim in Australia, is set on contesting Peter's will with regard to the painting and has lawyers working on a case to go before the Chancery Division of the High Court.

I gather the grounds for asking for the will to be overturned in respect of your legacy are twofold. Firstly as Peter had been diagnosed some months ago with the mild onset of dementia, Tim is claiming that he was not of "sound mind" when he wrote the will, and secondly that his intention was to leave you a picture that you had admired, not a secondary picture hidden within the frame that he almost certainly did not know the existence of."

She paused before adding, "I really am sorry about this Simon. Personally, as you know, I was happy to leave things as they were and if things worked out well, to toast your good fortune. But Tim is a bloody minded and determined man and persuasion won't sway him – I've tried, but I thought you ought to be forewarned. Frankly he seems completely obsessed above all reason about the bloody painting and I wouldn't put anything beyond him now in his attempts to gain possession of it," she paused to be more emphatic "so be warned and do take care – I never thought I would be saying such a thing about my own brother....but there it is."

Simon thanked her for telling him, pointedly did not mention the enigmatic letter that Peter had left for him and quickly ended the conversation.

It gave him more to think about. Someone else had now entered the lists as it were, to win ownership of the Tiepolo painting, as well as the person who had organised the assassination attempt in Venice.

But wait a minute, that was, according to the would-be assassin, someone living in Australia and hadn't Yvonne said that her brother lived there? Could this be the same person – it was confusing, to say the least.

His musing was interrupted by the phone ringing again, this time from an international number – it was Jeremy Idle with the worst possible news. The Tiepolo painting in its case had been stolen in Florence.

Chapter 12

Marie d'Albeigne Shawcross was a remarkable lady by any standards that you cared to apply. Now in her middle-fifties she was still very attractive with blonde hair framing a lightly tanned face with high cheek-bones, deep blue eyes and a smile that lit up a room. She was also witty and intelligent and carried with her a presence that belied her modest five foot four inches in height.

What made her unique however, was her ability, proven time after time to find missing masterpieces sometimes stolen, other times just lost. With a background in fine art history and experience gained working in gallery management at the Uffizi in Florence, the National Gallery in London and then as a consultant at Christie's in London and New York she possessed a unique talent and knowledge of fine art, the art world and those operating within its sometimes murky depths.

Invariably retained by companies specialising in the insurance of valuable works of art whenever they went missing, Marie worked alongside the police in Rome, London, Paris or New York or wherever investigations were underway to recover paintings or "objets d'art." Her reputation went before her and she was always welcomed by investigating teams whose files and intelligence were invariably opened to her.

Before Jeremy Idle had taken possession of the Tiepolo painting, he had asked Simon to take out an insurance policy with one of the specialist art insurers for one million pounds.

Needless to say, the policy was very restrictive in its coverage, requiring only named persons to be in charge and in sight of the painting – principally Simon or Idle – and when it was moved, a detailed programme of when and where had to be given in advance. Whenever the painting was "out of sight" details were also required of the conditions and security under which the painting was to be kept and again the people involved, with their contact number. These were very onerous conditions but ensured that the insuring company knew precisely where the Tiepolo was at any time.

After the favourable scientific report from the Courtauld Institute had been given, Jeremy Idle had taken the painting to a high security storage unit approved by the insurance company, whilst he made arrangements to put it before the Tiepolo experts and their advisors who between them would pronounce it genuine or fake. To accompany the painting, however, he needed a well-researched and verified provenance and that depended very much on what Simon had been able to uncover in Venice and elsewhere.

From telephone calls between them it was now apparent that sufficient information existed to confirm that Tiepolo had indeed painted another version of *The Last Supper and* that was the same size and contemporary with a group of six *The Life of Christ* paintings now hanging in the Louvre. But there were still gaps in the history of where the painting had been held in its early existence and again during the twentieth century which were troubling.

Idle had discovered that the next scheduled meeting of the Tiepolo experts committee to consider submissions from owners or galleries, was not due to be held for two months.

Although it was a disappointingly long wait, he had notified the committee secretary that he would be submitting Simon's alleged Tiepolo *The Last Supper* to their scrutiny at that time.

Four days after he had spoken to the committee secretary, Jeremy Idle had a telephone call from him, during which he told Idle that one of the two principal Tiepolo experts on the committee had expressed an interest in having a personal preview of the painting, before the formal examination, and asked if Idle would be prepared to bring it to Florence for a day or two. No reasons were given, but, bearing in mind the undoubted inconvenience that this would be to Mr Idle, the cost of the flights and his accommodation at one of the best hotels whilst in Florence would be at the expert's expense.

Although this was a most curious and unusual request, the man asking the question through the secretary was Signor Gregorio Ponticelli - without question the foremost expert on Tiepolo who also chaired the committee. Jeremy said that he would ring back shortly after he had conferred with colleagues but thought however, that such interest expressed in advance of the formal committee meeting could not be other than encouraging and gave Simon that opinion when he spoke to him on the phone and gained his agreement.

He also spoke to the insurance company who agreed providing that the terms and conditions on security under the policy were strictly applied. They also approved of the security arrangements for the safe-keeping of the painting when it was "out of sight" at the Firenze Porta Baltica Hotel where Idle would be staying and where it was proposed that Ponticelli would be examining the painting.

Jeremy Idle lost no time in ringing back directly to Ponticelli's private office on a number passed to him by the committee secretary, to confirm arrangements and two days later was Florence-bound on an Air Italia flight occupying two first-class seats one for himself and one for the painting in its case. A taxi from Peretola Airport brought him to the Porta Baltica hotel where he was slightly relieved to hand over the painting to an assistant manager whom he watched placing it into a safe within a strongroom, happy in the knowledge that it was in safe keeping until the meeting with Ponticelli the next day.

This was scheduled for ten a.m. in a private room on the first floor and having checked that this was ready, ten minutes beforehand Jeremy accompanied the assistant manager back to the strongroom and the safe to find that the picture had gone.

The police were called immediately and whilst awaiting their arrival Jeremy Idle first phoned the insurance company in London, then the number he had been given for Ponticelli's office to learn that he was, not unexpectedly, out, although it was now twenty minutes after their arranged meeting time at the hotel. It was then that he felt he could not put off the call to Simon any longer and rang him to tell him the bad news. Promptly Simon said he would fly to Florence as quickly as he could and join Jeremy at the hotel.

Meanwhile things were moving quickly, the insurance company had been in touch with the Italian police and also arranged that Madame Shawcross would be with them shortly after flying in from her home in Paris. Ispettore Superiore Ricci of the Carabinieri TPC Unit specialising in the investigation of art and antiquities theft, had arrived at the hotel with a forensic team.

After questioning Jeremy and the assistant manager concerned, the Inspector moved to question the hotel manager, the other assistant manager and the reception staff, whilst the forensic people dusted the safe and strongroom doors for unusual fingerprints.

The inspector was keen to understand the routine for opening and closing of safe and strongroom. Who held or had access to keys and who knew the numeric code that was used on the safe? He established that two keys were needed to open the strongroom door, the first of which had three copies held respectively by the hotel manager and his two assistant managers. The other key had two copies, one was kept by the hotel manager in a locked desk drawer until required with another copy lodged in a nearby bank. The numeric code for the safe was changed twice a month by the manager and given only to the two assistant managers.

It was an odd coincidence that Simon, who had left home in Gloucestershire that morning, should draw up in his taxi at the Porta Baltica hotel at the precise time that another arrived. This carried Marie Shawcross from the airport to which she had flown from Paris. With each of them pulling a wheeled suitcase behind them, they arrived at the stained glass doors together before they opened. Simon gestured for her to precede him and received a dazzling smile of thanks. Porters rushed to take their cases and they progressed to the reception desk side-by-side where an assumption was made that they were together. After explanations and apologies Simon and Marie exchanged smiles and Simon realised what an extraordinarily attractive woman she was and momentarily thought "if only."

As they were booking in, Simon caught her name which he recalled he had heard before, but it was only when she mentioned in her flow of immaculate Italian, the name Jeremy Idle, that Simon realised that this lady was the famed art recovery expert that Jeremy had mentioned in his phone call. Simon leaned across and held out his hand.

"Excuse me Madame, but I couldn't help hearing your name and your enquiry for Jeremy Idle. My name is Simon Brookes and I am the owner of the missing painting and will shortly be seeing Jeremy Idle here in the hotel. Might I suggest that we three meet up together over a cup of tea in say twenty minutes time here in the lounge to discuss what has happened?"

Simon was as surprised as Marie by his sudden presumptuous approach, but she shook his hand and agreed that it was an excellent idea. They shared a lift to the second floor followed by the porters and found that they were to occupy rooms on the same corridor. Simon phoned Jeremy in his room and told him of the arrangement and then arranged for tea and some Florentine speciality biscuits to be served in the lounge area in a quarter of an hour, before he unpacked and freshened up.

Jeremy was waiting in the lounge full of apologies, which Simon refused to accept, it being "not his fault," just as they were joined by Marie. Introductions made, they sat down to enjoy their tea and biscuits.

Jeremy Idle described again how he had witnessed the painting being placed in the safe itself within the strongroom the previous afternoon, and the events of the morning leading up to the unlocking of both strongroom and safe and the discovery of its disappearance.

He went on to describe the phone calls that he had made to the insurance company in London, to Simon and to the office of Gregorio Ponticelli. The first call to Ponticelli was some twenty minutes after he had been due at the hotel to commence his examination of the painting and the person answering the phone had said merely that he was out but couldn't or wouldn't say where or when he was due back in the office.

What with the flap in the hotel, the stress and shock of the painting's loss and the lengthy questioning he was subjected to by Inspector Ricci, it was afternoon before he had remembered Ponticelli's non-appearance and after checking with reception that he still hadn't come to the hotel, he made another call to the number he had been given only to receive a message that the number was no longer in service.

He tried again with the same result and checked on their website to find that the number there was almost identical, presumably in the same series, he rang and spoke to Ponticelli himself this time. He, Ponticelli, was astonished to hear what Idle had to say and quickly denied expressing a wish to see the alleged Tiepolo painting ahead of the committee meeting or that he had asked the committee secretary to arrange the viewing in Florence. Moreover, after a brief pause whilst he checked with the office personnel nobody had agreed to a date or a time, or had received a call from Jeremy that morning.

Idle had reported the matter to Inspector Ricci but had done nothing more, pending Simon's arrival. Whilst he had been talking, Marie had withdrawn a small notebook from her handbag, and had been writing in it and when he had finished, questioned him on several aspects of his story. Then she turned to Simon and asked him to tell her how he came to own the painting which he did as succinctly as he could.

He then described the search to fill in gaps in the provenance history, where it had taken him. and the things that had happened on the way.

Whilst he was talking Simon suddenly remembered that in all the rush and confusion he had left home without notifying the police in Gloucestershire, and felt he must get in touch with them quickly. The meeting over tea had fulfilled its main purpose and Marie said she must now seek out Ispettore Ricci, introduce herself and exchange preliminary impressions, whilst Simon rang the police in Gloucestershire.

The Inspector Morgan that he spoke to was unsparing in the way he castigated Simon for disappearing without notice. His absence was only discovered when the policemen were changing shifts and they checked to see he was OK. He had been posted up as an important missing person and extensive checks were already being made including with the Metropolitan Police.

Simon in apology explained the unusual circumstances for his lapse, the painting going missing and his sudden decision to fly to Florence which all happened so quickly. He also mentioned the phone call he had received from Yvonne with regard to the legal steps that her brother in Australia was taking to challenge their brother Peter's will and the connection that might be made between this brother and the man whom the would-be assassin Andreotti asserted had ordered Simon's shooting.

Morgan listened patiently to Simon's explanation and suspicions which he noted but was more concerned with his immediate safety and questioned whether Simon had spoken yet to the Italian police in charge of the investigation into the missing painting and told them of the threats to his life.

Simon responded with the fact that his interview was imminent, and he would certainly raise the issue. Before ending the call Morgan enjoined Simon to take special care and not leave the hotel for any reason, and then asked for the name of the Italian police officer in charge and whether he was still at the hotel.

It was three hours later that Ispettore Ricci found Simon and invited him into his temporary office in the hotel where once again he was asked to go through his story of events since first receiving the painting up to Yvonne's latest telephone call, and his suspicions. The Ispettore had many questions and made many notes before they seemed satisfied, then Ricci said "I have spoken to an Inspector Morgan of the English police and also to Commissirio Albertini of the Venice Carabinieri and I'm told by both of them that you should already be under police guard Mr Brookes, but I am now pretty certain that the threats to you come from two distinct directions – you are in double jeopardy."

Chapter 13

The Ispettore paused having made his dramatic pronouncement, awaited a reaction from Simon who merely commented "How come?"

"I believe that the shooting in Piazza San Marco in Venice, then the follow-up attack on Mr Marsden and the legal attempts to upset the terms of Mr Peter Bird's will, all seem to originate in Australia and are being investigated by the Australian police and others. It would indeed be a strange coincidence if these incidents were not linked.

However, I believe that the attack on Mr Burns in Gloucestershire was made to uncover information about the painting and your whereabouts, which was already known and being acted upon by the 'Australian connection.' Whoever had that Burns attack carried out, acted quickly to put you and Mr Jeremy Idle under surveillance awaiting a good opportunity to appropriate the painting.

That necessitated meticulous planning and an expertise that contrasts with the rather clumsy and ill-thought through actions of the 'Australian connection' person or persons. After discussion with my English and Venetian colleagues, I am confident that another party has come into play and it is they who planned and executed the theft of the painting from this hotel."

He went on "I think that you personally are not now in any great danger. 'The Australian connection' people must now know that the painting has been stolen and that you can know nothing about where it is, or who has taken it. I suspect anyway that your attempted assassination was a knee-jerk reaction by somebody who felt at the time that a legal overturning of the will of Mr Peter Bird would be made easier if you were no longer around.

Madame Shawcross, who I think you have already met and is helping our investigations, shares my current thinking and both she and I would appreciate your cooperation in staying on for the time being here in Florence."

Simon readily agreed. He was impressed with the way in which Ricci had assimilated all the background information and reached his current assessment in less than a day and was now more confident that the investigation was in good hands. He was in a happier frame of mind when he joined Jeremy for dinner that evening.

The next morning whilst having breakfast, he was approached by one of Ricci's team who asked if he would come to Ricci's office in the hotel when he had finished his breakfast. When he made his way there, he found that Ricci had Madame Shawcross with him, who greeted him with warm smile and a hope that he had slept well after a long day. Simon reciprocated with a smile and an assurance. Ricci then began by asking Simon if he had made contact directly with any art dealers or experts in the United Kingdom or in Italy after he became the owner of the Tiepolo painting, other than Messrs Benjamin Burns, Reginald Marsden and Jeremy Idle.

He thought carefully before replying "Well, as you know I was in Venice specifically to research the provenance of the painting and consulted several curators in museums and galleries. I was careful to avoid claiming ownership of the Tiepolo, although whilst over there it was announced in the papers and other media that a painting alleged to be a Tiepolo had been discovered and some of these people may have put two and two together. The only other people who I talked to and might be considered in a way "expert" as far the painting was concerned were Theo Manzini, whose family owned the painting for a long time and the family's major domo for many years Alessandro Pagnetti. I have already described my conversation with both of them."

Ricci agreed that he had, but Madame Marie was particularly interested in his meetings with the two men and had a number of questions she wished to put to Simon which he was happy to answer at length. She was interested in the manner and demeanour of both men when they were dealing with Simon's queries. Had they been hesitant or reluctant in describing what had happened or did they appear to be open and honest, holding nothing back?

Simon had no hesitation in saying that Theo Manzini struck him as being frank and straightforward in everything he had said, sometimes to his own detriment. He also reminded them that Manzini had handed over to him a formal letter giving up any residual claim that he may still have had in the ownership of the painting. Whereas Pagnetti was rather a reluctant witness and volunteered very little.

Something nagged Simon at the back of his mind as he finished his answer – it was something relevant and important, but he couldn't quite recall, until it came like a flash of lightening.

"There is one thing that I got from Pagnetti that may be significant. You will recall from what I told you that Manzini and his father before him had entrusted the sale of many of their paintings as the need arose, to an art dealer in the family, the younger brother of Manzini's mother, Angelo de Vincentti. He cleverly defrauded them and disappeared abroad with wife and family plus a considerable fortune. He was never heard of again but his eldest son Roberto de Vincentti, many years later emerged as an art dealer in his own right and he made contact with Pagnetti shortly after the Tiepolo painting had first come to light in England.

I got Roberto's mobile number from Pagnetti's old phone and transferred it to mine with the objective of making contact, and frankly had forgotten all about it till now."

At the mention of Roberto de Vincentti, Marie got a gleam in her eye and leant forward in her chair. "That may be very significant. So, you haven't rung the number?" she asked.

"No" he responded, "the police in Venice were very keen that I should leave Venice and their jurisdiction as soon as possible and I flew out the next day, and, as I say, forgotten all about it."

With another of her engaging smiles Marie addressed Simon with the words "Excuse us a moment," before turning to the Ispettore and engaging him in a rapid conversation in Italian, at the end of which Ricci shrugged his shoulders and nodded.

"Mr Brookes" she began…..

"Oh please call me Simon."

"Right thank you, Simon. I've suggested to the Ispettore that once the number has been checked and shown still to connect with Roberto de Vincentti, you ring him in our presence to try and arrange a meeting with him, ostensibly to talk to him about the provenance of the painting but hopefully to learn much more about his business and his interest in the painting.

"I hope I'm not being presumptuous in asking for us to be present when you ring him, but as his name has come up, I can tell you that he is well known to the police and by repute to me and may well be involved in some way with its theft. However, we do not know his present whereabouts and the longest possible telephone conversation that you could make with him would help the police pinpoint his location so that they can possibly detain him for questioning on several matters.

"No, of course not, I'm only to happy to co-operate in any way I can," said Simon.

"Excellent, I'll have the number checked out right away if you can let me have it," responded Ricci. Simon swiftly looked up the number on his mobile and the policeman copied it down before reading it out to someone over the phone with instructions. He replaced the receiver and paused, looking closely at Simon before going on "How well do you know Mr Jeremy Idle, Mr Brookes?"

"Not very well. My friend Ben Burns did some research on experts to consult after we discovered the old painting and came up with his name. As I recall, Jeremy didn't claim to be an expert on Tiepolo specifically but knew his work well as he did the work of several Italian artists of the period.

I think that Ben chose him to come and look at the painting and give us his opinion, as much to get his guidance on how I should go forward and the fact that he was based in England, which was handy.

As you know I agreed that because of his expertise and knowledge of how the market in old paintings worked, he should undertake to have the necessary scientific tests carried out and then submit the painting to the scrutiny of the committee on Tiepolo works to decide on its authenticity. It was also he who persuaded me to do the necessary research work to try and fill in the gaps in the painting's provenance. Why do you ask, have you reason to doubt his conduct or reputation in some way?"

Ricci batted away the question with a bland response "Just checking on everyone as a part of my enquiries." Then his phone rang and after responding "Ricci" said in succession "si.....si...... eccelente, molte grazie" and hung up. "That was confirmation that the number is still in use and is in the name of Roberto de Vincentti. Would you be prepared to ring him now Mr Brookes, from a neutral untraceable line from this office, so that we can listen in and record the conversation?"

Simon agreed and whilst a special instrument was brought in and assembled with two additional earpieces and a recording device, they discussed what Simon would say and how he could prolong the conversation if necessary, so that de Vincentti's location could be accurately traced. Having discussed all the foreseeable directions the conversation could take and with everything set up, Ricci commented that de

Vincentti would probably say that he would ring back and try and find out where the call came from before doing so. Simon rang the number.

"Allo, si?"

"Is that Signor Roberto de Vincentti?" said Simon. After a short silence came a response, "Si…. I mean yes. Who is this?"

"Thanks for speaking in English. My Italian, I'm afraid, is almost non-existent. My name is Simon Brookes and I obtained your number from Signor Alessandro Pagnetti. I should explain that I am the owner of a painting that I believe is by Giovanni Battista Tiepolo entitled *The Last Supper* and am engaged in filling in some gaps in the picture's provenance to stand beside the scientific tests when it is placed before the authenticity committee. As you have expressed interest in the painting in the past I hope that you may be able to help."

De Vincentti. Interrupted. "I'm sorry but I am in a meeting and cannot speak to you at the moment. If you give me your number, I will ring you back in half an hour, where are you calling from?

"From Florence. My number is 3955 790244."

"Thank you." Then the phone was hung up.

"You did well to string it out and gave him little chance to interrupt your introduction more quickly" said Ricci," but I fear it was too short to pinpoint a precise location. We'll hear in a moment."

"I think it has put him into a real quandary," commented Marie. "If he is involved in the theft, he will wonder why you haven't mentioned it and out of curiosity he might want to continue the conversation to learn what the police are doing and also what you learned from Pagnetti about him.

"Nothing much has yet leaked to the papers about the theft, so if he wasn't involved, he might not know the painting has been taken and would be very keen to learn as much as he could from you under the guise of helping you with the picture's provenance, so he might want to talk again on the phone or possibly agree to a meeting. Either way he is at risk of exposing his real interest."

There was a knock on the door and in response to Ricci's "Si" an assistant came in with a paper showing an outline map of Italy on which were superimposed four reducing circles, the smallest encompassing an area that included all of the Veneto and much of Bergamo to the west. He put this in front of Ricci with his comments in rapid Italian.

Ricci thanked and dismissed him and turning to the others said "As I suspected they hadn't enough time to trace exactly where in northern Italy de Vincentti was speaking from. Their best guess at present was that it was somewhere in the Veneto not in Venice itself, but there is a possibility that he is further west towards Bergamo. Using the area as starting point however means that another telephone conversation of a similar length would enable our people to zoom in on the location."

Ricci looked at his watch "My guess is that de Vincentti will spend the best part of half an hour trying to find where you are actually calling from and planning his strategy before calling back. Either way I would suggest Mr Brookes that you stay here by the phone, whilst I carry on with my questioning of people here in the hotel. I will be back as soon as the phone starts ringing." With that he left the room.

Simon discussed various possible scenarios with Madame Shawcross and during their conversation she asked him to call her Marie.

Then whilst he read an English newspaper, she made a number of telephones calls on her mobile in both French and Italian until the special phone started ringing. Simon let it ring four times before he picked it up which gave Ricci time to get back in the room and he and Marie were able to use the earpieces. The conversation was brief.

"Hello, Brookes here."

"Mr Brookes, I think it best that we meet. Would Friday this week suit In Florence, Café Rivoire, Piazza della Signora at 11 o'clock ?"

"That's fine.".

"Ask for me."

Then he rang off.

Chapter 14

It was now Wednesday, and the meeting was the following day. After a discussion between the three of them, Ricci suggested that Marie, who had never met de Vincentti, should go there with Simon but under an assumed name because her real name would almost certainly be familiar to an international art dealer. Ricci was frankly surprised that de Vincentti had a agreed to a meeting in such a public place, but would have the café put under surveillance from early in the morning by someone briefed on de Vincentti's appearance, who would note if the dealer brought anyone with him perhaps to sit elsewhere on the premises.

Simon agreed to be "wired-up" so that his conversation with de Vincentti could be listened to and recorded. Ricci said that as the art dealer was under suspicion in other cases, it was possible that his superior officers would insist on detaining de Vincentti for questioning, but it would depend on what came out during the conversation.

At five minutes to eleven on the Friday morning Simon and Marie made their way across Piazza della Signora to the Café Rivoire which was quite crowded both inside and out.

Nobody made an approach towards them, so Simon enquired of the head waiter whether a Signor de Vincentti had reserved a table.

"Ah. Mister Brookes is it?" he responded and on receiving an affirmatory nod went on "He apologises that he has been delayed and asks if you would phone him on this number," handing a piece of paper to Simon. They walked back into the piazza and Simon tapped out the number on his mobile which was answered on the second ring.
"Si"

"Signor de Vincentti?", said Simon, "This is Simon Brookes."

"Ah, so sorry I couldn't make our meeting at Café Rivoire, I was detained. I am still tied up momentarily but will soon be free, so could I ask you to you to take a leisurely walk along Via Vacchereccia to the junction with Via per Santa Maria and follow this road down to the Ponte Vecchio. If you then cross the road to the corner of the bridge and Lungarno degli Archibusieri I will pick you up from there in twenty minutes time. I prefer to meet you alone but you have a lady with you. Who is she?"

"She is a friend " Simon explained. "Jeanne Sablon, and I'm certainly not leaving her behind."

After a short paused de Vincentti said, "OK, see you in twenty minutes," and rang off.

As Simon was briefing Marie on the half of the call that she couldn't hear, his mobile rang, it was Ricci. He had listened in to the conversation and wasn't at all surprised that de Vincentti had postponed the meeting whilst he or his agents took a good look at Simon and anyone who accompanied him to the café.

However, he was not happy about Simon and Marie being picked up and being taken the Lord knows where. He would, of course, arrange to have the pick-up car followed, but this would have to be done very surreptitiously which could result in the trail being lost at some stage, This could put them both in considerable danger. In all conscience he could not agree to them going ahead.

As Simon and Marie made their way along Via Vacchereccia and then Via per Santa Maria, there continued a very animated if quiet conversation between the three of them over mobile phones. Despite Ricci's misgivings, both Simon and Marie were keen to go along with de Vincennti. Only that way, they argued, would they discover anything useful, and after all there were two of them. Eventually Ricci agreed that he could not stop them going if they were adamant.

They continued on towards the Ponte Vecchio and crossed the road to the corner of the bridge where they were to be picked up, with several minutes to spare. They agreed that Simon would do all the talking with Marie continuing in her role as the friend who was not involved.

Right on time a bright blue Alfa Romero drew to the kerb beside them and before it had even stopped, a tall smiling man in large dark eyeshades uncoiled himself and stepped out of the passenger door. He moved to open the rear door and ushered them both inside with the words "Quickly please – no stopping here." Once both were inside, he slammed the door shut, got back into the front seat, then, with a squeal of tyres they were off, fast.

After a few moments Simon leaned forward and began "Are you Signor de Vincentti?"

The tall man turned smiling again "No, no. We take you to him, yes?"

"Is it far?" asked Simon.

The man replied "Soon, soon" and remarked something in rapid Italian to the driver, a thickset man dressed all in black, and they laughed together.

Simon muttered sotto voce to Marie "I don't much like the feel of this" and she responded very quietly "nor I, having heard what he said to the driver."

Simon's request to know what Marie had heard was interrupted by the tall man turning with two black head coverings in his hand and the request that both the back seat passengers should put them on so that they did not see where they were being taken.

"Is this really necessary" asked an indignant Simon but as the reply came "If you want to see Signor Vincennti, yes," they reluctantly complied. During the next few minutes, they felt the car do a dozen quick left and right turns to completely distort any idea of the direction in which they were going, and no doubt to shake off any pursuing cars, before they came to a halt.

When they were relieved of their masks, both blinked in the strong sunlight before they were hurried through a door in a grey coloured wall and into some sort of warehouse building judging by the high shelving and the whine of fork lift trucks busy at work. They were led past anonymous offices at the side of the building where a dozen incurious people were working, all eyes concentrating on computer screens. The tall man knocked on a door before entering a large well-furnished office where a man sat at a splendid antique desk.

He put down the newspaper that he had been reading, stood and then walked round the desk to shake hands with Simon and Marie. He was a well-built man in his middle fifties with a pale complexion that somehow reflected the streak of white hairs amongst the black that ran from the middle of his hairline right to the back. This was matched by a similar patch of white in his neatly trimmed black beard. The overall effect was to give him a devilish look thought Marie.

He began, "I am de Vincentti. I'm sorry for the delays and the elaborate security arrangements but I'm afraid I find it increasingly necessary these days." He indicated that they should sit in armchairs that were placed beside a low table, and asked whether they would like tea or coffee. They both opted for coffee, and he passed on the order to the tall man, sat down opposite to them and went on, "I understand that your Tiepolo is missing?"

Somewhat taken aback Simon replied, "You are very well informed, how did you know that?"

"I have good sources Mr Brookes. And yet despite its disappearance you still come to me with queries about its provenance. I would have thought that you would be devoting your time to finding out, alongside the police, who has taken the painting and where it now is."

"Perhaps you could help us with that" retorted Simon.

"Me? How do you think I could help?"

"Well, you expressed considerable interest in it when it came to light in England in the early 1990's after it had been missing for many years before."

"Who told you that?"

"Signor Pagnetti. "

"Oh, that old fool. I should pay little regard to what you heard from him, he is a man consumed by a sense of self-pity and regret."

Simon stuck to his guns "But you did see him in 1992 when the painting had been re-discovered and talked to him about it, didn't you?"

"Yes, but only out of idle curiosity, as just one topic in our conversation."

"Yet Pagnetti was quite clear in his recollection of the offer you made to him in the event that the painting was to come into his hands. So you knew, or at least strongly suspected, that he was involved in having the painting shipped over to Venice. You even tried to have it picked up, ostensibly on his behalf, from the airport. Come off it de Vincentti, you were very keen to have the painting."

De Vincentti bridled at Simon's words and with attempted or real indignation snapped back "You are making some serious allegations Mr Brookes on the say-so of a confused old man with a bad memory, be careful."

After delivering this rejoinder de Vincentti picked up the coffee pot and turned to Marie with a wide smile "Some more coffee Madame —I'm sorry I've momentarily forgotten your name."

"It's Jeanne Sablon, and no thanks to the coffee."

"And tell me again Ms Sablon what is your connection to this business,"

"I am a friend of Simon's."

"But I'm informed that you spend a good deal of time in conversation with Ispetorri Ricci during his investigations. Not as Jeanne Sablon, but as Madame Marie d'Albeigne Shawcross the art recovery specialist. Is that not so?"

Marie replied calmly "Yes that is correct. But I thought it more appropriate to come here under an assumed name."

De Vincentti looked at her silently for a moment and then glanced at his watch, "It is time to move on I think," and then added " We will continue this conversation later elsewhere and I'm afraid that you will both have to stay as my guests for a while. Please hand over your mobile phones."

He signalled to his two henchman who approached, one pointing a handgun and the other carrying two pairs of handcuffs.

Marie and Simon began to protest loudly but the cuffs were quickly slipped on both their wrists. Marie's handbag was picked up and her mobile taken from it whilst the other man patted down Simon to find his mobile and inadvertently also detected the microphone and its micro-radio broadcasting device beneath his shirt. Ripping the shirt open he called to de Vincentti who was just leaving through the door.

He backtracked, looked at the devices and eyed Simon with a malevolent eye as he told his man to "Destroy it, and check them both for tracers" and then said to Simon "that was very unwise," turned on heel and left the room.

The tapes holding the microphone and mini radio transmitter were unceremoniously pulled from Simon's chest, each one painfully taking with it a quantity of chest hair, and the device was thrown to floor and ground to smithereens under the man's heel. They were both then checked over with an electronic detector which resulted in the tracer in Marie's skirt pocket being found and destroyed.

With head covers back in position they were led out and pushed into the back seat of a car which then moved off, no more than five minutes after they had arrived. Because of the head covers, conversation between them was impossible but to give a degree of support to each other, they each sought the other's hand, which were clasped together despite the cuffs for the rest of the journey.

That lasted for over half an hour, and they were bundled out, stiff and uncomfortable from the ride, and pushed and pulled up a path and into a building, up some stairs and through a door into a room before their handcuffs and headcovers were removed.

They found themselves in a small sitting room with a dining area at one end and at the other a window that was barred on the outside. The tall smiling man holding a gun, was standing with his back to the door through which they had come, whilst another man, whom they had not seen before, looked on.

The gunman, pointing his weapon alternately at Marie and Simon, addressed them in his somewhat disconnected English. "You will be good, yes? Then you will get meals. If bad, no meals and handcuffs on!"

Simon spoke up "How long do you intend to keep us here, only the police will I'm sure be onto you very quickly if you don't let them know where to find us immediately."

The tall man smiled again "I don't think so" adding "be good!" as he and his companion left locking the door behind them, followed by the sound of a bar being slid across.

Simon was disconsolate and turned to Marie "I'm really sorry I've landed you in all this."

She smiled and answered "Don't apologise. You couldn't have foreseen what was going to happen. It's not your fault, and anyway I came of my own free will." Then taking him by the arm went on "Come on Simon, let's have a look around our prison." She then led the way through a door in the long wall which led to a small lobby with a table on which there was tea and coffee making equipment and another two doors.

One of these led to a bathroom and the other to a bedroom sparsely furnished with a single chest of drawers, a rickety old wardrobe containing a spare blanket and a pillow, and a double bed.

Chapter 15

Ispettore Ricci had made good progress in his investigations. Suspecting from the start that the theft of the paintings from the Porta Baltica hotel strongroom had been, at least in part, an "inside job" he had the backgrounds of the most likely suspect employees thoroughly researched and found out that one of the assistant managers, Gustav Olivio, had a gambling addiction and was heavily in debt. By dint of continuous, cleverly contrived questioning the man had broken down and confessed that he had taken the painting in the early hours of the morning.

He already had his key to the strongroom and took an impression of the one held by the manager in a soft plastic material that quickly hardened and made it possible for a locksmith to create a duplicate for him. He knew the current code for the safe, so it took just two or three minutes to access the painting, re- lock the safe and the room and leave with the painting in its case. He then placed it, as instructed, inside a storeroom for the domestic staff on the same floor.

An envelope containing €1500 was pushed into the letterbox at his apartment the same morning to add to the €500 that had already been delivered after he had agreed to carry out the heist.

He showed Ricci the messages he had received on his mobile phone. The first arrived two days before the painting was brought to the hotel and, translated from the Italian read simply "Could you do with €2000 Euros, for performing a simple task that will take you less than five minutes?" This was followed less than four hours later by another "€500 Euros paid immediately and €1,500 Euros on completion. Learn more by replying "How?"

He had responded and received this reply "Its easy money, just take the painting from the strongroom safe at your hotel, between 2 and 2.15 am on the 23rd – the day after tomorrow - and leave it in the 1st floor chamber maids' cupboard near the lift under a pile of bath-towels second shelf on right. Respond "Yes" and €500 Euros will be posted into your home postbox."

Olivio admitted he hadn't thought long about it – he needed the money urgently, it was a godsend. He was scheduled to be on duty overnight between the 22nd and 23rd and had the time to borrow the manager's key make an impression and get a key made by a locksmith on the other side of town whilst he waited. To avoid being seen carrying the painting in its case, he took a suitcase into the strongroom with him and put the painting case inside it before making his way to the designated cupboard. It would not be an unusual thing to see an assistant manager carrying a guest's suitcase along an hotel corridor anytime, and the chances of meeting somebody on that short walk in the early hours of the morning were very small.

Everything went according to plan he said, and all the money was paid over as promised and at no time did he speak to his contact in person or over the phone, just contacted them by text. Olivio was arrested and charged with theft then released on bail awaiting trial.

All that Ricci got directly from this was a mobile phone number which, he anticipated correctly, was a "burner" phone and untraceable. He went up to the chambermaids' cupboard on the first floor where the painting had been placed and took a cursory look, but was more interested in the bedrooms opposite, 134 and 136. He got the manager to open both for him and squinted through the spy-glass fitted in their doors. In both cases one looking to the right and one to the left, gave a good, if slightly distorted view of the cupboard door.

Checking the room occupation list for the night in question, the manager showed that both were in use, one by a couple but the other, 136, by a single guest. Ricci asked whether there was any record at the time of booking that this single guest had particularly asked for room 134 or 136. The manager looked again into his records and expressed surprise that the guest concerned had indeed made a special request that he should have Room 136 which he claimed had a special sentimental attachment for him as he had stayed there with his late wife.

So strong was his plea that although the room had been allocated, arrangements were made to switch rooms to accommodate the request. Ricci took away the name, address and phone number from which the booking had been made, more in hope than expectation that they would lead anywhere.

He had been disappointed and frustrated earlier to find that the enquiries into the high-jacking of one of the telephone lines into the office of Signor Ponticelli, the eminent art expert, had been expertly done through the telephone company's junction box in the street outside. A knowledgeable engineer had diverted the calls for that particular number to a phone in a now empty office over a closed trattoria.

Whoever had carried out the work hadn't even bothered to disconnect the re-routing. Only one witness had been found who remembered seeing somebody working at the junction box a few days before, but the telephone company said that no official work had been carried out at that time and nobody at Signor Ponticelli' s office knew anything about it. There were just a few comments about the phones not working properly for a day or two.

One brighter spot was that the booking for Room 136 at the Porta Baltica was made from a landline number in Florence. Ricci immediately sent his deputy, Calassio, to see the account holder, a Mr Felix Holder,at the address and invite him to come to Ricci's temporary office at the hotel for questioning.

However, there was no response to a telephone call or insistent knocking on the door to the apartment. The concierge for the apartment block informed Calassio that Mr Holder only came to stay in his apartment five or six times a year for a week or so, but he allowed friends to use it occasionally and just recently an Italian friend of his – a Signor Tinteretto, had picked up the key and stayed for a few days. He had no information on the man other than that he knew he was genuine as he had phoned Mr Holder from the concierge's office and passed the phone over to confirm he was bona fide. The concierge described the man as best he could and gave Calassio Holder's phone number in England.

Back at the hotel Calassio rang Holder at his London office number to ask for his friend Signor Tintoretto's address and telephone number. Holder claimed to know nobody of that name but when Calassio explained the situation, he laughed and said that his friend had been joking when using the famous painter's name instead of his own.

He had no hesitation in passing over his real name, Antonio Castilenti, together with his address and telephone number in Rome.

The description that the concierge had given of Tintoretto/Castilenti tied closely with that given by staff at the hotel as the man who had occupied Room 136 on the night in question, even though the name he used was neither.

Calassio and Ricci discussed the next step and decided that after checking that Castilenti was in his Rome apartment, then Calassio would liaise with their Gendarmerie colleagues in Rome and go to question Castilenti with them and if necessary bring him back to Florence.

At this point Ricci turned his attention to Simon and Marie who had agreed to be picked up from the Pont a Vecchio by de Vincentti. He felt they were exposing themselves to unnecessary risks and argued strongly over their mobile phones to persuade them not to go, as they walked towards the bridge, however they were adamant. He made sure that cars were positioned to trail the pick-up vehicle from whichever direction it came and was comforted to some extent by the thought that not only was Simon "wired-up" but Marie also carried in the pocket of her skirt a tiny tracer beacon that would continue to pulse signals wherever they were taken.

Against the background of engine noise it was impossible to hear properly any voices other than that of Simon and more faintly Marie, but he heard Simon's questions and later his protests at the hoods.

The heavy traffic and the sudden changes of direction by the target car shook off the tailing police but initially the signal from the tracer beacon showed up on a screen overlaid with a map of Florence at the police station, enabling those watching to keep the pursuing car informed.

However, after a while the signal became fainter and more spasmodic and there was confusion when it seemed to have stopped moving in the middle of a trading estate before moving off slowly into a building. At the same time a message came in from a patrol that a car answering to the description of the pick-up vehicle, had just come onto the autostrada at a nearby junction and was driving fast away from the city. Arrangements were made to stop it at the next junction.

The tailing car reported that it was about five minutes away from the trading estate and the building into which the tracing beacon had been carried and Ricci was impatient for it to get there with all speed. He was able to hear clearly the exchange between Simon and de Vincentti and when Marie's identity was exposed. Then to his horror he heard the discovery and destruction of the wired device that Simon was carrying followed by the disappearance on the screen of the signal from the tracer that Marie had carried in her pocket.

They were obviously taken away quickly from the building as when the pursuit car arrived, they had already disappeared. Staff in the building were questioned but nobody had seen or heard anything that could be of use. The office that had been used for the meeting was quite often hired out for a morning or afternoon by anyone prepared to pay the price. On this occasion the room was booked by phone and paid for in cash shortly before people arrived, and they only stayed for ten minutes before leaving, after which police arrived.

It was booked in the name of Bellini but the Office Supervisor neither knew or recognised any of the people who came.

Ricci was now really worried because not only had Marie and Simon been kidnapped from under the nose of the police, but it now seemed that de Vincentti had an informant other than Olivio at the hotel, keeping him in the picture, at least superficially, on what was happening there.

The only staff who would know from personal observation or gossip between themselves, were the managers, the reception staff, the concierge and possibly bell-boys and porters at front of house, all of whom had been thoroughly questioned by Ricci or his assistants, which left only guests to consider. There was much to see in the beautiful city of Florence and most guests would be out and about for most of the day. Ricci and an assistant questioned the front of house staff to ascertain whether they had noted any guests who spent an unusual amount of time sitting in the central lobby lounge area or nearby where Ricci had his temporary office.

Several people working in reception, the concierge and the bell-boys said that there were currently two people who fitted that description, one an elderly man who came down to sit there frequently because his wife was unwell. She had been seen by the hotel doctor a couple of times, and her husband often left her to rest undisturbed whilst he read his newspaper or a book downstairs in the public area.

The other man, they reported, rarely went outside the hotel and was frequently in the lobby area or the adjacent bar when he wasn't having a meal in the dining room. He was particularly chatty and friendly with staff.

According to the hotel register his name was Signor Guido Foresta who had booked in on the same day as Castilenti and had said at the time he would probably be staying for "about a week." Two members of staff said that although there was no obvious connection between the two men, they had been seen in the bar together and on two occasions shared a short conversation in the lobby.

It was enough for Ricci who went into the lounge area where Foresta, ostensibly reading a folded newspaper, was seated in an armchair that commanded a view of all the comings and goings, and of the door to Ricci's office. He introduced himself and asked if Foresta could spare him a few minutes. Looking distinctly worried, Foresta laid down his paper and quietly followed the policeman back into his office.

" I understand that you live in Rome Signor Foresta," began Ricci, and when he nodded in the affirmative continued "and have you visited Florence many times before?"

Somewhat confused Foresta replied "Not many, a few, maybe two or three times."

"Yet I'm told you hardly ever go out to look around the city sights but are to be found in the lounge or lobby area most of the day. Why is that?"

Clearly embarrassed by the question Foresta was silent, his eyes darting furiously from side to side as he sought a believable response until he muttered "I'm hoping that my cousin is going to turn up soon and I stay down here so that I will see him coming in...." He knew that it was a lame excuse and delivered without any conviction, so that he could not have been surprised when Ricci came back sharply.

"Don't waste my time Foresta. You were deliberately sitting out there in the lobby keeping an eye on who was coming in and out of the hotel and my office and picking up information or gossip from the staff to pass on elsewhere. Have you already phoned in your report to Signor de Vinceniti today?"

Foresta's eyes widened with shock as Ricci's words struck home and whilst his meagre defences were tumbling Ricci struck again "You were seen talking to Signor Castilenti several times over the past few days and he is being actively sought in connection with the theft of a painting from the strongroom here at this hotel. Working with Catilenti you must know all about that and I am inclined to jointly charge you too with the theft."

"No, no, no" he exclaimed, almost hysterically "I had no hand in that I swear. I knew he was up to something, I've known him for years in Rome, but it was only after he'd booked out and then I heard about the theft and the police arrived here that I put two and two together and realised what he had done. I swear on the life of my sainted mother that I had no hand in the theft and did not know what Castelenti planned to do." By now Foresta had his head in his hands and was trying to stem his tears.

Ricci sat patiently waiting for Foresta to regain control of his emotions – he was either a superb actor or he was speaking, at least in part, the truth.

When Foresta sat up straight again Ricci resumed his questioning "But if de Vincentti had two people working for him in the same hotel at the same time it beggars believe that they weren't asked to co-operate."

Foresta looked surprised "But Castelenti wasn't working for de Vincentti......"

"But you said you knew Castilenti........"

"Yes, from Rome. We worked together for the same outfit in those days. I don't know who he was working for here."

Chapter 16

They both eyed the double bed looked at each other and then laughed before Simon said "I think it's the sofa with blanket and pillow for me tonight." Marie smiled and changed the subject "Let's have a cup of something, sit down and review our situation shall we?" As they sat sipping mugs of tea Simon began "So first of all tell me Marie, what was it that was said by one of the men that you found so alarming when they laughed together?"

"It was after you had asked how far they were taking us, and he replied 'soon,' and added *'com agnelli al macello'* – like lambs to the slaughter."

"Mmm. Not very encouraging I agree" Simon looked directly at Marie and went on "what do you think he wants to do with us."

"Well, I don't know whether you think the same, but I got the distinct impression that de Vincentti and his cohorts have not actually got the painting. He is very well informed, no doubt from somebody at the hotel, and was probably looking for an opportunity to grab it when a chance presented itself, but I believe someone else was ahead of him in the game. He may think that between us, we have a better idea of who that might be, and that we are privy to where the police enquiries have got to, hence his interest in us."

Simon thought about what Marie had said for a few moments before replying. "Yes maybe, he was of course, bound to deny that the theft was anything to do with him, but I too got the impression that he hadn't got the painting. Why should he bother meeting up with us if he had it, why not just disappear. Despite all his precautions before we met him, he was running a considerable risk of being arrested, and he cut short our meeting earlier because he guessed that the police could not be far behind, even though he didn't know at the time that either of us was carrying a tracker.

"If he had concluded that there was nothing useful that we could tell him why did he not just dump us somewhere in the country. Yes, I think he hopes to get something useful from us."

He went on to suggest that the idea that there were two distinct parties interested in stealing the painting was not a new one, indeed only the previous day Ricci had expounded the theory that the first was the 'Australian connection', involving Yvonne's surviving brother who was actively contesting his brother's will and was more than likely behind the shooting in Venice.

The second seemed to be a faction in which de Vincentti was involved – whether in his own right, acting for somebody else or a combination of both was not yet apparent.

They continued to discuss the possibilities and ramifications of this theory and then their predicament and the possibilities of somehow escaping, only to be interrupted by the sound of several pairs of feet coming up the stairs. The sliding bar was moved and the door unlocked before a voice shouted "Stand away from the door "and it was slowly opened to reveal the tall man wielding the gun.

After he had gestured for them to move to the far end of the room, he allowed two other men to enter carrying large trays which they placed on the table and left. The tall man smiled at them both before commenting "Good food. Enjoy" before he too left, locking the door and pulling across the bar again.

They both approached the table to find an array of food. Metal covers protected large plates of hot spaghetti carbonara, whilst other covered plates contained for each of them a mixed salad, a crème brulee, plus a plate of cheese and biscuits. Whilst one tray sported a cold bottle of Pinot Grigio, the other held glasses and two crisp new napkins and cutlery.

"Wow" said Simon.

"Well, whatever they have in mind for us it isn't to starve us" commented Marie "this is unexpected luxury." As she set the table, Simon opened the bottle and poured two glasses and proposed a toast "to us and our safe return" before the hungry duo tucked into an unexpectedly good meal.

Without the means to wash and dry the dishes, everything was stacked back onto the trays, and they went to sit in the easy chairs when Marie said, "I wonder whether they'll run to a decent cup of coffee?" Hardly had she finished speaking than the sound of feet on the stairs came and the routine of opening the door was repeated. This time when the tall gunman ushered in his colleagues, one bore a tray holding a tall pot of coffee, together with cups, saucers, sugar, cream and a plate of petit fours.

Both Marie and Simon chorused their thanks as the other trays were taken away and the smiling gunman said "Was good, yes? Now good night both" and left, securing the door as usual.

Over coffee their conversation ranged again over their present situation and in response to Marie's questions, Simon recounted in more detail what had happened before in England and in Venice during his quest to fill in some gaps in the Tiepolo provenance. In turn she told him about some of her previous successes in recovering works of art and a few of the strange characters that she encountered during her work. As the evening wore on, they continued talking and showing a real interest in each other's personal life.

Marie talked about her early, difficult years as the eldest daughter of the Duc d'Albeigne, the last male in the line of a very old but now landless and virtually penniless noble Italian house. Her father was widowed at an early age, her mother having produced three daughters, died exhausted of having to deal with a disappointed, often drunken and careless husband and father

Much of the task of managing the house and bringing up her siblings had fallen to Marie and only when the youngest was fifteen and she was twenty did she feel able to leave home to study fine art. She had married – hence the Shawcross – a wonderful, if considerably older man when she was in her late twenties. He had swept her off her feet in his ardent courtship and after their marriage had indulged her every whim, travelling with her as she continued to study art and then to hone her knowledge around the world thereby gaining her

145

reputation as a fine art specialist and in more recent times in the recovery of stolen or missing works of art.

She had been devastated by his death from a sudden heart attack ten years before and desperately missed him still, as did his daughter from his first marriage who was only a year younger than Marie. She was called Giulietta and was a lawyer in New York. Marie and Giulietta become very close friends even though they were step-mother and step-daughter.

Simon was fascinated by her story, so that he was somewhat startled when, after a period of reminiscent silence on her part, he heard her say "I've been doing all the talking Simon, now it's your turn. Come on -Simon Brookes his life and times, please!"

"Oh dear. I'm afraid it's not very interesting. How far do I have to go back?"

"To the very beginning of course" she demanded.

"Right. Born on the 22nd June 1956 in Woodford, Essex. I was the only child of Leslie and Joan Brookes, respectively an accountant and a teacher, both in their early forties so I was a late and much-loved arrival. Educated at The Forest School, I went on to read law at Durham. That's where I met Peter Bird who left me the picture.

When I got my LLB I decided for some reason I wanted to go into Maritime Law and through a stroke of luck managed to join one of the leaders in that speciality area Riley, Keats & Rawlins. You've probably never heard of them, but RKR have been one of the leading lights all over the world for many years in that branch of the Law.

In the early years I was based in London with a sprinkling of European work, then I was made a partner and lived and worked for a while at their offices in Australia and then in Singapore where eventually I became Managing Partner.

"Oh yes, and on a personal level I married the love of my life Pat Courtney in 1980 and we had three children.

A boy Richard, a banker now aged thirty and living the life of Reilly in Singapore, and two girls Beth, twenty-eight married with a little girl Debbie nearly two, and finally Viola now twenty-six, as yet unmarried, she's very picky her sister says.

She's a scientist, and because the girls are very close, they live not far from each other in Sydney. I see them all every year, usually when I go out there although they have all come over to England occasionally.

"I had a really good marriage, and I too was knocked sideways when Pat was diagnosed with cancer and died within six months. That was eight years ago. I retired early from my job about six years ago, live in the Cotswolds and have no problem filling in my time, walking, gardening, reading, theatregoing, working for the local Citizens Advice Bureau and of course more recently and excitingly, researching a provenance for my Tiepolo. All a bit dull I suppose, but there it is."

"On the contrary" said Marie "you have deliberately described the bare outlines of an intriguing career that I'm certain has many stories to tell, of a wonderful family life and a retirement that sounds far from empty or dull."

They talked on for another hour and more until they were stifling yawns which in no way indicated a lack of interest but rather the lateness of the hour. A glance at her watch showed Marie that it was now past one o'clock. She got up and crossed to where Simon was sitting and said "Thanks for a lovely evening despite everything" kissed him lightly on the cheek and left the room.

As she was occupied in the bathroom Simon took the blanket and pillow from the bedroom wardrobe and made up a makeshift bed on the sofa. As she went into the bedroom she called "Good night Simon, I hope you sleep well."

He reciprocated and followed her into the bathroom where the first thing he saw was some red underwear, washed and neatly folded to dry on a radiator. This served to remind him that he ought to do the same. Fortunately, there was soap and hot water, although an absence of toothpaste or toothbrush the same soap and cold water plus an index finger had to be substituted.

The sofa on which he had spread the blanket was a slim two-seater with hard, unforgiving arms and try as he may he could not get comfortable curled up between them – his six foot one length ended in either his head half on and half hanging out from the seat, or feet poking out to the extent that he was constantly in a state of falling off.

He attempted to get comfortable by putting the pillow on one arm and elevating his legs over the other, but it was initially uncomfortable and then painful. Another failed endeavour used two armchairs and two dining room chairs which gave extra length but an instability and a change in levels that led to collapse as soon as he turned over. Resigned to sitting in an armchair and just elevating his feet he dozed fitfully, until he decided to give up trying for a while and make a cup of tea.

He tiptoed to the lobby outside the bedroom door and was careful to make the minimum of noise in order not to wake Marie, but in vain, as the bedroom door opened as he was pouring boiling water onto a teabag in a mug.

"Ah, just in time I see" she began.

"Sorry I must have woken you. Would you like a cup?"

"No, I was awake, and yes, I'd love one please.

They carried their cups into the sitting room area only for Marie to comment on seeing Simon's latest arrangements to sleep "You poor thing, I don't suppose you've managed to get any sleep at all, but I thought you were going to use the sofa?"

Suddenly embarrassed by realising that only his shirt tail in front protected him from exposure, he grabbed the blanket from the chair and quickly wrapped it around him which brought forth a peal of laughter from Marie.

Smiling weakly in response, Simon explained his various failed experiments in finding a sleeping position that was tolerable. At this point Marie took one last sip of tea, stood up reached out a hand to Simon and with a "come with me" pulled him into the bedroom, pointed at the bed and went on "that's a Queen sized bed, plenty of room for two" and she added with her beaming smile, eyeing the blanket still tied round his middle "and you've got your trusty blanket for protection, should you need it.

Chapter 17

After the invitation, when Simon had slipped into the bed he had been careful to position himself as near the edge as possible without actually falling out, thus leaving a big gap between him and the recumbent Marie, and promptly fell into a deep sleep.

A loud and insistent knocking on the bedroom door made both of them instantly wake to find that during the night they had both moved to the middle of the bed where one of his arms had somehow found its way over her shoulder and his hand had been firmly grasped by hers. Unentangling himself, Simon called out "Hello" and received the one word reply "Breakfast."

Simon quickly disappeared into the bathroom to have a quick wash and to rescue his underwear before feeling a bit more presentable as he pulled on his trousers. In the living room he found another tall steaming pot of coffee and a selection of cold meats, cheeses, fresh fruit and spreads, with warm bread and rolls. He poured a cup of coffee, emptied the tray and reset it with a selection from the spread and took it into the bedroom where Marie was still dozing. He said "Breakfast is served Madame" as she came to, sat up and pushed her hair into place. She then accepted the tray onto her knees with a beaming smile and thanks. He lingered for a moment as she began to butter some warm bread.

"I've been thinking" he began "if you wanted to play semantics, last night we actually slept together, but in the colloquial sense we didn't – if you see what I mean."

Marie stopped eating and looking a picture of pseudo-perplexity, gazed at him saying "Didn't we, how would you know, sleepy head?" He went back thoughtfully to eat his breakfast.

Once showered and dressed, they sat down to play a game of chess, as Simon whilst exploring, had found a travelling mini-set amongst the paperbacks in the shelves of a bookcase. They were both competent, if rusty, players and soon became immersed in the games where they were evenly matched. It seemed that no time had passed when the sounds of feet on the stairs announced lunchtime had come. This time they were served with a thin steak and frites accompanied by a tomato salad and creamed spinach, a lemon tart, and to drink, a cold beer with coffee to follow.

It was all cooked and presented immaculately and Marie remarked to Simon that if one had to be kidnapped at gunpoint and incarcerated, she couldn't have possibly envisaged that it would entail such good food and charming company. She smiled at Simon and went on "Do you know, I've really enjoyed our imprisonment together, even though I wish it could end." Simon agreed and felt moved to come over and kiss her on the cheek.

Hardly had the cups, saucers and lunch crockery been stacked onto the trays than they heard the sound of feet on the stairs. They looked at each other with the same question on their lips – why was it only one person that was coming up, invariably it was two or three, with one carrying a gun.

After the bar was withdrawn and the key turned in the lock there was indeed only one man standing there - one of the men who usually carried up their trays.

"Come quickly" he said to them both, adding in fractured English "to escape while they away" and led them down the stairs pausing only at the front door to look left and right before gesturing them through. His last words were "Complimenti all'Ispetorre Carlini da Tomaso" (Compliments to Inspector Carlini from Tomaso) as he shut the door firmly behind them.

Astonished at the turn of events, they found themselves on a gravelled parking area in front of a large multi-car garage with rooms over that they had been occupying, adjacent to a large house with a Palladian front. A tarmac drive led down to a road on which they could discern other large houses amongst the trees.

"Come on let's get away from here" said Simon grasping Marie's hand as he began to move quickly down the drive and turned right onto the footpath beside the road. After walking quickly for a couple of hundred metres they came to a small park-like area of grass interspersed with trees and shrubs and found a bench that was almost totally hidden from the road. They sat down and Simon drew from his pocket with a flourish, a mobile phone.

"Where did you get that from" asked Marie. "It was lying on a small table in the lobby before we came out of the front door," said Simon. "So I helped myself. I hope it's charged up." It was, and he immediately looked up and rang the number for their hotel and asked to be put through to Ispetorre Ricci urgently saying it was Brookes and Signora Shawcross.

Ricci was both surprised and delighted to hear from them and immediately arranged for a patrol car to be diverted to pick them up, after Marie had spotted a road sign that pin-pointed their location.

Within forty minutes they were both sitting sipping a coffee in Ricci's office describing their experience and their extraordinary release. Marie remembered the man's parting words "Complimenti all'Ispetorre Carlini da Tomaso."

"I know the Carlini that he's sending his compliments to, I'll give him a ring and see what he has to tell us about Tomaso," said Ricci and picked up the phone. After a guarded response initially, Carlini told Ricci that Tomaso was one of his men who had infiltrated a gang who were engaged in drug and people smuggling amongst other rackets against whom the police planned shortly to take action. In the light of the events that Ricci described he would be moving more quickly.

Ricci, after listening to Marie and Simon relate everything that had happened, and questioning them further on details, surmised that de Vincentti had hired the gang led by the tall gun-toting man to first kidnap and then detain the two of them in a safe house until he could talk to them again. He tended to agree with their impression that de Vincentti had been forestalled by a rival and did not have the painting.

The fact that de Vincentti was so well informed on the coming and goings at the hotel and also on Ricci's investigations, certainly pointed towards another informant besides Foresta on the premises. It may also, Ricci suggested, be connected with Mr Jeremy Idles's sudden disappearance from the hotel the previous night.

Although Idle had been asked to remain at the hotel whilst investigations were at an early stage, he had told nobody beforehand of his intentions to go, which Ricci found strange and suspicious. He was now being actively sought for further questioning.

Ricci also told Simon and Marie that he had received some information from the Australian police who had been investigating the involvement of Tim Bird (brother of Yvonne and the late Peter) in the shooting in Venice, based on the admission of the gunman Andreotti to the police there. Andreotti had claimed that he had been hired and paid to shoot Simon Brookes (and had shot and injured his companion in error) by a contact in London who in turn had been instructed from Australia. Ricci had come to believe that the man behind this was Tim Bird.

In the light of Ricci's original suspicions of Tim Bird's involvement, the Australian police had some days previously interviewed him under caution and their report stated that he had vociferously denied any involvement in the shooting, although during the interview he had behaved erratically to the extent that the police had questioned his mental state. Bird confirmed that he was taking appropriate legal steps to have the terms of his brother's will overturned, as far as the gifting of a painting to Simon Brookes was concerned. He had stated that his late brother's ability to make rational decisions had latterly been undermined by dementia and that was behind his legal action.

Australian police had continued their enquiries and had established through telephone records and follow-up interviews that Bird had some time before, been in touch with people in criminal fraternity, allegedly trying to find someone capable of carrying out an assassination in Europe.

Whilst they were still investigating the matter, the police learned that Bird had "gone abroad," although neither his wife nor the staff at his Estate Agency business claimed to know where.

This report together with the information gleaned from the English police made Ricci all the more certain that Bird or his associates were now in possession of the Tiepolo painting.

Later that afternoon Marie told Ricci and Simon that two of her informants with contacts in the murkier underside of the art world had come up with some interesting news. Since the alleged Tiepolo had been reported stolen in Florence, there had been a spate of interest and some speculation about who the perpetrators might be, two of which stood out.

The first, not surprisingly, pointed towards de Vincentti and his associates, and the second was a French syndicate called Belvoir which had been linked to a wealthy Russian oligarch currently living in Britain - Dimitri Beltrovic. He was a keen collector of 18th century Italian art, particularly that of the Rococo masters, of which Tiepolo was the undoubted leader.

The acquisition of *The Last Supper* painting would be "the jewel in the crown" of Beltrovic's renowned collection. Most of this collection had been bought at auction, but many items were bought privately, often through Belvoir or other intermediaries. This made it difficult to trace the seller, the price that had been paid or the circumstances in which the purchase had been made.

Beltrovic was always at pains to ensure that his hands were clean, and anything shady or questionable about the acquisition of a piece of art was always several hands distant from him, so that no suspicion fell on him.

That was more than could be said of the Belvoir syndicate who had been at the centre of "art police" enquiries in several European countries as well as the USA.

It was frequently alleged that Belvoir had used both threats and strong arm tactics to persuade art owners to sell a painting when they were unwilling. Such claims were difficult to prove in court, particularly when the claimants had been paid very large sums of money for the works of art involved and the defendants invariably used the best and most expensive lawyers to ridicule the allegations in a Court of Law. So far, the defendants in all of these cases had been cleared of any charges and in a few, costs had even been awarded against the claimants.

Although the involvement of Beltrovic and the Belvoir Syndicate in the theft of the Tiepolo painting were just rumours at present, Marie was continuing to dig for more confirmation through her contacts. Simon asked her "Do you think that this syndicate is working with Tim Bird?"

"I think it's entirely possible, but we mustn't jump to conclusions until we know more" she replied. Ricci agreed and was about to enlarge on the actions he proposed taking when a knock sounded on his door and his deputy slipped in to say that Jeremy Idle had been found staying in another hotel in Florence and was at this moment being escorted back to the Baltica. Ricci told him to bring Idle straight in when he arrived and Simon and Marie left to go up to their rooms, change and freshen-up before having lunch together.

****

Ricci received a report from officers who had visited the house and garages where Simon and Marie had been held. There was nobody on the premises and no sign of recent occupation.

A few minutes later a rather sheepish Jeremy Idle was brought into Ricci's office and invited to sit down before Ricci launched into a frontal attack. "Tell me Mr Idle, why, when you had been explicitly asked by me, to stay in this hotel did you leave without any warning, and move yourself to another hotel in the city?"

"Err...just wanted a change of scene," he replied.

"I don't believe you. You had kept de Vincentti well informed on what was happening here for which I have no doubt you were well-paid, why should you give that up?"

Wearily Idle shook his head and made no attempt to deny the allegation. "Look I'll tell you the whole story" he began "I shan't be sorry to get it off my conscience."

"How de Vincennti learned of my mission on behalf of Simon Brookes I don't know, but it was just after I had left it at the Courtauld Institute for tests to be made that he first rang. I suspect someone on the staff there had been indiscrete about the "missing Tiepolo" and talked to an outsider and the word had got to a de Vincentti informant. Anyway, I told him I didn't want to talk to him about the picture and rang off.

He was very persistent however, ringing me sometimes twice or three times a day and got the same response, I didn't want to talk. Then I was having lunch in a favourite restaurant in London when a stranger stopped by my table and left me an envelope addressed to me, in which was a letter from de Vincentti." At this point he reached into an inside pocket of his jacket, pulled out an envelope and passed it to Ricci "and here it is."

Ricci took out the letter and read it aloud.

Dear Mr Idle,

May I sincerely assure you at the outset that in approaching you I have no wish or intention to upset in any way your arrangements and association with Mr Brookes in helping him authenticate and establish a provenance for his painting. On the contrary I wish you every success.

No, my interest is in legitimately acquiring the painting from Mr Brookes if he can be persuaded to sell. If you are able to help me in any way to this end you will be very well rewarded. My suggestion is that I pay you a retaining fee of £5,000 per month for initially, 3 months.

During this time you will use your best endeavours to suggest and persuade that he sells to me and keep me posted on the progress that is being made on authentication etc. and on his attitude to selling.

If you are successful and a sale to me is agreed, then I agree to pay you 5 percent of the selling price which is expected to be in excess of 3 million pounds.

I will be in touch again within a few days,

Yours sincerely

Roberto de Vincentti

When he had finished reading Ricci looked back at Idle and asked "So, what did you do?"

"To my shame I persuaded myself that it would not interfere with my work for Simon Brookes, indeed it might enhance it. So when Vincentti phoned two days later I agreed to help him in the way he had asked and the same day £5,000 was transferred into my bank account.

Thereafter he would ring me on my mobile every day or two and I would update him on the progress that was being made on tracing the provenance, the scientific testing of the picture and on its verification."

"Did you let him know about the invitation to visit to Florence that you had received ostensibly from the foremost Tiepolo expert so that he could see the painting before the committee met?" asked Ricci.

"Yes, he was quite excited about it."

"And when the painting was stolen, what was his reaction?"

"Well, I can't say that I looked forward to the conversation and delayed giving him a call that morning, but he rang me first having heard from someone else.

He was absolutely seething with rage, acting as if it was he who had been robbed. He demanded that I gave him chapter and verse about the theft, asking who the police suspected and so forth and of course I was able to tell him nothing at that stage, which seemed to anger him all the more. It was if he held me personally responsible for the loss, and over the following days he pestered me several times a day for the latest news and even began to threaten me personally when I was unable to satisfy him. It was after I had learned that Simon and Madame Shawcross had been abducted, apparently by his people, that I told him that I'd had enough. I moved hotels and took no more calls from him."

"So, you never met him, but have you heard from him again at all?" asked Ricci.

"No" answered Idle "he has rung numerous times on my mobile, but as I already said I didn't answer."

"You have a phone number for him I understand, can you give it to me now? asked Ricci and noted it down from Idle's mobile phone.

As he wrote it down he said "I think you had better tell Mr Brookes all that you have told me, if you want to have a chance of retaining his confidence. He and the Madame are back here safe and in the dining room as we speak" said Ricci and picking up de Vincentti's letter "and I'll keep this."

"Oh, thank goodness they are both OK, I'll go and see them right now" responded Idle and hurried from the room.

Chapter 18

Jeremy Idle walked disconsolately through the ground floor of the hotel to the restaurant at the back pausing momentarily as he passed the bar thinking that a stiff drink before he faced Simon might be a good idea. However, he walked on and stopped to scan the tables from the top of three broad stairs that led down into the restaurant and at first glance didn't recognise Simon and Marie.

Champagne flutes in hand they were leaning towards each other so that there was barely a few inches between them as they looked deeply into each other's eyes. He was almost embarrassed to interrupt them such was the intimacy of the moment, but Simon spotted him approaching the table and turned towards him. "Jeremy" he began "come and join us and have a glass of champagne" and gestured to a waiter to bring another chair.

Idle thanked him and after greeting Marie he admitted that he had come straight from Ricci's office to make a "heartfelt" apology to Simon and went on to tell them both about what he had done, which he now realised could be seen as a traitorous co-operation with de Vincentti. That had lasted until he learned of the abduction, when the full weight of his guilt and some responsibility for what had happened fell on him.

As was talking, Idle was conscious that despite his sorry tale, the happy smiles that had lit up both Simon and Marie's faces hardly lessened and when he had finished, instead of an expression of anger or even reproach Simon commented "Well whatever you did, it hasn't changed the situation one iota, so drink your champagne and be the first to congratulate Marie and me, as we've decided to spend much more time together and see what the future holds." Delighted to be let off so easily, Idle toasted them both and took a deep drink of the champagne. They went onto discuss the theft and where the police enquiries had got to when Marie suddenly directed a question to Idle "Do you know anything about Dimitri Beltrovic, or the Belvoir Syndicate?"

Jeremy didn't hesitate "I've heard of Beltrovic of course, but never met him. He's one of those Russian ogligarchs who made a fortune, like many others in the aftermath of the Soviet Union breakup and the privatisation of many industries in Russia. He is now a well-known art collector, particularly of some of the early Italian masters – he would be very interested in acquiring your Tiepolo, Simon.

"As for the Belvoir Syndicate – a shady bunch of operators that, it is rumoured, have been behind several works of art changing hands in unusual circumstances. Some say they are just a bunch of crooks." He looked at Marie and Simon quizzically and added "are they now thought to be responsible for stealing the painting?"

"It's a possibility" was all that Marie ventured in reply.

They left the restaurant together, Simon to arrange with reception for their luggage to be moved into a suite for their joint occupation, Marie to her room to sort her things, whilst

Jeremy set off for a visit to the Uffizi Gallery. A few minutes later Marie was back on the ground floor making for Ricci's office having received some information from one of her contacts. She told him that it was now strongly rumoured in the darker area of the art world that Beltrovic was indeed now holding Simon's Tiepolo, acquired with the help of the Belvoir Syndicate, and that he was now at his London residence in Belgravia.

Police in London, he said, were seeking Bird's whereabouts to question him on behalf of the Australian and the Italian police. They have been appraised of the rumours regarding Beltrovic and the painting and are keeping him under surveillance as there was, as yet, no firm evidence to confirm the rumours and suspicions about him.

Ricci leaned back in his chair with his hands behind his head "Although there is still much to do here in Florence helping to bring Beltrovic and company to justice for the theft, restoring the painting to Mr Brookes, finding de Vincentti and charging him with your abduction. However, the main suspects are no longer here, the caravan has moved on. I shall be giving up my temporary office here in the hotel and no longer require guests to stay on as my enquiries here have, at least for the time been concluded here.

I think that Signor Antonio Castelenti, the mysterious guest in Room 136 on the night of the robbery, who is now being questioned in Rome, may prove to be the final piece in the jigsaw in establishing exactly how and for whom the heist took place. In the circumstances I expect you will probably wish to travel on to London to liaise with the police there, and that probably applies to Mr Brookes as well though I've yet to talk to him."

Marie responded "I think you're right and that we shall both be going to London soon. By the way, before you hear it from someone else you should know that Simon and I have discovered a mutual attraction and have decided to spend more time together to see what might develop."

She smiled and went on "of course it means that you, Ispettore Superiore Ricci, are responsible for the whole thing, by bringing us together, perhaps you have been the Eros in our romance and for that and your work on the heist we owe you our heartfelt thanks."

Ricci had stood up as he listened to Marie and slowly moved round his desk. As she finished, he grasped her hands in his, kissed them and declared his delight at the news. "I had noticed, of course, that you got on well together, but I'm really pleased that in one aspect at least it seems our work, together with Mr Brookes has been successful."

A few minutes after she had left, Ricci's phone rang. It was his assistant, Calassio, calling from Rome where he reported that in company with the local police he had questioned Signor Antonio Castelenti at his the apartment. Not unexpectedly, he had denied that he had been a guest at the Firenze Porta Baltica hotel in Room 136 on the night of the painting heist and declared he had not even been in Florence. When faced with pictures extracted from the hotel's timed and dated internal CCTV tape, clearly showing him at the hotel reception desk booking in an out, carrying two suitcases, he went quiet and refused to answer any further questions.

Calassio said that he had charged him with complicity in the theft of the painting, and was bringing him, handcuffed in the back of his car, back to Florence where he hoped to arrive in about three and a half hours' time.

Looking at his watch Ricci told Calassio to take Castelenti directly to his office at the Palazzo Pitti in Florence where he would carry on the questioning, as he was clearing his temporary office at the hotel. It would be easier to keep the suspect cooling his heels in a handy cell overnight should he still refuse to co-operate.

Then Ricci phoned Simon and asked him if he would kindly step into his office which he was vacating shortly. As Simon came in, Ricci met him with outstretched hand. "I'm delighted to hear from Madame, Mr Brookes, that the two of you have decided, as she put it to see more of each other. I detected, as is my calling, so to speak, that there was a mutual attraction between you, but things have moved on and I wish you every happiness together – you make, if I may say so a very handsome pair."

"Thank you" replied Simon "you are very kind. I agree it has all happened rather quickly, but I must say I couldn't be happier."

Ricci gestured Simon to a chair and resumed his own "Onto other matters, I've brought Madam up to date, has she told you?"

"Yes, I've just left her."

"That's fine, but I wanted to see you before I give up this office at the hotel to let you know that I've just heard from Calassio who has arrested Castelenti in Rome and as we speak is driving him up the Autostrada back here to Florence. I shall be questioning him this evening at police headquarters. He has admitted nothing so far, but I have every expectation that he will, eventually, tell us all we need to know."

Simon thanked him for keeping them in the picture and for his excellent work so far and confirmed that within a couple of days he and Marie would be departing for London.

Later that evening Sourintendenti Calassio drove into the car park of the central Carabinieri station in Florence and marched Castelini into an interview room where he left him with a police officer whilst he went up to Ricci's office. After a brief conversation they both came into the interview room to find Castelini protesting vociferously to the attendant officer about his continued detention, and the lack of food or drink.

Ricci switched on the recording machine as they both sat down opposite Castelini who had gone quiet. Ricci introduced himself and Calassio for the record and went on to say that they were questioning Antonio Castelini in connection with the theft of a painting believed to be by Tiepolo, that had been temporarily held in the strongroom at the Firenze Porta Baltica hotel on the night of June 6th. He then began. "Signor Castelini would you like to make a statement at this point?"

"No, except to say that I have not had anything to eat or drink now for nearly five hours and that is inhumane."

"Well then, we must all press on with all speed to bring this interview to a satisfactory conclusion so that you can be served both. Perhaps you could start by confirming that you were a guest at the Porta Baltica staying in Room 136 on the night of the sixth of June this year?"

Castelini who at the time of his arrest had been immaculately turned out in a pale sand coloured linen suit a blue shirt and a bright yellow tie, presented a very different picture, his suit a crumpled mess and his tie slipped down and askew.

His swarthy face was beaded with sweat and his eyes looked furtive and apprehensive as initially he ignored the question. He sat silently for fully half a minute as the police officers watched him closely before he said quietly "No comment."

"Oh come on Castelini, we have pictures from the CCTV cameras showing you booking in and out, and half a dozen staff who recognised you. It is pointless denying the facts, make it easier on yourself by at least acknowledging that you were there" responded Ricci.

Castelini put his head in his hands for a while and when he looked up and across the table to Ricci said faintly "OK I was staying in that hotel for a couple of nights around that time" and with a sudden air of defiance added "but I know nothing about the theft of a painting!"

"And yet your old colleague from Rome, Guido Foresta who you bumped into at the hotel was pretty sure, after he'd heard about the theft, that you would have been involved."

"Pah! That old sod, he'd say anything that suited him" rejoined Castelini "he's a born liar."

"Look Castelini I may as well tell you that the assistant manager at the hotel Gustav Olivio has confessed to his part in the heist. That in response to the offer of a large reward he followed instructions to take the painting from the hotel strongroom and to leave it the chambermaids' cupboard near the lifts on the first floor. That cupboard is exactly opposite Room 136 and can easily be watched at the appointed time by someone looking through the spyhole in the door.

May I remind you that it was Room 136 that you were so keen to occupy, spinning a yarn to the reluctant receptionist when you phoned, that it was a room with a sentimental attachment for you.

"I put it to you Castelini that after you were told that the painting was going to be lodged in the Porta Baltica strongroom for a few days you moved into your friend Mr Felix Holder's apartment here in Florence where you planned every last detail of the theft. Your enquiries luckily led you to a susceptible hotel employee who had potential access to the strongroom and you made him an offer he found impossible to resist, then you booked Room 136 using the apartment phone, unwisely, as it was easily traced."

Ricci took a chance in his next clinching statement, banking on Castelini not being au fait with the technical advances that had been made in tracing calls. "We know that you used burner phones to send your text messages to Olivio, and that you have probably disposed of these, but of course we have the numbers and can trace back their location when last used – Holder's apartment."

Castelini looked astonished "You can't do that it's impossible."

"Technology marches on Castelini . Look you are in a corner and there is no escape. Do yourself a favour and cooperate with us, it will mean a lesser sentence when you appear in court and anyway we realise you are not the prime mover in this affair, so why bother protecting the Belvoir Syndicate or Beltrovic."

Castelini looked genuinely surprised "Who?" he asked.

Chapter 19

"Well come on then, who are you working for?" asked Ricci. Castelini chewed on his upper lip nervously as he eyed the two policemen and then came to a decision. "Look if I level with you and tell you the whole story, or rather what I know of it, will it reduce my jail sentence, and, because it will put me in real danger of being eliminated by the Cosa Nostra will you establish a new identity for me?"

Ricci replied "It depends on what you are able to tell us, but certainly if you cooperate in our enquiries it will lead to you being given a shorter sentence in court and if you can show that your life will be in danger as a consequence of that cooperation we can ensure that your evidence is given in a cleared court or by deposition so that you will not be identified in open court. We can also, if necessary, help you in changing your identity and settling in another part of the country – but it's got to be worth our while."

His mind made up then Castelini began "I live and work mostly in Rome and whilst I am not a member of the Cosa Nostra I am what they call "a connected guy" or a "goombah"- I carry out specialised assignments that for one reason or another cannot be carried through 'in house.'

It is generally work that calls for initiative with a combination of surveillance, discretion, careful planning and skilled negotiation." In reciting this as a list of his talents he positively preened, his head lifted and his no longer furtive eyes changed and shone with pride.

It had the effect of pricking an over-inflated balloon however, when Ricci retorted "or perhaps better described as spying, extortion and bribery. However, do carry on."

Castelini, rather disconcerted, looked askance at Ricci then shrugged his shoulders as if physically shaking off the comment and continued, " a week or so ago the capo of the biggest group of mafiosi in Rome asked me to meet him at the old Martis Palace Hotel off Piazza Navona to discuss an assignment. He'd got a private meeting room and was sitting in there with one of his top lieutenants who I also knew called Bianci. The capo told me that he had an important job he wanted me to handle for him in Florence starting immediately. It paid well, €50,000 at the start and a further €150,000 on the satisfactory completion plus a large expense fund that I had to account for."

"That would mean mainly bribes?" asked Calassio.

"Yes" agreed Castelini and went on "at this point the capo said that Bianci would give me all the details and information that I would need but reminded me from that moment on, Omerta would apply – absolute secrecy on pain of death," adding as he looked at each of the policemen in turn "hence my need for a new identity."

He went on "Bianci then produced several sheets of paper which he laid on the table and which he referred to as he talked. You probably know all this but briefly he said that a painting believed to be by Tiepolo, a famous 18th century Venetian artist was being brought to Florence in four or five day's time.

It would be kept in a safe within the strongroom at the Firenze Porta Baltica hotel. My task was to find someone, preferably an employee of the hotel who could gain access to the strongroom and safe, and persuade them to get the painting out, or if that was not possible arrange for strong arm tactics on the manager to force him to open up so that the painting could be taken away. The how and the when were left up to me to plan and execute."

He went on "Bianci had arranged for one of their people to run a rule over all the senior staff at the hotel and pinpoint any who were likely to be susceptible to blackmail or bribery and he handed me a short list of names. He also told me that the man who was currently in charge of the painting, an Englishman called Idle would, in a day or two, be persuaded to bring the painting from England to Florence, to show it to the leading expert on Tiepolo, and would, of course be staying at the same hotel.

"After briefing and handing over his papers to me, Bianci left the room and came back in with the capo and another man who was introduced to me by the capo as Mr Bird. He spoke little or no Italian, and it was left to Bianci to explain to him that I had been entrusted with the mission to reclaim the Tiepolo for Mr Bird, who claimed to be the true and rightful owner of the painting. He thanked me and wished me luck. Then we all shook hands and left, with me holding a brief case containing €250,000 in notes, my retainer and the rest for expenses. You probably know the rest."

"Yes maybe, but I'd like you to tell us for the record, including the name of the capo said Ricci.

Then Castelini continued to confirm much of what they had already discovered or surmised.

He had flown to Florence that same evening and began planning whilst on the plane. He confirmed that he had stayed at his friend Felix Holder's apartment using the name Tinteretto.

Amongst the notes that Bianci had handed over to him he said, was one outlining the way in which Mr Jeremy Idle was to be persuaded to bring the painting to Florence, this was to be paid for with a flight, hotel stay and expenses ostensibly to allow the eminent Tiepolo expert Signor Ponticelli to have a private view and examination of the picture in advance of the validation committee's review due some time later.

"To allow Mr Idle to consult the owner and the insurance people, he was to be given a special number to ring back on a line which he was to be told, was a direct line to the secretary of the validation committee who worked from Ponticelli's offices. In fact it was one of the sequence of numbers serving that office that would be diverted at a nearby junction box to another phone line in a temporary office.

"All this had already been set up or was to be arranged by Bianci's people, but I was frankly not happy, there was too much that was out of my control and much depended on getting everything organised and executed precisely from beginning to end. So once the phone diversion from Ponticelli's office had been made to this temporary office, I tended to work from there and took over myself the approach to Mr Jeremy Idle which went much more smoothly than I had anticipated. Then, through an agent and paid for in cash, I arranged his flights, hotel accommodation at the Porta Baltica, and for keeping the painting in their strongroom.

"Then having checked again the list of potentially malleable employees at the hotel, Olivio dropped conveniently into my plans.

"I never actually met the man, it was all done by text from disposable phones, cash in envelopes dropped into his home letterbox and it went precisely according to plan. Even to booking Room 136, the perfect observation post to see him put the painting into the storeroom.

"As you know" he concluded," I left the Porta Baltica early the next morning with the painting in a suitcase and went back to Felix's apartment. I spoke to Bianci from a public telephone to tell him I had his 'present' awaiting collection at the apartment, and he assured me that two of his men would call that afternoon and that as soon as I had handed it over to them, together with an account of my expenses and the balance in cash from the expenses advance, then the agreed transfer to my account would be made.

"After the handover I went back to Rome and since then have been trying to contact Bianco or the capo because the transfer of the money owed has not been made into my account, and I fear never will be, which is another reason why I decided to help you gentlemen, because they have gone back on their word. Unforgiveable."

After answering a few more questions including, reluctantly, the name of the capo, Castelini was charged with the theft of the painting and was taken into custody awaiting trial. After that, to his relief he was served with a hot meal in his cell.

Ricci then settled down to compose his official report, arranged for the whole interview to be set down as a hard copy and an English translation made to send on to Scotland Yard. Then he rang Simon and Marie at their hotel to put them fully in the picture.

He had quite a lot to relate and suggested perhaps it might be better if he called round the following morning. However, he didn't need a lot of persuading to join them for dinner an hour later, which just gave him enough to time to complete his report and make his way to one of Florence's most sumptuous restaurants where the couple were celebrating.

Sipping a glass of champagne and a simple grilled sole whilst Marie and Simon worked their way through more substantial starters and main courses, gave Ricci plenty of time to describe how Castelini had helped to fit those final pieces into the investigatory jigsaw and complete the story of the heist and those involved. Which, he added, brought to an end most of his, Ricci's, involvement – apart of course in co-operating as far as he could, in the search for de Vincentti, although that was being handled by another part of the carabinieri.

He would of course, keenly follow developments in London and help the police involved in recovering the painting and bringing all the criminals to justice. He also asked Simon whether he wished him to pursue a charge against Jeremy Idle for obstructing the police in their enquiries, or to let it rest and Simon agreed to the latter.

After listening to both their thanks and compliments on the way that he handled the investigation he pushed back his chair and stood to shake hands with Simon and with an Italian gentleman's customary courtesy kissed Marie's hand, bade them farewell and left them to leisurely complete their meal.

Later, returning to the Rosso Baltica, Marie went straight up to their suite whilst Simon sipped a malt whisky nightcap in the bar before following her up, feeling strangely, a little nervous. He needn't have been.
As he pushed open the door of their bedroom he barely had time to close it behind him before he heard Marie lying in bed with arms outstretched towards him call "Darling, where have you been. Come to bed." He lost little time before joining her, and they clung to each other with joy, relief and passion as the world stood still for a while.

The next morning, as they were breakfasting in their sitting room at the hotel, a call came to Marie from a French Insurance company asking her to cooperate with the Gendarmerie in the investigation into the theft from a Paris gallery of an early Gauguin painting.

Although they had planned to fly on to London together, Marie was in two minds whether to turn the job down or to go to Paris for a couple of days, to be briefed by the police and to get her own investigations underway. She also needed to make it clear that she could not devote all of her time and attention to the Paris theft until the Tiepolo case had been settled one way or another. When asked for his opinion, Simon said it was up to Marie entirely, he was happy to go along with her decision either way. She should not to be influenced by their new relationship but join him in London as quickly as she could.

In the end Marie persuaded herself that she needed to be in Paris anyway, however briefly, to go to her apartment, change the contents of her suitcase and use the washing machine. So, by mid-morning, after more than one long lingering kiss and professions of undying love, both had left the hotel at different times bound for the airport and flights to London and Paris.

Before Simon left, he had a brief talk to Jeremy Idle, who was relieved to learn that neither Simon or the Italian police were intending to take any action against him.

He stressed that should Simon feel that Jeremy could be trusted, he would be more than happy to help him in any way that he could. He too was returning to England later that day.

That afternoon, comfortably ensconced in a suite at the Grosvenor House Hotel overlooking Park Lane, Simon made contact with the officer in charge of the Art & Antiques Unit of the Metropolitan Police, an Inspector Nelson, and made an appointment to see her the next morning. He didn't know what to expect from this small unit of about six officers, compared with the three hundred strong equivalent organisation within the Italian carabinieri devoted to investigating cases of missing art and antiques in Italy.

He then phoned Marie in Paris who had just got back to her apartment after an afternoon spent talking to Insurance people and the police. They both claimed to have missed the other dreadfully and looked forward to being together again in a couple of days, and Simon described the view from their suite which awaited her.

Next morning with his appointment with Inspector Nelson not due until 11am Simon took the opportunity of speaking on the phone to Reggie, now home from hospital and feeling better by the day. During a long conversation Simon was able to update his friend on the many developments that had taken places since they last spoke. He also called Benjamin Burns and told him, but in less detail of what had happened recently. He too was feeling well, back at work and delighted to hear from Simon.

He took a taxi to New Scotland yard for his meeting, carrying in his briefcase a file that was almost bursting at the seams with papers and notes that had by now accumulated on every aspect of the missing 'Last Supper' painting, before and after the heist.

He was shown into a room where three people were already waiting, including one that came as a real surprise.

Chapter 20

As he paused in the doorway a woman stood, shook hands and introduced herself "How do you do Mr Brookes, my name is Sheila Nelson and I am a Detective Inspector in the Arts & Antiques Squad of the Met," and gesturing to the others seated went on "Detective Constable Price and Chief Inspector Ricci of the Florence Carabinieri I think you know."

As they all sat down Nelson went on to explain that she had received all the papers about the heist, including the confession from Castelini, plus a full report from CI Ricci, and had put it all together with the attempted assassination report from the police in Venice and other relevant matters. She had quickly realised that this was a complex and probably delicate investigation on her hands, now that the principal suspects in the case had come to London.

When Simon had telephoned from Florence seeking a meeting, Nelson felt it would help him and others concerned if CI Ricci could be persuaded to come to London for a day or so to attend the meeting and expand on his reports and thoughts, and he had kindly agreed.

Simon said "Personally, I'm delighted that that CI Ricci is able to join us today, his investigations in Florence were very successful in exposing those involved in the heist.It is through no act of his that, as he put it so well, the circus has moved on to here in London."

Ricci replied "Well, I'm pleased to help my colleagues here as much as I can and have told them that our close co-operation in Florence proved invaluable as it was with Madame Shawcross. I hope she is well by the way, and wonder will she be joining us?" Simon explained her brief diversion to Paris but told everyone that she would be in London shortly.

To start the discussion, Nelson suggested that she summarise the situation as she understood it, asking everyone to chip in if they disagreed or wished to clarify something. She began "The prime mover behind the heist of the picture in Florence appears to be a Mr Timothy Bird, an Australian known to the Police in that country as a dubious character and something of a con-man, although he has never been convicted of anything serious. His interest in the picture apparently stems from the discovery after his brother, a Mr Peter Bird, died and bequeathed a painting to an old friend – you, Mr Brookes.

"You took it to be reframed only to find that hidden within the frame behind the displayed picture was another painting - very old and potentially very valuable. It is not certain that Mr Peter Bird knew that the old painting was in there, except for some cryptic references, but when Mr Timothy Bird learned of its discovery, he was apparently furious that a masterpiece probably worth several million pounds had not been left to him and his sister.

"He was so steamed up about this initially, that clearly without much thought to the consequences, he arranged for

Mr Brookes to be shot at by a sniper, possibly even killed, only for the assassin to shoot Mr Brookes' companion in error.

At the same time Bird started proceedings to have his brother's will overturned in respect of the bequest to Mr Brookes on the grounds that Peter Bird was suffering from advanced Alzheimer's and was not of 'sound mind' when he signed the will.

"How Bird came into contact with Dimitri Beltrovic or the Belvoir Syndicate who we know do a lot of dirty work for him, we can only speculate at this point. But, without doubt, Beltrovich would be very interested in acquiring the old painting in question to add to his collection. Once he learned that the painting had come to light after being missing for many years, he may have alerted the Belvoir Syndicate of his interest. They in turn would have looked into the ownership, where the painting was being held, and whether there were other interested parties which would no doubt have turned up Mr Timothy Bird and Riccardo de Vincentti.

"Vincentti is a formidable rival and dealer who had probably already lined up prospective buyers should he acquire the painting, so there was no point in working with him, whereas Timothy Bird was almost certainly interested only in selling on to the highest bidder should he come into possession of the Tiepolo. He could be a useful associate, and it seems certain that contact was made, and an agreement of some sort reached that they would work together.

"The Belvoir Syndicate people would have quickly learnt that in a few weeks' time the painting was to be presented to the Tiepolo experts committee in Florence for their scrutiny and assessment to prove that it was genuine with a good provenance. They may well have felt that this would be a good time to execute a heist. Actually, it happened much more quickly than expected when Idle brought the painting to Florence.

The Syndicate is known to use only the best lawyers and other intermediaries to gain their ends and as the heist was now imminent and in Italy, they consulted the local mafia who decided to use a local man who had the expertise to plan and the ability to see it through – Castelini."

Ricci came in at that point "It may have happened just as you say but I'm intrigued to know in that case how The Belvoir Syndicate and Timothy Bird reconciled their aims. The Syndicate were interested in getting hold of the painting by any means for Beltrovic, who would pay them the "going" rate whatever that may be for a stolen painting. Bird, however, could only benefit if he was proved to be the legal owner of the painting in court. Only then could he legitimately sell it to Beltrovic or his agents.   Otherwise, why should they bother with Bird? "

"Good point" said Nelson "but maybe Bird approached Beltrovic or his agents, convinced them that his court proceedings to overturn the will would be successful and that he would then sell it to Beltrovic as legal owner. Confident that de Vincentti was after the painting, Belvoir Syndicate and Bird convinced Beltrovic that they must steal the painting to pre-empt him."

"Mm" said Simon doubtfully "although it's interesting to speculate it doesn't get us very far. Our best hunch at the moment is that Beltrovic has the painting with him in London, and it's surely no coincidence that Bird is also over here.

Chapter 21

Pieter Schott was almost invariably the first man on site in the morning, as there were almost always heavy building materials sitting on low-loaders queuing for his 400 foot high tower crane to swing them up high, and away to some precise point on the building site in the City of London where the drainage, foundations, and basement areas for a tall new office block were currently being constructed.

Every day Pieter started his shift and began to climb the stairs that were offset and encaged alongside each twenty foot section that made up the tower. He counted off each set by concentrating his mind on a different subject, switching from one to another during his brief rest before moving onto and up the next stairs, the whole climb taking up half-an-hour before he reached his cab.

This morning, however, was to be different. He had only reached the top of the eighth section when he spotted something odd in a corner of the site where they had been pouring concrete during the previous day. Normal practice when heavy rain was forecast after new concrete had been laid, was to cover the area affected with large tarpaulin sheets to deflect the rainwater which would otherwise adversely damage the drying out process.

As he looked down, he could see that there were four adjacent areas involved, three of which were adequately covered with blue tarpaulins but one showed that the sheeting had been removed and that area of unprotected concrete had taken the full force of the night's downpour.

He took out of his pocket his monocular telescope – an important aid in working over such a big site - to better focus on the scene and noticed a strange black object sticking up out of the surface of the concrete. He couldn't make out what it was but used his mobile phone to contact one of the managers on site to report what he could see.

The manager, Mike Davenport, walked over to look for himself and was startled to find that the black object was in fact a human arm still sleeved in dark suit cloth, that stuck up at an angle from the poured concrete. He immediately called the police and ambulance but had no hope that the rest of the person presumably embedded below in the grey hardening mass was alive.

Then he considered with his foreman and others who were now at the scene how best they could extricate the body from the tank of wet concrete. The arm and body beneath were situated about eight feet from the nearest edge and the consistency of the concrete, weakened by the overnight rain, was now like thick mud near the surface which would certainly not hold the weight of a man without pulling him down. After some discussion the construction of two rafts was begun, each using several sheets of particle board and long lengths of 4" by 2" to hold them side by side. Spreading the load over the concrete in this way would provide working platforms capable of holding a couple of men on each.

The first police car arrived as the rafts were nearing completion, and the two policemen lost no time in taping off the area and denying any attempt to launch the rafts and pull out the embedded person until the forensic people had arrived. Site Manager Davenport warned that the longer the person was left in the concrete the more difficult it would be to pull him or her out as it was rapidly hardening, a point he made again a few minutes later to DI Peter Percival and DS Riley as they arrived on site.

After questioning the Site Manager and Peter Schott, who had come down from the crane tower, about when the body had first been discovered, Percival and Riley accompanied them to where the tarpaulin sheeting that had originally covered the exposed concrete area had been found, together with two long lengths of four by two that were irregularly coated with concrete at one end.

The Forensic team had now arrived and after taking photographs from various angles, and seizing the abandoned tarpaulin and the lengths of four by two for examination, they agreed that the rafts should be slid out onto the concrete so that they lined up on either side of the body. With two men on each they would attempt to get a rope under the arms and lift the body clear.

It was, however, a bigger task than they had anticipated. The concrete had partially set and whilst that meant that the body was unlikely to slip further into the mixture, carefully digging out to expose the head and shoulders and get the rope in place, was hard going.

First the grey shape of a head was revealed, so slick with adhering concrete that no features could be distinguished, but

188

it was almost certainly a man. Once the shoulders had been exposed the men concentrated on freeing his other arm.

In all it took over half an hour before they were able to get a rope to encircle his chest but it proved impossible to get sufficient lift to haul the body clear. Having anticipated the need for more power from above, Pieter Schott had already started to work his way up the stairs to his cabin on the tower crane and twenty minutes later reported on his mobile that he was going to swing the arm and jib of the crane into position over the body.

Whilst waiting for this next stage to commence, Davenport, the Forensic team leader and Percival discussed some practicalities. The Chief Forensic Officer expressed his concern that too much strain might be placed on the body in pulling it from the hardening concrete, with a real danger of badly damaging the corpse. He would prefer that much more of the body be exposed before this was attempted. Davenport responded that, with the concrete drying out rapidly now, digging out was becoming harder and the angle at which the men were working was going to make progress much slower. A compromise solution was reached by which another foot or eighteen inches would be dug out around the chest and back of the body. Also, to weaken the rate of concrete hardening and make the digging slightly easier, a trickle of water would be directed around the corpse.

It helped and it was soon judged time to attempt the extraction. With the rope attached to the jib, upward pressure was gradually increased as the water trickled and the men dug, until first with a loud gurgle and then an enormous burp he came clear, dripping with water and shedding clumps of concrete.

Peiter swung him gently to a clear flat area nearby, where the forensic team were able to detach him from the jib and lay him on the ground. Then with another trickle of water helping, they began the task of clearing the congealing concrete from his head and face.

Very quickly they revealed what was almost certainly the cause of death. A bullet fired through the top of the head had exited through a now shattered jaw – he had been executed. At first glance he looked to be a man in middle age – perhaps fifty-eight or sixty years of age with thinning grey hair and a neatly trimmed beard. As the operatives continued to clear the grey soup-like deposit from the rest of his body down to his shoes, it became clear that even in its sodden state the suit was well cut from a light weight medium navy wool.

When the man's body and his suit had been almost completely cleared of concrete residue and most of the water mopped up, DI Percival asked them to search his pockets for wallet, papers and anything else to help identify him. However, there was nothing, although they probed and looked everywhere. Riley wondered whether the obviously bespoke suit had a tailor's name sewn in and a further search came up with a small discrete name "Sowerby, Jermyn Street, London W1."

After further photographs were taken, the forensic team allowed the ambulance to take the body away to the mortuary, to await an autopsy. They then loaded the long poles of 4 by 2 and the tarpaulin cover into a van and left the site.

The two policemen talked individually to the four men who had been involved in positioning the concrete mixing vehicles on site and directing the concrete being poured into the four parallel areas. They all told the same story and all confirmed that when they left the site at a quarter to five the previous afternoon, the tarpaulin sheeting was in place and secure over all four areas. Nobody else working on the site, including the gatemen, had seen anything of consequence during their shift, which for most finished at 4pm when a second shift continued to work principally on drainage work at the other end of the site from 4pm until midnight.

It was explained that later, when the foundations and drainage were completed, the site would be working three full shifts with many different trades working twenty-four hours a day but at this early stage that was not possible.

Percival and Riley wanted to question the Site Manager and the all the men working on the site on the second shift but that wouldn't be possible until 4pm. A policeman was left to see that nobody went within the taped-off area and the two detectives returned to their station to discuss what they knew so far, which was not much and mostly conjecture.

Summarised, it amounted to this. Sometime between 5pm the previous afternoon and 6am that day, persons unknown had brought onto the site the body of a man who had already been killed by a single bullet fired at short range into his brain.

They had removed the tarpaulin sheeting on the last of the newly laid areas then thrown the body into the mass. It didn't readily sink below the surface as they had hoped and anticipated, so they had found on site a couple of lengths of 4x2 with which they had managed to push the corpse deeper into the mix. They then left the site not bothering to replace the tarpaulin. The heavy overnight rain had not only retarded the drying out of the concrete but had probably watered-down the upper levels allowing the corpse or at least one arm to work its way up so that stuck up proud of the surface.

It looked to be a typical gangland killing and subsequent attempt to dispose of the body in what could have been a very effective manner but for the escaping arm. A trawl of missing person reports was already underway and a detective was even now visiting the premises of Sowerby the tailor in Jermyn Street to try and discover the identity of the corpse.

The big questions that remained to be answered were not only who carried out the crime but how did they gain access to the site and to the newly poured concrete area? Indeed, how did they know that such an area was available for their body disposal purposes. The two of them concluded that the perpetrators must have had a contact on site who had that information and passed it on. There were always two men on duty, checking vehicles and their loads in and out of the site's only entrance gate, and they changed with every shift. When the site closed, security men occupied the office by the gate and regularly patrolled the site.

Later that morning Percival received a report from the DC that had been to question the tailor in Jermyn Street, armed with a photograph of the victim and a description of his suit. One of the tailors instantly recognised him as a regular client and looked him up in the ledger. He was a Russian oligarch called Dimitri Beltrovich, with a home address in Holland Park, West London.

DI Percival and DS Riley were officers in the City of London Police, a small independent force dealing with every aspect of criminality within the square mile of this financial dealing and banking hub. Their leading world-wide expertise lay mainly in combating, fraud, illegal financial activities and associated areas. However, they also dealt with the more usual matters requiring police enquiries and investigation from parking offences to murder, but on a much smaller scale, bearing in mind that the working population in the daytime city increased tenfold the number of residents who were there overnight.

Surrounding the City Police area on all sides was a sea of Metropolitan Police districts and as a matter of courtesy, where an investigation carried the City Police over the border into Met territory, they would at least inform the District CID office of their presence and the nature of the enquiries they were pursuing.

Sometimes this would lead to the whole case being transferred to the Met, particularly if it was not clearly in the City force's area of expertise. If the enquiry was at an early stage most crimes of violence including murder would be left with City police.

It was something of a surprise therefore, that in phoning the CID office in the Met district police station covering Holland Park, DI Percival was immediately transferred to a Detective Superintendent Wilkins at New Scotland Yard. He was then asked if he could come immediately to a meeting there, bringing his evidence file with him. Having cleared it with his superior he left straightaway.

Chapter 22

At New Scotland Yard Percival was directed to Detective Superintendent Wilkins' office where there were already three men and a woman seated around a conference table. Wilkins introduced himself, then DI Major of the Serious Crime Squad and the other two, DI Sheila Nelson and DC Alan Price who he explained were with the Art & Antiques Section of the Met. He then invited Percival to tell them exactly why and how he had come to find the body of the man he had identified as Dimitri Beltrovich.

Percival went through the events of the morning. The report from the building site in the City of a body that was spotted with an arm sticking up out of an area of newly laid but uncovered concrete, an abandoned tarpaulin and two poles that had apparently been used to push the body beneath the wet concrete surface, the heavy overnight rain and so forth. How the body was pulled out and when cleaned off had no identifying wallet or papers, only a small tag on his suit jacket which gave the name of his tailor who then identified him from a post- mortem photo as Dimitri Beltrovich.

He added that he awaited the result of the autopsy but was quite sure that death was caused by a bullet fired at short range into the back of the head that had exited through the lower jaw.

He explained that he was returning to the site that afternoon to interview everyone on the night shift, during which the body had somehow been brought onto the secure site through the manned single entry gate, and for disposal, pushed down into the wet concrete.

After putting a few questions to him, Wilkins thanked Percival for a good, succinct report and went on "I expect you are wondering why I asked you to along this morning and why there are two specialists from our Art & Antiques Section here ."He continued, "I must tell you first that news of the violent death of Mr Dimitri Beltrovich came as a big surprise to those of us here at the Yard. We were already looking closely into the activities of this Russian oligarch who, amongst other things, is suspected of being behind the theft of a valuable old master painting. Other people were involved in the actual heist of the painting in Florence, but the latest intelligence strongly indicates that Beltrovich is now holding it either at his home in Holland Park or elsewhere in the country, and these two officers are running the inquiries," gesturing towards Nelson and Price.

"The death of Beltrovich doesn't alter the need to find the multi-million pound painting, but the manner of his death – a gang-like execution- throws up into relief other parties who are known to be interested in getting hold of the painting. So, finding out who carried out the killing, who their paymasters are and what you uncover in your investigations will be of particular interest both to our Arts team and of course to DI Peter Major."

Major, who had remained silent up to this point came in and addressed Percival, "We in the Met are happy to give you any assistance in the way of manpower or resources that you may need in your investigation but that may only become apparent after you have conducted your interviews on site this afternoon.

I am going to suggest that sometime tomorrow morning we reconvene this meeting to review our way forward. By then the death of Beltrovich will have become widely known through the media and will no doubt, as a Russian oligarch, spawn spectacular headlines, wild speculation and perhaps reaction from the Kremlin.

"Are you happy with that suggestion Percival?" asked Wilkins. "If so, I'll speak to your boss and put him in the picture, and in the meantime we'll leave you to your investigations and meet here again at 11am tomorrow."

Peter Percival agreed and, on his way out of the room, the two Art Squad detectives had a word with him to emphasise that their primary objective was to retrieve the old master painting and bring to justice anyone involved in the theft. Whilst the death of Beltrovich closed one door it may have opened up some intriguing lines of enquiry and they wished him the best of luck that afternoon in making progress through his interviews.

He left New Scotland Yard in good spirits. He had fully expected that Wilkins, after hearing his report, would have decided that as a major crime with possible foreign complications, he and the City Police would have been asked to pass the case directly over to the Met, but they obviously felt he was well suited to carry on – at least until the next day!

Later, having filled DS Riley in on the morning's happenings, they set off accompanied by a DC to the City building site in good time to see the day shift sign off and the night shift take up their duties. As there was only one of the portacabin buildings on site that could be used for interviews, the detectives had borrowed a police interview van for the day to speed up the process. They used the additional DC to help filter out those workers who were working well away from where the body was found or the entrance gates.

Percival and Riley initially concentrated on interviewing the site night manager, his assistant, operatives who had been working near to the crime scene, and finally the gatemen. It was only a chance remark made by one of these latter men that registered a chink of light through the dark blanket of ignorance of anything extraordinary being seen or heard that pervaded throughout the interviews. Having shown the detectives the meticulously timed and recorded in and out books for materials consignments and parcels, which were later uploaded onto a computer, he was asked if there were any visitors to site during that shift and responded "only the usual." Asked to expand he said 'the refuse truck' which came several times daily to take away full skips and leave empty ones, and the usual 'inspection team.'

"Who and what are the inspection team" asked Percival.
.

"Well, they come to the site two or three times every month on a spot check to see that all Health & Safety procedures and precautions previously agreed to between management and the authorities are all in place and being enforced, that site boundaries are still intact and adequately fenced and all that sort of thing."

"What are they called, these inspection teams?"

"Joint Site Inspection Company. I think it's owned and run jointly by the Health & Safety Authority and the Insurance Industry. You see their vans manned by their uniformed staff quite often where there are many building sites, like here in the City."

Percival went on "And what do you do when the inspection team arrives at the site entrance?"

"Ring the Site Manager to let him know they are here. Sometimes they want to see and talk to him first, but mostly they get on with their inspection. They know what they want to look at and who they need to talk to, so they drive round to various points on the site, do what they have to, make their notes, complete an inspection report which they give to or leave for the Site Manager and then bugger off 'til the next time."

"I see and is it the same team that comes here every time?" asked Percival.

"No, they seem to vary quite a bit. Lot of teams and a lot of sites."

Percival went on to ask the gateman whether he could identify anything distinctive or different in the team that came the previous day compared with other times. He shook his head "Same van with the company name and logo. Three guys in the same green waterproofs and hardhats with their big JSI logo as usual. I just let them in and left a message for the manager that they were on site. Come to think of it they were quicker than usual doing their rounds yesterday, usually

198

it is 30 or 40 minutes but yesterday they were barely twenty minutes here. I remember thinking when noting it down in the visitors' book that everything here must have been tickety-boo for once."

Percival asked him to make and sign a statement covering the essential points that he had made and then asked the site manager to come back into the interview room. Immediately Percival taxed him with the fact that there had been visitors to the site the previous night during his shift in charge, that he had not mentioned. He expressed surprise and asked who they were and when Percival told him he smiled and went on "Oh those people, bloody nuisance always popping up when least expected, but I suppose performing a necessary function."

"You didn't see them then yesterday?"

"No, the gateman left a message to say they were on site, but frankly I avoid them when I can, they're rather a pernickety bunch in my experience and unless they have got something specific to moan to me about, they come in, do their inspection and go leaving an inspection certificate which might make an odd comment, but invariably is stamped 'Satisfactory,' which suits me fine."

"I gather that during their inspection they sometimes talk to operatives or managers on site?"

"Yes, they do occasionally, to make sure that the guards on machinery or handrails at danger spots are always in place and that people are aware of the hazards and respect the safety procedures in force, but most of the time they just go and look and make their notes. Mind you if they do find anything amiss, they let me or one of my colleagues know in no uncertain terms. I must say they are very thorough, and as I said before they are a necessary encumbrance. Nobody other than the gateman commented on the inspectors' visit yesterday, they didn't speak to anyone otherwise I would have heard, indeed there were no comments about them being seen on site, which is unusual and they seem to have whizzed through their inspection in record time."

After he had gone, and all the interviews had been completed without any other useful information coming out, Percival remarked to Riley that quite obviously the finger of suspicion pointed towards the inspection team that had visited the previous day.

A team that seemed to have been invisible on site and got through their usual inspection routine very quickly – if indeed they bothered.

He looked at his watch, 6.25pm, which was well after most offices had closed for the day, however, the Joint Site Inspection Company because of the nature of their business had teams working outside the normal working hours and there could well be somebody still on duty. He looked up and rang a London office number only to receive a recorded message telling him to ring back after 8.30am.

It had been a full day and Percival was beginning to feel a little weary. Tomorrow was to bring an early start, so the three detectives returned to leave their van at headquarters and made their way home.

Soon after 8.30am the next morning Percival rang the London office of the Joint Site Inspection Company, explained who he was and said that he wanted to talk to the team who made an inspection two days ago at the site he named in the City. He was immediately put through to a manager who said that by a coincidence he was about to ring the police about that particular team as they had not reported in now for some 36 hours and checking with some of the sites they were due to visit during that period it seems they had never arrived.

It was not unknown for a team to go 24 hours without making contact with the office, particularly when it was easier for the team to take a van home with one of them to affect an early morning start rather than bring it in. Percival asked him for a description of the missing van and its registration number and after he had taken down the details told him that he would be with him in twenty minutes.

Percival saw to it that an APB about the missing vehicle was sent out, picked up his Sergeant on the way to his car, briefed him on events and they were quickly at the JSI offices in Camden Town where Trevor Davidson, the manager he had spoken to on the phone was awaiting his arrival. He had details about the three men who made up team that they were concerned about and their schedule of inspections, together with further information on sites where they had carried out their inspections on the day and others where they had never arrived.

By comparing notes, it became obvious that out of seven scheduled visits by the team to building sites in the City of London and north London that day, five of them reported that an inspection had been carried out and two were negative. According to the site contractor's records and the inspection sheet left with them, the last site visited by the team that day had been the one in the City where Beltrovich's body had been recovered.

Percival asked Davidson about the three team members and their reliability, to be told that they were all experienced and reliable. One had been with the Company for five years, the others three years each. Because of the changing nature of on-site work, as a building progressed, so did the need for different specialisations amongst the inspectors. Although they were all trained inspectors, their previous experience in the construction industry, perhaps in fire hazard, security or the safeguarding of machinery for example, meant that they all had their specialisations which were needed at different times on sites.

Most team members were between fifty-five and sixty-five years of age so there was a constant stream of men reaching retirement age and new inspectors in training and replacing them. With the membership of the fifteen or sixteen teams covering the Greater London area and beyond, teams were always changing.

It was a rarity for even two members of a team to meet up as part of another team over the years and almost unknown for the same three to be working together more than once.

"So, any three men providing they were in uniform and driving one of your vans would be admitted to a building site without much questioning?" asked Percival.

"Well yes, I suppose so" agreed Davidson.

"Which is what I believe happened on the City site yesterday. At some point your team was stopped in their van and abducted. They were probably taken somewhere locally, stripped of their uniforms and tied up. Then, three gang members donned their uniforms, and having placed the body of Beltrovich in the back of your van covered with a tarp or something, drove onto the site and to the area of newly laid wet concrete where they pulled away the protective sheeting and pushed the corpse under with the aid of two poles. All done and dusted in short time, they filled in the Inspection Report handed it to the gateman and left.

"I expect they parked up quite quickly, then changed back into their clothes, dumped the uniforms in some waste bins, cleaned up the van and left that somewhere where they had previously left a car and drove away."

Almost on cue Percival's mobile rang with message that a Joint Site Inspection Company vehicle with the registration number that was being sought, had been set alight on some waste ground in Hackney. It was a total wreck but there was nobody on board.

Percival calculated that the van had probably been dumped and burnt out only a short walk from where the escape car had been parked.

He guessed that this was probably not too far from where the absconded men had been taken and stripped of their uniforms, and where the Company van had been brought in to take on board the dead body before the gangsters drove off to the site. He tried his theory on DS Riley who thought it a strong possibility. Then, with the cooperation of the Met, he arranged for a search to be made of any empty premises factories, garages and warehouses that had a drive-in facility for vehicles, within a mile of the burnt-out van.

Because there were lives at stake, this was arranged quickly and thirty premises were identified as possibilities and visited by police personnel within a couple of hours. At one disused factory premises where there were loading bays that were fully under cover, a visiting police patrol was attracted by the sound of two windows being shattered in quick succession and the faint sound of voices asking for help. On inspection they found the three JSI inspectors tied up together all stripped of their long green waterproof coats and trousers.

One of them had managed to get an arm free and seeing the flashing police car lights outside, managed to pick up some pieces of scrap metal lying on an adjacent work bench and hurled them one at a time with all the force he could muster at a line of windows four yards away. Their ordeal had lasted for nearly two days and although they were all very thirsty and hungry, they were all in quite good shape.

Chapter 23

News of the inspectors' release was passed by the Met police to Percival who was quickly at the scene. The three men, swaddled in blankets, were drinking hot tea, eating sandwiches obtained from a nearby café and awaiting ambulances to take them for hospital check-ups. Percival took the opportunity to ask them some questions and the following account emerged.

The previous day, the team had just finished an inspection on a site in Dalston and were making their way down Shoreditch towards their next site, which was near to Tower Bridge. As they approached Folgate Street a large van pulled out in front of them and stopped. As they pulled up two men in hoodies approached each side window looking as if they were coming to apologise, but once the windows were down and they were close up to the vehicle they had both drawn guns. Very quickly they had pushed the two inspectors in the front, through the gap between the front seats to join their colleague in the back, followed by one of the men wielding his gun. The other gunman sat in the driver's seat and was able to set off immediately after the large van had moved.

The three men were made to stay down near the floor and couldn't tell where they were being taken, but it wasn't far, as after a few minutes they drove into the loading bays of a building.

They were ordered out of their vehicle, up a ramp and into a dusty old workshop where they were told to take off their distinctive baseball type caps, heavy green waterproof coats and trousers. They were then tied up together onto a wooden bench, leaving each man one hand free enough to lift a nearby litre plastic bottle of water to his lips. Finally, they were prevented from immediately shouting out, by duct tape sealing their mouths which took several minutes of meticulous picking and pulling with one hand to get rid of.

It had all happened very quickly, and they couldn't recognise any of the abductors, as each wore Boris Johnson thin rubber head and face masks with eye and mouth apertures. The abductors spoke very little but two of them had distinctive cockney accents.

Percival, accompanied this time with his boss DCI Leigh, was able to report on a very active twenty-four hours at his meeting at Scotland Yard later the next morning, but despite his undoubted success there were a lot of unanswered questions. Specifically, who had carried out the abduction and the murder of Beltrovich and who had previously grabbed the inspectors and were they the same people?

From where had the abductors obtained the information about the day and time of the JSI Company inspection at the site and when a large area of concrete was being poured? Not from anyone at the site, as they never knew in advance of any visit until the inspectors arrived, and not from the inspectors themselves as they only received the scheduled list of sites to be inspected that day at the beginning of their shift. The only people to know in advance of the day's list for each team were those people who drew these up or approved them at the local Joint Site Inspection Company office in Camden Town.

As the centre of the investigation had moved from where the body of Beltrovich had been found in the City to elsewhere in Greater London, DCI Major suggested that the Metropolitan Police should now officially take over the enquiry, but asked DCI Leigh if he would agree to DI Percival and his DS being temporarily attached to the Met for the duration of the investigations. They had already made a great contribution into the case and had acquired unique knowledge about some of the people involved. Leigh was happy to agree in principle.

In his new role Percival would be reporting directly to DCI Major to whom the team who had been carrying out the surveillance on Beltrovich and his home and now his murder, were already reporting. Since the discovery of the body, Major told the meeting that the Russian's home in Holland Park had again been visited, and his family and staff interviewed. They all told or confirmed the same story that, early after lunch on the day he went missing, Beltrovich was driven by his chauffeur/bodyguard to Hampstead Heath where, as was his custom, he went for a solitary walk lasting about twenty minutes before being driven back home.

This was a pattern most days, although he varied his walking area which was sometimes in Richmond or Hyde Park or another open space that had taken his fancy in or around London. He claimed it "cleared his lungs" and after he had been doing this for several weeks, his bodyguard stopped following him at a distance and parked-up to await his return, to both their satisfaction.

On the day in question when Beltrovich had not returned to the car after half an hour, the chauffeur/bodyguard went to search for him with ever increasing concern, for a further forty or fifty minutes, before returning to Holland Park and reporting on what had happened to Beltrovich's wife and his chief of staff.

There was no reply from Beltrovich's mobile phone, but they decided to wait for another hour in case he just turned up, before notifying the police.

Major said that when they responded, the Met team took the opportunity of searching the house, paying particular attention to his office and private picture gallery to try and find anything that would give an indication as to where he had gone or been taken. There was nothing that was of any help, even on his computer which was taken away for examination. The next day after the body had been found, a more rigorous search of the premises was carried out but so far had revealed nothing of value.

So far, the best prospect for making progress in the investigation seemed to be with Percival and his enquiries at the JSI offices in Camden Town and Major said he looked forward to having this report.

DCI Percival and DS Riley immediately left for Camden Town to see the manager, Davidson, at the JSI office and asked him first of all to describe how the teams of inspectors were selected and who was involved in the process.

"Yes of course" he began "it's a bit of an involved process as there are a number of considerations that we have to take into account. These include the inspectors we have available for the next month and their specialisations, the changing requirements of inspecting specific sites as work progresses and the need to ensure that as people retire or leave, the newly trained inspectors are always teamed up with two experienced colleagues."

He went on to say that to make up the fifteen or sixteen teams generally required, they had under contract approximately fifty-five inspectors to allow for sickness, holidays and with some involved in assisting in the training of new inspectors.

Once the complete list of sites for a visit the following month and their specific inspection requirements had been collated, those with similar criteria were grouped together and the selection of teams to meet these requirements began. A certain amount of shuffling and reallocation took place before everything was loaded with a specially designed algorithm into the computer and the team lists became available and the participants were notified two or three days before the beginning of the month. Finally, their site inspection list was issued to each team every morning, either at the office or by email.

The team selection and the collation of site information was in the hands of three people who began work on the following month's arrangements as soon as a new month began, and Davidson took Percival and Riley into a large adjacent office and introduced them to the trio. At first sight the greying 60 year old team leader, Jane Bradbury, seemed a humourless woman. She had a no-nonsense manner that somehow reflected the fact that she had been doing much the same work for nearly twenty years. Alan Schwarzkopf, balding, bespectacled and nerdy was a man of indeterminate age and of few words, in contrast to the third and latest team member smiling thirty-year old Olly Sinclair who seemed to rarely pause for breath between his jokey references and questions.

Percival and Riley soon realised that appearances often disguised the truth. Bradbury proved to be not just amusing but positively hilarious whilst illustrating some of the routines and intricacies of their work. Schwartzkopf, demonstrating the workings of the algorithm, not only proved his deftness on a complex computer programme but was concise and witty in his explanations. Sinclair was the enigma, his front as a talkative cockney-accented comedian was just that, a front or an act behind which there existed a shy, diffident individual yet with a razor-sharp analysing intellect. Together they made a formidable team and after listening to them, Percival and Price both realised that it was probably going to be a difficult task to find out which of them had been guilty of giving away the information.

Percival told them that he and DS Riley would be talking to them individually about something that had happened on a building site without, at that stage, disclosing what the two policemen were seeking. It was by any definition a delicate task as it was tantamount to suggesting that each one of them in turn had betrayed the trust that their work entailed.

After overcoming expressions of indignation, ridicule and anger from the trio, Percival patiently explained that the "leak" could only have originated from one of them or Davidson whether accidentally or intentionally. He explained why it was essential to question them all and investigate their contacts and connections. He didn't bother to add that their bank accounts and financial dealings were already being looked at.

All three were open and cooperative and at the end of the afternoon, on the basis of their enquiries and questioning so far, the two policemen were no further forward and began to question Davidson. He proved more hesitant and less straightforward in his answers than his colleagues had been until, at one stage, after being subjected to questioning for an hour and a half he gave a great sigh and said "I've been less than frank with you two gentlemen. I can't go on denying the facts.

I've been stupid a couple of times in the last few days and have passed on information about sites in Central London where large areas of concrete were being poured coinciding with when inspections were being made."

Percival sat up and quickly interjected "Did you phone someone, and have you the number?"

"Yes" replied Davidson and proceeded to pull a small diary from his pocket, which he consulted "It was a man called Ian Smith and on the three occasions I spoke to him it was on different numbers." He proceeded to read each of them out. DS Riley noted them down and passed them on during a conversation on his mobile phone. Percival continued "How were you first contacted by this Ian Smith and what did he say to you?"

"Well, it was strange, almost as if he was watching me and timing his call to my mobile phone. Every evening, sometime between 8 and 10.30pm I take my dog for a twenty-minute walk, it varies quite a lot depending upon what I'm doing or watching on TV. His first call came just after 8.30 on Sunday evening. I'd just left my house and his opening words were rather startling. After introducing himself, he laughed and said something like 'I don't usually spend Sunday evenings telling someone that they are going to receive a fee of £5,000 for supplying information that they have readily to hand, but that's what I'm going to do with you.'

"He assured me it was perfectly legal and ethical and went on to explain why he was doing this and the reason for secrecy. He said he was heading up some confidential research for the Concrete Society, concerned with newly poured concrete for the foundations of substantial new buildings under construction.

Because of the nature of this research, which involved spot tests on site, the construction companies concerned were only told about the tests when the testing/research team carrying the necessary authorisation arrived to do their work.

Secrecy, which was vital, could not be maintained if either the main contractor's personnel or the supplier of ready-mixed concrete for the site learned of the tests in advance and so the only people who knew of such sites and when concrete was being poured there were JSI. Because speed was of the essence, he explained, it was decided to approach Davidson directly and avoid all the delay and bureaucracy that a formal approach would entail.

Smith's story was plausible, although Davidson wasn't so sure about either the legality or the ethics of what he was being asked to do but he agreed after Smith mentioned that the £5,000 fee would be paid in banknotes and delivered by courier to his door.

Davidson confessed that his remaining doubts were overcome by the chance of earning some untraceable easy money in complete secrecy, in exchange for some information about a few sites. He only rang Smith twice, once to agree to his proposition and the other time to pass on information. The money was, as promised, delivered by courier the same night, and was still sitting in a drawer at home, untouched.

The two mobile contact numbers turned out to be burner phones and so untraceable, and the courier who delivered the money to Davidson had worn a black helmet and anonymous black motor cyclist gear and couldn't be identified, so the two detectives were no further forward. Until a lucky break in a completely new direction.

Chapter 24

Immediately DI Nelson had returned to her office after learning of Beltrovich's corpse being found on the building site, she had phoned Simon Brookes at his hotel to let him know about this surprising turn of events. She was also able to tell him that earlier, when the Russian had been reported missing, his house at Holland Park had been searched and there had been no sign of the missing Tiepolo painting. Nelson had promised to keep Simon abreast of the investigation into the missing painting and anything relevant to that, although she reminded him that, as this was now a murder investigation by the Met, some matters would remain confidential which may prevent Nelson passing on everything to him.

However, she was true to her word and had phoned Simon to appraise him of the situation after a second and more detailed search of the Holland Park house had taken place. Even examination of the computers and mobile phones that had been taken, had not uncovered any mention of the missing painting. She also told Simon that the murder investigation had uncovered how the body of Beltrovich had been taken to the building site and buried in concrete, but they had not, as yet, discovered who the perpetrators were.

This then was the situation described briefly by Simon when he was joined in their Grosvenor House Hotel suite by Marie after she had flown in from Paris, a day later than she had expected. The delight that was evident in both of them at being reunited culminated very quickly into a shedding of clothes on the way into the bedroom, where the height of their mutual passion took them both by surprise.

Later, showered, changed and relaxing in their sitting room over lunch and a glass of champagne, Simon described in greater detail what he had learned of the Beltrovich murder, the investigation and the unsuccessful searches for the Tiepolo. Marie asked him whether the Metropolitan Police Arts & Antiques section had been cooperative and he told her about the meeting he had attended at Scotland Yard and the subsequent conversations with DI Nelson. She said she would contact Nelson shortly but before that she wanted to make more of her own enquiries through her contacts in the London art scene to try and glean any scraps of information or rumours that would undoubtedly be in circulation by now.

****

A game of street cricket was in progress in Drovers Road, Bethnal Green, one of those in inner London suburbs that had been blocked off at one end with planters to stop through traffic and allow for a play area. It was such an unusual sight where games of football were almost always being played that the police patrol car passing by momentarily stopped as the two policeman looked on. At that moment, the batter smote the ball high and long over the planters and onto the road in front of the police car, pursued by a young boy resplendent in a dark green cap somewhat too large for him that fell into the road as he darted out without looking.

The officer on the passenger side got out to reprimand the boy for not pausing to look for oncoming traffic and then picked up the cap to hand back to him. It was an elaborate baseball-type with the large yellow letters JSI embroidered on the front and it rang an immediate bell.

"Where did you get this cap from" the policeman asked the boy.

"It was a present from me Dad" he replied.

"And what is your Dad called and where do you live?"

The boy hesitated before replying "Me Dad is Sid Atkins and we live round the corner in Creston Street." That rang an even louder bell in the policeman's mind, the Atkins brothers were key members of the Telford Syndicate, a notorious East London gang who were well known to the police. He told the boy "I'd like to talk to your Dad about this cap, so I'll hold onto it and call by when he's at home. Will he be home this evening about six?"

"Yeah, should be" the boy commented before running back with the ball to his game.

As he got back into the patrol car his colleague asked him "What was all that about?"

"Well I spotted that the cap that the boy was wearing belonged to JSI – you know, those building site inspection people, three of them were abducted and were only found yesterday or the day before. It may be a coincidence but when the lad told me he'd been given it by his father, who is Sid

Atkins of Creston Street I began to wonder, is there a connection?"

"I see where you're coming from. Are you going to call it in? Only the CID team might be glad of a lead, however slim."

"You're right I'll call it in."

When DCI Major was shown the report from the patrol officer about spotting a green and yellow JSI cap "a present from his Dad" being worn by a small boy in the East End who turned out to be the son of Sid Atkins, he knew that it could be an important breakthrough. He saw to it that that the policemen involved were thanked for their quick-sightedness, but told not follow up as this would now be done by CID officers already involved. He walked with the printed report and the cap in hand, into DI Percival's nearby office and placed them in front of him with the remark "something that could be really interesting."

He went on to give Percival more details about the background of Atkins and his associates – a particularly violent and ruthless gang known as the Telford Associates, to whom the abduction of the three inspectors would present no difficulty. He suggested that Percival and his sergeant get round to Creston Street pdq to ask Atkins where he got the cap and so on. He warned Percival that Atkins was a very volatile character and, if he felt he was being cornered might react in a hostile manner. Several immediate neighbours including Atkins' brother, were gang members who could be summoned.

In case that happened, he was warning a local police patrol to stand nearby ready, and gave an emergency number to Percival which would give him direct contact should assistance be required.

After Major had left him, Percival examined the cap carefully and inside the beige lining close to the peak were three small letters GTH. He checked his notes and found that one of the abducted Inspectors was called Geoff Harris. It was now nearing six o'clock in the evening and Percival left his office with the cap stuffed into his pocket, calling for DS Riley on the way down to his car where he told him about the new information, and they set off for Bethnal Green.

They drove the length of Creston Street noting that Number 37 was in the middle of a row of six red brick terraced houses all looking immaculate with doors, windows and downpipes painted a uniform light blue, giving the impression that were interlinked inside. The rest of that part of the street to the corner was occupied by a former pub now converted, as the small brass sign at the front declared into "The Telford Snooker Club. PRIVATE."

Responding to his knock and bell-ringing at the door of number 37 it was opened a crack and a third of a woman's face appeared.   Her eye looked them up and down before she said "Yes?"

"Is Mr Sid Atkins home?" asked Percival.

"Who wants to know?"

Producing his warrant card Percival responded, "Detective Inspector Percival and Detective Sergeant Riley of the Metropolitan Police." The woman paused before replying with "At the Snooker Club" and closed the door.

"Charming" remarked Riley as he followed his boss along the street past the side of the former pub to its front door round the corner.

As Percival pressed the bellpush and rapped on the door he commented "I'll be surprised if our presence hasn't already been announced." He was right, for after a minute of delay the door swung open to reveal a large shaven-headed man in a remarkably well-cut suit whose brutish face was surprisingly lit by a crooked smile that seemed to spread from ear to ear.

He stood back and beckoned them inside "Welcome Inspector Percival and Sergeant" and closing the door "I'll lead you in." He walked across the spacious comfortable lounge past a well-stocked bar and into a passageway beside it that led into a games room with four snooker tables, dart boards, table soccer, green felt topped tables for cards and hard tops for dominoes. Only one table was in use, where two men were continuing their unhurried game of snooker with an audience of another six men standing round and looking on. Their escort pointed to the table and stood back. Walking forward Percival enquired "Mr Sid Atkins?"

Having just potted a red ball, one of the shirt-sleeved players was just settling to a new position at the table in order to sink a blue ball into a middle pocket. The angle was perfect and the blue went down allowing the white ball to screw back to line up his next red. He stood up amidst a ripple of applause and favourable comments from the onlookers - a short, stocky figure with a pleasant smile which he directed at his visitors.

"Welcome to our club gentlemen" he began "and what can we do to help you today." He had walked around the table and extended his hand to Percival who either ignored it or didn't notice as he responded. "I'd like to ask you some questions" he said adding, as he looked at the onlookers, "somewhere private if we may."

"Certainly" said Atkins we'll go up to my office," and led the way back to the passageway, through a door and up a short flight of stairs to another corridor with several doors opening off. He took them to the far end where the door opened onto a spacious office where he took the swing chair behind a large mahogany partner desk and gestured for them to take two of the easy chairs that were positioned at its front.

A tap on the door announced the appearance of one of the men from downstairs – a younger version of Sid whom he introduced as Cyril his brother, and right hand man, "I never do anything without him. That OK?"

Percival did object, he would far rather have had Sid on his own, but he didn't want to make an issue of it at this juncture. The younger Atkins sat on a chair at the side of the room whilst Percival took one of the easy chairs. Before sitting, Riley looked at some of the many photographs of buildings, and of Sid Atkins holding a trophy or shaking hands with some celebrity. Others showed groups of people in which Sid figured prominently.

"Now. You have some questions for me?" began Atkins.

"Yes, thank you," said Percival and pulled the green and yellow cap from his pocket, passing it over to Atkins. "I understand you gave this cap to your son as a present. Where did you get it from?"

Accepting the cap from Percival reluctantly he immediately dropped it onto the desk in front of him and gazed at it silently.

"Do you recognise it?" pressed Percival.

"I'm not sure. I remember giving my lad a cap to wear for his cricket games, but where I picked it up I don't recall. Could have been anywhere. I get about in my work."

"Surely you remember this one, it's quite an unusual green colour and with the distinctive logo of the JSI -Joint Site inspection Company - in bright yellow. It would stand out in most people's memories I would think, wouldn't you?" said Percival.

"Well, I don't remember it" replied Atkins emphatically and passed the cap back over the desk.

"But you just said that you weren't sure. Is there a chance that it could be the one you gave to your boy?"

"I suppose it could be" came the cautious response.

"And where did you pick it up, you must remember that" asked Price. By this time Atkins was clearly uncomfortable with the questioning and fired back "I've already told you I don't remember." Percival came back "Mr Atkins where were you on Monday the 19th of this month?"

Somewhat relieved at the change in questioning Atkins said, "I'm pretty sure I was in the office all day but I'll just confirm by looking in my diary" and pulled an i-phone from his pocket and looked at it. "Yes, here all day, looking at figures with my accountant and then discussing my architect's plans for a new development." At this point his brother who had not said a word, got up and quietly left the room.

Sid Atkins waffled on about the difficulties of dealing with accountants and architects, then suddenly stopped and smiled in a sardonic manner at the two policemen.

"You're putting two and two together and making it five gentlemen. That was the day that the men from the JSI outfit were abducted and on the strength of that cap you're thinking that me or my people I had something to do with it, yes?"

"It certainly was a possibility that struck us, yes," agreed Percival.

"Gentlemen really!" said Atkins standing up from his chair "do you think that I would put my reputation in the property development business, my investment company and all my other enterprises at risk by me or my associates becoming involved in squalid abductions and murder. Come on."

"I really don't know at this point" said Percival "but I assume you would have no objection to our putting a few questions to your colleagues and associates here, plus your architect and accountant just to confirm."

"Not at all, you can use this office if you won't be too long" and Atkins wrote out the names and numbers of his architect and accountant which he passed to Sergeant Price.

Both Percival and Riley were aware that immediately after Cyril Atkins had left the room he had gone downstairs to the snooker room to alert everyone to what the story was about

Monday 19th – the boss was in his office all day and everyone else should dust off their alibis for that time. Cyril Atkins had also, no doubt, made quick phone calls to both professional advisors to note in their diaries and memories that they had been to see Sid in his office on the 19th at certain times.

It turned out to be much as Percival had foreseen, everyone had alibis that relied largely on the word of work colleagues or wives.

Even the accountant and architect when contacted confirmed that they had met Sid Atkin at his office on the day concerned. For the moment there was no progress to be made in that direction, but at least they had the names and addresses of the Atkins' closest cohorts, plus the names and details of those people providing alibis and could quickly return to these should new evidence make that necessary.

Before Percival and Riley picked up their things and left the office, Riley drew his colleague's attention to one of the photographs on the wall. It was of a dinner party table at The Raffles Hotel, Singapore two years earlier, so the caption read. A beaming Sid Atkins was easily spotted, sitting on the far side of the table, but it was his left hand neighbour that Riley pointed to asking "Do you recognise him?"

Percival looked and realised that the face was vaguely familiar without bringing a name or a context to mind. He confessed as much to Riley who said "I've only seen a couple of pictures in the files, of the Australian guy Timothy Bird who was in cahoots with Beltrovich and was said to be in Florence when the painting was stolen, and I'm pretty sure that's him – same heavy moustache and deep central peak of hair."

Percival took a longer look "I've also only seen those images in the files but there seems to be a good likeness. Well spotted. If it is Bird, it shows that he and Atkins knew each other a couple of years ago which may be quite significant. I'm tempted to ask Sid now about the picture and find out whether they are friends, but I think we should wait until we have had a closer look at Tim Bird now he's in London, and find out what he's doing here, otherwise Sid will get to him first and tell him of our interest.

"Remember, Bird is also suspected of being behind the shooting in Venice of a colleague of Simon Brookes, the owner of the missing painting. He is by all accounts a nasty piece of work and has had several run-ins with the Australian police but nothing too heavy. So far, in Europe although there are suspicions about his activities, there's no firm evidence to back it up.

The fact that he apparently knows Sid Atkins is not sufficient reason in itself to pull him in for a chat, so we must dig around to find something else, perhaps the Italian police can help us out."

They left the Snooker Club having thanked Sid Atkins and his colleagues for their co-operation and use of his office but added that they may be back.

Chapter 25

Simon and Marie at the Grosvenor House Hotel had been having regular updates from DI Sheila Nelson on the progress of the police enquiries as far as she had been able, but it was Marie's enquiries through her contacts that came up with some really interesting information. She learnt from two sources on the dodgy side of the art world's grapevine, that Beltrovich had been party to a big falling out with Timothy Bird a few days before he was killed.

Sources also told her of a strong rumour that it was Bird who had hired the mafia "heist" gang in Florence and had the painting brought to Beltrovich in London. Prior to that, it was said, the two men had agreed that on the basis of an independent valuation of the painting which might be in excess of £10 million, Beltrovich would pay Bird half of that final figure, and that immediately on receipt of the painting, the Russian would advance £5million to Bird, plus his expenses thus far.

But then it was reported that Beltrovich, now that he had the painting in his possession, welched on the deal and was prepared to pay over to Bird just £2.5million in full and final settlement for his services and his share in the value of the painting. At their last angry meeting It was all there in cash, packed into a suitcase.

Bird was pursuing a case through the courts claiming that he was the legitimate owner of the painting and thus theoretically would be able to sell it at auction providing him personally with something nearer to £10million profit. But this cut no ice with Beltrovich, who was confident the court case would fail and he would not budge from his offer.

The story went on that Bird, realising that he had not a leg to stand on and no chance of improving his pay-off, was furious and walked out of the meeting with the suitcase. He had the reputation of being a man with a quick temper that required speedy revenge for any set back. Certainly, on this occasion he immediately set about finding somebody who would accept a contract for the death of Beltrovich and discover where the painting had been hidden.

He was able to find someone very quickly who for a large sum of money in cash, agreed to take the contract. It was a meticulously planned and cleverly executed murder carried out in the three days before Beltrovich's body was dug out of the concrete. The search for the painting continued.

Simon had been worried about some of the dubious types that he knew Marie needed to meet with in her enquiries and it had not been without risk to her personal safety, so he was greatly relieved that she was safe and successful.

It was obvious that much of what she had learned would be of help to the police and they decided that Marie would phone DI Nelson and ask her to arrange a meeting with DCI Major and his colleagues so that she could update them on her findings so far. She wished Simon to be there as well.

Marie spoke to DI Nelson and within a short time Major was on the phone to her suggesting a meeting in his office at New Scotland Yard that afternoon at 4.30pm.

At the start of the meeting CDI Major said "It is most unusual to have non-police officers attending a meeting where progress into active investigations are under discussion, but the circumstances are unusual and the contributions that Mrs Shawcross is able to make through her unique contacts has always been helpful to the police here and in other countries. Similarly, as owner of the missing painting Mr Simon Brookes has been closely involved at every stage of the investigation and brings a usefully different perspective to bear. So, we welcome you both."

Marie then told the committee what she had discovered, emphasising that although much of what she had been told was based on rumour and hearsay its credibility had been enhanced by coming from at least two independent sources.

Major thanked Marie and went on to say that her findings fitted like jigsaw pieces into what the police investigations had turned up. If the strong suspicions and rumours were followed through and verified then they would not only have Bird earmarked as the man behind both the murder of Beltrovich and the theft of the painting, but also the London gang that were contracted to carry out both crimes and how they carried them out.

"We now need firm evidence to link in Sid Atkins' people and Timothy Bird to the actions we suspect they were involved in, and this is only going to come from persistent questioning of gang members and their alibis and, of course, Bird himself whose whereabouts in London have yet to be discovered I understand?" He posed the question to the room in general, but Percival answered.

"No, you're right, sir. When he first arrived from Australia, we've discovered that he was staying at a Kensington hotel but booked out of there several days ago leaving no clue as to where he had gone, even though all the staff there have been questioned and a couple of them thought he had hinted he was still staying in the London area. A search of all hotels, B & B's and so forth is still on-going."

He went on "You'll be interested to learn that Bird and Sid Atkins have known each other for at least a couple of years." He described how his sharp-eyed Sergeant had spotted the photograph in Atkins' office and explained that he hadn't yet questioned Atkins about this as he wished to use it when questioning Bird first. He said that the Italian police in Florence had also been helpful, in that the man arrested for the heist of the picture in that city, had told them that the man paying the mafia was nicknamed by them as the "*Aussie Uccello*", and they would be grateful if Bird could be asked on their behalf, why and when he was in Florence at that time. Percival ended with "That gives me more reason for seeking out Bird for questioning."

Major then turned to DCI Nelson "What progress has been made on finding the whereabouts of the missing painting?"

"Nothing definite so far," she began "but I am confident that someone in his household would know that he had a bank vault locker, a lock-up garage or another house somewhere in London where he would have taken the painting for safe keeping, possibly with other items that he didn't want to have on display. I'm hoping that DI Percival and I can go and question again those who are most likely to know something, like his Business Manager or his chauffeur" and looked across at Percival who nodded his assent.

Nelson continued "I wondered too, if one of Madame Shawcross' contacts might have an idea where Beltrovich had a hideaway for this and other works of art that he was holding illegally. After all, he was known for his confidential wheeling and dealing in such items and must have somewhere where he could take interested clients and collectors to view them that was away from his normal offices or house. Did anyone know about such a place? Marie said she would make some enquiries and see whether anything useful came to light.

Simon told the meeting that although he personally and others, had no doubts that his painting was a genuine Tiepolo it still needed to be officially authenticated and he had received some encouraging news from the chairman of the committee who would be making that decision. When the painting had been stolen in Florence, Simon had left with the Tiepolo committee a large dossier containing the results of all the tests that had been made on the painting and the research that had been carried out in respect of the picture's provenance so far.

Signor Ponticelli had sent him an email which said that although the committee could not of course authenticate 'The Last Supper' as a work of Tiepolo without inspecting the painting, the weight of evidence that Simon had provided was impressive and would help the committee a great deal in reaching their decision. He hoped that the efforts at recovering the painting would soon be successful and suggested, in the meantime, that it would be helpful if Simon could complete the provenance by confirming where and by whom the painting had been held during two critical periods.

As the meeting was breaking up CDI Major received a message which he read out. The police forensic people had been examining the inspection company's burnt-out van.

All the inspectors' clothing and gear had been doused in petrol and destroyed in the conflagration except for one of three hard-hats which by some fluke had not become fused into a mass of plastic like the others but had been missed by the flames.

The name of the owner was still discernible inside the rim and the straps and lining were intact, so much so that microscopic examination disclosed two distinct types of hairs were present, eight of one variety and two of another. DNA testing showed that the eight hairs belonged to the owner but the odd two must have come from another wearer. Could this be used to identify one of the abductors – maybe with luck Sid Atkins or one of his gang?

Chapter 26

Sid Atkins was not happy about Percival's request that he, his brother and all his associates at the snooker club give DNA sample swabs to the police forensic team. When he asked why, Percival's response had been just the usual "to eliminate people from specific enquiries," which told him nothing. However, he reluctantly acquiesced and the swabs were taken at roughly the time that Percival and Riley, accompanied by DI Nelson, arrived at the Beltrovich house in Holland Park. They had rung ahead to ensure that both the Business Manager and chauffeur were there and interviewed them separately in Beltrovich's office.

They talked first to Nicolas Bredask who had already explained his role with Mr Beltrovich in a previous interview as a mixture of "chief of staff, butler and business manager" and Percival began by referring to this.

"In your six years working for Mr Beltrovich which covered pretty much everything that went on in the household as well as his business activities you must have become a close confidant of his."

"Yes, I suppose this is true."

"So, you would know all about any other properties that Mr Beltrovich either owned or rented other than this house, the house in Suffolk and the villa near Nice in the South of France, all of which have been visited and searched by now?"

"There are a couple of apartments that he owns in Moscow and a Dacha outside the city I believe, but members of his family look after those so I have no details, not even their addresses.

Percival went on "As far as you know then he didn't rent or own a place like a warehouse, a garage or something of the sort in or around London?"

"No."

Nelson chipped in at this point "I'm sure Mr Bredask that you have always been a good and loyal employee to Mr Beltrovich over the years, but we are now investigating not only his murder but also the theft of a valuable painting that we have good reason to believe he knew something about. I would ask you to carefully consider the next question before answering. As you keep his accounts, is there any recurring item that comes up monthly, quarterly or even annually to be paid, probably for not much more than £200 per month. Although this is not a very significant amount, it is one that you perhaps have not had a satisfactory answer about if you have queried it with him."

Bredask fell silent and looked down at his hands folded in his lap for fully thirty seconds before he looked up at the police officers and replied "I have of course been aware that Mr Beltrovich has from time to time been engaged in in illegal art dealing and possibly other criminal activities but would emphasise that such activities were kept entirely outside the scope of my work for him.

Both he and I worked to ensure that there was a line that neither of us ever crossed in our dealings with each other. So truly, I know little or nothing outside his legitimate business and household concerns.

"However, in answer to your last question I will need to consult the accounts for recent months to check my memory is correct, but there are only two recurring amounts one for £8,100 per quarter and the other for £320 per month and, until quite recently I did not know what they were for. Both are paid through his lawyers, the first referenced merely '*re J*' and the second '*re NS.*'

"I raised my concerns with him that I could not properly allocate these items of expenditure unless I knew what they were for, and of course, would be unable to answer the auditors' queries should they arise, however he fobbed me off with "don't worry about it", but I did.

"Only two months ago he confidentially explained the quarterly payment of £8,100 to me. It appears that some years ago he had a fling with a lady called Jane who latterly had fallen on hard times, and he had been sending her through his solicitors £8,000 a quarter to support her. His wife knew nothing of this hence his wish for secrecy which I of course respected. However, he was not as forthcoming when it came to the monthly payment '*re NS.*' His response was to tell me to just forget about it."

Percival said "That sounds more like it. Thanks Mr Bredask, could you check your accounts now and confirm to Sergeant

Riley the figure paid to the lawyers, plus of course their name and address."

When Bredask left the room DIs Percival and Nelson exchanged grins with DS Riley and expressed their satisfaction at the information they had gleaned.

Sheila Nelson then stepped out of the office and asked Edward Holt the chauffeur/bodyguard to come in. He was a burly six-footer, only two years out of the Metropolitan Police where he been an experienced patrol driver.

As he sat down with the Percival and Nelson he remarked "I don't mind telling you sir and Ma'am that this business has really shaken me up, and I can't help feeling partly responsible for his abduction and subsequent death, being his protection as well as his driver. I let him down and he was a good and considerate guv'nor."

"You shouldn't blame yourself; you couldn't have foreseen what happened. It was just like any other day that you had taken him up onto the heath and he had asked you specifically not to trail him" said Percival "but I'm sure you would like to help us nail the people who did this."

"Yes of course, but I think I've told you all I know – which isn't much."

"You've worked for Mr Beltrovich for nearly two years now, isn't that right?"

"Yes."

"Did you drive him everywhere, in, and out of London or did he sometimes take a taxi."

"I never remember him travelling by taxi and even if he was being picked up by a limo driver to go to meeting somewhere I would often go along with him for protection – but that was very rare. No, I would say that 99 percent of the time he was out and about I was with him as driver and where necessary bodyguard, to business meetings, social gatherings or dinner with his wife, whatever."

As he was talking, DS Riley quietly came into the room and with a nod to Percival sat down.

"You must have worked some long hours, were you always on call?" asked Nelson.

"Most days I was here on standby, usually from 8am through to 5.30pm unless there were early flights or late pick-ups at the airport for example. I would receive a schedule the previous evening of where Mr Beltrovich was going the next day, with times and degrees of security required which would dictate whether I was to go into the function with him, wait outside or just return to pick him up. I rarely accompanied him on his business trips abroad. I handed over to another security team at the airport until I picked him up on his return.

"The days and sometimes weeks between his departure and return were my own – I was off duty, like I was on the frequent half or full days when Mr Beltrovich announced that he was not going out anywhere, which was almost invariably Sundays and some Saturdays. I have my own flat on the top floor here and come and go as I please. I generally eat with the staff and am very well paid, so as a single man I have been very happy. As I said before, he has been a good guv'nor to work for."

"I don't know what you mean, by storage elsewhere. As far as I know everything was kept in his gallery and storerooms at the back of the house. There is a separate entrance where the bulk of his paintings were brought in or despatched from by van. He has a security man there who looks after deliveries and despatches and also does minor repairs or re-framing in a little workshop adjacent to the gallery. He reports to Mr Bredask."

"OK fine" persisted Nelson "but just returning for a moment to when you were taking Mr Beltrovich to places he had written into the schedule, were they business addresses or private houses or what? And did you ever discover a name to fit any of the initials?"

Holt thought for a minute before replying "They were all sorts of places, offices, blocks of flats, private houses, cottages in the country – you name it. I didn't bother to tie up names with the initials, why should I, it wasn't necessary to know." He stopped and chuckled then went on "Except when, on several occasions he had me drive to an old curio and collectables shop in Sussex with the name over the window 'Christopher Allsop's which was a pretty good guide as to whom the initials on the schedule – 'CA' applied."

Percival smiled and said, "You've a pretty good memory for some of the initials I expect, particularly when you went to a place several times – does 'NS' any bells?"

"Now you've really hit the odd one out" replied Holt," he never gave me an address for that one, just told me to drive towards Finsbury Park in North London and drop him off either in Green Lanes or Seven Sisters Road somewhere near the junction, and then pick him up around the same spot a couple of hours later."

"Did you see where he walked" asked Nelson.

"Not really. I usually drove straight off and parked-up for a couple of hours in the Park or found a café, although I did see him once go into Manor House tube station shortly after I'd left him."

"Where do you think he went when you dropped him off and why was he so secretive about it, do you think?"

"I really don't know. Possibly calling to see an old friend and have a cup of tea, I just don't have a clue, and I wasn't particularly curious."

Nelson persisted "Were these regular occasions where you dropped him off near Green Lanes/Seven Sisters junction? Every week, fortnight or month perhaps? And did he take anything with him, a box of chocolates, a bottle of wine or something like that?"

Holt thought for a moment before replying "No there was nothing regular about it, sometimes he asked me to drive him there twice in a week and then he wouldn't go for four or five weeks but in the course of a month, on average he'd want to go there twice. He never took presents like you were suggesting, but a few times he carried a flat parcel with him like a picture wrapped in brown paper."

After thanking Holt the three policemen, pleased by the information they had gathered from the two interviews, talked animatedly in the car back to New Scotland Yard. They concluded that 'NS' was the person, the business or premises that Beltrovich visited from time to time, somewhere probably within a stop or two of Manor House tube station. Taking a short journey on the Underground was probably part of the security he observed to mislead his chauffeur or anyone else who might be watching him. Their guess was that he only travelled one stop, probably as far as Finsbury Park station, and that his ultimate 'NS' destination was nearby.

DS Riley had already rung Devrille, Archibald and Armitage, Beltrovich's solicitors and made arrangements to see the partner who handled Beltrovich's business that afternoon. Hopefully he and Percival would learn from him the identity and address of 'NS.'

Nelson was confident that it would turn out to be something like a garage or part of a warehouse where Beltrovich could hold any paintings or antiques which he had perhaps acquired illegally and wouldn't bear close scrutiny, and this part of his business he probably ran himself, secretly, with no assistance. The fact that Holt had volunteered that Beltrovich sometimes took a parcel that looked to be the shape of a painting with him to 'NS' lent credence to this idea. But no type of key had turned up in the various searches made and before Percival and Riley left for the solicitors she asked them both again about this.

Percival told Nelson that no keys of any sort had been found in the searches of Beltrovich's properties, even the top drawer of his desk had to be forced open in the absence of a key. Both Bredask, Holt and others had told the searchers that Beltrovich never carried a bunch of keys with him like most people, he didn't drive so he had no need for car keys, Holt or someone with him opened the front door with their keys or he rang the bell. So where, asked Nelson, did he keep his desk drawer key ? As the painstaking search of his office revealed nothing, then he must have had it somewhere on his person.

Percival didn't think so because when the Russian's clothed body had been recovered from the concrete, cleaned off and removed prior to the post mortem, any contents of his pockets would have been bagged, if there was anything. When he had first looked he found nothing at all, certainly no keys.

He had no objection, however, to Nelson having a re-check made at the store where bagged evidence was being held, and she lost no time in seeking permission for Beltrovich's suit to be re-examined.

Within thirty minutes she found herself in a temperature and humidity controlled room, plastic suited, booted and gloved like the custodian who brought a clear plastic bag containing the suit into the room and laid it on a wooden table.

He broke a seal and first extracted a slim record card from its interior which read "nothing in pockets" and a date. He added the words "examined with DI Nelson" and signed and dated it before carefully pulling out the light navy coloured two piece suit.

To ensure that the minimum amount of disturbance to the garment was made, to protect any evidential traces, only the worst of the wet concrete had been washed off and dried concrete made the material very stiff to handle with many bumps and lumps. With difficulty, together they examined and probed into all corners and crevices of the jacket's external pockets before turning their attention to those internally. Inspection of two large chest pockets and a small ticket pocket gave them nothing, then Nelson noticed at waist height close to the edge of the jacket, a well concealed zipped compartment which disclosed a small slim leather key wallet.

She unzipped it to find a desk key and a longer elaborately cut silver yale type key, neither of which had any markings.

But she was delighted. Her hunch seemed to have paid off

Chapter 27

Although the partnership of solicitors Devrille, Archibald & Armitage was founded in 1886 their strikingly modern offices in Red Lion Square near Holborn belied the firm's antiquity. The partner Tristram Ingram, whose well cut suit and polished Oxford accent reflected the sterling credentials didn't somehow He introduced himself to Percival and Riley as the partner who looked after Mr Beltrovich's legal affairs and after expressing his surprise and shock at his client's death, wondered how he could help them.

Percival explained that in the course of investigations into the death of Beltrovich, and his possible involvement in the disappearance of a valuable old painting, they had come across a reference in his accounts to a regular monthly payment authorised by Mr Beltrovich of £320 to your firm, who in turn, we understand paid a monthly bill rendered to you by a person or company for which we have only the initials 'NS.' We would ask you please, to give us the name and address of 'NS.'

Ingram looked at the two detectives for a few moments before responding. "Am I to understand that the information you are seeking from me, may help you to bring criminal charges against my client or rather his estate?"

"It is possible" said Percival.

"Then I'm not sure I want to co-operate at this juncture it may prove to be prejudicial to my late client's interests."
"I can get a warrant which will force you to disclose the information."

"Which I can oppose on the grounds that I have already stated, and that's going to delay your investigations if nothing else, which I guess would be very inconvenient to you. Look, I think we might resolve this in another way, would you excuse me for a few minutes" and Ingram slipped out of the door leaving Percival and Riley looking after him in some surprise.

A few minutes later a young woman hurried into the office carrying a piece of A4 paper with a few lines printed on it which she carelessly threw towards the desk in such a way that it fluttered down onto the floor, by which time she had already turned on heel and left the room.   Riley picked it up to return it to the desk and was struck by the first line in capital letters:

NS – NORTHAM STORAGE.
17, Chisholm Street, Finsbury Park, N4

"Hey boss, look at this" and as Percival leant across to look, Riley quickly wrote it down in his notebook.

"How extraordinary" exclaimed Percival "what next I wonder?"

Shortly afterwards Ingram returned and began by shaking his head from side to side. "I had the name and address of this company 'NS' looked up, and even had it typed out, but realised in all conscience I couldn't give it to you gentlemen. It could, in due course, lead to all sorts of legal complications. So, if you come across the name and address somewhere in the course of your enquiries – it didn't come from me or this firm. Do we understand each other?" With that he lifted the A4 piece of paper with the name and address and let it float again to the ground and with a cheerful "So sorry, goodbye," left the room.

His actions were quite clear to Percival and Riley. Ingram was willing to give them the information they sought, but for understandable reasons did not want him or his firm to be identified as the source. They let themselves out of the building, well satisfied with their visit.

As they were walking back to their parked car, Percival's mobile rang, it was Sheila Nelson to tell them that she had recovered two keys from Beltrovich's concrete-starched suit which she strongly suspected was precisely what they were looking for. One was a desk key and the other a Yale type although, sadly, there were no identifying marks on either.

Percival replied cheerfully that as they appeared to have now got the address of a storage facility in North London that Beltrovich had been paying for, they could hopefully match one of the keys to it. He gave Nelson the address and they agreed to rendezvous there as soon as possible.

Northam Storage facility was a mixture of old Victorian brick built factory buildings adapted to a new purpose and six blocks of modern steel buildings split into individual storage units of different sizes at the back of Chisholm Street. Percival and Riley arrived only a few minutes before Nelson and DS Price, and the four of them went into the small office situated in one of the old buildings where they met the manager, Giles Greville.

He was astonished and not a little daunted to be confronted by four Metropolitan Police detectives. Percival, however, quickly put him at ease and explained the reasons behind their visit. When he had finished Greville was somewhat confused.

"So, as I understand it, you have a key which you believe fits one of our hundred and four units but you don't know the number. Nor are you aware of the name of the person who is renting the unit and the bill is paid monthly on their behalf by a firm of solicitors – not that simple. But let's start with the key, may I see it please."

Nelson handed it over to Greville who examined it and commented "It certainly looks like the type of Yale double deadlock key that would be used to open most of our units, but as you see" pointing to the centre of the bow of the key, "the number has been ground out. Perhaps we'll have better luck in finding the name of the solicitors who are paying the rent, in our records."

Riley gave him the name and address and he excused himself to go into an adjacent office to use a computer. He was back in a few minutes to say that there was no sign in their records of a Devrille, Archibald and Armitage paying for a unit and he had gone back three years.

The four policemen exchanged disappointed looks before Nelson asked, "Are you sure that the firm's name has not got twisted round in some way like DA Armitage?"

"No, I'm afraid not, I've looked at all those sorts of alternatives. But look, we might be able to find the answer another way. Would I be right in thinking that secrecy is a big priority in disguising who the actual user is."

"You're right yes," said Percival.

"In quite a few cases," continued Greville, "the rental for a unit is paid for by a third party for all sorts of reasons. It could be relatives of people living abroad who have furniture and other belongings in store or it could simply be to add another layer of security and secrecy about the ultimate user by using another person, often a solicitor to pay the bill.

Some go further, and in such cases the solicitors will employ a third party to actually pay the bill, making it even more difficult to trace the identity of the user. I have three clients who pay in cash each month in advance through an intermediary."

"What sort of client would want to do that in this day and age" asked Riley.

"People who are VAT averse and deal a lot in cash transactions, like a small decorator who stores his gear and stuff in a small unit here, or a car mechanic who services or repairs your car at your home and again uses one of our units for storage and prefers to deal in cash. I've got four others who pay in cash – for whatever reason but they are all small firms and I just think it suits their business model re VAT.

But the fourth is a little unusual. My predecessor as manager several years ago converted one of the old Victorian single-storey buildings to suit the exacting requirements of two good clients. That left a strangely shaped space along the middle of the building lit only by a few rooflights and frankly not ideal for economic storage. Neither of the clients on either side were interested in taking it on and despite a bargain price he was not able to let the unit and it hung about unlet for months. Mind you, it is undoubtedly a funny shape.

"Then apparently a guy rings up looking for a unit around twenty five feet long and up to twelve feet wide and at the time we had nothing available but my predecessor half-heartedly described the odd shaped unit number E7, and the bargain price and the man expressed interest. He came in the next day to look and said it was ideal for his purpose - whatever that was.

However, my ex-colleague said that the man – a Mr Blake - had a number of requests. First he wanted to have mains electricity installed with a pay-in-advance meter put in near the front door – he would of course pay for any costs involved. He wanted to create a small lobby inside the front door so that the meter could be emptied etc. and have built a further security door beyond into the rest of the unit.

He would have special lighting and electric heating installed that could be dismantled and taken away when he wanted to give up the unit. Similarly he wanted to have a design team work to create a 'softening' as he described it, of the brick and plaster walls with fabrics to get the effect he wanted to achieve, here again these would easily be taken down when he vacated the place.

Whilst my colleague was considering what had been said, Mr Blake plonked down six months rental in cash - £1920, plus a further £500 for the installation of the electricity meter and any further inconvenience that may be caused.

That immediately made my colleague's mind up.   It was all a bit unusual, eccentric even, but nothing proposed would have a detrimental effect on the building which would be let at last!

He agreed and they shook hands, after which Mr Blake told him that after six months the rental would be paid in cash monthly in advance by an intermediary with the reference Blake E7.

"And that's how it has been every month now for several years. Would you like to have a look at Unit E7?" he finished.

"Yes please" said Percival "it sounds distinctly promising." Greville, opened a safe and took from it a small note book marked ' Codes - emergency use only,' and slipped it into his pocket. They then trooped across the area passing by several buildings before they reached the door to E7 which was in the centre of a solid brick building. Nelson produced her key which to general relief slipped into the lock easily and with two turns gave them access into a small lobby.

"Let's hope there's still some money in the meter" said Greville, as he went towards the light switch which he pressed and flooded the lobby with light. He took the notebook from his pocket and moved towards the other door where, on the adjacent wall, was a keybox which he flicked open to reveal a keypad and, consulting his notebook began to tap out the numerical code. He stopped after two digits as he realised the box was already open and on pressing the release button found that the compartment was empty.

"That's very careless" he said. "I let some electricians in to do some repairs two days ago and they left without putting the keys back in here." He pushed the handle of the security door, it was unlocked and swung open at his touch exposing an interior only dimly illuminated by a line of small roof lights and continued "Damn these electricians they didn't even have the courtesy to lock the doors behind them." He felt his way to the nearest light switch which lit up a corridor about ten feet long which then widened out before leading into a bigger area about twelve feet square.

The interior was draped in a matt-black, silk-like fabric that did not reflect the light. The whole space was furnished only with a black velvet upholstered, mahogany armchair on castors that sat in the wider corridor facing a wide five-sided, ten foot high column sited in the centre of the larger room at the end.

It was a strange sight with a rather funereal aura and as the five men made their way down the space, Greville switched on two further dimmer switches that directly shone spotlights onto the facing panel of the column, which on closer inspection had controls that allowed it to turn each of its five sides to the front.

DI Nelson spoke first "This is undoubtedly where Beltrovich held a stash of pictures that he had acquired by questionable means. He couldn't risk displaying them in the gallery at his house. No doubt he came to view them from time to time for his personal satisfaction and possibly showed them to potential buyers that he could trust" and then turning to Greville added "and it seems your electricians relieved him of the lot."

Chapter 28

Nelson demonstrated how paintings - framed or unframed - would have been attached to the various hanging devices on each of the panels, how the lighting could be adjusted according to the type and size of a painting, and the way the armchair could move on its casters from twelve feet away to within inches of a painting. Two temperature-controlled radiators together with equipment to ensure an even moisture level was maintained had been installed to keep paintings in the best possible atmosphere for their preservation despite the basic structure that enclosed them.

Beside the spaces provided for that number of paintings on the five-sided column, Nelson discovered an alcove behind the black drapery that provided a rack for a dozen more paintings, but they were also empty.

Meanwhile Percival and Riley were questioning Giles Greville. He told them that he had never been past the lobby of Unit E7 before and only held the keybox number in case an of emergency such as a fire in the building. Since he had been manager, he had never seen anybody entering or leaving Unit E7, on the other hand the site was open fifteen hours a day for unit renters' access and there was plenty of time in the evening up until 11pm for them to come and go.

He personally was there five days a week from 8am to 5pm. He employed two semi-retired night/weekend managers, both ex-policemen, one of whom would come in daily at 4pm and stay to lock-up the site at 11pm and alternate a Saturday and Sunday rota between them and cover for him when he was away during the day. In addition, a security firm had front gate keys and drove around the site several times between 11pm and 8am inspecting the outside of all units.

He had never seen the envelope containing the rental cash for E7 being delivered, it was invariably put through the letterbox in the evening.

Questioning then turned to the two 'electrician's' visit two days earlier. Greville related that they were both clad in blue overalls with the name 'Bridewell Electrics' emblazoned on their breast pockets and on lanyards that contained identity photos. They had presented themselves at his office and asked him to open the front door of Unit E7 for them so that they could carry out some repairs to the lighting. They produced a letter headed unusually 'From the office of John Blake" with an address on Piccadilly in the West End, addressed to Northam Storage and authorising operatives from Bridewell Electrics to be given access to Unit E7 to carry out lighting repairs, and signed by John Blake.

The men told him that they had been given the code to the keybox so they didn't require his assistance after he had opened the front door of the unit where he had left them. No, he had not seen their van which they'd parked elsewhere on the site, but they could easily have moved it up to the door of E7 and loaded up. He was not sure if he could identify the two men as he could not recall any outstanding characteristic of either, but of course he could try.

Greville was asked not to mention what had happened to anyone else and was asked to return to his office, look out the authorisation letter the men had brought, write out a summary of what he had just told the police and sign it. He was also asked to try to recall as best he could a description of the men. They would rejoin him there as soon as possible.

As she paused, DS Riley chipped in "I've checked, and as we expected there is no company operating as Bridewell Electrics."

"OK," said Percival "nor do I expect we'll find a John Blake having offices on Piccadilly, when Mr Greville produces the authorisation letter." He thought for a moment with furrowed brow before carrying on "Can anyone recall from discussions or reading through the files, who it was that the Italian police initially thought was responsible for the heist of the Tiepolo painting in Florence, until the mafia connection was discovered and pointed towards Bird and Beltrovich ?"

DI Nelson came in immediately. "That will be Roberto de Vincetti and you are right, he was the prime suspect and is still sought for questioning by the Italian police not least because he was responsible for abducting Mr Brookes and Madame Shawcross, but he has disappeared."

"That's the man," said Percival "do you think he is capable of finding out where Beltrovich was hiding the Tiepolo, here amongst other paintings, and organising the theft?"

"Based on his reputation I would say a definite yes to that" responded Sheila Nelson and I think perhaps Madame Shawcross might help us there. But how did the thieves get the code for the keybox?"

"They probably didn't have it" replied Percival "but with a good stethoscope in their tool box they could hear the tumblers fall as they rotated the dials, and if that failed I'm sure they would have happily smashed the box to extract the keys."

He remarked that they ought to have a word with the two ex-policemen who Greville employed as night managers as they may have seen or heard something useful, and asked his DS to get their details from Greville.

The four detectives went on to discuss the situation and their next moves in the investigation, before locking up and walking back to Greville's office. He had written and signed his statement which was lying together with the authorisation letter on his desk whilst he worked on drawings of what he could recall of the two men's features. Percival read through Greville's statement and Nelson looked over his shoulder as Greville worked on the portraits which were surprisingly good. When he laid down his pencil, the manager explained that he had thought really hard about both their appearance and demeanour and the harder he thought the more he remembered.

"This guy" he began pointing at one picture "was quite tall, certainly over six feet, rather swarthy and Mediterranean looking, but the thing I remember best about him was his hair. He was wearing a beanie but it was pulled well back on his head to show his black hair divided in the centre by a swathe of silver, almost white hair. That, together with his neatly trimmed moustache, and pointed beard, I recollect, leant him a rather devilish aspect. He never said a word, in marked contrast to the other guy" pointing to the other portrait "who did all the talking. Average height, a bit overweight, balding nondescript features and piercing blue eyes.

The only other thing I distinctly remember about him was a tattoo on the back of his right hand which was a serpent head with four tongues extending to the four fingers."

Percival heard the end of this description and came over to have a look. "Well, well, well" he said and chuckled "you've got him pretty well to rights - Ol' blue eyes Frankie they call him – although his real name is Walter Copp and your description of his tattoo was the clincher."

As the others gathered round, Nelson nodded her agreement and added "It's Frankie Copp alright. An intelligent, careful thief, mostly works alone, he's suspected of some remarkable heists of jewellery and objets d'art including paintings in a long career of villainy. But, through a combination of very careful planning, luck and good lawyers, the few prosecutions that have been brought against him have failed and other cases have never been taken to court through lack of firm evidence. I don't recognise the other guy though."

Nor did the others. Riley got the names, addresses and telephone numbers of the two night managers from Greville and as they were all about to leave Northam Storage the Police Forensic people arrived. As Percival and Riley let them into storage unit, Nelson and her sergeant left for Scotland Yard where they updated CDI Major. He immediately rang Marie and Simon at their hotel and invited them both to a meeting at

Scotland Yard the next day asking in the meantime if Marie could make some enquiries amongst her contacts to see if she could pick up anything in the light of the latest developments.

Next day as the meeting began Major handed copies of the portrait drawings that Greville had produced to Marie and Simon.

"These are the two men who gained entry to Beltrovich's storage unit and, we believe, took away not only the Tiepolo but a number of other paintings that Beltrovich didn't want to publicly display." As he was speaking they looked at the drawings and then at each other in astonishment. Marie found her voice first "This one" pointing to the picture of the bearded man, is without doubt Roberto de Vincentti, isn't it Simon?"

Chapter 29

"Now that is really a turn up for the books" began DCI Major. "Two arch-villains I would never in a month of Sundays have brought together, and yet it begins to make sense. De Vincentti, anxious to get his hands on the Tiepolo and having been denied in Florence, knows that Beltrovich had squirrelled it away somewhere in the London area. But, lacking the knowledge and contacts in this country de Vincentti no doubt made enquiries and turned up one of the best in the business, "Frankie" Copp, to help him achieve his goal. Which he did with extraordinary speed.

I know we have been concerned with a murder as well as in the recovery of the painting, but somehow Copp has managed to cut some corners and get to Northam Storage before us and we need to understand how, as well as finding both men and the picture."

"The only possible way to discovering where the painting was being kept, other than from Beltrovich himself, was through his lawyers, he had effectively covered his tracks in every other respect. That means Mr Tristram Ingram again," said DI Nelson.

"Not necessarily" commented Sergeant Price "someone on his staff could have the name and address of Northam Storage or have access to it, like the assistant or secretary who carefully dropped the information for us to pick up."

"Sounds a good line of enquiry to pursue," said Major who went on "but right now we must take steps to prevent the painting, and de Vincentti, leaving the country, if he has not already flown away with it."

DI Percival and DS Riley had now joined the meeting and were updated by Sheila Nelson. Major then went on to instruct the four officers involved to put out an alert, with copies of the portrait of de Vincennti, to all airlines operating flights from the UK to Italy to call in police and detain anyone answering that description. Similar requests were to be sent to all border control points, including cross channel ferry and train operators using the Channel Tunnel.

He doubted that de Vincentti would be parted from such a valuable painting because of its value and fragility and would probably take an additional seat for it or at the very least carry it on his knees for most of the journey by air or train and the operators should be informed accordingly.

He finished "Get on with that immediately please and then return here. You'll need assistance in getting it done quickly so use my name to get everyone available to pitch in."

When the four officers left the room Marie suggested that she used the next half hour to use her contacts to search for any reports or rumours that were circulating with regard to either de Vincentti or Frankie Copp.

The meeting reconvened forty minutes later when all the alerts with copies of the portraits had been put in place, and as she resumed her seat Marie had a smile on her face.

Major noticed this and asked her for an up-date and she responded "Yes, I've had some useful telephone calls. Before today I have not had a need to drop the names of de Vincentti or Copp into my conversations with UK contacts . When I did, not only was Copp's name well known, but to my surprise de Vincentti was also no stranger to many of my informants and had an unenviable reputation, even amongst shady dealers, as untrustworthy.

A previous association between the two men was not confirmed, but they had been seen dining together three nights ago. De Vincentti had apparently been in London for about a week, but was anxious to keep a low profile and nobody seemed to know where he had been staying. It is rumoured that he has suddenly left the country, one informant added a particularly intriguing morsel. He had been told that de Vicentti intended to go north aiming to catch a ferry to Ireland. Copp had dropped off the radar.

Major immediately ordered a double check to ensure that all passengers leaving from Fishguard, Holyhead, Liverpool and Stranraer to Ireland – North or South, were monitored against the pencil portraits of de Vicentti and Copp. Similarly, checks were redoubled at all airports with flights to Belfast or Dublin.

The meeting went on to review progress on building up the case of abduction and theft against de Vincentti so that he could be formally charged, and they also looked at the case against Bird. In neither case, despite the strong circumstantial evidence and some witness statements, did they feel confident of everything holding together in court yet.

DS Riley reported that he had made initial contact by phone with the two night managers at Northam Storage, one of whom seemed a bit edgy when he mentioned Unit E7.   He was seeing them both that afternoon.

After the meeting, Simon left for a lunch appointment with an old friend and Marie returned to their suite at Grosvenor House. As she pushed open the door she sensed there was somebody in there and called out "Hello" before letting the door close behind her. There was no reply and she walked on into the sitting room where a man rose from an easy chair levelling a gun at her. He stood in silhouette with the brightly lit window behind him so that she could not recognise him until he spoke.

"Excuse the manner of my visit Madame but I wanted a private word with you or Mr Brookes very urgently and this seemed the best way of getting to you without broadcasting my presence and leaving quickly after I had asked you both a very specific question."

Marie responded "No Mr de Vincentti, I do not excuse the way you have broken into our rooms and threatened me with a gun whatever your reason. Kindly leave now."

De Vincentti lowered the gun before continuing "Yes, I'm sorry for showing you this but you will, I'm sure, appreciate that at present I have to be very careful, and again my apologies for upsetting you, but I do need an answer to my question, from which both you and Mr Brookes can benefit."

Marie her anger subsiding, was intrigued "Well you can ask your question but I'm not guaranteeing an answer," and promptly sat down. "Good" said de Vincentti and also sat down without being invited. "My question is simple yet at present hypothetical.

What if the painting 'The Last Supper' alleged to be by Tiepolo, and owned by Mr Brookes was suddenly to be returned to him and no questions asked or sought ?"

"Would he agree on his word as a gentleman, to sell the painting to me, Roberto de Vincentti, a recognised art dealer, for £11 million – a figure that is at the highest estimate of what it would reach at auction, as you and Mr Brookes would recognise. This would also avoid him the bother of arranging for auction and the heavy auctioneers fees that would arise."

Without displaying the extraordinary surprise that she felt at this piece of blatant opportunism and effrontery, Marie responded calmly "So you are admitting that you have the painting in your possession?"

"No I am not, as I said it was a hypothetical question – a 'what if', if you like."

"But then, you will have taken all the risks involved in breaking in here just to ask a hypothetical question – I find that hard to believe."

De Vincentti smiled and continued "Believe it or not, I am here and looking for an answer to my question."

"I can't speak for Simon, he would have to consider his own response hypothetical or not, but I will pass the question on to him. However, even if he agreed to your proposition, it would not stop there. The police would continue their investigation and inevitably charge you with theft and the insurance company would look for recompense for the costs involved in their enquiries, even though there was no pay-out for the loss of the painting."

"Yes," said de Vincentti "I realise all that, but the police have nothing at present to substantiate their surmise that I have any involvement in the matter. I am just seeking the answer to a question which you have kindly agreed to pass on to Mr Brookes and please ask him to ring this number with his decision." He placed on table between them a card. "He just needs to tell me 'yes' or 'no'. If it is 'yes' he will be contacted."

He got up from his chair "And now I have to become thoroughly unpleasant again because I have to get away from here with at least a twenty-minute start and that means I'm afraid I shall have to use these." He produced a pair of handcuffs and led her firmly to a chair beside a radiator where he snapped them onto her wrists and around a pipe leading from the heater.

"I hope you won't be too uncomfortable for a while Madame, but you will understand my caution" he took something else from his jacket pocket and turned his back on her as she retorted "Well I can't say I'm happy about being left like this but as you have the upper hand I can't do much about it."

He turned to face her again with a length of duct tape in his hand and quickly put it in place across her mouth "Sorry about this but I can't have you shouting your head off when I leave. Thank you for not being difficult, and I look forward to hearing from Mr Brookes. Good-bye now Madam." He bowed and placed the handcuff key on the table before leaving.

Marie was not one to give up easily and accept that she was stuck in this situation for hours until Simon returned. She looked around for possibilities. Could she pull on the handcuffs in some way to loosen the pipe and/or the radiator? Experimental pulls showed that in her awkward position it was impossible to put much pressure on the pipe.

Pushing the back of the chair against the wall repetitively only made a slight sound that nobody would pay attention to, and anyway it was on an outside wall. It looked hopeless but then a thought occurred to her.

Her chair stood adjacent to a window, in front of which was a semi-circular rosewood table bearing a vase of flowers and a telephone. If she stretched out her arms and slid her legs across the space she might just be able to hook a foot or at least a couple of toes round the nearest table leg and pull it towards her. Her aim was to kick the vase out of the way and pull the telephone so that it fell onto the floor. She pushed off her shoes and moved painfully to try and execute her plan, and got into position, but the table didn't budge. She needed a better purchase on the table leg and that could only be done by bringing her other foot into play which was going to be difficult as she would need another two or three inches.

So far, she had used the chair to support her neck as she moved her legs and feet and the only way she could gain that extra length was to turn over and lean her wrists and forearms on the chair and feel with her feet to hook round the chair leg. It was both painful and exhausting as she tried several times to move the table and was on the point of giving up when she made one last extra hard pull and tipped the table so that the vase and its contents fell with a loud thump and splash to the floor.

Marie turned over to look and saw that the telephone had moved nearer on the table. She saw that it now might be possible to pull the telephone off the table using her hooked toe technique if only she could reach up there. She just managed to do that by kneeling on one knee whilst holding onto the chair side and letting the other leg and foot do the careful manipulation. It worked and the receiver and cradle crashed down next to the chair.

Her plan had worked and the means of communication lay at her feet – but she couldn't get at it with her hands tied and in her situation it was impossible for her feet to lift up the receiver. She looked down at it for inspiration and remembered that it was the '0' button for Reception, and if she managed with that very clever big toe of hers to press that button, she couldn't speak obviously but she could make a loud humming noise and keep knocking the instrument against the chair leg that might hopefully bring somebody up to investigate.

It all went well, and she was delighted to hear the receptionist's voice as he repeated several times "Reception. Hello" as she hummed as loud as she could and constantly made a noise against the chair leg, until he gave up and disconnected.

Exhausted through her acrobatic efforts and frustrated that she still couldn't make contact with anybody Marie knew that her best chances were still with people in Reception and that she must find a method of getting them to send someone up. First of all, she needed to make any noise she could organise louder and clearer in its purpose.

After thinking for a few minutes, she reached out with a foot and managed to roll the heavy vase towards her and retrieved one of her shoes in the same way. Then she manoeuvred the phone receiver in such a way that its microphone was just inside the wide end of the trumpet shaped vase. She slipped on her shoe and began experimental tapping with its heel on the outside of the glass, a sound which was magnified by its shape. She practised tapping out three short, three long, three short sounds – S.O.S. in morse code – it was very tiring on the leg muscles so she repositioned herself so that the tapping foot was partially supported by the other foot.

She rested for a few minutes before toeing the '0' button and when Reception answered began tapping the signal reinforced with her synchronised humming.

After a few 'hello's' the receptionist realised that help was required and within a few minutes, to her enormous relief, Marie was released and was on the phone to DCI Major.

Chapter 30

"How long is it since de Vincentti left you at the hotel?" asked Major. Marie initially thought it had taken her strenuous efforts ages to get free, but concentrating her mind, realised it can't have been much more than ten to fifteen minutes and said so.

Major thought that gave some hope that they could find him still in London and alerted all concerned with the search. One patrol car went to look at the recent cctv pictures at Grosvenor House Hotel's entrances. From Marie's description of what he was wearing they soon picked the Italian out leaving the entrance, walking to an adjacent car parked on Park Lane and being driven off.

It was a distinctive two-tone blue Range Rover which had set off in the direction of Hyde Park Corner although at this stage it was not possible to see the number plate clearly. However, DCI Major had immediately requested and been granted the power to 'hook' into and trace back pictures from cctv cameras in much of London including those overlooking the Hyde Park Corner roundabout. These not only showed the Range Rover turning into Grosvenor Place but displayed the rear number plate so that it could be read easily and noted.

Guessing quickly that the car was heading over the Thames, the tracers followed its route to Vauxhall Bridge Road and into South London. There, the multiplicity of possible roads that the car could have taken defeated them and it was going to need a much more detailed examination of all these before they could follow his trail through cctv.

Time for a quick reappraisal, as the police tracing via cctv were already about twenty minutes behind the Range Rover's actual journey. Meanwhile DVLA had found the registered owner of the car was a Michael Marchant with an address in Blackheath near Greenwich in south London – maybe that was where they were heading. A police car was quickly diverted there to find nobody at home, but a helpful neighbour volunteered the information that 'Mike' also had a cottage and a boat near Oare on the River Swale in Kent.

When that information reached Major and his team, they realised it was likely that was where Marchant and de Vincentti were heading.

Some of the team now concentrated on finding out more about Michael Marchant, his cottage and the type of boat he had. The tracers, with plenty of time in hand, hooked into cctv gantries or bridges overlooking both the M2 and A2. The Range Rover should be passing under one or the other shortly if their hunch was correct, and this should confirm that Oare was the destination. They also had a view through cctv at Junction 6 on the M2 where Marchant would turn off and into the town of Faversham where the car would have to pass-by en-route for the riverside at Oare. A message was sent to the Kent Police to appraise them of the situation and to request that any sighting of the Range Rover by their patrol cars was reported but not to intervene at this stage.

Unfortunately, this last interchange of messages between the Metropolitan Police and Kent Police was carried out on the 'open' police wavelength and as a precaution Marchant had put a radio receiver in the Land Rover tuned in to that wavelength precisely to pick up any police interest, and so he was immediately aware of what they were doing. He was on the A2 and immediately turned off at the next junction leading to Gravesend and pulled into a side road shortly afterwards.

"Bugger it" he said, "the police are on to us Roberto, you heard the broadcast messages." De Vincentti replied through gritted teeth "Yes, how did they find us so quickly I wonder and what do we do now?"

"They got lucky, I guess. But look we'll have to dump the Range Rover here and get a taxi or hire a car."

"But they'll be watching for us at Oare so we can't go there now, where do we head for?"

"You're right. We need to completely re-plan," said Marchant "I need to make some phone calls and consider our options. I'll just get out of the car for a while, you stay here Roberto and keep your head down and listen in to the Police waveband, I'll be as quick as I can."

After some intense phone conversations over the next ten minutes, as de Vincentti watched Marchant pacing up and down, he got back into the car.

"Right, it's all arranged but I'm afraid it's going to cost you another thou" he began looking at his companion for confirmation.

De Vincentti nodded his assent "if it gets me away it'll be worth it."

"A friend is taking you over the Channel in his boat which is moored at the harbour in Ramsgate and will drop you off on the other side as we had planned, near Boulogne. But first we need to get a train from the railway station up the road here in Gravesend to take us to Ramsgate. The trains run every hour and take about an hour and a half, so with luck it will still only be late afternoon when you set off from Ramsgate harbour".

"Now" he went on, " I'm taking a bit of a risk and driving us to somewhere nearer the station, it's only about a mile or so away and I'll park unobtrusively and pick the car up later this evening. The chances of us being spotted by the police are very low as they are looking elsewhere. It's too far to walk, and phoning for a taxi will take too long."

De Vincentti responded as they drove off "It sounds good, thanks Michael for the trouble you've had making these new arrangements. By the way you'll be interested to learn that there is now some confusion listening to the police radio because they had expected before now to get a sighting of this car on the A2 and are now hoping to spot it further on that road or the M2." They looked at each other and smiled, feeling safe for the moment.

Marchant managed to park between two vans in a line of cars lining a short street barely a hundred yards from Gravesend railway station. Then. wheeling de Vincentti's suitcase, they were quickly on the platform awaiting a train to Ramsgate due in ten minutes, ready prepared with coffees and sandwiches to consume enroute because neither of them knew when their next meal would be.

At Ramsgate it was an easy walk to the harbour where Marchant's friend Gary was awaiting them. Introductions made, he took them aboard his sizeable motor-yacht 'Moonbeam.' He made coffee and poured a shot of rum each whilst they confirmed de Vincentti's destination on a chart and concluded financial arrangements. De Vincentti paid out substantial sums from a stash of fifty-pound notes that he held in his suitcase, to both Marchant and Gary.

Followed by de Vincentti's profuse thanks Marchant left the 'Moonbeam,' helped cast her off and waved as the boat made its way slowly past the line of other boats in the marina, out of the harbour into the open sea, bound for France.

Back at Scotland Yard, some of Major's team, including Percival and Riley were awaiting an up-date on the Range Rover's progress along the A2. The plan had been that they would move off to confront and arrest the two men at Oare, their expected destination, after the local Kent police had detained them both at the holiday cottage.

However, the confirmation never came, no other sighting was reported and Kent Police patrols back-tracking on the roads towards London saw no evidence of a breakdown or accident involving the Range Rover, which had disappeared from sight.

Percival was the first to comment "Marchant has given us the slip. There is no other way he can drive to Oare excepting along the roads that were being watched, so he must have planned to mislead us by seeming to head that way and then changed direction, possibly south towards the channel ports. Alternatively, he has somehow learned of our surveillance – which is highly unlikely."

"I doubt that he will be heading for Dover or Folkestone or any other port with a ferry service serving the continent" commented Major "as he would know that we would be watching all those and the small airports in the southern counties, but nevertheless we should alert them again" and he told one of his staff to see this was done. "In the meantime, we should ensure that Kent and Sussex Police patrols are aware that he may be heading their way."

Simon returned from his rather long lunch to find Marie still both excited and exhausted from her efforts earlier and anxious to tell him of what had happened. He expressed both annoyance and anger at de Vincentti's effrontery and concern at the possibility that Marie had been hurt, but she brushed away his concerns as she continued her story. She explained how she had managed to release herself and communicate with reception, which he found difficult to understand until to his astonishment she was able to demonstrate her various moves and footwork.

When she had finished, he swept her up into an embrace that seemed to reflect his love and frustration at not being to hand to save her from her ordeal "I'm so sorry darling" he kept repeating.

When they had both recovered themselves, he said "I assume you have told the police, Percival or someone?"

"Oh yes, as soon as I was free, I spoke to Major and told him everything that had happened, that must have been the best part of an hour ago."

"What did he say?"

"Oh, he expressed concern of course, asked how long it was before de Vincentti left me and then quickly ended the call to "take swift action" but said he would be back."

Simon went on "Did he say anything about de Vincentti's question?"

"No, he was keen to get on and would come back."

"So how do you think I should respond to his question, darling?".

Her reply was interrupted by the phone ringing, it was reception saying that DCI Major from Scotland Yard – talk of the devil – was downstairs and wanted to see them both. She invited him to come up to their sitting room.

For the second time within a few minutes, Marie was to describe and demonstrate how she had freed herself from the restraints that de Vincentti had imposed on her, and Major congratulated her on her ingenuity.

He went on to say that that he hadn't a success story to relate and told them in some detail how the police had picked up de Vincentti on cctv about fifteen minutes after he left the hotel getting into a car and had traced the car to a Michael Marchant who had a cottage and large motorboat at Oare on the River Swale. A sighting had confirmed the car was heading out of London in that direction, but the car had been lost on the A2. Either the two men had guessed they were probably being tracked and deliberately misled their pursuers by suddenly changing direction, or they just got lucky, either way they had, for the moment avoided the net closing around them.

There was silence when he had finished his report until Simon said quietly "Frustratingly close."

But Marie had been distracted by something Major had said and asked "Was it Michael Marchant you mentioned that was the car and boat owner? Only it's a name that rings a faint bell."

"Yes" responded Major "do you know him from somewhere?"

"I'll just look through some notes on my ipad that should help my memory" said Marie getting to her feet and walking through to the bedroom.

Major then turned to Simon "I'm sure Madame Shawcross has passed on de Vincentti's question to you.   What may I ask, is going to be your response assuming that you are going to reply that is?"

"He's asked for just a one word response - yes or no - but we all know it's not as simple as that. You must be close to charging him with the theft of the paintings from the storage unit."

"Yes, we are moving in that direction but it's complex because nobody has claimed that the paintings have been stolen from Beltrovich as yet. Remember he kept them well hidden, so nobody knew for certain that he had them in his possession, and he can't answer any questions. In addition, your painting has been stolen twice, the robber robbed so to speak, and in those circumstances the law is not clear on a number of issues. But I expect you are wondering whether in dealing with him you would be putting yourself in danger of being complicit and at risk of being charged with that offence.

I can only say at this stage possibly. It depends how it is handled."

"So what is your advice, how should it be handled?" asked Simon.

"The fact that you have a line of communication open to him shouldn't be ignored I believe but before I make any suggestion, what do you think of the price he is offering of £11 million for your painting?"

"Well it's on the higher end of the speculative figures that have been mentioned should it go to auction and after auctioneer costs and VAT have been taken into account. I have to say that I wouldn't be unhappy at being paid a net £11million particularly as it has not been formally recognised yet by the Tiepolo committee as genuine."

"OK" continued Major "then I suggest you reply "Yes, to the question, adding two more words 'to discuss' that should encourage him to come back."

"And if he does…. Where do we go from there?"

"Ask him, if you agree to his terms, when and how he proposes to return the painting and how the transaction will be made, and the money paid over. Encourage him to open up."

At that moment Marie returned to the sitting room "encourage who to open up?" she asked.

Simon explained what they had been discussing and asked her opinion, to which she replied, "It seems a good way forward and keeps the ball rolling, I agree," and turning to Major "I have looked up Michael Marchant in my notes. I do know him slightly if it's the same man.

About ten years ago in France - we were living near Cannes at the time - he tried to sell my late husband a boat.

Several things made us suspicious of him, not least that he was not actually the owner. I only met him once and the lasting impression was a charming conman but as twisted as a corkscrew. Quite a suitable companion for de Vincentti I would have thought."

Chapter 31

Michael Marchant had dinner in Ramsgate before taking a train back to Gravesend station and then walking to his parked car. He was disappointed but not surprised to see that the space next to his Range Rover was now occupied by a police car and as he approached a policeman got out and asked, "Are you Mr Michael Marchant, sir?"

Having replied in the affirmative, he was told that he had been observed earlier in the day in the company of Roberto de Vincentti whom the police were actively seeking. The policeman went on to ask where de Vincentti was now and Marchant replied, "I have no idea." He was asked to follow the police car to Kent Police headquarters at Northfleet, just five minutes away, for further questioning. Shrugging his shoulders resignedly, Marchant got into his car and let the policeman into the front seat beside him before following the police car to Northfleet.

As luck would have it, DI Percival lived in Sidcup and he had just returned home when the pursuit of Marchant and de Vincentti had been called off. The police car driver in Gravesend had called in to say that they were bringing in Marchant for questioning and the duty sergeant had in turn phoned Percival, who immediately left home for the twenty minute drive to Northfleet.

During the drive in Marchant's Range Rover, the policeman accompanying him noted that on the floor behind the front seats was a scanner radio capable of picking up police, ambulance and fire service communications and reported the fact when they reached police headquarters. The report was passed onto DI Percival together with other information when he arrived a few minutes later.

Marchant was sipping a cup of tea when Percival joined him in an interview room and thanked him for coming into to answer a few questions.

"A!ways happy to help when I can" came Marchant's smug response.

"Do you mind then if I record our conversation?" asked Percival,

"If you find it necessary, not at all," agreed Marchant and looked on as Percival fiddled with the switches and then began "Do you know Signor Vincentti well?"

"Not well, but I have known him for some time" admitted Marchant. "This morning you were seen in your Range Rover parked, illegally on a double yellow line, outside the Grosvenor House Hotel on Park Lane for some minutes until Vincentti left the hotel and got into your front passenger seat before you drove away, is that correct?"

"Yes."

"If you didn't know him that well, how was it that you were prepared to wait outside the hotel and then drive him across London?"

"Yes well, it was a bit strange the way it happened. Out of the blue he rang me at home yesterday and asked me to do him a favour. He wanted me to pick him up from an hotel in Bayswater where he was staying, drop him off at Grosvenor House and pick him up there about twenty minutes later. If he was longer than that and it was difficult to park, he suggested I circled the block, but it wasn't necessary."

"Couldn't he have just got a taxi?"

"I had the very same thought, but he anticipated me by saying that he would have a large suitcase with him which had valuable contents and he did not wish to lug it into taxis or leave it unguarded in an hotel. He would happily leave it in my car whilst he was in the hotel, after which he wanted me to drive him to somewhere in Kent but didn't at the time specify where. As he was prepared to pay me handsomely, in cash, for helping him out I was very happy to agree."

"Do you know what he was doing at the Grosvenor House hotel?"

"Seeing somebody, he said."

Percival changed the subject abruptly "I understand you own a cottage at Oare in Kent on the River Swale, where you keep a powerful boat moored." Marchant gave his first sign of discomfort before he replied "Yes to both, although I wouldn't describe my boat as particularly powerful."

"Isn't it the truth that your original destination with Vincentti was to Oare to reach the boat in which you were prepared to carry him to France?"

"Good heavens no," interjected Marchant, but Percival went on. "Until you or Vincentti, using the radio scanner that is sitting on the floor at the back of your car, picked up messages that showed that the police were already tracing your progress and were correctly anticipating your destination. Then you changed course and drove to Gravesend Station where you caught a train together to Ramsgate, so my colleagues have been reliably informed by the station staff."

Marchant was clearly shaken by how far the police had got towards the truth in their observations, enquiries and deductions. However, he decided that a spirited offensive would serve him best, firstly in challenging their assumption that he had initially been headed for Oare, and secondly by agreeing that the police were right in certain limited respects, thus establishing him as a mere dupe in another man's plans.

He began "You're wrong. At no time was Oare mentioned between myself and Vincentti, he merely told me to head down the A2 and then onto the M2. I thought he wanted me to take him to Dover or another channel port. He had the scanner radio with him when I picked him up in Bayswater and he tuned it in to listen to police messages directly after leaving Grosvenor House.

As soon as he realised you were onto him and the car, he told me to turn off the A2 and head for Gravesend. He had me park near the Railway Station where he opened his suitcase and paid me from a wad of notes he had in there, and a further amount to cover fares because he insisted that I catch a train with him to Ramsgate where I would leave him."

"Was he meeting someone in Ramsgate" asked Percival.
"I don't know. He didn't share his plans with me" Marchant replied.

"So you didn't introduce him to anyone in Ramsgate?"

"No, we shook hands at the station, and I wished him good luck and caught a train back to Gravesend to pick up my car. The rest you know."

Percival looked questioningly at Marchant and commented "It seems very strange to me that having insisted that you travel with him to Ramsgate he says goodbye and you caught the train back to Gravesend when he left the station. Are you sure?"

"Absolutely. No wait - I'm wrong in saying that. Of course, I went into a restaurant near the station and had a meal before catching the train back."

"Have you got a copy of the bill?"

"No. But it'll be on my debit card account" and he proceeded to open the bank app on his phone and scrolled to an item for Ristorante Verona timed at 19.17 and dated that day, which he showed to Percival with a flourish.

Percival glanced at it and commented "Either that was a very long meal or you went somewhere else, before going into the restaurant, bearing in mind the time you arrived in Ramsgate on the train. Is there anything you would like to change or tell me Mr Marchant about what happened today" said Percival tapping his pencil impatiently on the desk.

"No, I think you've got everything that I know" he responded.

Percival terminated the interview but warned Marchant that he would have more questions for him, before they both left the police station.

* * * * * * * * * * * * * * * * * * * *

The destination of Gary's Moonbeam was a small inlet near Petit Fort-Philippe about twelve kilometres from Calais, where a small jetty made a quick landing possible without getting feet too wet.

Whilst the boat made its way across the English Channel, de Vincentti took his large suitcase into the cabin, opened it and laid out the contents. The first layer consisted of neatly stacked blocks and rolls of £50 and £20 notes and a similar quantity of 50 Euro notes, interspersed with padding provided by articles of clothing. Lying beneath these was a substantial metal framed navy blue backpack that occupied the full width and more than half the height of the suitcase. De Vincentti carefully unzipped the main compartment of the backpack to reveal an oblong flat package wrapped around with several layers of bubble wrap that had been nestling in a surround of clothes.

He cursorily examined this and then laid it aside as he changed out of his suit, shirt and tie into a brushed cotton shirt, pullover, waterproof trousers, woollen socks and stout walking boots, all out of the backpack together with a waterproof jacket and a beanie with a light at the front. All the remaining clothes, including the rolled up suit, went into the backpack surrounding the package and the rolls of money. He took the empty suitcase on deck and tossed it, open, into the sea where it quickly sank from sight.

As the Normandy coastline hove into view, Gary was careful to keep well away from the Calais approaches and, consulting the charts made his way to the little inlet where the faint moonlight illuminated the old jetty. He was able to bring the boat alongside and after a quick handshake de Vincentti was able to scramble onto it.

As the Moonbeam swung away and around heading out into the channel, he walked along the jetty onto the sand and then up and out of the low sandhills towards the main road, the very picture of a hiker walking the Normandy coastline towards Dunkirk.

Chapter 32

A meeting was convened in DCI Major's room at New Scotland Yard the following morning. DI Percival was able to update everyone on his conversation at Northfleet the previous evening with Michael Marchant. He was convinced that Marchant knew more about de Vincentti's present location, and that he had probably introduced the Italian to someone in Ramsgate who had taken him to somewhere in France or Belgium, although at present it was pure surmise and enquiries were on-going.

He added that, although Marchant strongly denied that the original plan was to take de Vincentti to Oare and then use his own boat to spirit the Italian over the Channel, he was unable to explain the presence in his car of the radio scanner tuned to police messages.

It was through this, he surmised, that they had almost certainly learned that the police were on to them, and the change of their plan. Marchant was also unable to explain his pointless rail journey with de Vincentti from Gravesend to Ramsgate if, as he insisted, they parted company at Ramsgate railway station.

Major remarked that Kent police had a team questioning people around the station, the harbour and the town centre in Ramsgate about a man pulling a large suitcase behind him around the time de Vincentti was there, but so far there had been no reported sightings.

Simon said that he had tried several times to get a response on the mobile number that de Vincentti had given Marie, but each time, so far, the call had gone to voicemail. As the meeting concluded he tried again, and this time got de Vincentti who merely said before quickly ending the call. "OK, I will be in touch shortly. I am no longer in England, be prepared to travel."

As Simon related the one-sided conversation, Major commented that it was as expected. De Vincentti, if he was to be believed, was now somewhere on the continent probably making his way back to Italy with the painting. He asked Simon, when he received the next contact number, to come back into Scotland Yard so that they could attempt to trace where the mobile was being used when Simon rang it, as had happened before. He agreed.

When de Vincentti pressed the button to end the call to Simon he was sitting on a bed in a Lille hotel where he had stayed overnight, and was about to leave. The previous evening, he had walked just over a kilometre inland from the coast to the junction of the D119 and D940 not far from Gravelines, where he had arranged for a taxi to pick him up and take him to Lille.

In the morning, whilst settling his hotel bill in cash, de Vincentti enquired where the nearest car hire offices were and walked a couple of hundred metres to find it.

There was a reluctance at the car hire firm to accept cash rather than a credit card, but as he was able to produce an Italian identity card and a driving licence (in a different name of course) they acquiesced.

He was soon on his way driving south for two days, through France and over the Alps into Switzerland and then into Italy and down to Bologna, where he returned the hire car and continued by taxi to a nearby village where he was currently living with his wife, in an isolated old farmhouse.

Having briefly relaxed, showered and changed, he lost little time before taking the bubble-wrapped package into the converted barn that he used as a studio/office. Carefully stripping away the packaging and padding he looked closely at *"The Last Supper"* painting and frame to check that it had suffered no damage on its travels. It was immaculate and he gazed in wonder at the artistry of Tiepolo (for surely there could be no real doubt, he felt, that it was the work of the master).

Covering the painting with a cloth he pulled back a curtain to reveal a concealed door which he unlocked, and walked into a small room that was environmentally controlled and placed the Tiepolo on a display stand with several other paintings before leaving the room, locking the door behind him.

From a bottom drawer in his desk he then pulled out a new packaged "burner" mobile phone, noted the number and sent a message to Simon Brookes asking him to ring that number the following day around 10am. For the next hour de Vincentti spent his time thinking through and then making arrangements for a brief meeting with Brookes. He would show him the painting, as he would, no doubt, require, and agree the choreography of payments that would follow.

Within one month of their meeting, he planned to pay Brookes the £11 million agreed and at the same time Brookes would pass over all the details of the provenance of the painting that he had researched.

De Vincentti then rang a wealthy collector in Monaco to assure him that he was now in possession of the Tiepolo, and received confirmation that the collector was still happy to pay him the previously agreed figure of Euro 13.5 million for full legal ownership of the painting and later its provenance.

Delivery of the painting would be made to him in Monaco in exchange for a payment by money transfer to be made in de Vincentti's presence. The provenance details would follow within the next fortnight. In this elaborate way all parties' interests would be safeguarded and he would have been paid before he had in turn to pay Brookes. This would leave him a commission of nearly one million Euros on the deal if everything went according to plan. It gave him a warm glow of satisfaction at the thought.

Meanwhile the Kent Police team had received three confirmatory sightings of two men, one pulling a large wheelie suitcase, getting into a taxi outside Ramsgate station at the appropriate time. Two further witnesses a few minutes later had seen the men getting out of a taxi on the harbour wall road near the East Pier.

One of the witnesses, who had been walking around the harbour wall, was particularly useful. He had paused to look out over the moored boats, saw the taxi draw up and the two men emerge, one of them trundling a big suitcase down an access slope to the gangways between moored boats.

He watched with interest the rather unusual sight of two smartly dressed men, neither seemingly sailing types, hauling this unwieldy case past two side gangways before choosing one that led to line of some larger boats, one of which they clambered aboard.

This witness had then continued his walk, returning the same way about half an hour later and glanced down to see one of the men, without the case, leaving the boat and walking slowly back along the gangways towards the harbour wall.

He then saw the man turn and wave, as the boat that he had just left emerged from the line, turned and went past him, slowly making for the harbour entrance and the English Channel beyond.   After watching its progress for a few minutes, the man had climbed up the ramp onto the harbour wall road, and continued walking back towards the town.

All the descriptions tallied, the timings were consistent and a taxi driver from a firm just by the railway station was found, who confirmed he had taken the two men and their case from the station the short journey to the harbour wall road and was able to give a good description of both men which confirmed that they were indeed de Vincentti and Marchant.

Marchant had lied to Percival as he had suspected, and he had some explaining to do. Armed with the Kent Police report. Percival and DS Riley immediately drove to Marchant's home in Blackheath. The door was opened by an attractive, smartly dressed woman who looked to be on her way out. In answer to Percival's polite enquiry as to whether Michael Marchant was at home, she had replied with another question "Who's asking?" On seeing the warrant cards and the recital of their names, she shrugged and queried "What's he been up to now?"

Before they had a chance to answer she carried on "Well I'm his wife and in a rush, he's in his office," and indicated a door off the hall before ushering them inside and then going out of the front door which she closed behind her.

Percival tapped on the door, and they went in to find Marchant sitting in a easy chair reading the morning newspaper. As he lowered the paper there was no disguising the look of shocked surprise that appeared on his face as he immediately recognised the Detective Inspector, but he quickly assumed his semi-jocular manner. "Ah Inspector" he began "some more questions?"

"Yes Mr Marchant. We're sorry to disturb you but since I talked to you yesterday, several things have come to light about which seem to be at variance with what you told me, and I would like you to explain."

"Yes of course, do sit down gentlemen. Can I get you something – tea, coffee? "

"No thank you sir" Percival replied and both he and Riley opened notebooks as he went on. "You told me that you left de Vincentti at Ramsgate railway station having travelled on the train with him from Gravesend, yet you were both seen getting into a taxi together with a suitcase, outside the station by several witnesses, and a cab driver described you both perfectly as fares that he took down the road to the harbour. There you were witnessed walking down the ramp into the marina with de Vincentti, him pulling the wheelie luggage, along the gangways between the boats and then both getting on board one of them. Is that what happened Mr Marchant?"

There was silence as Marchant stared down at the carpet before answering "I shall say nothing more until I have my solicitor present."

"Michael Marchant I am charging you with aiding and abetting a man actively being sought by the police on a serious criminal charge and of obstructing the police in the course of their duty. I must also warn you that anything you say." He carried on with the formal police warning, ending with "You will accompany us now to the police station for further questioning and your solicitor can join us there."

It was at breakfast time, five hours after dropping de Vincentti on the Normandy coast, that Guy Brodie on 'Moonbeam' re-entered the harbour at Ramsgate and slipped into his mooring. He had only eaten two chocolate bars in the last few hours to accompany numerous cups of tea and coffee and his mind was set on a full English breakfast in a harbourside café before doing anything else. However, it wasn't to be.

As he walked to the top of the ramp by the harbour wall, he was accosted by a young woman whom he vaguely recognised "Good morning, it's Mr Brodie of "Moonbeam" isn't it? I'm Jean from the harbour master's office and I walked across when I saw you coming in, as I wanted a word."

"Yes Jean, what can I do for you?" asked Guy.

"The police came here last night enquiring for you and your boat, or rather they wanted to know who was the owner of the boat that was usually moored in your space. Apparently two men were seen late afternoon or early evening walking along the gangways and then getting onto your boat.

One of them left, but the police said the other stayed aboard and shortly afterwards you slipped your moorings and went out of the harbour.

Of course, we had to give the police your name and address as owner of the boat, but I thought you would like to know, as we promised to give them a ring when you came back in."

Although he was far from happy at the news - the last thing Guy wanted at the moment was questions from the police - he managed to summon up a smile as he thanked Jean, and she walked back to the harbour office. He stood for a moment considering his options, should he take the boat out again and moor up somewhere along the coast until he had time to think and perhaps organise an alibi of some sort?

Going home was clearly not an option for the police were probably already there. Probably his best move now was to drive out of Ramsgate, stop somewhere along the coast, get his head down for an hour or two – he was suddenly conscious of feeling quite exhausted - then think about his situation over a meal. He started to walk in the direction of the boat owners' car park and suddenly wondered whether there was anything compromising left on the boat. and hurried back to check.

There was an exchange of emails with Marchant on his ipad that he often left on board, so he picked that up and then spotted a marked-up chart of the waters and inlets on the Normandy coast which he burnt in an ashtray and shook the ash overboard. Looking round he couldn't see anything else on board that would connect him to Marchant or de Vincentti and quickly left, thinking the police could arrive any moment.

He half ran, half walked to the car park with a very fast heartbeat and was sweating with tension and the exertion when he collapsed into the driving seat of his car minutes later.

He sat there for a short while regaining his composure before setting off, driving inland seeking a suitable spot off the main roads where he could pull over, and have some necessary sleep. He found the perfect place, stopped, and was fast asleep within seconds.

Chapter 33

DI Percival put his phone down onto its rest and swung round in his chair to talk to DS Riley who had just walked into the office "That was Kent police, they've pin-pointed the boat owner in Ramsgate who gave de Vincentti a lift, presumably to France, last night. The harbour master's office confirmed that the boat was back at its moorings early this morning and they went along to see the owner but there was nobody on board and he was not at his home address in a village a few miles inland."

"Did they give you his name?" Riley asked.

"Yeah, Guy Brodie."

Riley thought for a moment and went on "Does he have any form, did they say? Only the name seems familiar."

"Suspected of people and drug smuggling but nothing on the books."

"Will we pay him a visit?"

"When he turns up, but for the moment he has gone out of circulation. They'll give us a bell when he has been sighted.

How did your interviews with the two ex-coppers, turned Northam night managers go?" Percival asked.

"Extremely well with one, with the other nothing of note. I discovered they were friends, both ex-Sergeants with the Met, both retired in their late fifties and then joined different private companies in charge of security. Then when they turned sixty, one of them learned about the part-time jobs at Northam which appealed to both of them for different reasons, and they applied and got the jobs.

"One of them, Adams, is a bit of a plodder - incurious, unimaginative. He does the job by the book and never asks questions. He was a real contrast to his colleague McDowd – as bright as a button, very curious and keen to know what was going on. Thanks to him, I think we might very quickly learn how de Vincentti and 'Frankie' Copp got ahead of us in finding Beltrovich's storage unit."

"Go on" said Percival "I'm fascinated but get to the point."

"Yes, well, McDowd is a very social person, talks to anybody and everybody. He catches a Mr Evans some months ago dropping the month's rent for Unit E7 through the office letterbox one evening, as was his practice. They get into conversation and find that they were both ex-coppers, Evans was not his real name, it was actually Charlie Cleaver, and he did confidential stuff including private enquiries and the like for the solicitors Devrille, Archibald & Armitage

The two of them became friendly and Cleaver always brought his rental envelope in at times he knew Dowd was working and other times when he was passing by so that they could have a cup of tea and a chat together. "They were inveterate gossips and the link that had brought them together, Unit E7, was a subject that often beguiled them. They were curious who actually rented the place –Cleaver was never told, he was merely the rent deliverer in this case. Dowd had never seen anyone enter or leave that unit, indeed only once had he seen into the entrance lobby when he had let the electricity meter man in. Why was there so much secrecy and extra security involved they both wondered?

"Then one evening when doing his rounds, Dowd spotted someone approaching the door of E7 searching his jacket, presumably for a key. Dowd turned his torch onto the man asking if he could help. The man turned full face before holding his hand up to prevent being bedazzled, but it had given Dowd an opportunity to see him clearly, not that it meant anything to him at the time. The man thanked him and said no help was needed as he found the key, bent down to unlock the door and went in.

"A few weeks later the papers and tv news were full of the story of Beltrovich's death and Dowd recognised him from his picture as the evening visitor to E7. He did wonder momentarily if he should tell the police but couldn't see the relevance of the visit to their investigations. He didn't tell anyone except Charlie Cleaver and his colleague Billy Adams, neither of whom expressed more than a passing interest." He finished with the comment "But it's who they might have mentioned it to that would interest to us now boss, don't you think?"

Percival agreed, and asked Riley to go back and see Billy Adams again and get him to search his memory for any occasion since Dowd had told him about Beltrovich and Unt E7 that he had mentioned it to anybody else. Percival would do the same with Charlie Cleaver.

Percival contacted Cleaver by phone at the solicitor's office in Red Lion Square and was surprised to learn from him that, prior to Dowd's discovery, he had never known that Beltrovich was even a client of his employers and wisely, had not spoken to anybody at the firm, or elsewhere about him.

Riley found it was a different story with Billie Adams. After Dowd had told him, he had returned home to join his wife and daughters celebrating the youngest's seventeenth birthday with cake and prosecco. The daughter had invited her boyfriend to join them before the two of them went out to celebrate.

Adams made no bones about not liking the boy, not just because of his rather bumptious and superior manner but from a few enquiries that Adams had made about him, his associates were certainly not amongst the most desirable. However, his daughter was keen and as he had no desire to cause divisions in the family, he said nothing, but it led to awkward silences. It was to fill one of these that Adams, catching sight of a picture of Beltrovich on a muted tv playing in the background, related his colleague's discovery about the mysterious occupier of Unit E7 at Northam.

Riley picked up on Adam's remark about the boyfriend's undesirable friends, asking who they were, and learned that they were members of a notorious East-End gang. Armed with that information and the boy's name, Riley was able to dig further. Apparently, for several days after Beltrovich's disappearance and before his body had been found, rumours were circulating amongst London's criminal fraternity about a reward of £20K being available to anyone who could come forward with information about where Beltrovich kept his secret stash.

It could not be coincidence that the boyfriend came into possession of a brand new sportscar at that time. Riley pulled him in for questioning and his suspicions were quickly confirmed, and it was finally made it clear how de Vincentti and 'Frankie' Copp got to Unit E7 before the police.

Although it was now apparent that de Vincentti was somewhere on the Continent and had already made contact with Simon Brookes, Percival and Riley were keen to tidy up matters with regard to Michael Marchant, who had declined to answer any further questions without his solicitor present. A decision had to be made on the charges, if any, that could be successfully brought against him in a court of law.

They had deliberately delayed calling him to a further interview since it had been discovered that Guy Brodie was almost certainly the man who had taken de Vincentti to France in his boat. Although Brodie had since disappeared, the two detectives waited in the hope that he would soon turn up, so that during their next visit to Northfleet, they could include an interview with each of them.

Guy Brodie was still shocked that the police had so quickly got on to him and had no wish to be interviewed until he had sorted out in his mind just what he was going to say to them so, he had driven to his eldest sister's home near Brighton to stay a night or two and consult.

If he thought that he was going to get any sympathy he was wrong, she and her husband urged him to go to the police even if it risked landing him a prison sentence or at least a hefty fine.   The longer he left it the worst it would get, they insisted. So he made his way back to Ramsgate and went into the police station, and made a statement to the duty sergeant.

He then waited for twenty minutes and was then asked if he could make his way the next morning to police headquarters at Northfleet for a formal interview at 9 am.

Promptly the next morning he sat down in an interview room opposite DI Percival, DS Riley and a DI Warren of Kent Police who formally charged him with illegally conveying a man sought by the Metropolitan Police on various charges in his boat to France where he assisted him to land without passing through French immigration control, customs or security.

Percival and his sergeant were now only interested in tying up the loose ends and getting any useful information on de Vincentti's present whereabouts, leaving the Kent police to go forward with any charges that it would be appropriate to bring against Brodie. Percival began by saying that they had a full confession from Michael Marchant which included bringing de Vincentti to Brodie's boat in Ramsgate harbour where he left him. "Marchant watched" he said "as a few minutes later you cast off and went out of the harbour and into the English channel.

"Now" continued Percival "describe what happened from thereon."

"Not much" began Brodie "it was an easy crossing, light winds mostly cloudy but some moonlight. I steered well clear of any other boats and put him ashore near Gravelines."

"Did anyone meet him?"

"I didn't see anyone. But I heard him on his mobile making arrangements for a taxi to pick him further inland near a road junction from what I could make out."

"Did you talk to him much?"

"Very little. I tried to make conversation several times but he always ended it quickly."

"So, he didn't tell you anything about his plans, where he was going and so on?"

"Not a dicky-bird."

Percival persisted "So there you stood on deck, side-by-side peering ahead into the gloom without a word exchanged between you for hours?"

"Well not quite, he spent a good deal of time down in the cabin" replied Brodie.

"Doing what?"

"Well, some of the time he used to change out of his suit into hiking gear and boots and repacking everything into a large backpack. He slung the suitcase into the sea. The rest of the time down there he seemed to be reading a book. Oh yes, he made tea and coffee a couple of times, and produced tinned tuna sandwiches with some rather stale bread that I had on board. "

"So, it was neither an enjoyable or an entertaining voyage?"

"You're right. I only learnt one thing from him in one of his few sentences - that they don't make spaghetti bolognaise in Bologna they always use penne or something similar."

"Why did you take the job?"

"Because I was very well paid."

Quite sure that they had nothing more to learn from Brodie, Percival and Riley left the interview and went on to another room to interview Michael Marchant and his solicitor. They had made certain beforehand that Marchant knew that Brodie had made a full confession of his part in the business and that much of what Marchant had said was shown to be false, so he had decided to tell the police the truth about what had happened without reservation.

Nothing more was to be gained from Marchant that would help them in their continuing enquiries so both the policemen were happy to leave the formalities to their colleagues in Kent police and make their way back to London and new developments.

Chapter 34

Over breakfast, Simon's mobile phone pinged with a message from de Vincentti which gave him a number to ring "between 10 and 11 GMT tomorrow." He immediately rang Detective Superintendent Wilkins at Scotland Yard who asked him to come into his office at 9 am when he would arrange to track the call and hold a meeting of everyone concerned in the investigation, for an update.

At the start of the meeting, Wilkins introduced everyone to Police Commander Tom Hadfield. He had briefed the Commander on the twists and turns of what was proving to be a very complex case involving murder, abduction, assault, misrepresentation and the theft of a valuable Italian painting.

So complicated had the story become, he felt sure that he had inadvertently omitted important facts and developments in the telling and that it would be advantageous for everyone involved if he were to summarise what had happened to date. Questions could be asked where clarification was needed, errors or omissions could be corrected, and points enlarged upon. Much of the investigation work, he said, had fallen on DI Prentice and DS Riley who had done an exemplary job and he was sure would correct or amplify his summary.

He began "Some weeks ago an old friend of Mr Simon Brookes here called Peter Bird, died and left to Mr Brookes in his will a 1920's oil painting depicting a smiling girl in a garden. Attractive, but of little value. As it was of no consequence in the value of the estate, Peter Bird's sister Yvonne, an executor, handed over the painting to Mr Brookes after the funeral service and he decided to get it reframed as the picture was set into an ugly oversized frame.

The frame maker discovered, hidden behind the girl painting, a much older picture believed to be by an Italian master Tiepolo. If authenticated, this would be worth at auction, many millions of pounds.

Mr Brookes took advice and had the painting examined by experts who verified from scientific tests, that it was very likely by Tiepolo but that there were significant gaps in its provenance that would be detrimental to it gaining the necessary verification from the Committee on Tiepolo that sat in Florence. Mr Brookes set himself the task of doing the research to fill in those gaps and I gather has been quite successful." He lifted his eyebrows in question at Simon who nodded his assent.

"At the point when Mr Brookes was doing his research in Venice, his companion was shot at in mistake for Mr Brookes and badly injured. The gunman had been hired indirectly by someone in Australia. Ultimately this led the Australian police to suspect a Mr Timothy Bird, brother of the deceased Peter and Yvonne. It seems that Tim, reported to be a rather unbalanced and erratic man at the best of times, was so incensed when he learned that his brother had 'given away' this multi-million pound painting in his will, that he had a knee jack reaction to eliminate Mr Brookes or at least injure him. At the same time, he instructed solicitors to challenge his brother's will on the grounds of his mental competency, as he had just been diagnosed with early Alzheimers at the time the will was drawn up."

He went on "His case was complicated somewhat by the cryptic content of a letter, written by Peter Bird to Mr Brookes at the same time as his will, that inferred that he knew of the old painting hidden in the frame, without actually spelling it out. However, brother Tim was confident that he would get the will overturned and that he and his sister would become owners of the old painting. It seems that he then became obsessed with getting his hands on it as soon as possible, so that he could start negotiations with potential buyers.

Amongst those that he approached was Dimitri Beltrovich or his agents the Belvoir Syndicate, probably the latter, as Beltrovich rarely negotiated questionable deals at first hand. Anyway, Bird obtained a verbal commitment from or on behalf of Beltrovich that he would pay Bird half the valuation figure (expected to be about £12.5 Million) and moreover once the painting was delivered to him, Beltrovich agreed that he would hand over to Bird an advance of £4 Million plus his expenses in obtaining the painting. How this was to be done was left to Bird.

Through mafia contacts in Italy, Bird was put in touch with a clever thief – Antonio Castelini - with whom he drew up an ingenious and elaborate plan to bring the man currently in charge of the painting, Jeremy Idle, to Florence with the painting. Castelini, with accomplices, planned and executed its abstraction from the hotel strongroom and safe, and then its delivery to Bird who brought it back to England.

"However, unbeknown to Bird and his associates, there was another party interested in nabbing the painting should the right opportunity arise. Roberto Vincentti, a shady Italian dealer in fine art who had a particular interest in the Tiepolo painting, used his contacts and informants to keep him au fait with what had happened to the painting since its re-emergence.

The scientific testing, Mr Brookes research on the provenance and then the news of Idle's invitation to Florence. He immediately put two of his men into the hotel where Idle was to stay and the painting to be held secure, because he felt it might present a good opportunity to appropriate it, and was preparing a plan accordingly, not realising of course, that the Bird/Castelini scheme was already underway and worked perfectly as the Italian investigation has uncovered.

"De Vincentti was furious and tried to find out who had foiled him and now held the painting. He even stooped to abducting Mr Brookes and Mrs Shawcross in his efforts to find the perpetrator. In the meantime, Bird returns to England with the painting and brings it to Beltrovich who, we are reliably informed, welched on the deal that he had verbally agreed, and insisted that he was prepared to pay Bird only £2.5 million in full and final settlement, and that was to include all the money that Bird had paid out to set up the elaborate heist in Florence.

"Understandably, Bird was very angry but as he couldn't immediately do anything about it, he picked up a suitcase ready packed with the £2.5 Million and left Beltrovich and the painting behind. Bird is not, as we have realised, a man likely to forget or forgive easily and through an acquaintance with an East End gangster, the notorious Atkins, he immediately made plans to have Beltrovich abducted, and killed. The body was buried in concrete on a building site.

"However, Bird could not find out where Beltrovich had hidden the painting, despite his best endeavours. In that search he was beaten by his rival Vincentti who discovered and gained access to a storage unit on an industrial estate that Beltrovich had secretly rented to store some of his paintings. Vincentti stole the Tiepolo, along with several other paintings and left an empty unit.

Since then, we understand that he has escaped to France." Rather breathlessly he ended "I realise that I have left out a lot of detail but is there anything else of importance that should be mentioned?"

Most of those sitting around the table shook their heads, and made comments such as "excellent review," " good summary" or the like. DI Percival came in with "there are updates that I have reported on in writing to you sir, which may not have reached you yet."

Invited to give a verbal report, Percival told the meeting about his interviews with Marchant and Brodie and that that it had now been left to Kent police to make decisions on any prosecutions that would follow.   He then turned to the discoveries that he and Riley had made as a result of questioning the night managers at the Northam unit storage site that revealed how de Vicentti got ahead of everyone, including the police, in discovering where the painting was hidden.

DI Sheila Nelson had been keeping a watch on the progress of the action that was being taken by Timothy Bird in the

Chancery Court Division to overturn his brother Peter's will. She explained that Mr Justice Morris had called in the papers prior to a court hearing and was holding a meeting in chambers with legal representatives the next day. This may mean that he does not recognise that there are sufficient grounds so far put forward, to justify a full court hearing about overturning of the will and will dismiss the claim, but she said, we awaited his ruling.

DCI Major of the Serious Crime Squad reminded everyone that the investigation into the abduction and murder of Beltrovich was still ongoing.

The detectives who were working alongside DI Percival were steadily building a case around the involvement of Sid Atkins and his gang in both incidents but were still not able to "close the circle," largely because Tim Bird had not been found yet, although he was still believed to be in the UK.

After further discussion, Wilkins suggested that as it was now after 10am Simon should ring de Vincentti on the number that he had provided, with all the tracing equipment in position.

After only two rings the phone was answered – "de Vincentti."

Simon responded "Brookes here, good morning."

"Listen carefully," said Vincentti, "I shan't repeat as no doubt, you'll be looking to prolong our conversation and get a trace. To see the painting, catch the 9.50am flight from Heathrow to Guglieimo Marconi airport Bologna, next Tuesday the 22nd on your own. You will be met. No police." After 21 seconds the call was terminated.

Wilkins broke the silence "Well it seems he's back in Italy. Do you still wish to go Mr Brookes?"

"Yes, I want to see the painting is undamaged and discuss the price, but above all, it surely provides an opportunity for him to be caught."

"Good, and you're right of course," responded Wilkins "it should give us the best chance we have at present with our Italian colleagues to nick de Vincentti. But it needs careful planning, as he will certainly have his eyes peeled for any sign of a police presence. All that presumes he is in Bologna and it isn't a blind."

Percival chipped in with "Well on that point, Guy Brodie, the man who took him over the channel in his boat, only remembers one topic of conversation that de Vincentti seemed interested in, and that was the city of Bologna. He waxed lyrical on its attractions, history and food – to the point of Brodie's boredom. But he sounded like a proud resident."

Wilkins said "Bologna seems to be the place to start then. Does anyone, Mr Brookes and Mrs Shawcross in particular, know whether the jurisdiction of the Italian policemen Ricci with whom you worked in Florence extends another 50 kilometres north to Bologna?"

Marie responded "I'm sure it would as he is with the Carabinieri Art & Antique Unit and their remit covers the whole of Italy. Because he is familiar with case and knows de Vincentti it would be advantageous to have him 'back on board', so to speak. I'll begin my own enquiries through my Italian contacts to see what they can turn up about de Vincentti's current movements."

A tap on the door brought in a member of Wilkins' staff to say that the trace on the phone call got them as far as northern Italy towards Bologna but the call was terminated before they could get any closer. Still, it strengthened the feeling that they were starting in the right area.

After the meeting broke up, Wilkins asked Simon and Marie to stay behind whilst he phoned Ispettore Superiore Ricci in Florence to let him know that 'the caravan' had moved back to Italy, to update him on events and to set up a joint operation to hopefully, apprehend de Vincentti and recover the Tiepolo.

Chapter 35

As there were developments in the case which Marie was investigating in France, she decided to go back to Paris for a few days, hoping to join Simon later in Bologna or Florence after his meeting with de Vincentti. She and Simon left Grosvenor House Hotel together, she to take a taxi to Heathrow and a flight to Paris, he to Paddington Station and a train to Gloucestershire and on to his cottage for two or three days.

He planned to visit Benjamin Burns, still recovering at home from the injuries he had sustained when he was attacked. Police enquiries so far had found out nothing about the attackers or their purpose, but Simon was convinced that it was connected to the Tiepolo discovery and somebody seeking more information at the behest of Bird or de Vincentti.

As circumstances had changed, the police no longer believed that Simon himself was under threat, which was a relief. The local Gloucestershire police, during his absence, had continued to keep a regular watch on his cottage and a patrol car seeing the lights were on during his first evening at home had stopped to check all was well. It made him think momentarily of the arrangements that were being made by police in London and Italy in connection with his planned meeting with de Vincentti.

DCI Major had said that he would not be given any detailed information on police plans. He had just been told that he would be under surveillance from the moment of his arrival at Heathrow, going through immigration and security checks, onto and during the flight as well as when he arrived at Bologna. All in case someone made contact with him at some point en route. The general opinion was, however, that de Vincentti would get a message to Simon at Bologna airport sending him elsewhere to be picked up or asking him to ring a number. It would not be straight forward, that was for sure.

On the Tuesday, Simon arrived at Heathrow in good time, and went through the usual procedures, then waited around drinking coffee and reading the paper until his flight was called. All this time and during the flight he looked around now and again to see whether he could guess who was watching him, but of course it could be anyone.

Walking through Customs and out into the main concourse at Bologna airport, pulling along his wheeled suitcase, Simon looked along the line of waiting drivers and greeters displaying names but Brookes was not amongst them. He walked on slowly and then heard his name as part of an announcement coming over the public address system. His Italian was not up to understanding the context but fortunately the message was repeated in English – "Would Mr Simon Brookes travelling from London please come to the Alitalia desk on the main concourse."

He could see the Alitalia sign only twenty metres away and made his way over. He introduced himself to a girl behind the counter showing her his passport for identification purposes, and she handed him an envelope with his name written on the front.

He tore it open and took out the single sheet of paper on which was typed:

'Welcome to Bologna Mr Brookes, I look forward to seeing you.   Please carry on to your hotel – The Holiday Inn.   You will be contacted.   R.de V."

Simon thought it was quick work for de Vincentti to find his hotel booking, as he'd only made the reservation a day before. However, he needed to let his surveillance team know what the message left by de Vincentti was, without letting any other onlookers know. The instructions from DCI Major had been explicit - "after you have been contacted, if you wish to pass on a note or have a very quick word to one of our team go to the men's toilets on the concourse. Our man, in a light grey suit will be beside the third wash basin as you enter. Keep nil eye contact. If you have to speak, be extremely brief, three or four words. If passing a note leave it so he can see and pick it up quickly and unobserved. Take great care".

Simon carried them out to the letter. He wheeled his suitcase in front of the first basin, a light grey-suited man was washing and drying his hands two basins away. Simon, having observed nobody else approaching the line of basins, feigned a slight trip over his case which brought him adjacent to the other man to whom he said "Whoops. Sorry." Then he dropped the crumpled de V letter from his hand, between them. It was quickly picked up unobserved, and the man moved swiftly away. Simon caught a cab from the airport to the Holiday Inn and awaited de Vincentti's next move.

It came within the hour in the form of an envelope pushed under his door. Simon moved quickly to look into the corridor, but it was clear.

The note inside was brief merely telling him to phone a particular number, which he did immediately and recognised de Vincentti's voice answering.

"Now what?" began Simon.

"I think you have disregarded my warning and have brought in the police" said de Vincentti.

Simon who had become irritated by de Vincentti's evasions and high-handed manner, felt that an aggressive response was called for and replied "What nonsense. Look de Vincentti, I'm getting tired of being messed about. Understand this, if you don't show me the painting, and quickly, the deal is off."

There was silence at the other end, then de Vincentti, obviously feeling wrong-footed by Simon's words said "OK. I'll be back later with the arrangements for our meeting" and rang off.

Bologna is renowned for the number of excellent restaurants it has in and around the city, and Simon had spent some time reading about them before selecting one that was quite close to the hotel and booked for dinner. His mobile rang when he was still eating his delicious starter.

"I hope you are enjoying your dinner at *Il Cavaliere Verde* – an excellent choice," said de Vincentti "I'm sorry to interrupt and so late, but I have now completed the arrangements with the minimum of necessary security. A car will pick you up at your hotel at 10am tomorrow morning. Is that OK?"

"Yes. Fine." Simon replied and returned to his meal with relish.

Back at the hotel at 10.15pm precisely there was a tap on his door and through the spy-glass Simon saw a bar waiter carrying a silver tray on which was a cut glass tumbler covered with a napkin and a matching jug holding water and ice. Simon opened the door to hear him say "Buona sera signore," and then in heavily accented English "Your Talisker single malt whisky, where shall I put it down."

As the door closed behind him his manner changed as he asked "Has he been in touch?"

Simon told him quickly about the two calls and the arrangement for the morning, by which time the waiter was back at the door which he opened and whilst backing out bowed slightly and said "Grazie mille signore."

Simon was a few minutes early as he stood in the morning sunshine to the right side of the front of the hotel, remembering the last time he stood waiting for a car from de Vincentti with Marie in Florence. That had led to their abduction but with a happy ending, he smiled at the recollection. The meeting today would, he knew, be quite different, and quick. An examination of the painting, a discussion on price, possibly an exchange of documents and a quick departure, de Vincentti would not wish to hang around.

His thoughts were interrupted by a taxi sweeping by others and stopping immediately in front of him. The driver got out and opening the rear door said "Mr Brookes, sir," and ushered him inside.

"Are we going far?" asked Simon.

"No" came the accented reply "I take you to shop, you walk through to back door and get in another car, OK?"

"OK" replied Simon, knowing he would have to put up with one or two quick changes designed, no doubt to foil any following police.

A minute or two later they pulled up in front of a department store entrance which stood in the middle of a long line of shops and cafes. The driver leant back to release the car door which swung open for Simon who left with the words of the driver in his ear "Straight through to back, quickly please."

Once through the store doors it opened out into a much larger space than would be imagined from the outside, with many departments, displays and side passageways leading to them, but the way ahead was wider and less congested as he strode through the considerable length of the building to a rear entrance. Another taxi stood, with its engine running immediately outside. The driver beckoned and asked "Mr Brookes?" Simon nodded and as he got in noticed that on either side of him the road was fully blocked by large trucks – no doubt a further ruse to mislead or delay any followers.

His taxi turned ninety degrees up a narrow service road and sped away. Twenty minutes later they were in a smart residential area and came upon the entrance to a public park of some sort with ornamental gates outside which the taxi stopped. The driver opened the passenger door and indicated that Simon should walk through the gates to a "castle with a café, go into café. He is there. I will wait" and pointed up the pathway where he could see beyond a slight rise, the roof of a building with an abundance of turrets – almost Disney-like thought Simon.

As he crested the little hill Simon could see that the main building was some sort of Gallery or exhibition space to the right of which was a café.

There were very few people about, mostly couples but Simon spotted three men standing about or leaning against a wall as he went into the café. He had been seen because de Vincentti walked between the tables towards him, with a hand outstretched in greeting and a smile on his face.

"Good morning Mr Brookes. Not too uncomfortable a journey this morning I trust."

Simon ignored his hand and returned "No problem so far." De Vincentti gestured for Simon to precede him through into a curtained off private area where a table was set with coffee cups and a plate of pastries. They sat down and de Vincentti pulled over a case that was lying on an adjacent table. "And so to business Mr Brookes" he said unzipping the case, but stopped as a waitress came through the curtain with a large pot of coffee.

Having poured a cup for each of them and proffered the dish of pastries, de Vincentti completed his unzipping of the case lid and out a painting covered with a cloth which he pulled back with a flourish to reveal the *Last Supper* which he passed to Simon for his examination.

It looked just as he had last seen it, not damaged or marked in any way, and he remarked "It is nice to hold something as precious as this and know that it belongs to me even though it is not in my safekeeping." He paused and went on jocularly "In spite of my feelings towards you de Vincentti, I can't help admiring your colossal nerve, supposing the police were to arrive here any moment?"

"But I know they won't," said de Vincentti, "when you entered the first taxi you were checked for any wire or tracer.

"Also, any tails were lost when you entered the second taxi. So, they haven't a clue where you are."

Still holding on to the painting Simon said "When you abandoned Madame Shawcross at Grosvenor House in a very cruel situation – for which neither she or I will forgive you – the message you left for me indicated that as part of the overall deal you would hand back the painting to me as rightful owner, if only for a short time, no doubt to add an air of legitimacy to our transaction."

"Yes, I'm sorry I had to leave Madame like that, but of course I had to take necessary steps for my own safety, and you are right I did intend to pass the painting into your keeping as a gesture of good faith on my part. However, I have had to reconsider and regret that the risks of letting you take it away are now too great, but you have seen that the picture is in the condition that you last saw it, undamaged in any way, and I hope that is sufficient?"

All along Simon had found it hard to believe that de Vincentti would release the painting to him when it came to the point, so it was with the comment "I thought as much" that he handed it back to de Vincentti. He put it back in the case which he rezipped and pushed further back on the adjacent table. He then picked up a briefcase that lay beside it and placed it on his knee, took two sips of his coffee and then turned to Simon "So, are you happy to proceed?"

Apart from a reservation on the suggested price and subject to hearing how he was going to handle payment arrangements, Simon agreed to go ahead "in principle."

De Vincentti reiterated the point that £11 million net would be paid to Brookes without risk or encumbrance, represented a better deal to him than going to auction.

Whilst Simon might have got £12 or £12.5 Million at auction, this would be subject to the deduction of auction costs and VAT for something that at this juncture was not recognised by the Tiepolo Committee as genuine. Simon argued that more recent estimates of the painting's price at auction suggested a figure in excess of £14Million, which suggested that he should receive a figure of about £11.5 Million.

De Vincentti admitted that he had already agreed a figure at which he would sell the painting on to a private collector, and this inhibited his ability to negotiate with Simon. However, after much haggling they agreed on a new compromise figure of £11,250,000.

De Vincentti then went onto to detail on how payment and exchanges would be made, to which Simon agreed. Two copies of a previously drawn up Agreement were then produced by de Vincentti, amended, then signed by both parties and witnessed.

As they both stood and shook hands on the deal, Simon looked at his watch. Despite the haggling, it was barely fifteen minutes since they had sat down. They exchanged a few words more and then left the café, de Vincentti was joined by two other men and walked round the back of the building, whilst Simon walked down to the gates where the taxi was still waiting and took him back to his hotel, where an old friend awaited him.

Chapter 36

As Simon left the taxi and walked into the hotel lobby a figure arose from a sofa on one side and greeted him:

"Hello Mr Brookes. It's nice to see you again, even though we are back with the same problems, recovering your painting and arresting de Vincentti." said Inspettore Superiore Ricci.

Simon shook his hand enthusiastically and "Good to see you too back on the case. Quite a lot has happened since you were last involved."

"Yes I've had some long zoom calls with Detective Chief Inspector Wilkins who has brought me up to date. A couple of his people are now working with our team – DCI Percival who I gather has played a leading role in the UK Investigations and DS Price of the Met Police Art & Antiques unit.

We found where de Vincentti and his wife had been living in recent times, an old, isolated farmhouse in a village not far from here. However, when our men surrounded the place the birds, as you would say 'had flown,' and we are actively trying to find him."

Ricci went on "Of course we followed discretely after you were picked up from your hotel, but as you know, they had blocked the way around the back of the shop you went into and we lost you entirely. We had originally contemplated using a drone to track you from above but as soon as Vincentti or his accomplices had spotted it they would undoubtedly have aborted the meeting, which would not have helped. So, Mr Brookes tell me about the meeting and how you got on."

Simon suggested that they adjourn to the bar, and they sipped their drinks whilst he described his journey to the park with the café and told Ricci all that had happened during his conversation with Vincentti, including the deal that they had struck on the painting. Ricci made notes and asked a number of questions. He also asked after Madame Shawcross and was pleased to learn that she would be flying in to join Simon in Bologna the following day as her business in Paris had been concluded quickly, and they planned to spend a few days in the city.

The following morning Simon hired a car and drove out to Bologna's airport to meet Marie off her flight from Paris, planning to take her for lunch at a renowned restaurant in the countryside a few miles outside the city.

Later that morning a lady presented herself at the Bologna Holiday Inn reception desk asking for Marie d'Albeigne-Shawcross to be told that she had not yet booked in but was expected any time as she was flying in from Paris. After showing the receptionist her passport that recorded her as Giulietta d'Albeigne-Knox and persuading the girl that Marie was her stepmother and that she could be trusted with a key card, she went up to the second floor in the elevator and entered the suite.

Walking through into the small sitting room she was taken aback to see a young woman was sitting there in an armchair, who was equally surprised.

Recovering first, Giulietta said "I think there is some mistake. This room is reserved for Madame d'Albeigne-Shawcross I believe."

"Yes. I'm sure you're right."

"Then who are you and how did you get in here?"

"I'm Viola Brookes, Simon Brookes' daughter. I think this suite must be booked in both names as the man on reception was happy to give me a keycard so that I could wait for him in here."

They laughed as Giulietta had a similar story to tell. They shook hands and Viola explained that she lived in Australia and was attending a scientific conference in London. She had had a free day and on the spur of the moment decided to fly to Bologna where she knew her father was staying, hopefully have dinner with him and fly back that evening or early the next morning. At the same time, she wanted to have a look at this woman that her father was spending so much time with.

Giulietta began to laugh again before commenting "Two minds with but a single thought. I live in New York and came to Rome to see some clients. I thought I would take the opportunity to see my step-mother who had told me she was staying in Bologna for a few days and it's a quick flight, so here I am. I'm also keen to meet this man who she seems completely enamoured with, Simon Brookes – your father."

As it was now lunchtime, they decided to go down to the restaurant for something to eat, leaving a note on a table in case Simon and Marie returned.

It was a great surprise for both of them to walk into their suite a little later and find who was waiting for them. There followed much delight in introductions, laughter and conversation before they went out for a celebratory, high-spirited dinner together.

Viola was going to have to leave mid-dinner to catch her plane back to London, but between them Simon and Giulietta, rearranged matters so that Viola travelled on Giulietta's later flight to Rome, stayed overnight and flew early the next morning back to London. That evening, by the time they reached Rome they were firm friends and both gave a thumbs up to the relationship between one's step-mother and the other's father.

It was a couple of days later that Simon learned from Detective Sergeant Price that Tim Bird's plea to the Court of Chancery to overturn his brother's will had been rejected by the judge in chambers before the case even came to court. Simon's solicitor had claimed that Bird's claim was very unlikely to succeed but, nevertheless, Simon was pleased that his ownership of the Tiepolo was not now legally in doubt. Confirmation by letter from the solicitor followed a few days later.

As there was nothing to keep Marie and Simon in Bologna as the search for de Vincentti and his wife went on, they decided to take a few days in a leisurely drive north to Milan then down to Verona, Padua and up to Castelfranco in the Veneto before turning east to Venice, where Simon was keen to do further research on the provenance of the Tiepolo painting to try and fill in some gaps.

Even though he had agreed to sell the painting, Simon wanted to pass it on with as complete a provenance as possible. He believed that de Vincentti could be found and arrested at any time and the painting recovered, but it was still important to have the best provenance. They told Ricci about their plans, and he promised to keep in touch with them if there were any significant developments.

It was a couple of days later that Simon received a panicky call from Yvonne Simmonds, Tim Bird's sister. Bird had written to her a rambling, and in places unintelligible letter in which he made it clear that he held Yvonne responsible for giving away the old painting, and Simon for not relinquishing his bequest. There followed vague threats against both of them for denying him his rightful ownership. The ruling of the judge in Chancery had made him angrier than ever.

Yvonne was very conscious of the strange behaviour of her brother in recent weeks and had begun to wonder whether he had become mentally disturbed. Her husband had persuaded her to contact the police about the letter and her concerns. He was still, of course being sought by the police but they promised her that they would redouble their efforts to arrest him and would help her with her security because of the threats. Yvonne was anxious that Simon should know of the threats against him as soon as possible so that he could take precautions. Simon told her that he was in Italy at present and unlikely to be at much risk, however, he would inform the police in both Italy and the UK and thanked her for her warning.

He spoke to both Ricci and Wilkins in London the same day and told them about the call, and Wilkins commented that he thought Yvonne Simmonds was probably right in her suspicion that her brother was mentally disturbed.

Wilkins had always thought that Bird's reactions to events had not always been those of a man who was fully in control of his emotions.

Both Marie and Simon were enjoying their leisurely drive in northern Italy, the captivating towns, the gorgeous scenery, the historic associations and not least each other's company. They were in the Veneto near the old town of Castelfranco when Simon saw a sign to Frezzati and on an impulse swung the car down the narrow lane.

"Where are we going?" asked Marie as they plunged more deeply downhill with trees on either side and meeting overhead, giving the impression of travelling through a dark tunnel. Simon was forced to turn on his headlights to penetrate the darkness that lay ahead, in such contrast with the bright sunlight and blue sky that they had left behind.

"It's that name Frezzati," he replied. "When I was talking to old Teodoro Manzini at the palazzo in Venice, he spoke about his late wife Carlotta, who you remember was a de Vincetti, her younger brother was Angelo whose son is Roberto de Vincentti. Carlotta and Angelo's parents apparently had a sizable estate hereabouts with a house that was razed to the ground in a big fire in 1932 in which both the parents died. The children were fortunately away. As we were passing by, I thought it might be interesting to have a look."

The oppressive tree tunnel gave way to more scattered trees and sunshine, so he turned off the headlights as they entered a hamlet with a couple of cottages and a farm.

"This must be Frazzati" said Simon "I think I'd better enquire where the de Vincentti property is or was" and pulled up by the farm house."

"Are you sure that your Italian is quite up to rustic chit-chat, darling," asked Marie "or shall I lend a hand?"

"You're probably right, thanks," he replied.

The farmer's wife was both knowledgeable and helpful. She told them that the de Vincentti estate had been sold off many years before, and confirmed that the old manor house had been destroyed by fire way back in the 1930's. The trees and hedges that had marked the edges of the estate could still be clearly seen and if they wanted to see the remains of the old house, they could go to the drive which began beside the Lodge House, only a half kilometre from where they were standing, adding that family of the last lodge keeper, Bascalso, still lived there and might tell them more.

Giacomo Balscalso was initially suspicious when they said that they wanted to have a look at the old house ruins, because they had heard what a great place it had been. He was more forthcoming when they told him that they knew Roberto de Vincentti.

"Ah Roberto, how is he now?" he asked and went on "He hasn't been here for four years or more, when he promised me he would have all the stuff moved from the store room at the back which has been there, cluttering up that end of the lodge for the best part of a hundred years, ever since the fire in fact. Roberto's father Angelo asked my dad if he could leave the stuff here temporarily." He gave a contemptuous laugh, and repeated the word "temporarily."

"What sort of stuff is it?" asked Marie.

"Mostly bits of furniture, mirrors, porcelain, all sorts of things that they were able to get out from the ground floor during the fire, and quite a lot of books, files and so on. Come and have a look."

He grabbed a key from beside the front door and led the way round the back of the lodge building to a single storey extension that had been built on with its own entrance. When he opened the door you could barely see anything in the gloom until he switched on a central light and the cause of the darkness became evident, with pieces of furniture stacked high against the windows. There was no sense of order, with all sorts of furnishings leaning against each other or stacked haphazardly one on another. The surface of several small tables and a big desk were cluttered with an assortment of framed photographs, Sevres and Royal Worcester porcelain, elaborately carved ivory statues and wooden pieces in proliferation. It was a sort of Aladdin's cave of beauty and craftsmanship that took their breath away.

"This is a remarkable collection" said Marie "I'm surprised that no-one has gone to the trouble of sorting it out during the last century, some of the items must be quite valuable."

"I know and yet neither Angelo nor his son, Roberto seemed to be that bothered. About ten or fifteen years after the fire and the war, my father said that Angelo would come occasionally, about every year or two and sit at the big desk which was his father's and work on papers, but he never took anything away apart from oil paintings.

Father said there were three really big paintings which he took away with five or six others. When Angelo died Roberto came two or three times to take a look over the years but despite him agreeing to move the stuff out, he's done nothing."

Whilst Balscalso was talking, Marie and Simon had been examining various objects, some of which Marie declared were spectacular. Simon was particularly drawn to a handsome mahogany box inlaid with ebony, rosewood, and mother of pearl with elaborate brass strapping. On the top was inset the striking enamel emblem of the de Vincentti family, the rearing horse against the blue background.

Instinctively Simon felt in his jacket pocket, where he always carried the little key, and brought it out. It looked right and, standing in such a way that Bascalso could not see what he was doing, he deftly thrust the key into the keyhole. It fitted and turned smoothly and with a click it became free and he was able to lift the lid.

He glanced inside and right on the top of a bunch of papers was something that made his heart miss a beat and then begin to beat faster and faster as he stared and tried to bring his excitement under control.

Chapter 37

It was a small square of yellowing paper attached by a tassle and pink string to documents beneath. At the top right was a date, June 13, 1973 and it read:

UN MESSAGIO DA CARLOS:
Signor Angelo Vincentti,   Ho il piacere di allegara una provenienza completa cho ho ricercato per il dipinto dell'Ultomo Cena creduto di essere da Giovanni Battiste Tiepolo. Ho incluso alcun idocumenti originali, altri sono copie verificate.
Confido che troverai tutto soddis facente.   Il mio account seque.
Cordiali saluti,
Carlos

It was the words *'provenienza completa'* coupled with *'dipinto dell'Ultimo Cena'* that struck Simon so forcibly even with his scrappy Italian. A complete provenance for the painting The Last Supper – it was incredible. But there it was, he had to read the note two or three times over to make sure he was not imagining things.

His thoughts were interrupted by Marie's voice as she moved towards him "Is everything alright darling? Signor Balscalso was wondering if we had seen enough, I think he wants to lock-up."

Simon, pointed to the box and said "Just to confirm that that note on top says what I think it does darling, can you quickly translate into English please, before I talk to Signor Balscalso. She looked down at the note and read out :

A MESSAGE FROM CARLOS
"Signor de Vincentti, I have pleasure in attaching a full provenance that I have for the The Last Supper painting believed to be by Giovanni Battista Tiepolo. I have included some original documents and others are verified copies. I trust you will find everything satisfactory. My account follows. Sincerely, Carlos."

"Thanks" said Simon to Marie and walked across to Giacomo, who was standing open-mouthed with surprise as he could see that the wooden box had been opened somehow. He struggled to speak "How you open the box?" he asked.

"With a key that I had" answered Simon and went on to explain about how it had been embedded into the frame surrounding a picture that he now owned called 'The Last Supper' — "the very painting that is referred to in the note in this box." He moved over with Giacomo and pointed into the open box and to the note, which Giacomo read. Then he scratched his head and said "But this box and everything else in here belongs to de Vincentti you shouldn't be opening it."

"I realise that and apologise to you for doing so without your knowledge or permission," said Simon. "I confess that when I realised I had the key in my pocket, the temptation was too great," he admitted.

Giacomo muttered something under his breath and then said "OK. You lock-up the box and we say no more."
"Before we do that, will you kindly allow us to read through the papers relating to the provenance of my painting and make some notes, because some of the research referred to is almost certainly of great importance to me ."

"I don't know ; they are private papers."

"And they will remain just as they were, locked in a box that nobody has looked at since the death of Angelo Vincentti many years ago. If it would salve your conscience, I will write a statement guaranteeing that I will not tamper or mark the papers in any way and as a guarantee I will give you two hundred Euros."

It was probably the promise of the Euros that settled Giacomo's mind as he nodded his acceptance and Simon opened his wallet and passed over the money.

"You will stay in here and read them, then lock the box, and let me know when you have finished" he said and they both agreed, but when Simon asked for some paper to write out his guarantee statement he merely shrugged and left them to carry on.

Between them Simon and Marie cleared more space on the large desk so that they could systematically go through all the research into the provenance of the painting that Carlos had carried out. Simon carefully photographed each document with his iphone.

It was very thorough and comprehensive, covering the period from its completion by Tiepolo through to 1972 and included an early fly-poster for Galleria Aspidistra listing names of artists whose work they claimed to handle including Tiepolo. There were posters for exhibitions where *'The Last Supper'* was listed as on show sometimes with the then current owner's name.

Sometimes it was listed as by Tiepolo, sometimes as 'school of or 'after', demonstrating for how long the work had been questioned as genuine. Several documents were certified copies of entries from auctions or catalogues. Simon and Marie checked them all, and most, Simon was pleased to note, confirmed his own findings but there were others he had no prior knowledge of and all gaps were filled up to 1972.

That was the year after Angelo de Vincentti had been asked by Manzini to sell the painting, but had retained it himself whilst falsely claiming to have made a private sale. Aware of the lack of a convincing provenance, he had obviously instructed 'Carlos' to carry out the necessary research and his report was put into the box. Why Angelo decided to keep the box and its contents away from the painting but buried the key in the frame, is a matter for conjecture, but he seemed to have told nobody about it, not even his son.

For obvious reasons, Carlos' report gave no clue as to where and when the painting passed into other hands after 1972. Other papers in the box were mainly concerned with other painting sales or purchases that he had negotiated – possibly ones of dubious origin, hence the need to keep some records in a secret place. However, there were some notes made at various times, often dated, which related to possible deals and requests from potential collectors. Four of these were headed *D'U C* (Della'Ultimo Cena?) which translated read:

D'U C

2/10/78 Stainter, Philadelphia - suspects I am still holding it! Or could obtain it. He is interested in acquiring. $500,000 plus.

9/7/82 Oscar Bernstein, Berlin- expressed interest in adding this to his collection if it became available.

6/8/94 Quinton Leasdon, London/Bahamas - convinced I have it, suggested deal around £2 million.

18/2/95 Quinton Leasdon, London - Persistent, now offers £2.5M, is retiring shortly. Deal tempting. Maybe 5 yr loan with claw back clause?

Simon recalled that in his conversations with Manzini he had been told that Angelo had disappeared in 1974 with the painting and was believed to have died in about 1997.

He knew that somehow the painting had passed into other hands during the period 1974-1983 before Wendell spotted it, and he guessed Lambertini hid it for a while before selling it privately to somebody very quietly. So, when and how could Angelo de VIncentti have been in a position to sell or loan it to Leasdon in 1995. Had he re-acquired it? Or did he know who held it at that time and was this someone who could be persuaded to sell to him so that he could sell on with a profit? The notes were not clear.

Although Simon's photos now gave him an almost complete provenance, with only small gaps from the time it was painted by Tiepolo up to 1995, it would be much more satisfactory if he had certified scans of everything. But would Giacomo agree to them taking the documents away so that these copies could be made?

Two hundred euros had overcome his initial reluctance to them going through and photographing documents, perhaps more money would gain his agreement?

To prepare the ground, and using Marie's fluency in Italian, Simon drew up a document stating that he and Marie had borrowed certain papers as listed, all concerned with the provenance of the painting that he owned, to have them scanned and certified.

They undertook to return the papers as soon as possible and certainly within 24 hours and as a token of their honest intent would leave with Giacomo their passports, their watches and several items of personal jewellery, in addition to financial recompense for Giacomo for his help and cooperation.

Simon went and found Giacomo, explained what they wished to do showed him the document that he had signed and dated. He also passed over a further three hundred euros to Giacomo and that seemed to make his mind up. They left behind with him an envelope containing all the items that guaranteed their return and drove off to Castelfranco, the nearest town where they would stay the night, get the certified copies made and return to the Lodge as soon as possible.

By noon the following day, they were driving away from the Lodge having restored the documents to the box, recovered their belongings and said farewell to Giacomo. Simon's phone pinged. It was a message from Yvonne Simmonds brief and to the point 'Please ring Urgently' followed by a number.

Simon pulled off the Autostrada at the next opportunity, and rang the number to find Yvonne in a state near to panic. When he had calmed her, she managed to tell a frightening story.

The previous night she and her husband were asleep in bed when they were woken by the sound of breaking glass. Her husband went to investigate and was half way down the stairs when the sound was repeated and as he walked into the hall he saw that the sitting room carpet was a mass of flame, rapidly spreading to encompass a table and an easy chair.

He went to get a fire extinguisher they kept in the kitchen and directed it at one area of fire, where it was effective but of limited help as the flames advanced quickly, accelerated by another missile filled with petrol came crashing through another window into the room.

Yvonne had followed her husband down the stairs and immediately phoned both the Fire Brigade and Police, and in a vain attempt to assist began to throw buckets of water onto the conflagration. As they watched helplessly, another flaming petrol torch was flung into the dining room also at the front of the house. Yvonne's husband went to the front door to see a figure standing in the front garden holding a full bottle of petrol into which he had lit a fuse - a Molotov cocktail – preparatory to throwing it through a window. Seeing Jack he threw it directly at him, hitting him on the shoulder before falling to the ground beside him and bursting into flame.

Jack staggered away from the explosion, but his dressing gown splashed with petrol was alight down one side. He managed to beat the flames out, suffering slightly from burns to his arms and side. Meanwhile the man in the garden, clad in black and wearing a balaclava, had run from the house down the drive, got in his car and driven off.

Both Fire Services and police arrived within a few minutes and the former soon had the fire under control but the damage to the two rooms was extensive.

The police lined up in the front garden four more Molotov cocktails that had been prepared with fuses in place and also a hastily made cardboard notice that read:

'Yvonne. Retribution.   You had been warned'

She was sure that it was the work of her brother Tim and was concerned that because he had been similarly warned, something similar might happen to Simon and his property and had informed the police accordingly.

Simon thanked her, hoped the damage to her house was not as bad as it was thought and that it could soon be restored and assured her that he would phone Gloucestershire straight away to check on his cottage, as he was still in Italy.

He told Marie and then phoned the police near his home. He was told that nothing untoward had been reported but that an extra patrol car would regularly call by in the light of the new circumstances.

They continued their journey eastward to Venice leaving their car in Pizzale Roma and taking a water taxi to their hotel, a favourite of Marie's – The Concordia.

As they sat on the balcony overlooking the water, as the sun descended, sipping their cool wine, Simon was unusually quiet and Marie questioned his mood, "You should be jumping for joy tonight I would have thought.   An almost complete provenance for the picture that will, I'm sure, more than satisfy the verification committee, a selling price that, if all goes well surpasses your wildest expectation and yet here you are in romantic Venice with someone who loves you looking so sad."

"Sorry darling" he began with a big smile "you are quite right, I should be over the moon with everything – particularly having you - but I can't help wondering if I'm doing the right thing. Selling to that rogue de Vincentti despite what he did to you, to both of us, knowing he is a thief and a fraudster.

On top of that I will be giving him a well-nigh perfect provenance to present to the committee alongside the painting. I'm not happy about it." He paused before going on "You haven't said very much about my predicament, darling, what do you really think?"

"It is something that only you can decide upon Simon. You are not acting illegally, and it is irrelevant to bring into consideration his actions before, because this is, as I see it, is purely a business transaction with moral implications that wouldn't trouble most people. Whatever you decide to do I'm with you one hundred percent. She leaned over and gave him a kiss.

"Thanks. That's made me feel much better," said Simon and took a large swig of wine.

Chapter 38

The following day Simon and Marie were walking through St Mark's Square towards the Correr Museum, when Simon's mobile phone pinged. It was a message from Inspector Morgan from the Gloucestershire Police who asked him to phone him as soon as possible.

They went and sat at a table outside a nearby café and ordered coffee so that Simon could return the call. Morgan had an interesting story to tell. Through the sharp observation by a near neighbour, an attempt to damage Simon's cottage by fire had been averted. This neighbour, returning with his wife from an event in Cheltenham just before midnight, was closing his garage door when he noticed some activity in the front garden of Simon's cottage fifty yards away and a strange car parked nearby.

He knew Simon was away, and his suspicions were aroused, so, pausing just to collect his dog from the house together with a pad and pencil for his pocket he walked down the road towards the cottage. He stopped when he could read the strange car's registration number and made a note of it and then as he drew nearer, peered into the cottage garden to see what was going on. He could make out a figure lining up what appeared to be some bottles.

The neighbour challenged the person, whose head was covered in a black balaclava. He was clearly startled by the voice and took off at high speed out of the gate and into his parked car and away. The neighbour went into the front garden and saw that the bottles lined up were in fact Molotov cocktails all with fuses attached and ready to light and throw. He immediately rang the police and because he was able to give the car's number, they traced it within minutes to a car hire company in London.

Although it was now past midnight the police got the manager of the company to go into his office and look up details of the hirer, which was given as Timothy Beard staying at a nearby hotel. Two hours later Metropolitan policemen were waiting in the hotel car park in London and arrested Timothy Beard, who was in fact Timothy Bird, initially on a charge of arson and attempted arson.

He resisted arrest by punching one of the officers on the head and attempting to run past him but was floored by the other policeman who quickly handcuffed him. Morgan ended the call by asking Simon if he intended to returning to England in the next day or two, as it would be helpful if he was able to attend the first court hearing when more charges would be brought. He might be asked to give evidence to ensure that Bird was referred to a higher court - possibly the Old Bailey - on all charges including conspiracy to murder. Simon said he would ring back again shortly and after terminating the call, told Marie, who had only heard his end of the conversation.

They discussed the situation and agreed that as there was nothing happening on the search for de Vincentti and he was unlikely to be in touch about the painting for a week or two, there was nothing keeping them in Venice.

Simon felt the need to get back to his cottage and thank his neighbour for his timely intervention, besides which it was a good time to show Marie the cottage and introduce her to the pleasures of living in the Cotswolds. Also, he would not only be available to attend the court appearance of Timothy Bird and give evidence if required, once back in England he could try and find out about this man Quinton Leasdon and his possible acquisition *of The Last Supper* painting. It was not that he wanted to do de Vincentti any favours by filling in the remaining recent gaps in its provenance, it was more for his own satisfaction in completing what had been a fascinating journey of discovery.

They phoned Inspettore Ricci to tell him of their plans following the incident in Gloucestershire and booked seats on a flight to London the following morning. Inspector Morgan was pleased to hear that Simon would be back in Gloucestershire in a couple of days.

Following a two-and-a-half-hour flight and an hour and a half train journey, plus two hours waiting around at various points, a taxi from Stroud Station brought them to Simon's cottage the next evening, tired and hungry. After quickly sorting themselves out, Marie was introduced to a typical country pub down the road, where they had dinner. She found both pub and cottage quaint and delightful and a unique experience to her.

Simon had already googled Quinton Leasdon, and found out that he had been a wealthy businessman who died at the age of 87 in 1998. If Angelo de Vincentti had made some sort of deal with him before his own death in 1996, Leasdon had enjoyed having the painting only for a very short time. Simon needed to find out if the painting had indeed been passed to him and what happened to it after his death.

The latest edition of Who's Who for the United Kingdom incorporated between its covers a *Who was Who* section that listed distinguished people that had featured in earlier editions. Simon quickly found a brief entry from which he learned that Leasdon had had a son with the unusual name of Isambard, It rang a bell – wasn't there an architect making a name for himself internationally, called Isambard Leasdon? Surely there couldn't be two or more with that name. He turned back to the current listings in the volume and found him, now aged 58 and indeed the son of Quinton. The entry also said that he lived with his wife and three children in Oxfordshire – couldn't be much better, an adjacent county.

A few more enquiries gave him the address – just over the border near Burford - and a telephone number which he rang. Isambard was not at home, but was expected about seven that evening. Simon briefly explained to Mrs Leasdon that he was the owner of an old painting that he believed had once belonged to her husband's father and that he was trying to piece together a provenance. He said that he would be grateful for any information that he had. It was left that Isambard (Izzy) would ring him back.

When he did so he expressed himself intrigued by Simon's story and suggested that rather than continuing the conversation over the phone, particularly as Simon had mentioned that he lived quite close, that they meet up on Saturday morning at Leasdon's house, if that was convenient. It was, and when Simon asked if he may bring along his French partner, Marie was included in the invitation.

Leasdon and family lived in a Georgian manor house close to the charming old Cotswold town of Burford which Marie remarked as they drove through was a "delight to the eye."

As was the Leasdon house, classically Georgian at the front and extended at the back with a design that was undeniably modern though seemingly making a perfect blend between the two styles.

They sat, the four of them, Simon, Marie, Izzy and his wife Pat in a long sitting room that gave wonderful views over the garden and beyond to a rolling Cotswold landscape, which caused much of their early conversation. However, after Pat brought in coffee, the big bronzed architect with a crown of curly grey hair began "I'm afraid I can't tell you very much about that painting *The Last Supper*. I remember it of course, although it was one amongst many paintings that my father collected and on the odd occasion that I remember he talked to me about various pictures, that wasn't one he seemed to feature.

"But Simon, I gather it is now yours and you've had quite a job getting a provenance together for it, perhaps you would tell us about that before I add my little bit of information. Oh yes, and wasn't it that particular painting, according to an article in The Times, that had come to light after being missing for years?"

Simon smile and replied "Well it's yes to your last question, and whilst I am happy to tell you the whole story I have to ask, do you want the summary or the whole works including attempted murder, abduction, theft and fraud, because it takes a while in the telling and you may be bored by the end."

Izzy and Pat chorused "the whole story" and after taking a swig of coffee, Simon began with finding the old painting hidden in the frame of another painting that he had been bequeathed to him.

Nearly half an hour later, Simon, who had only halted his dissertation to answer a few questions said "That brings you pretty much up to date," sat back and took another swig of a fresher cup of coffee.

There was silence which was first broken by Izzy applauding and calling "Bravo, wonderful, extraordinary" before his wife joined in. When they had stopped, Izzy went on "You know so many unusual and dramatic things have happened to you and Marie over recent months and weeks that if you read about them in a book of fiction it would seem quite incredible. Wow!"

Marie spoke up. "Sometimes Simon, and to a lesser extent I too, have found that what has happened has been extraordinary, and dangerous at times, but on the plus side it brought us together, for which we are profoundly thankful." Which brought an "absolutely right" from Simon.

"After that tour de force my contribution to your research is, I'm afraid, pretty meagre," said Izzy. "As I said, I remember the painting quite well, but it didn't feature amongst my father's favourites. I had the impression that he was a bit disappointed after its acquisition somehow and described it as *after the style of* Tiepolo with its lack of provenance.

"He bought it, I believe, in 1995 and died in 1998. I was away at university at the time and came home for the funeral when my mother announced that she was selling the house and its contents as soon as possible. To her it was too closely associated with my father for her to carry on there, living mainly on her own. The fact is that she never really liked the house and the Norfolk countryside very much, since my father had bought it on a whim. She preferred the smaller house that they had down in Devon where she spent most summers and a week at Christmas.

She said I could have anything I liked from the Norfolk house, furniture, paintings or whatever, but as I said I was at uni in Manchester sharing a furnished house with two other students and the last thing I wanted was extra furniture or other clutter.

I went back one weekend and packed up all my clothes and personal things, most of which went down to Devon. My mother lost little time in putting the house on the market and arranged for all the furniture and other contents to be catalogued and then sold off at auction, including all the paintings. I could kick myself now for not taking a greater interest in what was going on, particularly with the paintings but like my mother, I was not that interested in fine art and happy to leave it to the auctioneers in Norwich to get the best prices they could for father's collection.

Some years later I was going through various papers after my mother's death and came across the auctioneer's accounts. "The Last Supper" was described as "in the style of Tiepolo," presumably in the absence of any accompanying documentation. It sold for the meagre sum of £110,000, which contrasts with two modern paintings in his collection which achieved £260K and £340K."

"You don't happen to know to whom the Tiepolo was sold I suppose?" asked Simon hopefully. "Afraid not," responded

Izzy, "but the auctioneers – Dakins, can probably help you, providing that they have kept the records after twenty five years or so. If it helps I'll give you a letter of introduction."

As it was now lunchtime, Pat invited Simon and Marie to eat with them, during which Izzy returned to the subject of Roberto de Vincentti. "So, you've both met this rather dodgy gentleman who is illegally in possession of the Tiepolo painting?"

"Yes, more than once" replied Simon.

"But despite his history and the way he treated you both, you have now agreed to sell it to him and make his possession legal?"

"That's right. I suppose it seems a bit odd or even questionable that I should be doing so, but believe me, I have thought long and hard about it. Putting to one side his treatment of both of us, which will not be forgiven or forgotten, you should understand several things. Firstly, he has not been charged or convicted of any crime yet, and I want to sell the painting that he is holding and he has offered me a good price.

Whilst it legitimises his position regarding the painting and rewards me, it doesn't in any way lessen the police wish to arrest and charge de Vincentti with various offences including theft and abduction. They have encouraged my contact with him and believe that it gives them the best chance of tracing and catching him."

"Yes, I see what you mean," responded Izzy.

It had been an enjoyable time for all concerned and when Simon and Marie left with the letter to Dakins, it was with promises to keep the Leasdons informed on how things developed and that they would in any case get together again before long.

The next morning Simon first rang Inspector Morgan to see whether a date had been fixed for Timothy Bird's initial Magistrates' Court appearance and found that it had just been arranged for the following day in Cheltenham. He went accompanied by Marie, but he was not called as a witness. In fact the hearing lasted no more than twenty minutes and the case was sent to a higher court with Bird held on remand.

It was the first time that they had seen Timothy Bird, who made a strange sight sitting between two policemen in the dock. He seemed to pay little attention to what was going on in the courtroom between scratching his head and gazing into space.

He had several sessions of rapidly opening and closing his mouth for a couple of minutes at a time and two or three times he got up with the apparent attention of leaving the dock until restrained by the two officers.

As Marie observed, he had all the signs of somebody with a mental disorder, or he was a very good actor. Inspector Morgan, in thanking Simon for attending, said that he didn't anticipate the case being heard in the higher court for some months when no doubt other charges would be added.

Back home, Simon rang Dakins, the auctioneers in Norwich, to find that they did still hold their auction records from 1998/9 in their archives and in the circumstances would look them out for him to examine. A few days later, with Marie at his side, Simon set off on a drive across England from the west of England to Norwich.

Chapter 39

Dakins were an old established auction house and estate agents. Their head office occupied an old Tudor building in the centre of Norwich, behind which was a much more modern, utilitarian structure with a large basement that housed the archive storage, a mass of twelve feet high shelves on wheels closely packed together.

The archive manager, David Barber was clearly proud of his empire, which he declared to be, "A Treasure Trove, 150 years of memory". His excellent cataloguing made it an easy task to pull out the shelves housing 1998 and 1999 auction sales. An earlier check following Simon's telephone enquiry had led him to two volumes - one in October 1998 for the house contents other than paintings and sculptures and another in February 1999 for fine art paintings and other objet d'art which included those from the Leasdon house.

It was in the latter volume that he pointed out the item:

No 36. *The Last Supper* in the style of Giovanni Battiste Tiepolo 1696-1770.

Owner: Mrs Letitia Leasdon. Sold to: 123 Leddingham.
Hammer price: £110,000

"Is that all?" remarked Simon. "I was hoping for more detail about the buyer than just his auction card number and a surname."

Barber smiled, "perhaps our archival magic can oblige" and after Simon had written out the meagre detail, he pushed back the shelf and pulled out the next in line. These consisted of shelves containing foolscap and later A4 sized hard backed books dated by the year. He pulled out the one dated 1999, turned to the inside front cover and explained that listed there were the names and personal bidding number for regular attenders at their auction sales. These included 123 Lord Leddingham, Dellshott Hall, Blewdon, Norfolk.

"Magic indeed" said Simon "that's more like it" and copied down the information. In thanking David Barber for his help, he asked where Blewdon was situated and received explicit directions.

Dellshott Hall was only twenty miles away and they were both curious so they decided to drive there and had lunch in the Leddingham Arms, an old coaching Inn in the village. They were sitting drinking coffee after their meal when Simon's mobile phone rang, it was from a number he didn't recognise but replied:

"Simon Brookes"

"Hello Mr Brookes, this is David Barber, the archivist at Dakins. I saved your number from the time of your original enquiry and I'm sorry to bother you, but I think I, or rather my assistant has come across something that I know you will be very interested to see regarding the painting. Can you possibly call back this afternoon or tomorrow morning and have a look? I assure you it will be well worth your while."

"Sounds intriguing, and yes, we could call in say at 9.30am tomorrow if that's OK."

Barber responded. "That will be fine and it's extraordinary as well as intriguing, but I'll explain it all when I see you," and rang off and Simon told Marie what the call had been about.

"Curiouser and curiouser. Life is never dull I find when I'm with you, I have discovered, darling" she commented, and went on, "Perhaps we ought to begin our enquiries about Dellshot Hall now, whilst we have the time. She started with the receptionist. Unfortunately, she had only been in the job for a few weeks but referred her to the elderly head waiter who had lived locally all his life and more importantly, had made a study of local history and of the Leddingham family and the Hall. He would, given the opportunity, have talked about the family from the grant of the peerage to a John Leddingham in 1680 and the move by a descendent James and family to Dellshot Hall in 1721, but without being too rude they hurried him on to talk about more recent times.

He told them that Lord Lionel Leddingham would have been the holder of the title in 1998/99, and he died in 2012. Lionel was a keen collector of various things including notably butterflies and yes, paintings. His eldest son Lord Richard Leddingham now held the title and lived at the Hall with his wife and a large family. Like his father before him he had never bothered to take his seat in the House of Lords, preferring to spend his time managing the large estate and live the country life.

He was well liked locally and supported the local villages in various ways. On the off-chance, Simon phoned him, explaining who he was and what he was seeking, and half an hour later he and Marie were driving up the long tree-lined drive to the Hall.

Richard, Lord Leddingham, came out to greet them as they drew up. He looked more like a farmer in his brown corduroy trousers and a shirt with a frayed collar, than the latest scion in a distinguished line of the nobility.

He was very affable, showing real interest in Simon's search, and took them into the estate office where an assistant had gone through the family archives and discovered an inventory dated 2001 listing all the works of art, statues, antique furniture and other items of note in the house. Amongst the paintings listed was '*The Last Supper*' attributed to '*school of Tiepolo*' and a note '*acqu. Dakins 1999. £110,000.*' Confirmation that it had been in the family collection, but where and when did it go elsewhere?

The next inventory had been made five years later in 2006 and there was no record of the Tiepolo amongst the paintings, so sometime between 2001 and 2006 Lionel had disposed of it.

Lord Richard discussed with his assistant where a note of the sale during that period was to be found and they agreed that there was no certain answer. It could be in the estate accounts or more likely in his father's personal accounts and papers which would entail a lot of research and he didn't have the staff to make it a priority, so, whilst they would do the search it might be some time – possibly weeks before they could work their way through five years of records.

He apologised but promised to write and let Simon have details of anything that they found relevant to the painting. It was disappointing, but Simon and Marie hoped for interesting revelations from David Barber the following day.

The archivist could hardly contain his excitement when they were shown down to his basement that morning. He explained that, to make their records more easily accessible, Dakins had been working for some time on digitising some of their archived documents.

One of his assistants, who knew of their interest in *The Last Supper* painting had come across an earlier reference to possibly the same painting. He went on to show them the record for a November 1983 auction sale:

147 *Christ and Disciples at the Last Supper.*
Oil on canvas. Italian late baroque style.
Possible copy of a Tiepolo.
Seller : Hearn & Miller
Buyer : Mr Marcus Welland
Hammer price : £1,720.

The clincher was Marcus Welland's name, Manzini's agent in the UK. It tied in precisely with what the old man had told him, and Simon was delighted. He asked who Hearn & Miller were and whether they were they still in business, to be told that they were a firm of house clearance agents and dealers in second hand furniture now no longer trading. How the painting, clearly unrecognised for what it was, had come into the hands of a house clearance company remained a mystery. Having taken a photograph of the 1983 auction entry and thanking Barber and his assistant for their help, Simon and Marie went into a nearby coffee shop for a reappraisal.

Simon expressed his frustration, complaining that every step forward filling in the gaps in ownership seemed to lead on to yet another question mark and more research and sometimes contradictions or complications.

For example, they knew that Angelo de Vincentti had the painting with him when he disappeared in 1974, so what happened in the years up to 1983? How long did he keep it, how did it leave his possession, and how did it go on to be sold at least once, unrecognised at auction?

Then even more strangely how and when did he get it back, so that he could negotiate its sale or loan to Quinton Leasdon in 1995?

Marie countered his pessimism by pointing out how much he had learned since he began his research only a matter of weeks before. On reflection he agreed, and his mood improved. But then he posed the question "Where do we go from here? The house clearance people who put the painting into the auction in 1983 are now out of business and there's no chance of finding out where they got it from."

"Come on" said Marie stretching out her hand "let's take a walk around the city centre, it might cheer you up."

They walked around the centre in the bright sunshine and then she led them to a rundown district where new houses and other buildings were slowly replacing the old. At one point Simon asked where on earth he was being led, when she pointed at a road sign Oldfield Road and further along an old disused stone and brick church. "That is The Old Chapel,

Oldfield Road where Hearn & Miller ran their business from, I wonder who has it now?"

As they drew nearer the sign outside told them 'A D Turner. Antiques and Collectables.' Inside they found an eclectic mixture of items ranging from a fin de siècle French clock to an old leather football commemorating a championship win in the 1930's.

There were copper bedwarmers, ancient lacrosse racquets, postcard collections, tea caddies, an Indian carved table with inscribed brass top, and some Clarice Cliff teacups. They took in the myriad assortment as they walked down the central aisle.

"Is there anything in particular that you are looking for" asked a man emerging from behind some furniture "or are you just happy looking around?"

"Well we were fascinated by the variety of things that have in here" began Simon "have you brought it all together yourself?"

"Oh no, quite a lot of the stock belongs to dealers, particularly those in cases up in the gallery upstairs. Most of the furniture is mine and some of the ceramics and curios, I take the best that comes from people doing house-clearances and small dealers."

"Like the business that occupied this building some years ago, Hearn & Miller, I suppose?" asked Marie.

"Yes that's right.   Did you know them?"

Simon chipped in "No not really, it's just that I learned today that they had sold at auction a painting that I now own, through Dakins, and I'm trying to research its history by finding out who or where they got it from."

"Was it valuable?" asked the man who by now had introduced himself as Alan Turner. "Fairly" replied Simon. "I ask" said Turner, because H & M did handle a lot of junk as well as some good pieces and paintings which they invariably sold through Dakins.

I know about the junk" he added "because when old Hearn died and this place went on the market it was full of junk that, when I decided to buy the premises, I had to get rid of which was not a happy experience I can tell you."

He thought for a moment before going on "when did you say the painting was auctioned by Dakins?"

"1983" said Simon. "Then old Billie who works for me, might remember," said Alan Turner. "He was here at that time working for H & M, probably called young Billie then. He's out the back making tea, I'll ask him to come and talk to you" and walked to the end of the chapel and through a side door.

A couple of minutes later, a big burly man with silver speckled black beard emerged and made his way to them. "I'm Billie Wardle, how do you do, Mr Turner tells me you want to test my memory of working at Hearn & Miller's."

"Yes, well it's on the off chance really because you would hardly remember one painting that they sold at auction through Dakins back in 1983."

"Try me, I've a pretty good memory," he replied.

Simon named and described the painting and observed, as he was talking, how Wardle's face changed and ended up looking down at the floor.

When he had finished Billie looked up, his face the picture of dejection. He began, "Of all the pictures that Dakins sold for us, you would have to bring up that one. It wasn't really my fault but I copped most of the blame, but I'll tell you the whole miserable story.

I was twenty and had been working for Hearn & Miller for about three or four years in 1983, and my boss Mr Hearn began to trust me over the other lads in the business with taking charge of some house clearances, sales and entering suitable items into Dakins auctions. Mr Hearn had a good eye for paintings and had quite an interesting collection at his home. I think it was mainly through that interest that he became friendly over time with a local man called Harold Jenkins who was an obsessive art collector.

He made a fortune making top end handbags for woman with more money than sense I believe.

Anyway, Jenkins was a bit of a recluse, lived in this crumbling old house in the sticks, on his own with his art collection. He became ill and had to go into hospital for an operation and arranged for someone to go and live in the house and keep an eye on things whilst he was away. However, he couldn't bring himself to entrust his most prized possession, the painting you have described as 'The Last Supper' to the house-sitter and asked his old friend Mr Hearn to keep it with his art collection for the time being.

Mr Hearn picked up the painting himself and brought it into the old chapel intending to take it home that evening. Unfortunately, he left it propped against the wall next to a collection of stuff – two other paintings, a gilt framed mirror, two small tables, an elaborate coat stand and some vases and ceramics. I can remember it all as if it were yesterday. I loaded up the van, old paintings and the rest and took them to Dakins for their next auction a few days after. We always left the catalogue descriptions to Dakins who obviously didn't recognise Jenkin's painting as anything special and it was sold.

Why Mr Hearn didn't remember that he'd left the painting leaning against the wall I don't know, but he was inclined to be a bit absent-minded and just forgot I expect. It was a couple of days after the sale that news came of Mr Jenkins' death during his operation. That reminded my boss that he had put his friend's painting somewhere in the Old Chapel, and he quickly learned from me that it had accidentally gone into Dakin's last auction and been sold.

He went hairless, fired me on the spot after describing me as the worst son of a bitch he'd ever set eyes on and several other phrases I'd rather forget. I tried to explain how it had happened and that it wasn't entirely my fault, but he wouldn't listen.

However, he came round to my house the next day and took me on again, saying that it couldn't be helped now, that the least said now that Jenkins was dead, the better, and that I was to forget it and not mention it again. I have tried to do just that until today, but I hope it answers some questions for you."

"It does" said Simon "even though it must be something of a painful memory for you to recall, thank you. This Harold Jenkins, do you recall his address, and do you happen to know how long he owned '*The Last Supper*?'"

"Yes, he lived at The Grange, Aggletham. I don't know where or when he got the painting, but I think it was several years before."

Simon and Marie thanked him again and, before leaving the Old Chapel went up into the gallery to look at the wide variety on display. Marie spotted a Victorian silver ring carrying a well-cut ruby in its design and as a little celebratory gift and thank you for a successful visit, Simon bought it.

As if on cue, as they left The Old Chapel and began walking back to the town centre, Simon's mobile phone bleeped. It was an email from Inspector Morgan, prefacing another twist in the tale.

Chapter 40

Inspector Morgan's email was giving advance notice that a date had been set, three weeks hence, for Timothy Bird's trial at the Old Bailey, to face a murder charge for Dimitri Beltrovich and other offences in this country. Other charges, he wrote, are also pending in Italy as the police there hoped to be bringing charges for the attempted murder of Simon Brookes and the shooting of Reginald Marsden.

Such a quick criminal trial at a Crown Court after a referral from a lower court was highly unusual. Morgan explained the reasons for this would become apparent at the trial. As *'The Last Supper'* painting had been the subject of dispute between Beltrovich and Bird, Simon may be required as a witness and a formal request for his attendance would follow.

A few minutes later, Marie's mobile phone rang with a similar notification, and a request that she attend the trial in case her evidence was required. That afternoon Simon and Marie were due to go and visit Reggie Marsden at his home outside Norwich. He was still recovering from the effects of the shooting in Venice when he took two bullets in the leg.

Simon knew from their last phone conversation that Reggie was still fascinated by the story that surrounded the old painting. To show him where he had got to, Simon drew up a timeline to illustrate the owners or keepers - both legal and illegal -- and locations when he knew them.

It was whilst he was compiling this that that Richard Leddingham, the farming Lord from Blewsdon, came into the hotel reception and asked to see Simon if he was there, and Simon came down to see him in the hotel lounge.

"Glad I've caught you Simon," he began "I've interesting news about what we found only yesterday, much more quickly than we anticipated, amongst my father's private papers. It appears that in 2004 he was approached by the Palgrove Society & Gallery in London who were at the time, planning to put on an exhibition of mid 18th century Italian artists. They were asking if he would loan 'The Last Supper' painting to them for the exhibition, which was to run in London for a few months and then was expected to move to other venues in the UK and Europe over the following two years, still under the management and care of Palgrove.

According to the initial correspondence, which I have copied for you, my father agreed that they could keep it on loan for up to three years. As you know he died two years later, just about the time that Palgrove were running into financial difficulties which not only caused the end of the exhibition and tour but eventually the collapse into bankruptcy of the whole organisation in 2007. There is no trace of any correspondence from Palgrove to my father amongst his papers about this state of affairs.

All owners who had loaned pictures to the Gallery should have been asked to prove ownership and then had their paintings returned by the receivers. However, my father did not appear to have had received any letters or forms regarding his painting, even though the Receivers claim to have sent them.

I discovered most of this having spoken to the Receivers who handled the bankruptcy. They told me that father's painting, unclaimed, and after due notice, would have been sold at auction by Bonhams or by private sale alongside Palgrave's own stock of paintings. After I pressured them, they looked it up and were able to tell me that it had been sold privately for £2.2 Million to an organisation called the Belvoir Syndicate acting "on behalf of an anonymous client."

He handed over several photocopied papers to Simon and commented "That helps you a little with your research, I hope. I must say that personally, I am annoyed that my father didn't keep a proper account or even a copy of the loan agreement with Palgrove. If their letters were actually sent to the correct address, together with those from the Receivers, there is no sign of them being received at the Hall where they would have all been acted upon urgently, before or after my father's death.

In the circumstances, without even a copy of the contract, there is little or nothing I can do now, Palgrove having gone bust and the statute of limitations for contracts well past the 6 year mark. On top of which the Receivers appear to have done all the right things regarding the ownership of the painting. So, I just have to give a shrug and be philosophical about it all."

"Yes, I can understand your frustration and disappointment now that you have discovered what happened. It's a great pity," said Simon. But you're right about it being a help in my research.

The name Belvoir Syndicate gives me quite a good pointer towards the next owner of the painting if my hunch is right and thank you very much for bringing me the news."

When Leddingham had gone, Simon thought for a moment. It was the mention of the Belvoir Syndicate that had made his heart miss a beat because of their association with Beltrovich, but of course this was way back, before Peter or he owned it. A lot had happened between 2007 and 2022 when he knew that Beltrovich had acquired the painting, probably with help of both Belvoir and Tim Bird. However, it was likely that Belvoir, whose business depended on being well-informed, had kept track of 'TLS' after they had acted for the new owner in 2007.

He went upstairs to tell Marie what Leddingham had said and ended, "I thought momentarily that I'd got a real breakthrough when he mentioned the Belvoir Syndicate and immediately thought of Beltrovich for whom, as you know, they often acted, but of course it was much further back in time."

"Well, it's a bit of progress darling" she responded with a sigh and went on "so how near are you to finding the last brick in the great wall of provenance to mark the end of your tortuous search?"

"Almost there" said Simon and then questioningly went on "do I detect a hint of irritation or annoyance?"

"Not with you, my love, but <u>for</u> you, it seems to have become so important in your mind that it affects your moods, and your usual sunny disposition suffers."

Simon was genuinely shocked "Sorry, I had no idea I was reacting like that, although I do agree it has weighed quite heavily on my mind of late."

He smiled, walked over and gave her kiss. "But I'm all but finished, and if you don't mind, I'll just finish up that summary of progress so far before we go and see Reggie."

"See what I mean?" she gestured with a smile as he resumed and updated his timeline:

1738 (circa)	The Last Supper by Giovanni Battista Tiepolo completed	Venice
1739/40	Exhibited in Aspidistra Gallery	Venice
1741/42	Acquired by Manzini family	Venice
1742-1972	Held in Manzini family collection at Palazzio Manzini	Venice
1972	Angelo de Vincentti instructed to sell the painting. He reported sale to private collector for $22,000, but appears to have kept it	Venice
1974	Angelo de Vincentti disappears presumably with painting. Location unknown.	Unknown
Between 1975 and 1980	Painting passed to Harold Jenkins	Agglesham, Norfolk
1983	Jenkins dies, Painting is sold through Dakins Auctioneers, Norwich, unrecognised and unacknowledged, to Marcus Welland, agent for Teo Manzini. Price: £1720	Norfolk
1983	Welland orders and pays for a special frame to be made to accommodate a new painting in front and 'TLS' hidden behind, from Burlinghams of	East Anglia

	Norwich, He retains the receipt and 'TLS' intending to insert it into its special place in the new frame before shipping it back to Manzini. However, he dies of a heart attack	
1983-1992	TLS remains hidden at Welland's secret cottage in East Anglia. New frame awaits collection at Burlingham's	East Anglia
1992	Investigators working for Lambertini and Pagnetti discover the location of Welland's hideaway in East Anglia, and Lambertini goes there, finds the receipt and the 'TLS' painting. With the receipt he claims the new frame from Burlinghams and has them despatch it to Pagnetti in Venice, but without the Tiepolo.	
Between 1992 and 1995	Somehow 'TLS' comes into the hands of Angelo de Vincentti again	
1995	'TLS' acquired from de Vincentti by Quentin Leasdon for his house in Norfolk. Price circa £2.5 Million	Norfolk
1999	TLS' sold by Mrs Leasdon through Dakins auctioneers to Lord Leddingham, of Blewsdon for £110,000.	Norfolk
1999-2004	'TLS' remains in Leddingham collection	Norfolk
2004	Leddingham loans 'TLS' to Palgrove Gallery for a three-year term of exhibitions. All papers missing	
2006	Leddingham senior dies – family in ignorance of loan arrangements with Palgrove who go bankrupt. No notifications received at Leddingham home.	
2007	Receivers sell painting privately to anonymous buyer fronted by Belvoir Syndicate for £2.2Million	
2013?	Somehow TLS comes into the possession of Peter Bird, who knowingly (?) keeps it hidden within the frame of another picture	

2022	Peter dies and bequeaths the picture 'Laura' by Lawrence Dence with TLS hidden beneath to Simon Brooke	
2022	Picture is stolen from hotel in Florence	

Reggie, who was now able to walk with the aid of a stick, came to the door to greet Simon with an affectionate hug, and he in turn introduced Marie. Reggie's widowed sister, Adele, had come to look after her brother during his convalescence and after introductions led them into a sitting room overlooking a colourful garden, where the tea things were set out.

They talked about many things – life in Norfolk, when and where Marie and Simon had met, her work, and then the shooting in Venice and Reggie's recovery, before Simon was able to launch out onto an account of his latest research.

He produced his timeline notes for Reggie to read, commenting as he did so, at which point Marie and Adele went for a walk around the garden.

Reggie was impressed by how much Simon had found out and said, "Surely you have enough here to convince the most sceptical of authorities over the picture's provenance, when you get the chance to present it with the picture?"

"Yes, I'm pretty confident I do" agreed Simon. "The provenance is now quite strong but there are still small gaps which, for my personal satisfaction I would like to fill. The biggest niggle being how did Angelo de Vincentti in Italy, get hold of 'TLS' again to sell it onto Leasdon in Norfolk in 1995?"

He continued, "and another thing that puzzles me how the Tiepolo and the special frame with the girl in the garden painting were reunited after Lambertini sent the frame without the Tiepolo to Pagnetti back in '92?"

"Yes, it's a puzzle, but you have surely done enough now, and you mustn't let the thing become an obsession."
"You are sounding like Marie now."

"Well, she's right, and incidentally what a charming lady you've got there. Do I sense romance in the air?"

"I suppose you do. We're very attracted to each other but just letting things progress as they may."

"Well, good luck to both of you – you seem well suited. Now tell me Simon, how are the police doing in their search for Roberto de Vincentti and the picture?" So Simon brought him up to date and he had just finished when Marie and Adele rejoined them.

An hour later Simon and Marie left for their hotel after promises were given to return soon. As they passed through reception, the girl behind the desk held up a large, elaborately decorated gold envelope for them and said that it had been delivered a short time ago by a young man. It was addressed to Mr Simon Brookes and Mrs Shawcross. Simon slit it open and drew out a copperplate handwritten invitation to them both from Roberto de Vincentti.

Chapter 41

The card read:

Roberto de Vincentti
cordially invites
Mr Simon Brookes & Madame Marie Shawcross
to
A Reception and Buffet
at
The Hotel Palazzio Gustavo, Venice
In celebration of and tribute to "The Last Supper "
by
Giovanni Battista Tiepolo
on
Tuesday, June 13th, 2023, 5.30pm to 8.00pm

RSVP by phoning 64072333 and leaving personal contact number Please bring this invitation with you.

Attached to the card was a handwritten note:

"I do so hope that you both can come to this event, to which a very small, select group of people have been invited. All guests are connected in one way or another with this painting, but none as prominently as you Simon. I'm quite sure that you will find the proceedings surprising, interesting and entertaining, hence this pressing note. For obvious reasons, security will be very tight at the venue, and I will be participating via Zoom. Our agreed arrangements regarding the painting Simon, will unavoidably be delayed for two or three weeks. I will be in touch.

Sincerely,

Roberto

After they had both read the invitation and note they looked at each other in astonishment and Simon said, "I have to give him full marks for audacity." Marie retorted "I think he has a colossal nerve."

As they got back to their room Simon went on "He says that he will be taking part via Zoom, why then should he need such tight security at the hotel?"

"Perhaps he anticipates that the police or somebody else would be able to trace where he is speaking from if they get into the room," said Marie.

"Not if he uses a number of intermediate relays. But I'm fascinated by the reasons why he is doing this risky thing. Is it intended as a display of personal triumphalism, a play for respectability, or what? He claims that we will find it surprising, interesting and entertaining. Can we even contemplate missing it, darling?"

"No, I think it's a must, and it is two weeks after the appearance of Tim Burns at The Old Bailey, so there is no clash of dates."

Back in their room, Simon phoned DI Sheila Nelson at Scotland Yard to let her know and read over to her the wording of the invitation and the accompanying note.

Her response was "Wow, he likes to keep you guessing, doesn't he?. But why is he doing it? Just showing off, or is there some other reason we don't know about? I see he's not appearing in person, but will you and Madam Shawcross be going?

" Yes, we both plan to go – I must confess we're fascinated by what the villain is up to now and wouldn't like to miss it." Nelson went on "I suppose the arrangements he refers to are his payment to you for the painting and you passing over to him the provenance? Do you trust him?"

"Nobody who knows him and his reputation could entirely trust de Vincentti. On the other hand, it will be greatly to his advantage to legitimise his ownership of the work, and I can't see him backing out at this stage."

"Right. Well thanks for letting me know. I'll tell all my colleagues here and be in touch."

Simon then rang Inspetorre Superiore Ricci to put him in the picture. However, his office said that he had gone for the day and Simon left a message asking him to ring the following morning.

They were driving back to the Cotswolds from Norfolk when Ricci returned the call, Marie took it and turned it on speaker as Simon was driving.

Ricci had already learnt of the de Vincentti Reception from another invited guest but was particularly keen to see the wording of the invitation and note that they had received and Simon promised to send copies. Ricci went onto say that he had already started discussions with his colleagues in Venice on what steps the police could take, although it had been made clear by the hotel that this was a private party to be held in their famous ballroom with its own security arrangements. Accordingly, police presence in the ballroom was neither required nor desired.

As Vincentti had confirmed that he would not be there in person, it lessened the importance of the occasion for the police although they would be keenly interested in what went on, if only from their presence elsewhere in the hotel. Before ending the call Ricci said he looked forward to seeing them both when they came to Venice.

The next week passed quickly for Marie and Simon as she had to spend four days in Holland, investigating for an insurance company the theft of a landscape painting by Jacob van Ruisdael from a private collector. She was quite quickly able to trace through her contacts who had got it, and a speedy swoop by the police led to arrests and the uncovering of a plot to swindle the insurance company and she was back at the cottage in the Cotswolds within the week.

Marie had two younger sisters. Both were married with children and living abroad, one a medical specialist in

Capetown and the other married to a lawyer in Sao Paulo, Brazil.

They didn't meet up that often but regularly spoke on the phone or by Zoom and it was during one of these sessions that Marie mentioned that she and Simon were going to be stuck at an Old Bailey trial as witnesses for possibly days or even weeks on end, and she just didn't know how long they would be living in an hotel.

Now, Marie knew vaguely that her sisters and their husbands had, some time back, jointly bought an apartment in London so that they could all get together once or twice a year, or for one or two of them use when on a business visit. Marie's business mainly required her to spend only a day or two in one place before moving on elsewhere, and then perhaps briefly returning to check on progress, or begin another investigation, so staying in a succession of hotels had been her most convenient option.

So, it came as a complete surprise when both her sisters chorused "why don't you stay in our apartment, it's in the City Road/Old Street area quite close to the Old Bailey - you'll love it, St. Pauls Cathedral and lots of bits of Old London everywhere."

So that is why Simon and Marie found themselves, a couple of days before the trial was due to begin, ensconced in a very large luxury apartment with every service on hand – spa and large swimming pool, squash and tennis courts, and a choice of restaurants in the building. It made a pleasant change from hotels.

The day before the trial began, Simon and Marie and a number of other witnesses and police officers met the leading prosecution barrister, Archibald Sykes K.C. and his junior, at the DPP offices. They recognised several of the police officers present - DCI Major, DI's Sheila Nelson, Peter Percival and DS Riley, but none of the other witnesses were familiar except Yvonne Simmonds, the prisoner's sister, and Jeremy Idle.

The eminent K.C, Sykes, greeted everyone and thanked them for coming to the meeting that gave him an opportunity of briefing them all on how he felt the proceedings would pan out.

"It is likely to be an unusual hearing. Mr Justice Ruskin is presiding, and he has made it clear that he wishes to hear or consider the affidavits of all prosecution witnesses, even though the defence is offering only one witness – a psychiatrist who will ask for the action to be dismissed on the grounds of the prisoner's mental deficiency.

"I have no means of knowing," Sykes went on," which witnesses he will wish to call on to speak, but he has a reputation for being thorough, so I expect there will be quite a few."

He was right.

Those people who had been the in the Magistrates court some weeks before to see Tim Bird's preliminary hearing were intrigued to know whether his eccentric behaviour would be repeated.   Initially though, he appeared calm and disinterested, his expressionless face and slow movements suggested that he was heavily sedated.

The first day was largely taken up with swearing in a jury, and a reading of the charges, which included the following:

"Joining with others in planning and carrying out the murder of Dimitri Beltrovich, issuing threats and attacking and destroying part of the premises of Mrs Yvonne Simmonds, issuing threats and planning to similarly attack the premises of Mr Simon Brookes."

Sykes also pointed out to the Court that there were affidavits that had been sent to the trial by the Italian Courts from witnesses and police officers that involved Timothy Bird, whom they wished to bring to Court in Italy.

The sworn statements alleged that the prisoner conspired with Ernestino Andreotti in the attempted murder of Simon Brookes in Venice and in the shooting and injuring of Reginald Marsden at the same time. The other charge that the Italian affidavits referred to was that, with Antonio Castelini and others he had planned and executed the theft of a painting 'The Last Supper' from the strongroom of the Hotel Firenze Baltica in Florence.

When the charge was put and Bird was asked how he wished to plead, he looked blankly towards the judge and said nothing. Junior counsel had to go and have a word with him so that when the charge was put again, he mimicked the counsel's mouth movements and said somewhat incoherently "not guilty."

In his opening statement Sykes said that he would show the jury how an all-consuming desire to possess by fair means or foul, a valuable eighteenth-century Italian painting, had led Timothy Bird with others to plan and carry out these crimes.

Witnesses that he would call and affidavits he would show to the jury clearly showed that he was guilty as charged.

The defence barrister in his statement said his client was pleading "not guilty" to all the charges on the grounds that he had not been responsible for his actions, as the balance of his mind had been severely disturbed. He would be bringing expert medical evidence to make that point.

Sykes first called Simon to give evidence of how the picture had come into his possession and the chain of events thereafter with a particular emphasis on Bird's involvement. He posed many relevant questions during Simon's account. The judge was particularly interested when he mentioned the Chancery Divisions rejection of Timothy Bird's application to have his brother's will overturned on the grounds of him "not being of sound mind". Judge Ruskin called for all the relevant papers from the Chancery case to be produced for him to read through overnight and adjourned the case for the day. After an hour and a half giving his evidence and answering questions, Simon was exhausted and only too happy to get back with Marie to their apartment.

When they were discussing the day in Court, Simon remarked that he hadn't looked particularly closely at Tim Bird in the dock and asked Marie whether she had noticed any change in his demeanour or attitude. She said that, as the afternoon wore on, the effects of his sedative lessened, and he began to make the popping noise when he opened and closed his mouth rapidly and his eyes seemed to become more focussed not on the proceedings but on individuals in the well of the court and in the public seats beyond, to whom he would wave and point occasionally. To sum up she added "he's either a consummate actor or off his rocker."

As it had taken so long to get the trial underway the previous day, with only Simon called to give evidence, he and Marie envisaged that it was going to be a long and tedious trial with more witnesses called upon to give verbal evidence, rather than counsel relying on sworn statements. Simon hadn't even been questioned by the defence as yet.

However, when the Court re-convened next morning, two things happened to change their view.

First the defence counsel when asked if he had any questions to put to Simon replied "No, m'Lud." A pattern that he followed after other prosecution witnesses had given their evidence, unless they had mentioned Bird's temper or eccentric behaviour, when he questioned them closely. One such witness, later in the morning was Yvonne Simmonds, Bird's sister.

The second reason was something that His Honour Judge Ruskin said at the beginning of proceedings.

"As the evidence given yesterday by Mr Simon Brookes was so valuable in its range and content, I have decided that I shall not require some of the witnesses to give their evidence in person, but rely on their affidavits, unless prosecuting counsel think otherwise, Mr Sykes?"

"Quite happy with that M'Lud. May we confer on the list?" responded Sykes.

"Right now, if you please. Recess for twenty minutes."

When the court reassembled, quite a number of witnesses had been told that they would no longer be required to stay, including Marie and several police officers. It was clear that the judge wanted to get a move on with the trial.

During a break in the proceedings, Yvonne Simmonds joined Simon for a coffee where they discussed Tim's obvious decline in health and acuity amongst other things. Before they went back into court Yvonne said, "By the way Simon, when you asked me where Peter had obtained the 'Laura' picture, I told you I didn't know. In fact, I do now recall Peter telling me that it was left to him by an old friend from his Singapore days." Another piece of the puzzle fell into place.

Most of day two and the morning of day three was taken up with evidence given by the police – principally DI Peter Percival and DS Riley and a surprise witness called Terry Muldoon.

Muldoon was a member of Sid Atkins' gang, whose identity had been discovered from forensic examination of two hairs that been recovered from the hard hat that had miraculously survived the burnt out JSI van.

The DNA extracted showed that he had been a member of the three man crew that had abducted the three inspectors, then used their uniforms and the van to get into the City building site and bury the body of Beltrovich In concrete. Under the pressure of police questioning and the assurance that his giving evidence would mean a shorter sentence and police protection, he told them everything the police wanted to know. Sid and his brother had abducted and killed Beltrovich, and as it needed three to impersonate a JSI team, he was pulled in to make up the number. All three had now been charged and were being held on remand awaiting a Crown Court trial.

Evidence followed of the firebomb attack on Yvonne Simmond's house and the attempted one at Simon's cottage, for which Bird was identified as the perpetrator. That ended the prosecution case, which was damning.

The defence barrister reiterated that Bird had not been responsible for his actions due to mental disturbance and called in evidence a leading psychiatrist who at some length described his illness and his inability to control either his actions or emotions.

In his summing up and directions to the jury, Judge Ruskin reminded them that they were to consider whether Bird was guilty of the offences he was charged with on the evidence, They were not asked to give their opinion on his mental state as that was for experts to decide.

They went to the jury room and were back within ten minutes, their unanimous decision was that he was guilty as charged.

Judge Ruskin said that before sentencing he was sending Bird for further psychiatric investigation and reports and that the Court would reconvene in six weeks. All over in three days, what a relief.

Chapter 42

Marie and Simon decided to stay for a few days in Venice around de Vincentti's Reception and chose a small but luxurious boutique hotel along the Grand Canal a short walk from the Hotel Palazzio Gustavo. Although Venice was busy, the full impact of the summer tourist invasion had not yet begun, and they spent a full day showing each other their favourite and secret places in Venice.

On the morning of June 13th, they were to join Inspettore Superiori Ricci for coffee, when they hoped that they might learn a little more of what to expect that evening, but he was able to tell them very little. Apparently, there was to be quite a spectacular show with lights and music and a large screen had been installed on a platform erected at one end of the ballroom for film, video and of course his Zoom appearance, but he had no details.

The police were keeping a low profile with just a few plain clothed officers in the hotel itself and as a concession, a line had been taken from the ballroom to a small office off reception where the police could listen in to the proceedings. He hoped they would enjoy the Reception and looked forward to hearing their impressions afterwards.

Early that afternoon they each received a message on their mobile phones from de Vincentti, Simon's said:

Greetings,

Be assured a warm welcome awaits you later this afternoon, commencing at 5.30pm at The Royal Palazzio Gustavo. For reasons of security please bring your invitation plus an identifying photograph (e.g. identity card, passport, driving licence) and give your personal password to the attendant. Your personal password is S7B

Roberto

Marie's was identical except for the personal password which was M8S. "Bearing in mind that he's not coming in person and presumably only showing the painting via Zoom as well, the emphasis on security seems extraordinarily high don't you think Simon?" said Marie after reading it through.

"There must be a reason darling, and I shall be interested to see what it is," replied Paul.

Palazzo Gustavo is one of the older buildings lining the Grand Canal that had been converted into an hotel. It had retained much of its character from when it was a private residence, including at the rear a ballroom, rising to the equivalent of three storeys, topped with a glass dome.

Keen to take stock before the start, Simon and Marie went into the hotel entrance at 5.15 pm and walked through towards the ballroom, which had been blocked off from the rest of the hotel in order to channel guests through a security checkpoint.

Here everyone's documentation was checked, metal detectors walked through, handbags examined and finally a quick body pat-down, before they were allowed to pass through the doors into the ballroom, which was spectacular.

The whole room was subtly lit from different angles and tints that gradually changed between colours of the rainbow, in such a way that the drapes that covered the back of the stage and all the windows seemed to slowly change their shape. To one side of the stage a small orchestra softly played classical pieces.

There were only two rows of seats, each with about fifteen chairs, more than half of which were already occupied, and they were shown to theirs in the front row, numbers 7 & 8. Much of the front row was now full or filling up except for the seat next to Simon. He regularly looked up and down the rows but failed to recognise anyone at a quick glance.

With only a few minutes to the start, a familiar figure walked along the front with the aid of a stick and an attendant holding his arm and stopped at chair 6. Simon stood to grasp the newcomer's outstretched hand and said "Delighted to see you again Signor Manzini" who reciprocated the greeting, and shook hands with Marie before taking his seat, then spoke and shook hands with two men seated to his right. Manzini attempted to speak again to Simon and introduce his neighbour, but the lights dimmed and momentarily the room was plunged into darkness, the music ceased, and the show was about to begin.

As the lights came up, those that had been changing colour stayed at a muted blue, but the stage was lit up. Spotlighted in the centre was a well-known presenter on Italian television who alternated in Italian and English her welcome and introduced all that was to follow, which was colourful and varied.

Two young talented tenors sang arias from operas and songs from the musical stage and screen, sometimes together and sometimes as solos, switching from one genre to another with enviable skill and grace accompanied by an augmented orchestra.

A well-known Japanese maestro of the violin played three contrasting pieces that showed off her virtuosity. This was followed a brief flurry of magic from a magician and illusionist whose patter was as clever and funny as his tricks, judging by the loud laughter and applause that followed his act. An unusual mixed acrobatic and conjuring act with four participants was applauded for its originality and extraordinary skill, and that led to the final act. An internationally well-known singer performed not only her popular hits but a whole range of songs in English and Italian, to the appreciation of most of the audience.

The whole programme had been illuminated by spectacular colour laser lighting and was adjudged a lavish entertainment by the audience, who had moved across during the interval to the buffet tables laid out on one side of the ballroom. From these, security guards now disguised as waiters, filled plates from a plethora of dishes loaded with small portions in seemingly infinite variety, and brought them with wine to tables nearby.

Simon and Marie sat at a table with Manzini and the two other elderly men who had sat next him in the audience. Manzini lost no time in introducing Simon and Marie to them

"This gentleman you have met before if I'm not mistaken Mr Brookes – Alessandro Pagnetti, and the other is Guido Lambertini my former agent in England."

Simon was momentarily taken aback as he shook hands, surely the last person that Manzini would wish to associate with was Pagnetti, the man he had last seen on the island of Murano.

At that time Pagnetti had been very bitter towards Manzini who in his turn had accused his former major domo of dishonesty. What had brought them together, animosity apparently forgotten? He was gradually to find out from their conversation. It was a burning hatred of de Vincentti.

In Manzini's case it had been transferred down from Vincentti senior – a cheat and a liar - to his son – a thief and confidence trickster. To which list Pagnetti added – double-crosser. Not to be outdone, Lambertini not only agreed with everything that the others had said, he explained that he had been blackmailed by Angelo de Vincentti, who threatened to expose Lambertini's theft of the Tiepolo unless he handed it over to him. Lambertini had lost a fortune by complying. This explained to Simon how Vincentti senior had got hold of the painting for a second time.

Marie had spotted amongst the guests two people she knew, one the Director of a National Gallery and the other a London art dealer and went over to speak to them.

The heat and anger displayed by the three old men Simon found disconcerting, but he couldn't resist asking them as a group "If you dislike and despise de Vincentti so much, gentlemen, why did you come to this affair?"

They looked at each other as if at a loss how to answer the question until Manzini broke the silence with "Well, we shall see how the second half goes, that might tell you." The other two nodded in agreement."

Disturbed by their attitude, Simon felt in need of a cold drink, and walked over to the bar, where he was surprised to find Lambertini had followed him.

"I wanted a quick word," he began. "In case the Tiepolo comes back into your possession, you might be interested in finding the special frame that hid it behind another painting."

He went on "when Angelo de Vincentti took the Tiepolo from me in 1993, he left the frame behind, and I held on to it until 2008 when I was approached by an agent who was researching the provenance of TLS for a client called Warburton, living in Singapore.

He claimed to be the current owner of the picture and produced a letter to prove the point. I was able to help him a little, and mentioned I still held the frame. He immediately offered to buy it for his client, and I agreed. But I still wondered whether the frame and pictures were ever brought together."

"Yes, they were," confirmed Simon. "They first came into my ownership through a bequest from an old friend who had in turn inherited the picture from Warburton. Thanks for filling in more details, they answer a lot of questions."

Simon and Lambertini returned to their seats, and he addressed the three elderly gentlemen. "However, you feel about de Vincentti personally, and believe me I have no reason to shout his praises, you must agree he has put on a splendid show so far and the buffet is quite superb, don't you think?"

"Yes, but why do it" one of them asked "it's just self-glorification and trying to redeem himself for past sins."

"Most of the people here" said Manzini "are important people in the art world, the sort of people he wants to impress and through them he hopes to become respectable and more acceptable."

Finally, Simon couldn't resist asking the trio "and why do think he invited you three gentlemen, he must know that none of you are exactly friendly?"

Manzini replied "I think we may in some way be featured in the next part, as will you I should think. All in self-justification of his past actions and behaviour."

"Yes, and it may not end as he would have hoped "added Pagnetti enigmatically, to which the others nodded their agreement.

Simon could not continue his questioning as the audience was asked to resume their seats in front of the stage as the second half was about to begin and everyone started to move. Marie sat down beside him and asked Simon "What was all that angst about?" to which he replied, "I'm not at all sure but maybe the next session will tell us."

As the presenter was talking, the big screen was moved forward centre stage and she turned to it saying, "Here is your host of the evening who requires no introduction, please welcome through the medium of Zoom – Roberto de Vincentti!"

The big screen then lit up with an overwhelmingly large picture of Roberto de Vincentti looking even more devilish than usual as the lighting seemed to emphasise the streak of silver coming down through his black hair and into his neatly trimmed beard. He was immaculately attired with black tie and a white tuxedo, carrying a rosebud in his buttonhole.

Lifting his hands in greeting he said, "I hope you enjoyed the first part of our programme," and paused whilst a ripple of applause went round the room "Let me again welcome you my friends, to this, a celebration of the work of Giovanni Battista Tiepolo born exactly 327 years ago tomorrow and in particular his *The Last Supper* painted in 1738."

The screen split into two as he showed several of Tiepolo's paintings including the series of six representing his Life of Christ that hung in the Louvre and finally he held up *The Last Supper* now in his possession.

As he did so he said "This is not only a remarkably fine picture, but it has an extraordinary story to tell of the many hands through which has passed since it was painted two hundred and seventy-five years ago.

"Most of this has been uncovered through the sterling work of Mr Simon Brookes in tracing its provenance." As he was speaking Simon's name, a spotlight picked him out on the front row temporarily blinding him with its concentrated beam. "And it is from Mr Brookes," de Villiers continued, "that I acquired the painting."

"And not yet paid for it," thought Simon.

De Vincentti went on "for two hundred and thirty years between 1742 and 1972 it stayed in the collection of a distinguished Venetian family" and the spotlight came on again this time illuminating the occupant of seat 6 as he continued "the Manzinis, whose present head is Teodoro Manzini who is with us this evening."

He then began to list the names of people and institutions that had held the painting over the years including, to his embarrassment and annoyance, Guido Lambertini who was also spotlighted.

He emphasised the deep affection that his own father Angelo de Vincentti had for the picture which he had owned twice during his lifetime, something that had led to his own acquisition of the painting 'when the opportunity arose.' "That's a convenient way of putting it," thought Simon.

As de Vincentti continued to recite his list and comment on how the painting was lost to sight several times, there was a growing rumbling anger from the three seats to his right as the three elderly men muttered aloud. Then de Vincentti apparently came to the end of his talk and announced. "I must now beg your patience for a few minutes before I continue," and disappeared from the screen which then went blank and the lights in the room became brighter.

Manzini turned to Simon "Other than President Putin I can't think of anyone who can turn the truth on its head and present lies as facts that seem believable to those people who don't know – my colleagues here are spitting blood at his version of history." Simon replied "I can understand their exasperation, he's very glib with his lies and half-truths. I've been puzzled by why he's bothering to put on this extravaganza though and I believe now it is partly to justify the high price he is asking of the next owner of the painting."

They stopped speaking as the house lights dimmed a little and those directed on the platform brightened, as onto centre stage, under a spotlight, strode de Vincennti himself carrying aloft the *'The Last Supper'* painting, to scattered applause.

The three elderly gentlemen next to Simon could hardly contain their delight at his appearance, Pagnetti, rubbing his hands and remarking "I knew he couldn't resist showing up in person, now let's see."

De Vincentti put the painting onto a stand and turned to the audience and began "I wanted to join you briefly in person before I left, and to thank...."

He didn't finish the sentence as two shots rang out in quick succession, the sound reverberating around the domed room, as he fell to the floor, his head split open from two bullets that killed him instantly.

Security guards ran to the stage, whilst the audience was for a moment shocked into a stunned silence until several ran to the sides of the room in panic, whilst others looked around to try and see where the marksman had fired from. Simon and Marie both thought that the shots had come from the gallery that ran round beneath the dome but could see no signs of movement up there. Simon turned to Teo Manzini and was surprised to see him exchanging smiles and little 'thumbs up' signals with the two others.

Pagnetti leaned across to Simon and said above the hubbub that was now all around "As I said before, things do not always end the way that people hope."

The police had secured the painting and now joined the security guards in ushering the audience out of the ballroom, taking names and addresses and asking if anyone had seen anyone up in the gallery or the flash of a rifle being discharged up there. Nobody had.

Marie felt unwell after the shock, so they stayed in the Palazzio Gustava bar to have a cognac and coffee before walking the short distance to their own hotel. She soon felt better, and Simon thought he could mention his suspicions to her. "Did you notice Manzini, Lambertini and Pagnetti's reactions to de Vincentti's shooting?" he asked.

"Yes, from what I could see they looked pleased," she replied, and Simon went on to reiterate what Pagnetti had said before and after the shooting and the real hatred that they all displayed towards de Vincentti.

"I do wonder whether perchance the three of them had organised the assassination," he ruminated. "We shall never know, darling, so I suggest you keep your thoughts to yourself, particularly when we talk to Ricci tomorrow," responded Marie.

It was the following evening before Ricci was able to break away from the investigation at the Palazzio Gustava and to tell them some details of what had happened. The shots had been fired from the gallery, access to which was via a wrought iron spiral staircase that ran from behind a door leading off the ballroom. The security guards and police found it had been partially dismantled by someone cutting out a section. It took twenty minutes to secure a temporary ladder to bridge the gap and reach the top and then open the heavy locked door. There was of course, nobody there.

The gallery was nowadays closed to the public and used as a storage area but there were signs – a camp bed, table and chair, the remains of several meals, water and wine bottles and even a temporary toilet – that showed that someone had lived up there for forty eight hours or more.

He or she had escaped through an inspection tunnel that led out to the dome base from which a rope ladder still dangled down to the ground. The police forensic team might get a DNA result from what the assassin had left behind but unless it was on a database they were left without a clue.

Simon kept his speculations to himself, but was distinctly cheered when Ricci said that there was no reason for the police to keep the painting now, and as rightful owner he could pick it up the next day if he wished!

****

Three weeks later, His Honour Judge Ruskin resumed the trial of Timothy Bird whom the jury had found guilty on all charges, which would in normal circumstances mean 25 years imprisonment. However, the psychiatric report said that his mental condition which had been worsening over recent months now made him wholly incapable of reasoned thought. In the circumstances, the judge pronounced that Bird was to be held in a secure facility for the mentally afflicted at the King's pleasure. Which meant Broadmoor for life.

****

Simon's painting *'The Last Supper'* (together with its complete provenance) was verified by the Tiepolo official committee as being by Giovanni Battista Tiepolo, and was sold by Christie's at auction two months later for £15 Million.

****

Marie retired from her work with insurance companies and she and Simon got married with the enthusiastic approval of their families.

They now split their time between the Cotswolds, Paris and a newly acquired house on the coast in the Le Marche region of Italy when not visiting family around the world.

****

Simon always declared that the discovery of the 'Message from Carlos' contained in the carved wooden box was the most significant find in his search for a provenance that ultimately led to the very successful sale of the picture.

Printed in Great Britain
by Amazon